MARVEL

BLACK WIDOW
RED
VENGEANCE

MARVEL

BLACK WIDOW
RED
VENGEANCE

BY MARGARET STOHL

Los Angeles • New York

First Edition, October 2016

10 9 8 7 6 5 4 3 2 1

FAC-020093-16239

Printed in the United States of America

Library of Congress Cataloging-in-Publication Control Number: 2016932664

ISBN 978-1-4847-7347-5

Reinforced binding

This book is set in Sabon.
Designed by Tanya Ross-Hughes / Hotfoot Studio

Visit www.hyperionteens.com
www.marvel.com

SUSTAINABLE FORESTRY INITIATIVE
Certified Sourcing
www.sfiprogram.org
SFI-00993

THIS LABEL APPLIES TO TEXT STOCK

THIS ONE IS FOR
SARA MARGARET STOHL
ZERO PERCENT SIDEKICK
ONE HUNDRED PERCENT BUTT-KICK
FUTURE HERO

ACT ONE: WIDOWED

"I IMAGINE DEATH SO MUCH IT FEELS MORE LIKE A MEMORY. . . . IF I SEE IT COMIN', DO I RUN OR DO I LET IT BE?"
—LIN-MANUEL MIRANDA

HIGH-DENSITY TARGET AREA, MIDTOWN MANHATTAN RADIATION ZONE ZERO, ZERO HOUR

Nothing like the Christmas tree at Rockefeller Center, thought Natasha Romanoff—for terrorists, crackpots, and basic criminal scumbags. As always, there were no visions of sugarplums dancing in the Black Widow's cold red head. The S.H.I.E.L.D. agent glanced up at the green-needled monolith—dusted with snowflakes and twinkling with lights and Swarovski crystals, the centerpiece of Manhattan's annual holiday party—and thought two words.

Merry Christmas? Try: target package.

Natasha knew that the famed Rockefeller Center tree was larger-than-life in a score of dangerously useful ways. Symbolic significance? *Check.* Media coverage? *Check,*

check. Mass casualties? *Check, check, check.* She sighed and touched her earpiece. "Black to base. No sign of their Alpha."

"Copy that, but don't park your sleigh just yet, Black." Coulson's voice crackled into her ear as she moved through the crowd. "And check in with Red. We've lost her signal."

"Copy that, base. Black out." She kept moving.

A sea of raised arms, all holding cell-phone cameras, now saluted the hundred-foot Norway spruce from every side, as if the yuletide monstrosity had crash-landed on some worshipful alien planet and assumed the role of supreme leader. *Yeah, a planet of sardines, more than a million a day, all packed squirming into one snowy city block,* Natasha thought.

And for what? To see a freaking plant.

It was a stormy Saturday afternoon in December, a bad time both for crowds and weather, which meant these were die-hard tree people—Natasha just hoped not literally.

Tourists plus terrorists? That always ends well.

The potential for disaster was staggering. Eyes up, defenses down—not one dazed worshiper was looking anywhere but the supersized tree—even though there was an entire holiday parade moving down Fifth Avenue at the far edge of the block.

Ever since the yuletide crowd had begun to surge and climb over the sludge-banked metal barricades at the edges of Rockefeller Center plaza—the corner of Forty-Ninth and Fifth—the NYPD had given up. Now they just cursed the cold afternoon, waiting out the end of their shifts on the safe side of the roadblocks, their breath curling upward in raggedy white puffs. *And they're strictly donut patrol, not top command.* That had probably also been a factor in the strategic acquisition of this target, she thought. *Human gridlock with only Paul Blart on your tail—*

Natasha touched her ear again. "Red, what's going on? Ava? You lost?"

All she got back was static.

That's not a good sound—

"Hey, happy holidays," said a harried-looking mom in a cheery red fleece, pushing a stroller zippered in plastic up the curb next to Natasha. "Great snowsuit—"

Natasha nodded, eyeing the kid as the patch of red disappeared into the snowflaked crowd. *Don't get distracted, Romanoff. Do your job and maybe this time nobody gets hurt.* She hitched her pack higher, pushing on toward Fifth Avenue.

Yeah, right.

The odds were good that this op was going to end in casualties—and that, soon enough, the red in the snow wasn't going to be fleece. Natasha's hooded "snowsuit" was a CBRN (Chemical Biological Radiological Nuclear) state-of-the-art mop suit that only resembled snow gear; really, it was lined with filtering charcoal and striped with M-9 detection paper so she could gauge what was being thrown at her in any given hot zone. And the goggles around her neck weren't for skiing but surviving—a mouth guard flipped down from inside, like a collapsible gas mask. (Dire biological functions aside, the whole getup also lowered the odds that one of the Black Widow's many superfans would recognize her infamous red hair. *Oh, the price of super hero superstardom . . .)*

But it was the contents of her rucksack that really set her apart. Her requisition S.H.I.E.L.D. ruck held an M183 demolition charge assembly with enough C-4 (sixteen charges in all) to flatten a city block, if that's what it came to.

Unlike the rest of Manhattan, Natasha Romanoff hadn't come for the tree. She was there to take out the unknown number of hostiles who were plotting to use Rockefeller Center as holiday bait for civilian casualties. Her alpha priority was their leader, who had threatened to launch the largest and most sophisticated chemical-weapons attack in the nation's history.

When it hit, the Northeast Megalopolis, the Boston–Washington corridor that was home to more than fifty million people, would be flooded with aerosolized chemical particulates. The invisible, odorless microbes would seize control of human neurons and eventually destroy them— unless Natasha could destroy the as-yet-unidentified dispersal device before the Alpha triggered it, somewhere on this street, sometime on this day, at some point during this parade.

But no pressure.

This wasn't the first time she had carried a satchel charge through the streets of a populated area; off the top of her head, there had been Pristina and Grozny and Sana'a and Djibouti and even Bogotá before now. She had infiltrated

Serbian revolutionaries and Chechen guerrillas and Yemeni pirates and Somali armed forces and Colombian mercenaries—but then, they had already known they were at war. It didn't make the ops any less devastating, only less of a surprise; those buildings had long been riddled by bullets, roads ravaged from IEDs, walls chiseled with rat holes for hostiles at every turn. Those cities had become operational theaters way before she'd gotten the call; everyone who could leave had already left.

At least, that was how Natasha had rationalized it to herself.

This, on the other hand, was midtown Manhattan. This was a holiday attack perpetrated on American soil in the clear light of day during prime traffic for the highest-density urban population in the country. It was the sort of bad business only attempted by a depraved coalition of psychopaths grasping for global attention—because it worked. Every lethal move the opposition made brought them closer to achieving the desired result, to producing the headlines—THE WORST! THE DEADLIEST! THE BLOODIEST!—that could shape or rule an era and force a country to its knees.

Not if someone stops them first.

She checked her watch.

Come on, Ava. Where are you?

They didn't have this kind of time to waste. For the next two hours, the parade would still be going, and Rockefeller Center would still be jammed with civilians. The timing wasn't an accident. *Pearl Harbor was hit at 7:53 a.m.; the first of the Twin Towers was 8:45 a.m.* If the attack succeeded, today would be worse by an order of magnitude.

From where Natasha stood, she knew she could shake up a Coke and spray fifty people without so much as tossing it. If she had to use it, the effect of a single stick of C-4 in a place like this, on a day like this, at a time like this, would be unimaginable. If she didn't use it, the number of people affected by the chemical attack would probably be worse. There was no easy answer, and there never had been.

Twenty-eight years of peace. She'd read it in one of Ava's S.H.I.E.L.D. Academy assignments, citing a journalist named Chris Hedges.

That's all the quiet this planet has known, since the beginning of recorded history. How can one person change that?

Even if that one person happened to be the Black Widow.

But it's not just you; there are two of you now, she scolded herself. *I don't know why you keep forgetting that. Red and Black, remember? You don't always have to be so alone, Natashkaya—*

"Natashkaya!" She heard Ava's voice while her back was still turned. "I found the Alpha. Right around the corner. There's just one thing—"

Natasha heard it in Ava's voice before she saw it. The flinty hardness, the push of adrenaline that inflected every syllable.

The betrayal.

Her hand went immediately to the back of her waistband.

7

It's not there—

Now the voice was louder, harsher. "Touch one hair on that Alpha's head and I'll shoot," Ava said. "I mean it."

"I know," Natasha said, raising her hands in surrender. And as she slowly turned to face all that remained of her family, she also found herself staring down the barrel of her own Glock revolver.

REWIND:
WEEKS EARLIER
IN SOUTH
AMERICA

S.H.I.E.L.D. EYES ONLY

CLEARANCE LEVEL X

CONFIDENTIAL: PHILLIP COULSON

CLASSIFIED / FOR OFFICIAL USE ONLY (FOUO) / CRITICAL PROGRAM INFORMATION (CPI) / LAW ENFORCEMENT SENSITIVE (LES) / TOP SECRET / SUITE AB ENCRYPTION / SIPRNET DISTRIBUTION ONLY (SIPDIS) / JCOS / S.H.I.E.L.D.

** FILE COPY OF INCOMING TRANSMISSION ** FROM THE PENTAGON **

Phil, buddy:

Just heard from the Oval. It's not good. Keeping a potentially dangerous "controlled specimen" under wraps is off the table. What did you think POTUS would say? [CODE: REDROCK] is still too hot with the press.

What I can do is declare [CLASSIFIED SUBJECT] a Restricted Handling Asset, and name you to run the After Action Assessment. AAA is an easy sell, you have the expertise. Wrap it up, control the narrative, it all goes away.

Otherwise I'm hearing that [CLASSIFIED SUBJECT] faces quarantine in 1 of 3 high-security research facilities:

- Amundsen-Scott S.P. Station (INT)
- Superkamiokande (JP)
- CERN (SUI)

BUT: lab protocols would require [CLASSIFIED SUBJECT] to undergo a cerebral wipe and to be declared legally DOA— rough stuff, even for S.H.I.E.L.D.

We are, after all, talking about a child.

That's the fallout from the [CODE:REDROCK] crapstorm. The NSA vultures are circling. Good luck.

Stay low. Head down.

ARTIE

OFFICE OF THE JOINT CHIEFS OF STAFF
9999 JOINT STAFF PENTAGON
WASHINGTON DC

ROMANOFF: What am I doing here, Phil? I don't have time for this.

COULSON: You know the protocol. There's always an After Action Assessment. You're an SME now—

ROMANOFF: Subject Matter Expert? No, let's leave that to the wonks on the tenth floor.

COULSON: The real battles don't end on the battlefield. We need to lock down this story. Start at the beginning.

ROMANOFF: Why?

COULSON: A beginning is a delicate time.

ROMANOFF: Is that a quote? Are you quoting at me?

COULSON: Dune. Frank Herbert. You know it?

ROMANOFF: Not unless you're talking about a Desert Storm field manual.

COULSON: The beginning, Agent. There are people asking questions, and this doesn't end until we answer them.

ROMANOFF: I filed a report. Classified. Top Secret. Encrypted. You know, the kind they keep in the little drawers with the combination locks?

COULSON: So let's just talk. I've been your friend longer than I've been your AIC.

ROMANOFF: You going Hallmark on me, Phil? Now you're that guy?

COULSON: You know I was always that guy. Start with the truth. They say it's out there.

ROMANOFF: Phil—

COULSON: I'll get you started. It ended in a national disaster and a global emergency. It began in Recife. Just tell me the truth about Recife.

ROMANOFF: Some stories aren't just classified. They're also personal.

COULSON: I think we both know you're not just a person anymore.

ROMANOFF: Okay. You want the truth? Then forget Recife. It started in Rio.

RIO DE JANEIRO, BRAZIL
CHRIST THE REDEEMER MONUMENT,
MOUNT CORCOVADO

You are one huge stone dude. *You know, you kind of remind me of this big green friend of mine—*

Natasha bit into a wild guava as she stood at the base of the massive stone Cristo overlooking Rio de Janeiro. She contemplated the statue, sucking on the ripe pinkish fruit, dribbling juice off her chin. The polished, graying soapstone arms were outstretched, as if the forty-meter giant of a messiah looming from the mountaintop above her truly believed he could gather up the entire city for a group hug. *Aw, bring it in, you guys—*

"Tell me why we're here again?" Ava Orlova, the S.H.I.E.L.D. Academy rookie currently under Natasha's immediate supervision, glanced at the guava in Natasha's hand. "Huh. Wow. You don't seem like a fruit person."

"I'm a fruit person. Of course I'm a fruit person." Natasha swallowed. "What does that even mean?"

"Let's see." Ava began moving through the swarm of tourists crowding onto the observation deck with them, high above the city of Rio. "Thick rind. Sweet and mushy in places, I guess," she said, straight-faced. "Slightly seedy at the core, rotten in parts—"

"Funny." Natasha scowled. "What did you think I ate? Rocks?"

Ava moved along the railing, looked over her shoulder as she slipped away. "I don't know, rounds? Washed down with jet fuel?"

Natasha tried not to smile as she turned back toward the view. Their relationship had softened into an easy familiarity since they'd left New York. It made Natasha nervous. *Don't get to know me enough for opinions, kid. Everyone who does ends up dead.*

The Widow eyed the pale sprawl of the city that unfolded below her, the broad blue sweep of ocean beyond that—and hurled the guava skin into the sky. It arched and fell, rolling down the mountainside. She wiped her sticky lips with the back of her sticky hand, still taking in the view. She always came up the hill at least once every visit; she had for years. Despite the number of times the job had brought her here, she had never gotten used to the way Rio looked—especially not from the Cristo at Mount

Corcovado. It had always meant something to her, as silly as that was, and she'd wanted Ava to see it.

How can the world be so messed up and still look so magical?

It was true; the coastline seemed to be one of those surreal hand-drawn maps you might find in the front pages of old fantasy books. Everything she could see was too sharp or too steep or too brightly colored to be real.

Reality wasn't usually all that pretty.

Yet here it was. The vertical plateau of Sugarloaf Mountain rose up in front of her, sheer rock and cable cars and all; Ipanema (like the song) and Copacabana (like the other song) occupied the broad stripe of sand directly south of that—and then the curving seam of land and water broke into an abrupt handful of tiny jagged hills that poked up from the shallow surf, well beyond the row of grand beach hotels.

If she looked hard enough, she could just make out the Copacabana Palace hotel, where back in the 1950s Howard Stark had fallen in love with the view of the sea (or, more likely, the women who swam in it) and purchased the sixth-floor penthouse Natasha and Ava had been using as a base of operations for weeks now.

Natasha had told Coulson she was taking Ava out of S.H.I.E.L.D. Academy so they could combine fieldwork with vacation, but the truth was clear: they had come to South America for one reason.

Vengeance for Alexei.

Ivan Somodorov was dead, but his network of terror remained. The Widows were here to follow the trail of intelligence—what Ava now called the "fact story," since her Academy training—that could bring Alexei's murderers to justice and crush Ivan's network, and with it his infamous Red Room—the spy school that had destroyed both of their lives. The loss of Natasha's younger brother and Ava's first love had sent them each reeling in different ways.

And in some of the same ways—

After nothing but setbacks and dead ends in their investigation—questions without answers—today Natasha had decided to take a few hours off. She'd dragged Ava up here on the back of the Harley, disregarding the oppressive afternoon heat, without being able to put into words why.

A feeling.

Natasha only knew she'd experienced it before—once, during a routine S&R (surveillance and recon) op, while climbing over a tiled rooftop at the edge of Havana at sunset.

Another time, she'd sensed it when, on the way to an RDX (rendezvous) she'd flown an Apache low enough over the green-green of a Myanmar rice paddy to interrupt a family of elephants during bath time in the River Mali.

She'd gotten it again while flattened on a rooftop for a recce (reconnaissance mission) in Aleppo, watching the sun rise over the partly destroyed minaret of the Great Mosque as the Syrian city echoed with the dawn call to prayer.

Later, she'd found it in the sudden warm draft of cinnamon and coffee from a nearby *vatrushka* bakery as she rappelled down from Zhivopisny Bridge to the frozen Moskva during the exfiltration of a compromised Support Asset from the wintery, hostile *Rodina*, the motherland.

While each of those moments had struck during a Denied Area Operation, Natasha had to admit she'd found something undeniable as well. The remnants of a dream, or maybe just a hope. *If the world can still feel like that—even now, after everything—then who knows?*

Maybe the cold, orbital ball of nickel and iron and silicon—the worn gravity-bound rock that had miraculously outlasted everything she'd ever cared about—could one day again be something more. *Not just death and loss and betrayal and pain. Not loneliness and isolation . . .*

Natasha stared out at the world in front of her, trying to see that now. They had both had a rough year, in a lot of ways, since Alexei had died. Her family was gone, and her friends were divided. If Ava really did plan to keep calling herself the Red Widow—to use her newfound powers for the greater good, or even just for whatever Maria Hill or Coulson had planned for her—the kid would have to find hope somewhere.

Maybe that was what this afternoon was about.

Natasha took a deep breath, focusing on the bright wash of sky in front of her. *Give it a rest, Romanoff. What's wrong with you? You really are turning into some kind of fruit person—*

Natasha looked away. Somewhere in the crowd a radio

was blasting the city's unofficial anthem, a moody, crooning bossa nova number from João Giberto. You couldn't take a cab or walk through a hotel lobby anywhere in the city without hearing it; the melody had been stuck in her head for weeks now. *Tall and tan and young and lovely, the girl from Ipanema goes walking—*

"*Desculpe—*" The crowd of tourists moved, and a dark-eyed, dark-haired young woman in a fitted, retro-looking green shift found herself being shoved toward the railing—dipping perilously close to the edge of the sheer rock hillside—and knocking her elbow into Natasha's shoulder in the process. Off balance, the girl teetered to one side, over the rail—until the Widow reached out, grabbing her by the arm. Natasha felt the girl's fingers close around her wrist as she steadied herself.

"Watch it," Natasha said. "The view's less pretty from an ambulance." The girl couldn't have been much older than Ava.

"*Desculpe! Desculpe—*" The girl switched into heavily accented English. "Sorry, yes, to excuse. She is to make the accident," she said, backing away. "She is to distract by the angels."

"What?" Natasha looked at her. "Angels?"

"She is to mean the sky. English not to be her language." The girl's eyes had gone wide; she was clearly panicking. "Forgiving you." She turned and fled into the throng of tourists.

Natasha watched her go, automatically registering the face. Three seconds and she had it; *pronounced bone structure, widely spaced eye sockets, large features, sharp horizontal profile, the accent.* She spoke Portuguese, but she was more likely Russian, certainly Eastern European, aside from just her dark hair and eyes. *Definitely a trace of the Urals in there, some part of the Caucasus.* But there was something else, something off about her, for a girl in—what, her late teens, early twenties? *Maybe the speech? Could it be the second language . . . ?*

Frowning, Natasha reached up and felt her shoulder. *Was that a brush pass? Do I feel a transmitter? A bug or a mic or a tick?*

Was that an encounter with foreign intelligence or a klutz?

She let her hand drop again. There didn't appear to be anything there. She shook her head. Maybe this South American op had finally gotten to her; Coulson had been telling her she was paranoid since she'd left Istanbul, more than a year ago.

Then again, you can't really call it paranoia when that many people are actually trying to kill you. And I could have sworn the girl was playing trip-and-tag. Not to mention there aren't a whole lot of Russian tourists in Brazil. . . .

"Natasha! Look!" Ava waved at her frantically from across the platform; one of Rio's many stray monkeys had climbed up on the wall next to the teen and was now photo-bombing her selfie, screaming at her with his wide, elastic monkey mouth. "Monkey!"

"Congratulations." Natasha shook her head. "Both of you monkeys." Ava was in rare form today; Natasha hadn't seen the kid smile this much since Istanbul. *But monkey selfies? Was I like this at the beginning?* It had been too long; she couldn't remember. *I just hope she stops talking about going to look for capybaras now.*

Natasha looked around again, but the girl in the green dress had vanished.

Strange. She began a closer inspection of the crowd—

Her wrist began to vibrate, though, and she turned to check the Widow's Cuff peeking out beneath the army surplus jacket she wore over her light-fiber, moisture-absorbing jumpsuit—despite the heat—because heat was better than mosquitoes. *And much better than malaria or chikungunya or dengue or zika.* (This far south of Panama, even the Black Widow had no choice but to abandon her black leather.)

Seven p.m.? Crap—

She'd almost missed check-in. *Again.*

Natasha pulled her sunglasses down over her eyes and turned back to her Cuff, tapping a tiny screen to initiate her S.H.I.E.L.D. Sametime connection—secure military real-time communications, using shared tech originally borrowed from the CIA. The U.S. government had a few versions of private internet, and none was more private than Sametime—even if Tony Stark called it *lame-time.* He didn't trust anything the government (or anyone else) made without him.

She eyed the crowd immediately surrounding her, then leaned forward over the railing for a little public privacy, pretending to check her phone. She let the tiny camera on her Cuff scroll its thousands of microscopic lasers over her right retina. A low tone sounded, and she pressed her left thumb to the sensor on the inside of her wrist, using her right hand to slide her S.H.I.E.L.D.-issue earpiece into one ear.

"Tony Stark is the greatest, bestest friend I've ever had," a synthetic version of Natasha's own voice said in a calm monotone, rattling up from her inner ear. It was her Synth, a digital doppelgänger whom she thought of as Fake Natasha, assigned to secure her comm link. Maria Hill had allowed Tony to add Stark Industries' own rigorous security protocols to all forms of S.H.I.E.L.D. secure communications he used; otherwise, he refused to use them. As a result, Tony had access to everything, which was how Natasha always ended up with voice-match samples as idiotic as this one.

Real Natasha sighed, pressing her earpiece. "Tony Stark is a class-A megalomaniac who wouldn't know a friend if she bit him in the—"

"I'm sorry, Natasha, that's incorrect," the Synth interrupted smugly. A buzzer sounded, and Real Natasha jumped, startled. It felt like someone had hammered a tiny nail inside her eardrum. *Wrong answer.*

"Fine. Whatever. Tony Stark is the greatest, bestest friend I've ever had," Natasha repeated sullenly, uttering all the requisite vowels and consonants for her voice match. She knew it had worked when the sound of applause rumbled inside her ear. "Very funny." She rolled her eyes. "And I'm going to kick his greatest, bestest butt if he doesn't stop writing himself into my Sametime security protocol."

The protocol rolled forward. "Match is one hundred percent. Line is secure. Daily *lame-time* check-in initiated, Natasha."

"Just like clockwork, along with Tony's daily lame joke." Natasha touched the side of her glasses now, and the S.H.I.E.L.D. interface unfolded in a hologram, occupying most of her field of vision. "What do you have for me?" She tapped twice on her Cuff, moving through the interface as she did. Rows of numbered transmissions appeared, now hovering above the skyline of the city.

"Retrieving. One hundred forty-one unread data bursts, Natasha."

"Sounds like a drag." Natasha scrolled through a pile of memos as she stared off into the view. "Do I want to read any of them?"

"Seven highly classified. Thirty-eight classified. Ninety-five top secret," the Synth answered brightly. "Fourteen in the CurrentOps mailbox marked *From Phil, with love*. Seven in the box marked *From Tony, with no love*."

"Send the Phil files to my Cuff. Other than that, can we speed this up? I won't be able to get to most of these until later."

"Hill, Maria?"

"File, *OpSec*."

"Banner, Bruce?"

"File, *personal*."

"America, Cap?"

"File, *stressful*."

"Marvel, Cap?"

"File, *GopOps*." Danvers ran their highly classified Girls Only Poker Night Operation, and half the mail she sent to Natasha's box was about whose turn it was to host this month (Maria) or what particular junk food She-Hulk was craving. (Salt-and-vinegar something? Or was that Quake? Natasha had lost track.) It was a small, select crew, but on the nights Natasha was in the city and Carol could be persuaded to make her way down from her command post at Alpha Flight station, where she kept watch over Earth's first line of defense from orbit . . .

Well, look out—

You couldn't be expected to put up with all the crap that came with being the world's mightiest female super heroes and *not* have a safe space to compare notes. For the lucky few members of Go Night, as they usually called it, that space was an old conference/poker table in the basement of the New York Triskelion. Conveniently located in the same complex as S.H.I.E.L.D. Academy (for Natasha, who had become a lurker of practically parental proportions, thanks to Ava) and at the bottom of what everyone jokingly called Carol's private Wonkavator, her transport from Alpha Flight to the Triskelion and back, Go Night was nonnegotiable.

Natasha smiled to herself. Ava was still too green for

Go Night, no matter how badly she'd wanted in the game since she'd first heard about it. *Which is why the first rule of Go Night is that there is no Go Night. Danvers never should have told her about it, that softy . . .*

Natasha paused. "That all?"

The Synth whirred as it searched the server. "One more, Natasha. UNSUB?"

"Say again?" Natasha covered her other ear, trying to hear.

"Correct, Natasha. The data burst originated with UNSUB," the Synth repeated. "UNSUB is online now."

"Wait—an UNSUB? As in, Unknown Subject, on our Sametime? That's not possible." Everyone at S.H.I.E.L.D. was assigned a single digital profile, and every profile was highly tracked. There were no unknowns—not ever—on a secure line. *That's the whole point, isn't it? What could get through Sametime and Stark-time?*

"Pull it up," Natasha said, suddenly turning to check the crowd for Ava, who was busy taking panoramic pictures of the view, spinning herself and her cell phone in circles at the edge of the platform.

"Enabling S.H.I.E.L.D. Sametime message now," the Synth confirmed.

A second text box appeared on the horizon in the center of the screen, and Natasha opened it.

UNSUB: WHEN YOU EXPECT MORE FROM S.H.I.E.L.D. SAMETIME'S
    FIREWALL . . .
UNSUB: OR THE AVENGERS' BLACK WIDOW . . .

Okay—

Natasha concentrated on the line of text in front of her. As she spoke her answer carefully into the mic, the corresponding words appeared in her holographic field of vision.

N_ROMANOFF: SORRY TO DISAPPOINT. WHO IS THIS?

There was no answer, so she tried again.

N_ROMANOFF: WHAT DO YOU WANT? HOW DID YOU GET IN HERE?

Still nothing.

But the user was flagged as active. Someone was lurking in her Sametime account. Ghosting. The name on the account was fake—*UNSUB* was a military term for an unknown person or persons during an operation—but whoever it was might as well have been waving a red flag.

The next three transmissions didn't make her feel any better.

UNSUB: #HEROESALLFALL
UNSUB: #LIKETHEWALL
UNSUB: #PAYATTENTION

Pay attention? Natasha frowned. *I always do. Who are you?*

She watched through her glasses as the projected words glowed in the three-dimensional hologram in front of the rapidly darkening sky. She no longer saw the view.

What are you looking for?

How the words—this person—had made their way through firewall after firewall, relay after relay, into Natasha's only truly secure account, she had no idea. All she knew was that they were there now, which meant they had access to everything. . . .

Suddenly a third dialogue box appeared—this time lit in glowing red.

A new message from UNSUB.

She watched the letters rapidly appear, one by one—and she was hardly surprised when they no longer assembled themselves into English.

UNSUB: ZHIVOYE OTOMSTIT' ZA MERTVYKH, NATASHKAYA
UNSUB: THE LIVING AVENGE THE DEAD, NATASHKAYA
UNSUB: HAVE A LITTLE FAITH, PTNETS . . .
UNSUB: WE HAVE MISSED YOU.

Ptnets—

Only one person had ever called her that. She felt her body begin to shake, the oxygen leave her lungs, her head—

But I fired a bullet into his skull. I saw him die with my own eyes.

At my own hand.

Natasha had no idea she was holding her breath until the voice of her Synth startled her back to reality. "Security protocols have been violated, Natasha."

Real Natasha hardly listened—her mind was already racing. "Activate Protocol X, security."

"Affirmative, Natasha. Protocol X is activated. Taking X Action now." Then the Synth seemed to hesitate, which Natasha knew was impossible. "Updating: UNSUB has copied and deleted eighty-four percent of your secure personal files, Natasha."

Natasha's face went white, but she stayed outwardly calm.

Every action is a message. So is every attack.

You can't be Ivan Somodorov, so what are you telling me?

I'm listening.

"Compromised files reaching ninety-four percent, Natasha."

She frowned. "What happened to the protocol? Lock it down, security."

Play your best hand, go on.

No matter what you try, you won't stay an UNSUB for long—

"Protocol X has been overridden, Natasha."

"That's not possible—"

Instinctively, Natasha began to thread her way through the crowd toward Ava, who still had her eyes glued to her phone. The veteran agent's heartbeat stayed on double time, and she knew it was panic, though it wasn't a sensation she'd felt often. The only other thing she felt was a mounting frustration that was capped by fury—and that one, she knew well.

Is that it, UNSUB? You can get to me, but I can't get to you?

Think again, friend.

The moment that Natasha reached Ava, she grabbed her roughly by the arm. "Time's up. We're rolling out."

Ava tried to wave her off. "Wait up. Did you know, if you catch the sunset at exactly the right second, it glows green instead of orange? Like, bright radioactive slime green. Alien green. Why is that?"

The Synth spoke up through Natasha's earpiece. "Personal files are one hundred percent deleted, Natasha. So are the following: classified records, medical records, records of service, files flagging Natasha Romanoff, files cross-referencing Natasha Romanoff . . ."

As bleak as the announcement was, Natasha didn't care about her files. She kept a copy—three copies, in fact—of everything she cared about in one or another of three external drives stored in three safety-deposit boxes outside of New York City: in Zurich, in London, and in Hong Kong. There were also passports and a few old photographs, plus rubber-band-wrapped envelopes of cash for emergencies—ten thousand euros, ten thousand pounds sterling, and twenty-five thousand American dollars, to be exact. Not enough to arouse suspicion, but enough, in a pinch, to lease a *masseria* farmhouse in Puglia, the southeastern heel of the Italian boot, for a year. If she had to.

More important than the security breach was the reveal—the fact of what it said about the crime against her, and the person committing it. The trained-operative side of Natasha was fascinated, even if the rest of her wanted to scream.

Interesting. So our UNSUB only wants me—or they want a certain piece of information from my files—or to disappear that certain piece of information?

Or maybe they really just want to mess with my head?

Any way you looked at it, it was useful. She pressed her earpiece. "How are we doing on the protocol?"

"I've isolated your data string now, Natasha. Remaining firewalls appear to be secure."

"Copy that." Natasha sighed. "Better loop in S.H.I.E.L.D." As she began to pull the glasses off her head, a white flash temporarily blinded her—and she stumbled.

Ava caught her by the arm. "Whoa—you all right?"

The hologram shifted, and a pixelated graphic of a winged skull now appeared in front of Natasha.

UNSUB: DO NOT WORRY, PTNETS.

UNSUB: KRASNYY ANZHEL PRIKHODIT DLYA VAS

UNSUB: THE RED ANGEL COMES FOR YOU

UNSUB: DOCH' SVETA

UNSUB: DAUGHTER OF LIGHT

UNSUB: REBENOK SMERTI

UNSUB: CHILD OF DEATH

UNSUB: ENJOYING THE VIEW?

S.H.I.E.L.D. EYES ONLY

CLEARANCE LEVEL X

SPECIAL CIRCUMSTANCES & INDIVIDUALS (SCI) INVESTIGATION
AGENT IN COMMAND (AIC): PHILLIP COULSON
RE: AGENT NATASHA ROMANOFF A.K.A. BLACK WIDOW
A.K.A. NATASHA ROMANOVA
AAA HEARING TRANSCRIPT
CC: DEPARTMENT OF DEFENSE, SCI INQUIRY

COULSON: Red Angel.
ROMANOFF: Daughter of Light, Child of Death.
COULSON: Poetic.

ROMANOFF: Twisted messages. I wish I had understood at the time.
COULSON: You can't blame yourself for what happened.
ROMANOFF: How can I not?

COULSON: So that day at the Cristo was your first indication that you had been targeted?
ROMANOFF: Yes. We had believed the Red Room was operating in the region, but we didn't know we were stepping into their crosshairs.
COULSON: Not until that day.

ROMANOFF: It was almost funny. Before the Cristo, we'd had no leads pan out since we'd gotten to South America. We were about to give up on finding any.
COULSON: And people say there is no irony in special ops.
ROMANOFF: Go figure.

COULSON: Now can we talk about that poker game?
ROMANOFF: Above your pay grade, Coulson.
COULSON: How far?
ROMANOFF: Friend, that's one clearance you will never have.

RIO DE JANEIRO, BRAZIL
CHRIST THE REDEEMER STATUE,
MOUNT CORCOVADO

Ava watched in shock as Natasha ripped off her glasses and shoved her toward the monument staircase in almost one fluid motion. "What's *wrong* with you?" Ava said as her phone went flying out of her hands.

"Run. Now!" Natasha barked.

Ava looked surprised, but once she caught a glimpse of Natasha's face, she was up and sprinting after her. She knew that look well enough not to ask any questions or take any chances. The agents skidded down the stairs two at a time—Ava's cheap sandals slapping on the stone—all the way to the parking lot next to the ticket kiosk and the shed of restrooms where Natasha's Harley waited.

Only paces away, Natasha stopped short, grabbing Ava with one extended arm. "Wait." She pulled a keyless remote out of her pocket and clicked a button.

Ava held her breath, though she didn't really know why. *What are you expecting, for the thing to explode? You've got to be kidding me.* But the starter button hit, and the bike's ignition kicked in, and the engine rumbled like usual. Both Widows looked relieved to hear it.

Natasha slung one leg over her bike. "Get on."

Once again, she gets to drive. Ava hopped on, just behind Natasha. "You want to tell me—"

"Nope." Natasha grabbed the clutch and gunned the bike out of the parking lot. Ava barely held on to her shoulders—she was so surprised by the suddenness of the acceleration.

What happened?

Natasha careened the Harley out onto the twisting mountain road, narrowly avoiding a rattling truck full of jackfruit—which slid, rolling into the street with every bump. A wild marmoset monkey screeched from his perch atop an abandoned Dumpster as both truck and bike passed, leaping clear over the Harley to chase the road-kill fruit. All Ava knew, as she hung on for her life and dodged flying green produce the size of watermelons, was that Natasha had to be driving like a maniac for a reason.

Something has gotten her attention. The mission. Something big.

Ava ducked behind Natasha's back as the Harley dove forward, ignoring the S-curve of the road by shooting straight down the center axis. *Krasnaya Komnata? Red Room? Is that what this is about?* As the highway curved in front of them, she considered the shadowy group that had been funding Ivan's rise to power, his research, his tech, his whole army. In other words, the organization they had sworn to destroy—

Something to do with Ivan Somodorov? And Alexei?

Ava's stomach lurched and roiled, and the wind bit her face as they raced toward the long shadow of the mountain, spraying gravel behind them. She pulled her chin up over Natasha's shoulder to see ahead of the bike.

Only then did Ava notice the Widow's Cuff sparking and smoking. She pointed, shouting, "Look, your Cuff—it's on fire!"

"What?" Natasha glanced down. The Cuff began to burn red-hot, smoking against the skin underneath it, where it had come into contact with her throttle grip. She swore, pulling her left hand away from the handlebar, continuing to curse as she held it out from her body. She didn't stop the Harley, though—she drove faster, steering the bike with only her right arm.

"Natasha!" Ava shouted. "You have to get that thing off—"

"It's stuck." Natasha leaned to twist her arm back behind her. "You try—"

The bike swerved as Ava reached up to fumble at the jammed release on Natasha's Cuff. It burned the pads of her fingers, and she winced. *How is she not screaming? How high is the Romanoff pain tolerance?*

33

As she tried the clasp again, the Harley's back wheels hit a gravel patch and skidded out. For a moment, Ava thought that Natasha was going to inadvertently lay the bike down on the road.

She closed her eyes. *Pazhalsta*— Please—

"Ava," Natasha yelled.

The energy flowing through Ava—that was always flowing through Ava, ever since the O.P.U.S. blast in Istanbul—pulsed and convulsed from the center of her chest, finally surging, uncoiling all the way down her arms and up her legs, wrapping its tentacles from her neck to her wrists and ankles. Though normally the light found its way out through her blades, which functioned more or less as basic conductors, now she let it escape through her fingers.

When she opened her eyes again, her pupils glowed with the now-familiar iridescent blue light. Even her lips and fingertips burned with cold blue fire.

Natasha glanced over her shoulder. "Ava, what are you—"

Ava reached for Natasha's Cuff again, this time barely touching it. The Cuff began to stream black smoke from all sides—

It exploded open, flying off Natasha's wrist and shooting high into the air over their heads—

Ava ducked forward with a shout. "Watch out!"

Natasha winced and yanked her wrist away. A split second later, the Cuff exploded into a billowing cloud of soot and flame.

Oh no, not again, she thought. She had overdone it. *Quickly. Shut it down, before you make everything worse—*

"*Der'mo—*" Natasha cursed, and Ava saw that now the left throttle had ignited as well. The flames were spreading, and Natasha had to control the Harley again with only her right hand. "Oh, come on," she shouted at the bike, annoyed.

You lit a whole motorcycle on fire this time? Great. With your luck you should just be happy the whole thing didn't explode—

Ava shouted up into the wind. "Pull over!"

If this thing does blow, I don't want to be remembered as the person who killed an Avenger.

Natasha shook her head. "Can't. They're here, and we have to put a little mileage between us and whoever wants us to be roadkill." As she spoke she gunned the bike.

Roadkill, Ava thought. *Who wants that?*

The burning Harley sped through the center of the smoke, dipping dangerously to one side. Natasha's hair fluttered in the wind as she leaned to swing her weight far to the left. Ava followed, until they pulled the bike back up to a vertical axis.

The bike lurched, smoking and coughing up gravel, but managed to stay on the road. Ava's eyes were watering in the wind, and it was difficult to see. She could feel her entire body tensing into a tight fist of clenched limbs.

Is someone after us?

She looked over her shoulder. There was a crater in the

asphalt behind them now—and above it, a coiling black snake of smoke and ash. She turned back around to see the fire spreading across the front of the bike.

That can't be me. Not all me.

Someone rigged her Cuff, and I set it off.

Her throat and lungs burned; her eyes stung. The air around her smelled charred—or maybe that was her hair—and she could hear (and feel) Natasha coughing up smoke in front of her. "You okay?"

"*Ideal? No,*" Natasha yelled back. *Perfect.*

Of course. How Russian. Ava tried again. "What was that?" *I'm guessing a direct action assault, not that you'll admit it. Not while we're sitting on a burning Harley meters from the attack site—*

Natasha accelerated again. "My Cuff. Someone got to it."

"No kidding," Ava shouted back. "But what *was* that?"

"Magnesium."

"What?" Ava yelled. "I mean, how?"

There was no answer until they came out of the next turn. Then Natasha leaned halfway toward Ava. "Magnesium trace concentrate. You were just the lighter. Can we talk about this later?"

So they rigged your Cuff—? You, the great Natasha Romanoff? Ava shook her head. *And they knew I would set it off? Whoever it is, they know about me?*

Natasha swerved again, this time cutting left off the main road into what looked like a long private driveway. The flames on the left half of the handlebar were spreading into the main chassis of the bike now. Natasha's tough black boots only protected so much; Ava's legs were bare, and she curled them up as high as she could, keeping her feet propped on the wheel covers. *We can't keep this up for long—*

The bike chewed and bumped its way past a ranch-style house, then through the shrub-covered hillside beyond it. Pebbles and roots and dust went flying. With every revolution of the wheel, the flames spun farther down from the handlebars to the body of the bike. Ava leaned forward to shout in Natasha's ear. "It was the girl, right? Back at the monument? The one in the green dress? Who tried to pull a brush pass?"

"What?" Natasha glanced over her shoulder, startled. Ava felt proud for a moment—and then humiliated. *She didn't think I noticed. She doesn't think I'm capable of anything.*

"Brush pass," Ava shouted.

"Yeah." Natasha turned her attention back to the rocky hillside. "Think so." *Classic Red Room move—right out of Ivan's manual.* But Ava also knew that Natasha understood that manual better than anyone, so she knew what must have happened next. She leaned forward once again.

"Did you tag her back? Tell me you tagged her back, right?" Ava shouted.

Natasha angled her head slightly to one side and smiled. "Is that even a question?"

Of course you did, Ava thought. Knowing Natasha, she'd stuck her standard-issue adhesive RFID tag on the girl before she could walk away. Hopefully, within twenty-four hours—or as long as it took S.H.I.E.L.D. to find the right frequency—they'd be able to pinpoint her location. Radio frequency IDs were the classic go-to in data-pushing surveillance, and Natasha always kept one handy; it was the size of a grain of rice, lodged in a niche at the base of the tiny silver ankh ring on her left hand. She wore it the way other people would wear a wedding ring.

Lucky for both of us, she's married to the job.

Ava thought back over the attempted plant again now; at least, what little she had seen of it. The dark-haired girl's elbow, bumping Natasha's shoulder. She imagined the bump was the decoy, or what Natasha had taught her was the sucker's move. You had to keep an eye on the other hand, the one slapping the magnesium tab on the under-side of the Widow's Cuff. That was the shot that mattered.

It's always the second move that counts, isn't that what you said, Natasha? The second shot, the second flank, the second attack? See, I was listening—

They powered through a row of jacarandas and burst out onto the road again, just as it curved around the bottom of the rising hills of Corcovado. The Harley bounced over and over—and Ava's body slammed against Natasha's from the impact. *"Smotret eto sestra!"* Watch it, sister! *You just might kill us before anyone in the Red Room can—*

"Yeah, you should talk, *zhivchik*—" Natasha shouted back. Fireball.

Ava's face burned with embarrassment.

Natasha accelerated wordlessly out of the landing, speeding into the oncoming chaos of Rio's evening traffic. Their tires were smoking; their chassis was fully on fire.

Ava turned once more to check out the road behind them, and then shouted back up to Natasha. "There's no one there. We're clear. You have to stop—this whole thing is going to blow, *man'yak!*" Maniac. She suspected that Natasha's boots were burning, close to melting, even. They were out of options.

But we aren't the only ones, she thought.

Now the Widows sped weaving past the cars in front of them. Nobody could stop Natasha Romanoff when she was in this mood.

Whoever you are, girl in green, I hope you know what you've done, Ava thought. A siren began to blare in the distance. *Because this means war . . .*

Natasha jammed down her one working throttle and plowed the bike up the back of an unsuspecting Fiat.

Ava screamed and the Harley went flying into the air.

She squeezed her eyes shut as they smashed through a chain-link fence and landed wheels down in the deeper end of the ancient, low-lying swimming pool of the Piscina do Casarão—

Hissing and steaming, metal hit water. Both Widows went under, barely touching the concrete beneath their ten-foot tsunami landing.

Ava opened her eyes in the murky water to see Natasha's Glock sinking slowly down to the pool bottom.

. . . and war is how she wants it.

S.H.I.E.L.D. EYES ONLY
CLEARANCE LEVEL X

SPECIAL CIRCUMSTANCES & INDIVIDUALS (SCI) INVESTIGATION
AGENT IN COMMAND (AIC): PHILLIP COULSON
RE: AGENT NATASHA ROMANOFF A.K.A. BLACK WIDOW
A.K.A. NATASHA ROMANOVA
AAA HEARING TRANSCRIPT
CC: DEPARTMENT OF DEFENSE, SCI INQUIRY

COULSON: Unbelievable.

ROMANOFF: I know. One day, two encounters. HUMINT and SIGINT.

COULSON: I was back on the whole "driving a flaming Harley down a mountain and into a swimming pool" thing, but okay—

ROMANOFF: Two encounters, both direct assaults. I didn't know why.

COULSON: I don't know why there aren't more action figures of you on flaming Harleys.

ROMANOFF: Coulson. The attacks were messages, like I said.

COULSON: And the message was, screw you?

ROMANOFF: More like, we can screw with you.

COULSON: How'd that go over?

ROMANOFF: Pretty much like you'd imagine.

COULSON: I have a vivid imagination. I'm imagining grenades.

ROMANOFF: I held it together. After it happened, the only thing I pulled a pin on was Stark, when we got home.

COULSON: To Howard Stark's Copacabana Beach penthouse?

ROMANOFF: Yes.

COULSON: The one with the butler and the rooftop pool?
ROMANOFF: Didn't notice.

COULSON: What came next? You had to locate the tracker you stuck on the operative?
ROMANOFF: I handed that off to the guy who owns half the world's airwaves.
COULSON: Ah yes, our man of iron and butlers. Let me guess, he was happy to help. . . .
ROMANOFF: I wouldn't say happy. . . .

COPACABANA BEACH, RIO DE JANEIRO
THE STARK PENTHOUSE,
COPACABANA PALACE HOTEL

"**N**o, Tony, I don't *happen to think* you're my IT guy." Natasha bristled, wrapping the electrical burn on her wrist with a roll of gauze from one of Howard Stark's many steel-encased first-aid kits. "*I'm* my IT guy."

"That's great because, as I told you, I'm kind of in the middle of something." Tony's face looked down from the wall-size monitor behind her; behind him, wherever he was, she could see a massive, concrete wall—maybe part of a basement? His voice echoed in what seemed to be a cavernous space. "Six million volts of electron energy, to be exact—and probably my best shot at a Nobel Prize in physics, or whatever. You know, CERN? The Large Hadron Collider? But no big deal, I guess it can wait because you need your *email fixed—*"

CERN? What is Tony doing in Switzerland? As the quantum entanglement link between Natasha and Ava had been one of Tony's longest-running open investigations in quantum physics, she was suspicious—but she also knew the look on Tony's face. He wasn't talking.

At the moment, she was too impatient to care. Natasha looked at him. "Are you through?"

Tony shrugged. "I guess."

"Has your server finished tracking the data path yet?"

He consulted a panel on his digital tablet. "Almost," Tony said. "Hang tight."

Natasha shook her head, frustrated. "I can't just sit here. Something's happening again. I can feel it, even if I can't see how it all fits together yet."

Last year, it had been hard enough to locate the hidden synapses between a Ukrainian shipping company and Moscow's black-tape military-industrial complex—not to mention between a future-tech underground Turkish laboratory and Ivan Somodorov's legendary school for spies. It was overwhelming to try to see how that all connected to what had happened today.

How it connected? Who do you think you're kidding, Natashkaya? Everything in your life connects back to one place and one time.

The Red Room.

She'd guessed the Krasnaya Komnata would come for her the moment she had taken out Ivan Somodorov, hadn't she? For all she knew, the Russian girl at the Cristo could be Red Room, herself. Beyond that, Natasha had only one true piece of intel to go on, the same tip that had brought Ava and her to Brazil six months ago. A few words taken from a dispatch that had been translated from an unfamiliar Ukrainian dialect.

KRASNAYA KOMNATA POTREBNOSTI YUZHNOY AMERIKI DEN'GI—

THE RED ROOM NEEDS SOUTH AMERICAN MONEY.

Moscow Station had bumped it to S.H.I.E.L.D., and Maria Hill had tossed it to Natasha. It hadn't come from any confirmable or reliable source, and they hadn't determined if it was true, yet. All of this, plus the hack, plus the girl, could still amount to nothing. *But—*

It also could be a first tremor, a single stray thread, or a hairline crack that might eventually bring the whole wall crumbling down.

And the one thing Natasha Romanoff knew about walls was that they tended to come down, especially when the Avengers were around.

This could be exactly what we've been waiting for—

"You think it's them?" Ava asked. She didn't have to say the name. There was no one else.

"That's what we need to find out." Natasha looked at her. "What do we have—a face if we can recognize it, a digital record if we can trace it?"

"What about Rio's city security footage? The Cristo's a public monument, right? They could have something," Tony said.

"Already got Maria Hill on it. She said to give it a day." *Though I'm not sure I have a day.* "Let's focus on the girl." There was something about Green Dress Girl that bothered her—a nagging feeling, a faint sense of déjà vu—even if she couldn't place why or how she felt it . . . or even what precisely she felt, yet.

"You think she's Red Room's latest model? Or a cutout?" Ava volunteered. "And yes, I know what a cutout is," she said, trying not to sound too proud of herself for pulling out her Academy vocab.

"Right," Natasha said. "Which means she could be nobody and know nothing—except to follow her orders and keep her mouth shut. That's the S.V.R. way."

S.V.R.: Sluzhba Vneshncy Razvedki. The Foreign Intelligence Service of the Russian Federation. She let the shiver roll through her body as she said the acronym; even after all these years, she still felt the pull of cold, industrial dread whenever she heard those three letters.

The K.G.B. had been no different before it, neither was the G.R.U., now. The characters bore a significance hammered from iron and snow; they stood for words that could never be spoken and pain that must forever be endured. *That's how it works,* Natasha thought. *The alphabet of fear.*

Ava looked anxious. "You really think Green Dress is S.V.R.?"

"Would the S.V.R. be stupid enough to try a move like that on you?" Tony looked at her skeptically.

"Who do you think taught me those moves? Someone in the S.V.R.'s Directorate X, the Division of Science and Technology—and in their Directorate S, the Division of Illegal Intelligence," Natasha said.

"Stop," Ava said, shaking her head.

But Natasha couldn't, and the words came spilling out. "Ivan Somodorov was deputy director of both, at one time or another. He was born to it, his father was K.G.B., and his mother was a political officer for Stalin—a spy of spies. He once said even his brother was Spetsnaz." Russian Special Forces. "What other kind of person could have run the Red Room?"

"I don't know, but it makes me think of a worse question. Who is running it now?" Ava sounded miserable.

"That," Tony said, "is one of those questions you really don't want answered."

"So maybe that's what this little meet-and-greet is about—the announcement of a new regime." Natasha looked at the screen. "And to answer your question, people like that would do anything to anyone."

"But it's not anyone," Ava said, suddenly. "It's you, and they know that. So they'd predict that you'd see their move coming, wouldn't they?"

Tony nodded. "Absolutely."

"And if they did, then was their first move the goal, or was your countermove? Were the attacks meant to scare you away or draw you in?" Ava frowned.

She's learning. That's good. "They trained me as a spy—so if I had to guess, I'd say they wanted to give me something to spy on," Natasha said.

"So your countermove was the point." Ava nodded. "To draw you in by launching your investigation for you. Because it's always the second—"

"—the second move that matters. Exactly." Natasha nodded. Ava smiled.

"So the girl at the Cristo was trained," Tony said. "By someone who knows you, or who took the time to profile you. Someone who knew you'd visit the monument. That you'd be wearing your Cuff—and that Sparky here would be . . . sparking."

Neither Widow answered. It was a sobering thought.

"Okay," Tony said. "Green Dress had training. Green Dress had intel. Green Dress had access, right? A supply network. I mean, people don't sell magnesium on the street corner."

"No, they don't. But we'll know more soon. I planted that RFID tracker on her. She has to turn up soon," Natasha said.

He shook his head. "Those things are so old-school we have to work through radio waves, not even satellite. We'll be lucky to find her, even with that. It could take days."

"Data is data," Natasha said. "And 'old-school' just means so old they won't trace it back to me."

"Speaking of data . . ." Tony held up his tablet. "The Stark servers have just confirmed the trace on the data package." He looked at Ava. "That's the Sametime message N-Ro got—"

"I know what a data package is," Ava said crossly. "Don't *Tonysplain*."

"Okay, okay. I don't have the spy-school syllabus," Tony said. "Snippy."

"So you confirmed the trace? And?" Natasha asked, impatient.

"Then my network tracked that data package backward, through the first series of relays, as it connects again and again through almost every continent," Tony went on, scrolling through the endless code. "The path almost doesn't seem to stop."

Natasha nodded. "So they're good."

"Very good. That's some clean code, nice work," Tony said. "Almost a crime that it's a crime. I'd hire them in a second. Well, maybe five seconds, realistically speaking. A second is actually not very—"

"Thought train," Ava said. "It's leaving the station."

He got to the point. "Right. Eventually, the data tracks back to a series of ghost accounts owned by other ghost accounts, which isn't a surprise."

"Ghosts?" Ava looked at him strangely.

"The surprise is that it's a loop," Tony continued. "It's programmed to rewrite over and over itself so you can't find an origin. It's the chicken and the egg of big data."

"So we're screwed," Ava said. Natasha wordlessly sat back in her chair.

"More like scrambled." Tony arched an eyebrow.

"Except this is me, so, please. Have a little faith. I think I can unscramble the data and try to step out of the loop. Just a sec—"

Natasha looked up. "Go on."

"I asked my network to compare data streams. Not what we're getting from the hacker's ghost sites, but what those sites are getting from the rest of the web." Tony tapped his screen. "I can't get past the ghost accounts, but it looks like one particular spam website can."

"What?" Ava asked.

He studied the screen. "Our hacker must have clicked on it once. Either way, it's the only IP address sending anything that the fake hosts have in common." Tony shook his head.

"And? What is it?" Natasha asked.

He looked up with a grin. "*Meows of Moscow.* And sadly, that is actually not a joke."

Ava looked incredulous. "What are you talking about?"

"One pop-up. That's all it takes. Our hacker opened one pop-up, possibly because he was sloppy but probably because he's *meowy funny.*" Tony hit a few keys. "Now I'm asking my network to compare that site back against everything else it visited on the data path."

"And?" Natasha looked at him.

"And . . . looks like there is one . . . two? . . . no, just one IP address not accounted for."

"Which is?" Ava moved in front of the wall screen.

Tony studied the tablet. "It seems most of the heavy lifting here originates from an IP address owned by an account named ZeroHour, who also happens to be—and I'll let you guess—"

"Yeah, not guessing," Natasha said.

"Well, too bad. If you had said *expert in zero-day vulnerabilities and other cool surveillance party tricks*, you would have won a prize." Tony said. "Instead, all you get is his snazzy web profile." He held his tablet up to the monitor, and a tabloid photograph of a Russian guy with sunken eyes, pale skin, and an even paler bleached Mohawk appeared in his place. "And I ask you, who thinks neck tattoos are ever a good idea?"

"Wow," Ava said. "*That's* our hacker?"

"*Maks Milosovich?*" Natasha read off the screen. "I know that name. The Moscow party boy?"

"Mosc-*meow*," Tony corrected her. "But I've been accused of staying with a joke for too long."

"That," Ava said.

"No. It can't be him." Natasha was convinced. "All that Maks guy does is dance on tables and date live Barbie dolls."

"And yet you say that like it's a bad thing," Tony said dryly.

Natasha looked at the caption beneath the photograph. "Zero-day expert? I think this one's just a zero."

"*Zero day?* What does that mean again?" Ava asked.

"Private tech security," Natasha said. "Maks heads up a digital security company funded by his father, Vladimir Milosovich, a.k.a. obscene oligarch of the Russian new world order. They say Putin himself is jealous of his oil holdings."

"Go Vlad the Dad." Tony whistled.

"The Milosovich clan is from Moscow, right? Which means a Red Room connection isn't out of the question." Ava looked at Natasha.

"Vladimir Milosovich is said to have made his fortune in tech stocks after working for Directorate X. You know the drill: sell your secrets to the government, then turn around and sell the government back their own secrets," Natasha said.

"Wait." Tony looked at her. "Didn't you just say Ivan Somodorov was a deputy dog or whatever in Directorate X?"

For a moment, no one said a thing. Then Natasha shook her head. "That's too easy, isn't it? A rich Russian hacker comes after us because Ivan knows his father?"

"You think they know each other?" Ava was startled.

"Easy? What about that was easy? My ability to synthesize information? Yeah, I think you're confusing *easy* with *certifiable genius*," Tony said. "As is so often the case."

"I never said you weren't certifiable." Natasha looked at him.

"Well, I vote this is our guy," Tony said. "So have S.H.I.E.L.D. check it out. Confirm the intel. Listen to the chatter, or whatever it is those guys do up on the tenth floor." He shrugged. "I feel like it's definitely something about chatter."

"Don't tell me about chatter. All we've gotten around here is chatter," Natasha said, frustrated. "We need actual leads to follow. I want to know everything about our hacker and our girl in the green dress—and what they have to do with each other."

"Synthesize that," Ava said, looking up at digital Tony.

"We'll figure it out," Tony said. "We always do."

We have to, Natasha thought. Once again, the familiar ache overtook the empty space in her chest. *Alexei's gone, and they have to pay. All of them—*

She wanted a reckoning for her brother, an evening of the odds. More than that, she wanted payback—for Alexei and Ava and herself. *Vengeance for our shared broken heart. And justice.* That's what she wanted now.

But since when, she asked herself, *have you ever gotten a single thing you've wanted?*

COULSON: So, the Russian.
ROMANOFF: The Russian.
COULSON: Why is there always a Russian?

ROMANOFF: You know that's what the rest of the world says
about Americans, right?
COULSON: Maybe it's the vodka.
ROMANOFF: This guy had bigger problems than vodka.

COULSON: And Ava—how was our girl? After almost getting
blown up?
ROMANOFF: This wasn't her first almost-getting-blown-up
rodeo.
COULSON: They start to add up, though. After a while, every
death you've avoided—and every one your team hasn't—it
takes a toll.
ROMANOFF: Tell me about it.

COULSON: You spend enough time with S.H.I.E.L.D. and the
ghosts are everywhere.
ROMANOFF: I don't believe in ghosts.
COULSON: But you're fine with gods and aliens and big green
men?
ROMANOFF: Yeah, well. I know those guys.

COULSON: What if you knew the ghost? Or what about Quantum ghosts? The ghost of Schrödinger's cat?

ROMANOFF: Would I have to feed it?

COULSON: Technically, I think you'd have to both feed it and not feed it at the same time.

ROMANOFF: That would and would not be all right.

COULSON: Think about it. Isn't quantum entanglement just the possibility of matter resonating in two different places at the same time? How is that different from a ghost?

ROMANOFF: Science, that's how.

COULSON: One day Tony will science the crap out of ghosts and then you'll see.

COPACABANA BEACH, RIO DE JANEIRO
THE STARK PENTHOUSE,
COPACABANA PALACE HOTEL

This place is a maximum-luxury, maximum-security prison, Ava thought as she retreated back outside, past the soundproof Plexiglas living room walls to the hot, damp shade of the terrace on a Copacabana afternoon. Tony and Natasha were still online, trying to find a way to track down the hacker. When they had gotten hung up on arguing the finer merits of the Doomjuice worm versus the NIMDA virus, Ava had excused herself.

She unrolled a monogrammed towel—A.E.S., for Anthony Edward Stark, though Natasha liked to pretend to misread it as A.S.S., as if that joke never got old—and settled into a canvas-padded chaise longue that overlooked the beach far below. Ava pulled out her comic book and her music (the playlist her best-and-only friend, Oksana, had made for her) and tried to tell her brain to shut up.

She had no complaints about their accommodations. Excepting its rock-hard couches and space-age Howard Stark furniture, the penthouse was insane. Aside from adding monster-size plasma screens to every room, Tony had left the already impressive features of his father's sixth-floor Brazilian getaway completely intact. The two-bedroom suite had its own rooftop pool, sauna, butler, and most conveniently, helipad, where a S.H.I.E.L.D.-registered (and highly armed) Sikorsky chopper was currently parked and waiting. Howard, aside from being a fan of Rio's breathtaking beaches, had clearly had a taste for the finer things. *It's a long way from the basement of the Fort Greene Y,* Ava thought.

Not that she was entirely enjoying it, though she wasn't sure she could say why not, aside from her general mood ever since Alexei died.

Stop. Not now. Don't go there.

As Ava put in her earbuds, she stared down at the embarrassingly bright floral pattern of her matching tank top and board shorts. *Look at you. Some intimidating operative you are.* Ava had a harder time than Natasha outside of New York. Natasha had come to expect Rio's inferno blast of heat and humidity; beyond S.H.I.E.L.D.-issue gear, she'd insisted they pack nothing and buy all their clothes from the cheap shops and stalls of the Bazar

Centro do Saara—even shoes, though she rarely took her own motorcycle boots off. Natasha was fine with it, and always managed to look cool. Ava, in her neon tank top and awkwardly-fitting Velcro surf shorts and flimsy leather sandals that would fall apart in a minute if she tried to strafe and roll, did not.

"This is fieldwork. You're blending in. Deal with it," Natasha had said when Ava had protested. "As long as you have enough pockets to hold your gear and a loose enough shirt to conceal your blades, what do you care what you're wearing?"

But it wasn't just the shorts. Ava put down her comic and stared out at the soft blue-and-white-striped Brazilian sky. After today's events, she couldn't pretend anymore. The truth was obvious.

We both want the same thing, but I can't help her find it. I'm only slowing her down—when I'm not lighting her on fire.

The reality was that Natasha had been targeted and attacked today. She had been the subject of some kind of foreign intelligence op, while Ava was distracted with what? Trying to take pictures of the sunset? Or a monkey? And as they fled the scene, her one big contribution was what? Torching her Harley? Helping Natasha unclasp her *spy jewelry?* Ava had barely gotten a look at the girl in green. She didn't even know the hack was happening until it was over.

What would Agent Coulson or Maria Hill have said about that? Where was your Academy training when you needed it today? Have you shut down your whole S.H.I.E.L.D. brain?

Ava wondered. Would she have noticed a targeted polonium-210 poisoning, like the one that took down the Russian spy Litvinenko in London? An umbrella that fired dioxin, like the one that had struck the politician Yushchenko in Ukraine? A one-shot kiss-of-death lipstick gun or a poison pen, as in the K.G.B. case studies she'd read in her Cold War counterintelligence seminar? How about a precision aerial drone strike on the entire Cristo monument? Would she have heard it? Would she have even seen that coming?

I don't know why Natasha hasn't sent me back to the Academy already. She probably wants to.

For a second, Ava considered the possibility of taking advantage of their Quantum link to see exactly what Natasha thought of her. . . .

"You know it's more complicated than that," a voice said.

Ava looked at the empty chaise next to her. Alexei Romanoff—or rather, the ghost, the memory, the soul of Alexei Romanoff, she no longer knew what to call him— sat on the edge of the cushion, shielding his eyes from the sun with one hand. He was as breathtakingly handsome as ever, and now looked tanned and fit and pleased with himself—or at least, pleased that he'd been able to just show up on the rooftop like this. Alexei still loved a joke.

"Is it?" She rolled her eyes, but as he grinned at her, the

familiar sadness uncoiled itself deep in her body. She had gotten used to his visits, though she had thought she was losing her mind when they'd first begun, the night after his funeral, when he'd curled up next to her and whispered soothing words into her ear until the sun came up again. *I'm here. I'm still here. You aren't alone, Mysh. You never will be. I'm here—*

Now she'd made her peace with only being marginally, secretly insane. He came to her most often at night, in the moments just before she fell asleep. He also had a habit of turning up when she was super stressed, or very upset. Frightened. Sleep-deprived.

Or crashing burning bikes into swimming pools, she thought.

Apparently.

"I'm a liability. Admit it," Ava said to what she knew, deep down, was just an empty space on an empty chair. Still, it was better than an empty heart, which is what she'd had until Alexei had reappeared.

"It's only been a year," Alexei said. *"You have to remember, when I left my sister in Istanbul, I left her with more than just a* razrushennoy *heart." Shattered, yes. More than broken.*

"Exactly," Ava said. "You left her with me, and now she's stuck with a little sister she never wanted. And I drive her crazy, because I'm a half-trained rookie moron, and I barely know what I'm doing. I can barely control my own powers. So yeah, I'm a liability."

"She's not stuck with you. And you're not a rookie moron. You're the Red Widow, remember? She's just looking out for you, like I told her to."

Ava's eyes flickered toward him. *I don't want to talk about this. Not with you.* She wanted to fling herself at him—hide in his compactly muscled arms and kiss his sunburned face—but she had learned by experience that it only made her feel that much more alone. *When I reach for your warmth and feel only air—*

So instead, Ava tried to keep her eyes on the sky. "Are you ever coming back to me, *moya lyubov?*" My love. Their sweetest words always seemed to stick to Russian, as if they still needed to speak in code, even now.

Instantly, he was close by her side, sitting right next to her. She could smell him, the mix of his sweetness and sweat as he held his face only just apart from hers. "You tell me, lisichka. *Did I ever really leave, little fox?" He smiled.*

Ava wondered at the clarity of his gaze; though brighter, even the sky had more clouds. When she turned toward him, it was difficult to not look away, and she found herself fingering the edge of her towel distractedly. "*Pervaya lyubov.* You were my first love. My first broken heart."

"Da, pervaya lyubov," *Alexei agreed. "You still are."*

"Maybe that's enough. To have been in love, even once." She studied his face carefully now. It seemed to soften as she spoke. "I'll never have that with anyone else."

He smiled sadly. "That's not true. You have Natasha and everyone at the Academy. At least three of your classmates ask about you, every day. And of course, Sana and Dante." Dante had been his closest friend, just as Sana had been hers.

"They love you best, and they know us both." He *reached out to touch her face.*

Knew, she silently corrected, and with one word, the anger she worked so hard to keep in check burned back up to the surface.

"Ava."

She looked him in the eye now. "I swear, Alexei. I'll kill everyone who had anything to do with taking you away from me. The Red Room, the military—the whole country if I have to."

"Don't." He sounded wistful.

She frowned. "Why shouldn't I?"

"Ivan's gone. It's over," he said, softly. *"I'm gone, too."*

"If it's so over, then why are you here, *moy prizrak?"* My ghost.

Alexei sat back on his heels. "Ava Anatalya. Vesti sebya." Behave.

She put her hands to her eyes, rubbing away the brightness of the sun. "You know it's not over for your sister—or for me." *Vengeance and hatred, Alexei, that's the nature of our Widows' bond. I accept that, why can't you?*

Her head ached with the weight of it all.

He shook his head. "Nyet. But that's not true—you know it isn't only grief that binds you to my sister, Mysh." No, Mouse. *"And it isn't only me that binds you, either."*

Ava rolled to her other side. She didn't want to think

about quantum entanglement, though it wasn't far from her mind. The two Widows were trapped together in Ivan Somodorov's never-upon-a-time world; they had been since the day their psyches were first linked. Ava's and Natasha's conscious and subconscious minds, thanks to what Tony liked to call the mad science of Ava's quantum physicist mother, Dr. Orlova—not to mention the sick machinations of Ivan himself—were still connected in ways the two of them could only partly comprehend.

Quantum ways.

They could sometimes feel what each other felt or dream what each other dreamed. Other times they simply remembered. The two Widows had tried to sever their linked psyches once, but since they'd arrived in South America, months ago, their connection had only gotten stronger—a fact neither one of them had yet to openly acknowledge to the other. Whether it was proximity or something else, Ava knew, for instance, that Natasha was still reliving the night of Alexei's death in her nightmares—seeing his pale face framed by a spreading puddle of scarlet, over and over again—

"But so are you, Ava Anatalya," Alexei interrupted.

"Of course I am," Ava said, looking at him. "I probably always will. You left. Ivan Somodorov and his army of killers took you from me. My life ended that day, too."

"I don't want that," he said sadly. "Not for you."

"I can't help it. I don't have a choice. I can't control my nightmares, and I can't stop your sister's. At least the memories only come in the day." She didn't want to admit the cost—trauma, exhaustion, unyielding sadness—that the grim parade of images exacted, not even to herself. She imagined it was no better for Natasha. She knew it wasn't, actually, from what she had seen of her mentor's psyche.

The price of the Widow.

Most often, they dreamed of Alexei's death. Sometimes it was Ivan's, or for Natasha, the bombing of the Romanoff family home. Other times they saw the faces of girls who had died in the Red Room, whether from savage beatings or hypothermia or starvation—or from their role as human guinea pigs for the military/scientific/industrial complex served by Ivan and his laboratories.

Why so much darkness? Why is it only the nightmares that linger? Why can't we let them go?

She stared up at the flat blue of the now cloudless sky.

"Because you think they make you powerful, but they don't. They only make you suffer, and you've suffered enough," Alexei said reluctantly. *"You don't have to remember. I wish you wouldn't."*

"How could I forget? How could I even want to?" Ava avoided looking at him. Instead, she studied her own toes. Anything to not see his eyes.

Where's the S.H.I.E.L.D. training for forgetting the eyes of the dead?

Training aside, Ava knew S.H.I.E.L.D. was still a problem, just as it always had been. A shared psyche was inconvenient and sometimes embarrassing, but in the classified, compartmented, eyes-only life of a spy, especially with the Avengers Initiative and global security involved, it was also potentially lethal.

"None of this is your fault," Alexei said, reappearing on this side of the chaise and startling her. *"You don't need to be so worried."*

"How do you know what I need?" Ava said. But she was worried; in fact, the longer they were out in the field, the closer they got to the looming possibility of going home, the more anxiety Ava felt about it.

"How wouldn't I know? I know everything about you, Ava Anatalya." He smiled.

She thought about it. What *was* the issue with going back to New York? She didn't want to fail Alexei by allowing the Red Room to remain operational—and she knew Natasha felt the same way. But Ava also didn't want to go back to the Academy if it meant returning to a life of pretending she wasn't a thousand times more broken than everyone else around her. Beyond that, she didn't want to think about what Tony Stark—who had taken it upon himself to monitor their shifting quantum entanglement—would have to say about the Quantum connection now.

Nothing good.

She looked through the Plexiglas doors to see Tony's face on the monitor, while Natasha stood with her arms folded in front of him. *Probably beating their heads against the wall—*

"Yeah, Tony will probably have you both wired up to a monitor the moment you land at the East River

Triskelion," Alexei agreed. The Triskelion base, stretching for the most part deep beneath New York's East River, was also the home of S.H.I.E.L.D. Academy, where Ava had spent part of last year training. *"Don't let him burn the whole place down. You know he could."*

"As if anyone could stop that," Ava said. Tony had, in fact, burned down his lab the last time they were there together.

Alexei grinned again.

"Anyways, he can try whatever he wants—it won't help. Nothing does." She felt like giving up. "Even if he won't let it drop."

"Don't say that."

"Your sister and I will probably always be linked—and I'll always be a mess." *Because I'm the rookie. I'm the one setting fires and sparking like a downed power line.*

It was true.

"Stop it," Alexei said. *"You're doing the best that you can. How could you do any better? You're at the top of your class. You're training in the field. You're on a mission."*

"This isn't the Academy, Alexei, and I don't know what I'm doing." Truthfully, even the Academy had taken some getting used to; Ava's chest still pulsed with a seemingly free-flowing electrical charge, as it had ever since Istanbul. The current of blue light that coursed through her body carried with it an explicable charge and newfound powers she had only begun to explore. When Ava had it all under control—when she wasn't under attack, or hyperemotional, or otherwise chemically surging—she appeared to be a normal girl, if you didn't look too closely.

Or so she hoped.

It was only when you caught the glints of electricity sparking in her eyes—or the slightest waves of crackling sea-colored light that rippled over her skin—or, okay, when everything around you was suddenly burning—that you realized what she was. Or what she wasn't . . .

"Normal," she said out loud. "I'll never be normal. Not even for a Widow."

"Compared to what? And who cares?" Alexei shrugged. "I don't know any normal people. Not one."

"But you're dead. In your case, that's sound logic."

"In my case, I'm a talking ghost. That's your idea of logical?" Alexei smiled.

She sighed. "Well, in my case? I'm just a freak." There was no answer. She rolled over. *Even my subconscious knows it's true.*

When she looked back again, Alexei had disappeared into the sunshine.

S.H.I.E.L.D. EYES ONLY

CLEARANCE LEVEL X

SPECIAL CIRCUMSTANCES & INDIVIDUALS (SCI)
INVESTIGATION
AGENT IN COMMAND (AIC): PHILLIP COULSON
RE: AGENT NATASHA ROMANOFF A.K.A. BLACK WIDOW
A.K.A. NATASHA ROMANOVA
AAA HEARING TRANSCRIPT
CC: DEPARTMENT OF DEFENSE, SCI INQUIRY

COULSON: Did you know Ava was hallucinating?
ROMANOFF: Quantum entanglement, remember? Our secrets were never very secret from each other. Not that this one would have been easy to miss.

COULSON: So you didn't say anything?
ROMANOFF: What could I say? "Hey, I know you're losing it, but this is a covert military intelligence organization, so no crackpots allowed—we're going to have to cut you loose"?

COULSON: You could have told me.
ROMANOFF: So she could get sent home for needing a shrink?
COULSON: If S.H.I.E.L.D. did that, we'd have no agents, Agent.

ROMANOFF: Send someone to battle and there will be scars, whether or not Uncle Sam allows you to admit it.
COULSON: Believe me, I know.

ROMANOFF: So I guess you also know I was in no position to judge.
COULSON: Because of your own scars?
ROMANOFF: . . .

COULSON: Say no more.
ROMANOFF: I wasn't going to.

COPACABANA BEACH, RIO DE JANEIRO
THE STARK PENTHOUSE,
COPACABANA PALACE HOTEL

Natasha had to give it to Maks Mohawk; even if he was the person they liked for the hack, he wasn't the easiest guy to find. According to her last image search for him, he had disappeared completely online as of twelve months ago.

There were zero photos of him, not clubbing with models or posing at the wheel of half-a-million-dollar race cars or brandishing color-coordinated platters of sushi on his private jet. Not since last year, and not anywhere—not in the searchable databases of the print trades, not online.

Vlad the Dad wasn't giving anything up, either. According to Credit Suisse, Vlad's wealth management consultants—whom Natasha had rung, after Ava saw their names dropped on a *Moscow's Fun Percent* streaming documentary—Mr. and Mrs. Vladimir Milosovich had been on an extended "corporate health retreat" at a private *riad* at the swank La Mamounia in Marrakech for months now. The fact that Morocco enjoyed a healthy nonextradition treaty with the United States was probably also not a coincidence. And Vlad the Dad was apparently a fan of the pigeon soup.

Natasha shuddered.

What sends an oligarch running to the desert? Or gives his weak-chinned son the backbone to disappear? She had no idea.

After a fifteen-hour digital database search, the Widows had decided to regroup. Now they sat at the kitchen table across from each other, eating room-service Wheaties out of eggshell-thin china bowls, with silver pitchers of foamy milk. ("Wheaties? Now you're a Wheaties person?" Ava had asked. Natasha had glared. "It's the breakfast of champions. You got a problem with that?")

"So something must have happened," Ava said. "Something big."

Tony's voice crackled up from the speakerphone on the table next to her. "And our rich Russian kid of Instagramsky vanished."

"Maybe Maks messed with the Russkaya Mafiya?" Ava asked.

"Maybe. *Bratva*'s got a long memory," Natasha said.

"Or the S.V.R., the G.R.U.? A little questioning in a basement of Yasanevo?" Ava shivered. The infamous former headquarters of the K.G.B. was nowhere anyone wanted to visit. "That's what they did to my mother. It would send me running."

It did, Natasha thought. *You've been running ever since. I know, because I know that feeling. And that basement—*

"That kind of big trouble is, you know, *big* big." Tony was mulling it over. "So big he couldn't handle it. So big he erased himself."

"Whatever it was, unfortunately for us, it made him realize he had to be less stupid," Natasha said. "Not stupid enough to use an Amex or keep a sim card in his phone. Nothing that could help us get a read on his G.P.S. or on any other kind of digital signature." She stirred her cereal in the bowl.

Ava looked at her. "Then how are we going to find him?"

"Don't ask me," Tony said. "You're the ones with the Wheaties. Last time I had breakfast, it was a thirty-five-year-old Scotch."

"Ew," Ava said. "You're disgusting."

"Excuse me, you're talking about a 1977 Single Malt Highland that I would have dumped Helen of Troy over."

"As if Helen of Troy wouldn't have dumped you first," Natasha teased.

"In my defense, I would have made one heck of a Trojan horse," he said. No one could argue with that, and they didn't.

The conversation paused—

"That's it. Of course." Natasha let her spoon clatter to the table. "I've got it. We're not going to find Maks Milosovich. Maks Milosovich is going to find us."

"How?" Ava asked.

"The girl in the green dress is our horse." Natasha leaned closer to the speaker.

As she did, the perfectly circular Carrera marble table-top reflected the bright morning sunshine of the kitchen window, and she wondered for the first time if things were going to start falling into place. *Because when has that ever happened?*

"I thought we couldn't find her?" Ava looked at Natasha.

"We're trying to, and we will eventually. But we don't need to locate her to use her server to get a message to our hacker. We just hide ourselves in her digital signature," Natasha said. "Right?"

"Huh," Tony mused.

"Huh?" Ava asked.

Natasha's brain was racing. "I mean, it's a long shot, but it worked for the Spartans, didn't it?"

"Hold up. The Spartans had digital signatures? And the Green Dress Girl would be the messenger?" Ava looked puzzled. "Why would she agree to do that?"

"If this goes down the way I hope it will, she'll never know." Natasha drum-rolled the table with each of her idle fingers. The adrenaline was kicking in. "We're not asking her, we're *being* her. At least, as far as our hacker friend knows."

"Of course. It's so obvious, now that you put it like that." Tony had no problem keeping up with her in the operational calculus department, but then, he liked to hang out at Large Hadron Colliders. She smiled.

"Obvious how?" Ava asked.

"Obviously, if we jack the signal coming from the tracker N-Ro planted on Green Dress Girl, it should pick up her network whether or not we can locate it. It's our back door into whatever she's using to encrypt her communications with the hacker—as long they're communicating," Tony said. "Nice."

Natasha was still figuring it out as she spoke, which also meant the tabletop was still rattling. "There's a chance she might not notice if we get in and out quickly enough. We piggyback on her wireless, use it to send a message through her own network to him, then track his location when he responds."

"If they're in contact, he'll get it. You're some kind of evil genius," Tony said, approvingly.

"If it doesn't work, it doesn't work," Natasha said. "Still, we might as well try. If Green Dress isn't the person who directly hired Maks Milosovich—"

"You mean, if she's a cutout," Ava interrupted.

Again with the vocab. "Sure." Natasha smiled. "Even then, there's still a chance she reports to whoever put out the contract."

"Especially if its Krasnaya Komnata," Ava said. "Which we can't be sure of. And she could also just be onto us—she could have found the tracker and ditched the signal already. For all we know, she could be manipulating us into a trap."

"Either way, it's worth a shot," Tony spoke up. "Seeing as, you know, we don't have any others. The Brazilians aren't exactly jumping to share the feed from their street surveillance cameras with us, my excellent relationship with local law enforcement notwithstanding. . . ."

Ava looked at Natasha. "He's right. We've got nothing else."

Natasha pushed back her chair and stood up. "Then it's settled. We hack the hacker."

Hours later, the penthouse wall monitor was covered with lines of illegible code, all leading up to a single, blank text box.

UNSUB:

Now they just had to compose a fake message to an unknown hacker from a girl they also didn't know.

Tony worked remotely from Geneva via the monitor. Natasha sat at the weird white table on the side of the room, the one with the bottom shaped like a vase. Ava sat on the hard leather rectangle of a couch.

"The message has to be simple, almost generic. We don't want to duplicate a past transmission," Natasha said, staring at the screen.

"And we don't want to expose ourselves by getting some obvious detail wrong," Tony agreed, his voice projecting over the visible text.

"Like we're catfishing." Natasha nodded. "When impersonating someone online, less is more."

Tony thought about it. "So what's something our hacker can't double-check?"

"Something he's afraid of?" Natasha wondered.

"Some breaking news?" Ava asked.

"Nothing too big. Nothing he'd react to in a way that she'd notice," Tony said.

Ava thought about it. "A joke? A meme? An emoji?"

Natasha snorted. "Seriously?"

"Come on, N-Ro, are you telling me you can't give that idea three trophies and a cat with heart eyes?" Tony flashed her a thumbs-up onscreen.

"You think you're going to smoke out our hacker and maybe the entire Red Room by texting them a little iron and a man?" Natasha said, annoyed.

"And a big green fist?" Tony said. "I wish."

"The emoji would have to be yellow," Ava corrected him. "Or brown. There's no green fist."

"Try telling that to the people who have seen it," Tony said with a smirk.

"Forget emojis. I'm not tweeting our hacker, either." Natasha sat back down in her white tulip chair. "Hashtag: *So Black Widow*."

"Hashtag: *Black Panther Is Lit*." Tony smiled.

"Hashtag: *When Old People Make Hashtag Jokes*."
Ava sighed.

Natasha frowned. "I somehow don't think any of this will do it." She eyed the massive screen. "What else?"

"Okay, wait. I got it. Perfect." Tony typed—only two letters and a single punctuation mark—

UNSUB: HA!

"Ha?" Natasha stared at him. "That's your big idea?"

"Not 'Ha?' It's not a question. Bolder. It's an assertion. 'HA!' " Tony repeated.

"I don't get it." Ava looked puzzled.

"Trust me. I use that 'HA!' all the time." Tony sounded confident.

"Why?" Natasha asked. "For what?"

"Pepper wants an answer from me and I don't have time to read some codrafted eyeball-numbing ninety-page brief on whatever a team of junior analysts think Stark Industries' latest widget crisis is? I write back 'HA!' " Tony winked at Ava. "Focus issues, remember?"

"And that works?" Ava looked interested.

"Sure. Someone wants me to pull resources from my Like Minds R&D think tank? HA! Buy an island? HA! Get Iron Man to take out a foreign government? HA! It's perfect."

"It is?" Ava asked.

"Nobody ever knows what you mean—but they think

you think they do and they don't want to admit they don't—so it buys you a full week, minimum." Tony grinned. "I bet they don't teach you *that* at Stanford Business School."

Ava looked at Natasha. "It's your call. He lost me back at *widget crisis.*"

"Ha!" Tony replied. "See?"

Ava swallowed a smile.

"We could try it, I guess. Seeing as it doesn't matter what Maks says, just where his transmission originates from," Natasha said, finally. "I can't see that we'd have that much to lose."

"Is that a yes?" Ava asked.

Natasha regarded the blinking letters.

SEND MESSAGE_Y/N

"Okay. Fine. Do it," Natasha said.

"You're sure?" Ava asked.

"No," Natasha said, sitting forward. "But do it anyway."

They heard the wheels of Tony's desk chair squeak—and as the cursor on the screen flashed to *Y*, the text box disappeared.

The screen went black.

It suddenly seemed a little anticlimactic. "Now I guess we wait," Natasha said.

Ava kept her eyes on the screen. "I'm just trying to remember how this whole Trojan-horse thing turned out for Troy."

"Back then, I'm pretty sure it all came down to which god was on your side." Tony's voice echoed down from the monitor. "So you're in luck. The folks at Troy had Neptune. You kids have me watching your back."

"Lucky us," Natasha said. Then the screen unexpectedly lit up again—

KOS_16: HA?

Natasha froze. Ava sprung to her feet and moved closer to the screen.

"Tony?" Natasha said, raising her voice. "You seeing this?"

Tony's voice was low. "Oh yeah. He took the bait. That was fast."

"So that's our guy?" Ava asked.

"Looks that way. Which means our friend Maks was just sitting there waiting for her to reach out," Natasha said.

"That, or he's a habitual social media butterfly," Tony said. "That's a hard habit to break."

"Some of us manage," Natasha said.

Tony grinned from the bottom of the penthouse screen. "Either way, I'm on it. Tracing the signal back down to Earth now."

Natasha could hear the sound of Tony's fingers flying across the keyboard, all the way over on the other side of the world.

"Okay. Got it," he said, finally. "We're looking at . . .

South America . . . Brazil . . . Pernambuco . . . and the winning city is . . . Recife. A cell tower near the beach, to be exact. Got the address . . . right . . . here." He was positively beaming. "You're welcome."

Ava looked at him in shock. "You mean that *worked*?"

"As soon as you're finished congratulating yourself—" Natasha began.

Tony interrupted, "Deleting our phony message from Green Dress's server now." He hit a final keystroke. "Ah . . . HA!"

Natasha stood up and began to pace. "We don't have long. Maks probably changes location every few days. I know I would."

"Maks Mohawk's not a field agent," Tony pointed out. "He's a hacker. Which means his first priority is his online footprint, not his IRL one. For all we know, the guy is hitting the same Starbucks for his Flat White every day."

"Even so, we've got to get there before he figures out what just happened," Natasha said.

"Sending you his address," Tony said, hitting another key.

"No. Let's keep this offline. I'll get a pen and write it down," Natasha said, quickly.

"Why?" Ava looked spooked. "You think they're still in our network?"

Natasha shrugged. "We're in theirs, aren't we?"

Ava shivered.

"You're overthinking this," Tony's voice crackled back at them. "Just go pick up our pal Maks Mo. We'll put the screws on him when you get home. You'll get your answers."

"You got it," Natasha said. She just hoped they got there in time. *And that Maks Milosovich has something to tell us.*

Now the words disappeared from the screen—three trophies and a cat with hearts for eyes in their place.

And Tony's voice: "Knock him dead, Sparta."

Natasha was already halfway out of the room. "Thanks, Helen."

Nobody was laughing now.

COULSON: So that's when you made your move from Rio to Recife?

ROMANOFF: We took off that afternoon. Two and a half hours by chopper. Up along the coast to Espírito Santo and Bahia, then cut inland to Pernambuco.

COULSON: That's a long way to go based on a single hacked transmission.

ROMANOFF: It only took three words for Turing to crack the Nazis' Enigma code.

COULSON: So that's what this was now? Another world war?

ROMANOFF: I was playing the only hand I had, Phil.

COULSON: Hands come and go. Take it from a guy who knows. Boom.

ROMANOFF: At that point, we were just trying to stay in the game.

COULSON: So—did things turn out like you expected?

ROMANOFF: I never have expectations, Coulson. You know that.

COULSON: They say that's the key to happiness.

ROMANOFF: Low expectations?

COULSON: Or cats. I hear some people really like ghost cats.

ROMANOFF: I'm more interested in birds, maybe Black Hawks. I like my pets damage-tolerant and full-spectrum crashworthy. And heavily armed.

COULSON: In that case, you're probably wise to stay away from kittens.

COULSON: So hunting Maks Mohawk brought you to the Recife airstrip?

ROMANOFF: Well, we weren't there for the ghost cats.

COULSON: I'm guessing this hacker wasn't damage-tolerant, either.

ROMANOFF: Not exactly, no.

RECIFE, STATE OF PERNAMBUCO, BRAZIL COMFORT HOTEL UZI RECIFE

There was nothing like hugging a few walls to introduce a person to the painful world of surveillance, or so Ava had learned. Hug enough of them and you'd pick up a few things pretty quickly. Jagged bricks could cut like a knife; soft plaster could cave in on top of you. Wood splintered into your skin; stucco bit through your clothes. Whitewashed cinder block was the South American standard, but in this particular alley, no one had even bothered with the wash.

"Yeah, because no one ever sees this place," Alexei said. He had appeared as soon as they'd landed, and seemed to be in no hurry to leave. "Which is exactly why my sister picked it, right?"

Ava blew the hair out of her eyes. She knew better than to answer when Natasha was this close. Even at that moment, Natasha raised a hand above her shoulder and pulled it into a fist. Hold up. She'd been in full operations mode since they landed on the dirt airstrip outside of the city.

"I'm holding, I'm holding," Ava muttered behind her. They waited as a spluttering motorcycle passed them by, then began to move again, all the while flattening themselves against the back of what now appeared to be a sleazy hotel's parking garage—the location for their current mission.

Natasha edged one combat-booted foot forward at a time, keeping her eyes on the building in front of her. COMFORT HOTEL UZI RECIFE. The lit neon letters ran unevenly down the side of the concrete structure.

"Check out that name." Alexei laughed.

"Seriously?" Ava whispered. "I mean, I know the *Comfort* part is a joke, but *Uzi*?"

"Zip it," Natasha answered, looking over her shoulder.

Ava whispered back. "Our guy's on the run and he's staying in a dump named after a machine gun?"

Natasha shrugged. "It's not like he named the place."

Ava raised an eyebrow. "Yeah? What's next, the *Marriott Kalashnikov*?"

"No, I got it," Alexei grinned, poking her in the ribs. "The Motel MI6?"

She tried not to look at him.

"What's next is that we have work to do," Natasha

answered, still eyeing the lit windows of the building. A stray cat watched them lazily from its perch on top of the parking-lot wall, too sluggish from the heat to move. Ava didn't blame her; it was well past midnight and the weather was still unbearable; this time of year, it was only after the sun went down that the Brazilian day began.

"Can you blame them? I'm so hot I want to die, and I am dead." Alexei sighed.

Ava ignored him again.

Traffic had picked up considerably since they'd staked out the alley; she could hear the cars crowding down the busy avenue that separated the front of the hotel's concrete box of a building from the brightly lit sand of Boa Viagem, the popular section of beach on the other side. Now and then, screams drifted over the road, followed by cheering. A football match in the sand, she guessed; many Brazilian beaches became football fields at night.

Oh, Alexei, you would have liked that.

"I did. I still do." Alexei smiled at her.

Ava caught her mind drifting—a realization that was inevitably followed by self-loathing. She bit the inside of her cheek and fixed her eyes on a random balcony in her line of vision. *Focus:* they were here for a fast recon, actionable intel, and a casualty-free, close-quarters grab and bag. Nothing all that out of the ordinary.

Even if Alexei was extraordinary, she thought.

"Don't be such a goof." Alexei frowned at her. "You don't have to do this for me. You don't have to do anything for me. I would rather have you be safe."

You need to go away. I can't do this with you in my head.

She dug into the tender skin between her thumb and forefinger until it throbbed with pain.

I have to focus. Right now—

Alexei disappeared.

She turned her attention to the current op. She had watched how carefully Natasha had plotted it, as always; there was more to a Black Widow than a steady eye and a deadly shot. People seldom realized that there was a whole lot about the S.H.I.E.L.D. life that nobody ever talked about—dreary necessities, primarily involving research, math, and Google Maps. Line-of-sight and field-of-fire calculations. Probability algorithms and casing reports. Supplies and tactical plans. Hugging walls and waiting for orders and lurking around alleyways in tropical weather . . .

The fun stuff. Good times.

Ava eased up her cramping legs, stretching until she stood tall. She was hot, sweating through the thin material of her black field suit—lighter than the usual combat gear. Ava thought they looked like they belonged on a safari rather than an urban beach, but *as usual,* Natasha could care less. Now the agent kept her eyes trained on a lit window cut from the concrete, two floors up.

Ready and wound to eleven, Ava thought. Natasha had been like that, lately—ever since Rio. *If we come up empty again, she's going to snap.*

Natasha glanced over her shoulder to Ava, lowering her

voice. "All right, then. You keep your eyes on the prize while I reach out to our new friend."

Ava nodded, looking past her to the balcony.

Natasha pulled a small black box out of her utility belt, and pressed a button like it was a remote on a television. She looked up to the building in front of her . . . and as she did, the illuminated letters spelling out the name of the hotel went dark. So did the hotel windows, the crumbling concrete balconies, even the streetlights on either side of it.

Everything but the moon, Ava thought when she saw it.

She was surprised. S.H.I.E.L.D.'s remote kill switch lived up to the name; it basically turned off the world around them.

An improvement, in this dump of a neighborhood.

"What do you think? Thirty bucks a night in this place? That's what I'm going with." Ava studied the row of now-dark hotel balconies. "Are we a go?"

"Thirty? Really?" Natasha raised an eyebrow. "Because I have to say, this is more like a twenty-buck alley. Twenty-five, tops." Over on the beach someone must have scored another goal, because as she spoke, the cheering floated on the breeze into the alley.

"Thirty for the beach view," Ava said, her voice still low. "Alley view, I'd say twenty-five."

Natasha made a slashing motion with her hand at the level of her throat. Kill the conversation. Ava nodded. She understood. *Now.* Natasha dropped her hand into two fingers, pointing forward—then up. *We're a go.* Time for tactical to kick in.

Ava took a breath.

Natasha yanked a grappling hook from her waist, unspooling a length of black nylon cord. She tossed it into the air, and it arced toward the second-floor balcony, catching the cinder-block railing. The sound it made as it fell was so quiet it could have been a palm tree thumping against a roof tile in the wind.

Ava was impressed. She'd only just learned that same toss at the Academy, right after the rope climbing and before the rappel wall. She probably still had the calluses to prove it.

Natasha pulled the cable tight, attaching the lower end to a length of drainpipe protruding from the asphalt and gravel beneath their feet. Their target was in range, directly above them. She pointed two more fingers up toward the now-dark balcony, and Ava nodded.

Here we go, she thought, grabbing the rope.

In front of her, Natasha had rappelled up the crumbling side of the building in the shadows before Ava could even get a decent grip on the line.

It wasn't as easy as it looked. Ava tightened her hold, hooked her feet beneath her, and pulled herself up slowly, meter by painstaking meter.

Didn't learn this one yet—

By the time she passed the first-floor balcony, her arms were on fire. By the second, they felt like they were ripping out of their sockets.

When Ava's progress came to a halt, just below the concrete patio where Natasha stood, the veteran agent reached down and yanked her over the balcony railing with one hand. Ava rolled soundlessly to the tiled floor, gulping for air.

At least I've got that part down.

Natasha held a finger to her lips, and Ava nodded. She raised her Glock, and Ava got to her feet, moving her hands to grip the handles of her blades. Ready position.

Natasha was so fast that even a trained agent would have been hard-pressed to see her actually pull the trigger.

Two quick blasts—

POP POP.

The glass shattered into fireworks in front of them.

Their target was a real *geardo*, a hard-core one, especially for a civvie. Half the hotel room was taken up with the guy's cov-com crap, his covert communications equipment—not to mention more surveillance gear than anyone could personally put to use. Some of it was marked with American flags, some with Kanji. A few dented metal crates bore the faded stamp of a red hammer and sickle. All from the usual circuit of black markets, Ava guessed.

Between Russia, China, and the United States, we supply the whole world's superweapon supermarket.

She'd learned that in Criminal Axis & Access 101.

Then Ava realized that Natasha had her Glock pointed across the room, and hastily managed to raise her blades.

"What the—" Maks Milosovich, a.k.a. Maks Mohawk, a.k.a. ZeroHour and Meows of Moscow Lover, cowered on the bathroom tile farthest from the balcony. When he finally dared look up, he dove behind the sink counter. There was really nowhere to hide.

On the other side of the room, still half-hidden by shadows, Natasha picked up a black metal box with her free hand. "Stingray. Military grade. Nice dirtbox. You're pretty nosy for a little rich boy, aren't you?"

"If I was a rich boy, do you think I'd be staying in this dump? Whoever you think I am, you're making a mistake," he spluttered in English, covering his head with his hands. Now sporting a mangy beard and a full head of post-faux-hawked, dyed black hair, along with a rumpled black T-shirt and black jeans, the hacker no longer looked like a playboy from the pages of *Hello!* magazine, Russian edition.

"Save it." Natasha tossed the Stingray to the ground. "That's a Moscow accent and a five-million-dollar Hublot watch. I can see it from here. Just looking at you makes me feel like I've crashed a Ferrari into the VIP room at Garage."

Almost immediately the hacker began to pull himself together. "Nobody goes to Garage anymore." He shrugged. "And it could be fake, the watch."

"But it's not," Natasha said, picking up a small, black-lidded pot of shampoo from the side of the bed. "Because this crap is Russian Amber Imperial, and that's going to set you back at least a hundred American dollars. Probably more. Pretty swank for this one-star bedbug-bag."

"I could have found it. I could have stolen it," the hacker said.

"You could have, but you didn't. I saw you wearing it at the Krysha Mira last summer, when you ran out without paying your bar tab," Natasha said, tossing her head. "You were with Vin Diesel, if I remember."

"*You* were at a Moscow nightclub last summer?" Ava asked. Natasha's eyes flickered over to her, code for "shut it."

"They let *you* into Krysha Mira?" the hacker asked.

"You know Vin Diesel?" Ava asked the hacker.

Natasha glared at both of them. "Yes, yes, and now I feel like shooting both of you, so . . ." She raised her Glock and shot out the bathroom mirror from across the hotel room. The hacker covered his head again as mirrored shards went flying.

He cursed.

"Hold up. Can we go back to the whole watch thing? Did you say *five million*?" Ava was incredulous. *"Dollars?"*

"I didn't say rubles," Natasha said.

"But for a *watch*?"

"They make that thing out of only diamonds, even the moving parts. It's like a special flag for jerks to wave at other jerks. Like a Lamborghini," Natasha said.

"But you can't even *drive* it," Ava said, dumbfounded.

"Americans." The hacker rolled his eyes. "That kind of craftsmanship is art."

"Yeah? Is that what you think you are, *Maks*? An *artist*?" Natasha began to move forward, striding out of the shadows and toward the hacker. Ava cringed; she knew what was coming.

"*Chto ty ot menya khochesh'?*" What do you want from me?

The answer was a flying right hook.

S.H.I.E.L.D. EYES ONLY

CLEARANCE LEVEL X

SPECIAL CIRCUMSTANCES & INDIVIDUALS (SCI)
INVESTIGATION
AGENT IN COMMAND (AIC): PHILLIP COULSON
RE: AGENT NATASHA ROMANOFF A.K.A. BLACK WIDOW
A.K.A. NATASHA ROMANOVA
AAA HEARING TRANSCRIPT
CC: DEPARTMENT OF DEFENSE, SCI INQUIRY

COULSON: I like the right hook—but I like the watch more. What a collector's piece.

ROMANOFF: We were more interested in collecting the stolen files.

COULSON: So you just took it upon yourself to decide Ava was ready for field ops?

ROMANOFF: Moscow rules. I was going with my gut.

COULSON: What about Rio rules? You were supposed to take time down south to heal.

ROMANOFF: Widows aren't supposed to heal, Phil.

COULSON: That doesn't mean you both don't need to.

ROMANOFF: Maybe it's better to keep the wounds fresh. Maybe pain is power.

COULSON: One, you do need to read Dune, and two, I don't buy it. Ava wasn't ready.

ROMANOFF: Was I ready to infiltrate the London Rezidentura at fifteen?

COULSON: Some would argue you were born ready.

ROMANOFF: To recruit Berlin operatives twice my age at sixteen?

COULSON: Some would argue you were twice your age at sixteen.

ROMANOFF: Maybe Ava and I went on that op to find closure. Is that touchy-feely enough?

COULSON: For her or for you?

ROMANOFF: All I knew was that we had to see this thing through to the end.

COULSON: Even if you were the one ending it?

RECIFE, STATE OF PERNAMBUCO, BRAZIL ROOM 217, COMFORT HOTEL UZI RECIFE

"**K**ak ty menya nashel?"

How did you find me?

The hacker rubbed his jaw as he spoke, lying flat on his back in the shards of plaster and mirrored glass. Natasha noticed he used only Russian now, which she took as a sign that he had given up pretending to be anyone other than Maks Milosovich.

"Find you? HA!" she said, straightening up. A faded stripe of moonlight crossed her face. It was just enough to give the floored hacker a look at her.

"You?" He tried to scoot away from her, even rolling

over to his hands and knees in an attempt to crawl out of the bathroom.

Natasha could tell that he'd recognized her. Hence his expression, and his cursing. "*Vot der'mo. Lisus Khristos,*" he cussed. "Romanova." She shrugged.

Ava stepped in front of him at the edge of the bathroom. One wave of an electric blade and he dropped back to the floor, cowering, hands over his head. Ava tried not to look too proud, but Natasha could tell she was.

"All right, tough guy. Let's talk," Natasha said.

After that, Maks wasted no time. He nodded his head toward the bedroom. "My money's in there, wrapped in duct tape. Inside the chair cushion, you'll see, euros and dollars. Tell me, whatever your contract is, listen, I'll triple it. *Ya bogatyy chelovek.*" I'm a rich man.

Natasha leaned over him, her red curls falling away from her combat suit. "Trust me, *neudachnik.*" Loser. "You can't afford what it will cost you." *Show him you aren't messing around.* She pulled back one boot and dug it into the side of Maks's rib cage.

"*Oy! Bozhe moi?* You crazy?" My God. The hacker looked shocked, even outraged.

"Yes. Now—clothes off." Natasha gestured with the Glock.

"*Idi k chertu.*" He shook his head. Go to the devil.

"Let me tell you about crazy people, Maks," Natasha said, pulling a suppressor out of her utility belt. She made a great show of screwing it onto the barrel of her pistol.

"We don't like hidden mics, pocket transmitters, wires—and being told we're crazy. So take off your shirt."

Maks recoiled. "This is a mistake—big mistake—I'm telling you." He looked over to where Ava stood behind Natasha now.

"Oh, she's made bigger," Ava said. "Trust me."

The hacker grabbed the bottom of his black T-shirt, apparently giving up. "Who are you with, Triad? S.V.R.? G.R.U.?" He yanked it angrily over his head. "Whatever they've promised, it doesn't matter. They won't do it. They'll kill you first."

His pale, bare chest was glistening with sweat, and as Natasha watched him, she noticed the tattoo over his heart, a small trident inked to look three-dimensional. Not the familiar tattoo of the U.S. Navy SEALs, but similar. She made a mental note of it; it was the sort of thing she wished she'd had for Green Dress Girl, that one incriminating detail that the entire S.H.I.E.L.D. Triskelion database could organize itself around.

"Pants," was all she said. "Faster."

"*Eto bystro!*" This is fast. Maks peeled off his limp black dress socks; only his jeans remained. "If you think you can trust anyone north of the Moskva, you're out of your—"

Natasha raised her Glock and shot out the shower door behind him in answer. Maks rolled to his side on the floor, shielding his head from the explosion of glass. "Stop, stop—"

Ava ducked, covering her ears.

"*Psikh?* Out of my mind? Me?" Natasha looked at Maks. "You're the idiot who thought he could hack S.H.I.E.L.D." She waved the gun in front of his face. "Then again, they say you're also the idiot who counted cards in a Triad-run casino in Macao."

Maks rolled onto his back like an overturned beetle, now squirming out of his black jeans. Natasha angled her arm so she didn't have to see his pale, spindly legs or his leopard-print jockeys. Ava looked away.

"Macao? That's all talk. It wasn't about cards," Maks scoffed.

Ava frowned. "You were there for vacation?"

"I had a job, and then I stuck around to watch some pro circuit. Johnny Chan, you seen him play poker? Ten times World Series champion?" He whistled.

Natasha scoffed. "What is it with Russians and champions?"

"Two things Moscow loves—the best, and the most," Maks said. "World champions might as well be human caviar."

Natasha nudged him with her foot again. "Why mess with the Triad, then? It's not like you needed the money." *Keep him talking.*

"*Moy golubushka,*" Maks said. My darling. As if she didn't have a boot on his chest and a pistol in his face. "There are better reasons to take a job than money."

"Like what?" Ava asked. "Because you're afraid?"

"Afraid of what?" he scoffed. "Getting shot in the back of the head and buried in an unmarked grave?

By who—Stalin? Jason Bourne? You've seen too many movies."

"The movies she likes are the ones where she's doing the shooting," Ava said.

Natasha shrugged. "Why did you take the job? You tell us, Russki."

The hacker's eyes focused on the water-stained bathroom ceiling. "Let's say that I had a client who needed something. Something difficult to obtain, requiring a great deal of my expertise."

"So you had to steal something? And you couldn't just say no?" Natasha asked.

He looked at her. "Let's say there would have been . . . consequences."

"Ah," she said. "Those."

"Let's say that the Triad had in their possession a server containing the location of the required items. Let's say accessing that server required a certain . . . *proximity*. In that case, a trip to Macao to watch Johnny Chan play poker might be useful, no?"

"So you raided the Triad's server *while* counting cards in their casino?" Natasha whistled. "Bold move, Mohawk. I'd be impressed except—well, here you are. So what went wrong?"

"Your hands," Ava said suddenly. "Show us—"

As Maks held up ten fingers, Natasha saw that every knuckle was discolored and strangely lumpy. "Triad handshake? They break those one at a time?" She almost felt bad for the guy.

"They tried." He dropped his hands. "By then, I had what I needed."

"And the card counting?" Ava looked at him.

"Triad's cover story. Better than admitting they were hacked." He waved it off.

Natasha studied him. "So now what? You're going to spend the rest of your life in a one-star hotel room in Recife with a target on your back?"

"I was thinking about Orlando," Maks said with a smile.

"Yeah? Think again, unless you tell me why you hacked my Sametime account," Natasha said.

"That had nothing to do with me." Maks held up his hands. *"Tol'ko poslannik."* Only the messenger.

"Talk like that won't even get you to Tampa," Natasha said. She pointed her Glock at the toilet this time, looking back at him inquiringly. "Try again."

"I'm not lying!"

BOOM!

Natasha fired—and porcelain exploded into powder.

"Ty chto blya?" What are you doing? Maks flung his hands in front of his face; his scraggly beard was now covered with finely powdered toilet shrapnel. "I don't know! I told you, I have a client, it wasn't my idea!"

"The one who sent you to Macao to steal the server?" Natasha looked interested.

"Yeah, a real *cyka*." It wasn't a compliment. "Someone who found me through my father, that's all I know."

"Someone you were really so afraid of that you'd rather

hack the Triad than disappoint them? Sounds like a keeper," Natasha said.

"Exactly," he said. "I didn't ask for the job, and I didn't want it. But like I said, I couldn't say no."

"What was it? The job?" Ava asked.

He didn't look at either one of them. "Identity wipe. Classified military server. It was supposed to be totally secure."

"So you mean me," Natasha said. "I was the job. You were the UNSUB."

"Yes." He nodded. "I didn't write the *cyka* messages, though. I didn't even understand them. I just relayed them."

"Not good enough," she said, moving her gun closer to his head.

Maks twisted his head away from her. "Look, I have the digits of a bank account in São Paulo where my paycheck was wired. That's it. One and done. You can take it all. Don't kill the messenger. Please—"

"Shoot the messenger," Ava corrected him.

"Oh, you can shoot him, that he can live with, he's Russian. Just don't kill him," Maks said glumly, staring up the barrel of Natasha's Glock.

"I want everything you have, every record of that job. The numbers of the account. Any records from your client or your father," Natasha said. "The whole op."

"Look. You don't get it. You seem like a nice person—" Maks began.

This is taking too long. Natasha stepped back and fired

three times in rapid succession. Once on each side of his head, once just above it. The linoleum tile curled up from the floor, from the impact.

"Nice? Really?" Ava asked Maks. He was shaking now.

The guy started to babble. "Take my advice and forget it. Go home to Orlando. Have your Starbucks. Be an American. You don't want this. Trust me, I'm giving you an out." He was really rattled. "This isn't about money. I can't buy them off and you can't stop them."

"Stop them?" Ava stared. "Stop what?"

"This! What happens next! What do you think? Leave now or you're going to end up just like me. Maybe worse," he said. "You're going to end up dead. Both of you, everyone."

"You seem pretty sure about that," Natasha said.

The hacker looked away. "How about we talk about something else. Anything else. Moscow? Military secrets? From the S.V.R. and the G.R.U.—or the CIA? You pick? Two-for-one special?"

"What's that, a going-out-of-business sale?" Ava asked.

"We'll pass," Natasha said.

He shrugged. "Your grave."

"Speaking of graves, one more thing," Ava spoke up, this time in Russian. "Do you know the name of the operative who tried to blow us up? Maybe a young girl? What about the name Somodorov? Does that ring a bell?"

Natasha knew every prisoner had a breaking point, and at that moment Maks Milosovich reached his. He snapped right in front of them. His eyes went wide as he lunged for the door, frantically grabbing at the knob—

POP—

He went down on her first shot. Natasha heard the bone splinter and crumple just beneath his right kneecap.

He screamed—and with one look, rolled himself over the edge of the balcony.

"Maks!" Ava shouted. But it was too late.

There were some things more frightening than the two of them, apparently. *We just need to find out what—or who.*

Ava looked at Natasha, panicking. "He just—but he was just—"

Natasha sighed. "Come on." But even she was unsettled, because she knew she now believed Maks Milosovich.

What did he say? I can't buy them off and you can't stop them?

What does that mean? What did he want to buy? What do we need to stop?

And what makes a person become so hopeless?

Or who—?

They found Maks unconscious but still breathing, wedged deep in the hedge between the hotel and the alley. After they dragged him back to the parking structure, they brought him to his own BMW—a mint-condition $200,000 race car hidden beneath a custom cover.

So much for keeping a low profile.

He was going to fit right in, in Orlando, if he ever made

it there. In spite of everything, Natasha found herself starting to hope that he did.

The keys were under the floor mats.

Two hours later, Maks Milosovich was sedated and loaded onto the body of a Stark cargo plane out of Recife. Back to Coulson and temporary protective custody, pending arraignment. Hands secured with cable ties *and* duct tape, to be safe.

Over in Maks's dump of a motel room, the Widows were in no rush. Natasha found two high-intensity work lamps among all the military gear and flooded the small rooms with uncomfortable light. "Now the real job begins," she said, shoving a laptop toward Ava and opening up one herself.

Ava studied the computer screen. "What are we even looking for? Something about Green Dress Girl?"

"Not specific enough. Look for decrypted files. Check all the image attachments—you can hide encrypted text above or below or inside most jpegs."

"Got it," Ava said. She hit a few keys. "At least this hard drive isn't fried."

"Then search for key words. *Somodorov. Red Room.* Any of the IP addresses we've come across. The old port warehouse in Odessa. The lab in Istanbul. The O.P.U.S. project—" Natasha said, absorbed in what she was seeing on her own screen. "Or what Maks talked about. His father, or the Triad hack. Or something about this *cyka* boss."

"Isn't this what the tenth floor is for?" Ava asked. The tenth floor was the wonk room at the New York Triskelion. "Or one of Stark's nerd herds?"

"First we see what's there," Natasha said as she worked. "Otherwise we don't even know what to bring back with us."

Ava kept scrolling. "Well, there's nothing encrypted on this hard drive. It's just scans of paperwork filed in random folders that seem to belong to some kind of holding company. I'm not sure what any of this is going to tell us."

Natasha looked back up. "A holding company? What kind of company?"

"I don't know," Ava said, peering at the screen.

"Maks owns more than a few holding companies. So do his clients, probably," Natasha said.

Ava frowned. "If this was important, wouldn't he have hidden it better?"

"I don't know. This drive is completely encrypted. Maybe whatever we're looking for is here."

"I hope so, because I've only got scans of some kind of receipts. They're pretty much all the same." Ava scrolled through more. "It looks like these are manifests for some kind of global shipping group. Veraport."

"Veraport?" Natasha looked up. "Luxport was a container shipping group, remember? Ivan Somodorov's front for the Red Room in Ukraine. Maybe they're related?"

Ava scanned the screen. "Like I said, these aren't even hidden files."

Natasha shrugged. "*Somodorov.* Just search for the

word. You might as well try, you never know." She didn't look up from her own screen.

"Okay, searching files now." Ava typed in the name, then hit a few keystrokes and sat back in surprise. "Look at that. You can't be serious—" She looked across the room. "You had better come see this."

Natasha was already crawling through the boxes, and found a spot on the floor next to the computer. "What did you find?"

Ava shook her head. "You're not going to believe it." She zoomed in on a word at the bottom of the page. There it was.

The name.

In the signature for a Veraport cargo pickup originating at what was described as a "rubber factory" in Amazonas, Brazil.

Y. SOMODOROV.

"Ivan's brother. From the Spetsnaz," Natasha said slowly. "There it is. That's our connection."

Yuri Somodorov. Ivan's little-known, little-seen brother.

The name was signed on one line of one hard-to-read scan of one almost illegible document. That was all—and it was still more than they'd ever had.

It's the most we've been able to give Alexei since his death. But he deserves this, and more.

"Is that even possible?" Ava breathed.

"It has to be," Natasha said. "It's right there in front of us."

Ava studied the scan. There was no address for the

warehouse, only the name of a region. "*Amazonas— Manaus—Parque Nacional do Jaú.* Do we know where that is?"

"Amazonas is the Brazilian rain forest, in the north— and Manaus is the biggest city up there," Natasha said. "Look it up."

She did. "Parque Nacional do Jaú is a national park near Manaus," she said. "By the Rio Negro."

"Just because it's a protected area now doesn't mean it always was, especially when it comes to the rain forest," Natasha said. "There could easily be an old 'rubber factory' somewhere around there."

"It's huge," Ava said, pointing at a map on the screen. "Twenty thousand kilometers, the biggest protected forest in Brazil."

"And that entrance looks to be, what? Maybe two hundred kilometers from Manaus?" Natasha stared at the map. "That has to be where it is."

"How do we get in there?" Ava asked. "Looks like no roads." She scanned a profile of the preserve. "Eight hours by speedboat from Manaus, and you can only travel the park by water. It's slow going. The rangers live on houseboats."

"Then we'll go by chopper," Natasha said. "I know S.H.I.E.L.D. had a satellite base in Manaus. A command post, disguised in some kind of condemned housing project, by the riverhead. It should have a landing pad, and then we'll find a place to touch down in the park from there."

"Actually condemned?" Ava asked.

"Could be worse." Natasha sighed. "The Malaysian satellite office used to be in a trailer, not even a double-wide. I spent three weeks in that thing with Hawkeye, once. And that was before he figured out *sambal petai* means 'stink-bean stew.'"

"Yeah, didn't need to know that," Ava said.

Natasha looked back at the screen. "We can be there by tomorrow."

"Why wait?" Ava said. "I'm ready now."

"When you say *ready*, you know it will be hotter than Hades with bugs bigger than your old cat, right?"

"Sasha Cat wasn't all that big," Ava said, pulling herself to her feet.

Natasha snapped the laptop shut. "You don't have to come with me. I could head up to Manaus and pull a fast recon without you."

"I know," Ava said. "But you won't."

Natasha rose slowly from the floor. She was now facing Ava, and the two Widows stood eye to eye, both pale as ghosts and sharp as the blades Ava carried. "He was all the family I had, Ava. I know you feel like you lost your whole life when you lost Alexei, but you're young."

"*Sestra*," Ava warned. "Don't."

Natasha held up a hand. "We aren't fighting the same fight, *mladshaya sestra*." Little sister. "Just because I have to go down with this ship doesn't mean you have to. Alexei wouldn't want that for you."

"You don't know what Alexei wants," Ava said. "Or

wanted," she corrected herself. "And you don't get to tell me what I'm fighting for."

"That's part of the problem. I don't know anything for certain," Natasha said. "Not like I used to. I'm not . . . right." She took a breath.

I'm not right in my head, because I'm stuck back in Istanbul. I'm lost in the cisterns and I'm beginning to think I always will be.

Every time I see you, I have to remember that again. I have to remember him again—

"It doesn't matter. This isn't about us," Ava said, firmly. "I'm not going home until we find what we came looking for—and we end it, the Red Room, and the Somodorovs." She took a deep breath. "And I don't care what Alexei wanted, because that's what Alexei deserves."

Natasha stayed silent until the steel composure of the Romanoffs fell back into place. "Fine. Don't say I didn't warn you."

Ava said nothing at all.

Natasha shoved both laptops into a storage crate. Then she looked at the rest of the worn-looking hotel room, what remained of it. Every surface was covered in a layer of white plaster dust, like a can of talcum powder had exploded inside. "We take as much as we can and torch the rest."

Ava nodded.

It was only when they were walking away from the burning building—and she felt the heat at the back of her neck—that it began to sink in. They had a real lead. A name and a place to find him. *This is happening. This is really happening.*

Finally.

Natasha slung one arm over Ava's shoulders. "Welcome to the real S.H.I.E.L.D., kid. Your first jungle op. Let's make some memories, as Coulson would say."

Adrenaline memories. The kind that last forever—

As they disappeared into the shadows of the alley-way, the Black Widow took a deep breath, inhaling the darkness.

COULSON: Ivan had a brother.
ROMANOFF: And a partner.

COULSON: So you dumped the hacker on me and went to
check it out.
ROMANOFF: I had to put the Russian somewhere. When I've
got a big fish and no pond, you're the guy.
COULSON: I'm your big-pond guy?
ROMANOFF: One of them.

COULSON: Maybe we should have tossed him back to the
Triad.
ROMANOFF: For a death sentence? That was Stalin's
approach, right? No man, no problem. The Triad use the same
playbook.
COULSON: Makes for a fast read.

ROMANOFF: Either way, we bagged the tech and shot up
Maks's place, so that anyone who came around would know
we'd taken him.
COULSON: Speaking of sending messages.

ROMANOFF: After Recife, things got interesting.
COULSON: Romanoff interesting?
ROMANOFF: Amazon interesting.

CHAPTER **8**: AVA

S.H.I.E.L.D.
SATELLITE OFFICE, MANAUS
AMAZONAS, BRAZIL

Ava looked out the window as Natasha guided the Sikorsky down through the cloud base toward the uneven steps and layers of industrial rooftops. They'd been flying for what seemed like an eternity, and the longer they'd stayed up, the lower the sun had faded into the horizon.

"There," Natasha shouted from the pilot's seat, pointing down into the sea of stacked building tops. The sound of the rotating chopper blades was so loud that you had to shout to be heard, even when you were sitting right next to each other. The gray-green standard-issue DC aviation headsets they wore only partly helped. "The top of that old hospital, see it?"

"The one with all the broken-out windows?"

"You got it." She circled the building, dropping lower. Ava gripped the side of the chopper as her stomach flipped over. Natasha was right, though; as their altitude fell and the humid air cleared, Ava could see a white *X* painted on a graying square on top of the decrepit building. A landing pad. *Sort of.*

"What if it collapses under our weight?" Ava shouted.

"Won't be the first time." Natasha grinned.

She stared down at it. "I'm more worried about it being the last—"

The chopper dropped its nose, pushing down toward the painted roof.

Here we go—

They didn't even have to break down the rooftop door. Miraculously, the rusting steel security hatch was still running current S.H.I.E.L.D. protocols; it was even calibrated to open for Natasha's fingerprints.

Why bother? Who cares about the inside of a condemned building?

The moment they were in, though, Ava realized that the building's wrecked facade was an elaborate deception. Though no Triskelion, the interior space was clean and modern and bright; air and electricity had kicked in the moment the Widows had opened the hatch.

The station consisted primarily of a large rectangle of open space occupying the top three floors of the old hospital. There was a kitchen stocked with dehydrated food and coffee, and a bunk room offering clean, worn sheets; a locker room full of camo combat suits and body armor; a storage room shelved with floor-to-ceiling weapons and ammo—even military-issue rucksacks and sniper-style drag bags to carry it all.

The Widows ate their reconstituted rations while sitting on neighboring cots in the bunk room, atop blankets as scratchy as steel wool. Ava pointed with her fork to the row of exterior windows facing their beds. "How come the windows are all broken on the outside, but they look fine from in here? Is it a hologram? A projection? Some kind of three-dimensional distortion—"

Natasha put her bowl down on the polished concrete floor next to her cot. "I'm guessing paint on glass, the old-school S.H.I.E.L.D. classic. I'm not sure when this station was built or even recently used."

"What happened? Why is this place such a ghost town?" Ava asked.

"Priorities change. Threats move. World War Two starts and Moscow's your ally to fight Berlin; then the Cold War starts and suddenly West Berlin's on your team against Moscow." Natasha shrugged.

"It sounds insane when you say it like that," Ava said.

"By the time the wall falls and you agree not to nuke each other, Moscow's moving on Ukraine and China's flexing on the South China Seas and the Arab Spring's becoming the Syrian Winter—and now what? You find you're fighting too many Cold Wars to fight any," Natasha said.

"And that's all before you factor in alien races and sentient machines and Entangled armies," Ava responded gloomily.

"Not to mention Tony and Cap," Natasha added.

"How can you save humanity from the rest of the universe when you have to spend so much time saving it from itself?" Ava asked.

"Good question." Natasha sat back against her pillow and stared out at the empty room. "And after all that, we end up with empty places like this, built for what? An old administration's War on Drugs? Who can even remember? But we don't tear them down, either, because we know the theater of war will just keep on moving, and we could all end up back here again."

Ava was incredulous. "How many buildings like this are there?"

"More than you would believe. So they sit and wait— and all you can do is hope they stay empty as long as they can."

As Natasha spoke, Ava noticed she was wearing her new Widow's Cuff, the one that had been waiting inside the facility's secure safe, courtesy of a military courier earlier in the day.

And she just puts it back on and keeps going. She just keeps fighting. Someone has to. We all have to.

"We should crash. Early start tomorrow." Natasha abruptly rolled over and killed the lights, even though they were both still fully dressed.

Ava curled up in a ball, listening to the air rumble

through the vent over her head. She didn't know what tomorrow would bring, and she didn't know how to think about it. Either way, it didn't seem like sleep was going to come anytime soon.

Ava looked to her side, and saw Alexei lying next to her, his hair scattered across her pillow.

"This is getting strange," Alexei said.

She moved a finger to her lips. *You think it's strange? You're the dead boyfriend. Imagine how I feel,* Ava thought. *Because I almost can't anymore.*

"Got it," he said.

Then he smiled. "Strange never stopped us before, Mysh."

Ava tried not to think about how close she was, at the moment, to both of the last Romanoffs—even if only one knew it.

What would Natasha say if I told her? Would she think it was a dream? Would she think I had gone mad?

Then Ava had a more terrifying thought: *What if she knows already? What if the Quantum link connects her to how I see him, too? What if she's been listening to everything we've been saying to each other?*

She rolled the other way, lying with her back to Alexei now.

But when she stole a look at Natasha, she seemed to be sleeping, and Ava felt momentarily relieved. *It's impossible. That link goes both ways.*

I would know, wouldn't I?

"Of course," Alexei mumbled in her right ear. *"You*

would know." He smiled. *"You know her as well as I do—almost as well as you know yourself."*

Then she squeezed her eyes shut and pretended to sleep while she lay next to her dead boyfriend imagining her first mission into the Amazon.

Like any girl would—

S.H.I.E.L.D. EYES ONLY

CLEARANCE LEVEL X

CONFIDENTIAL: PHILLIP COULSON

CLASSIFIED / FOR OFFICIAL USE ONLY (FOUO) / CRITICAL
PROGRAM INFORMATION (CPI) / LAW ENFORCEMENT
SENSITIVE (LES) / TOP SECRET / SUITE A ENCRYPTION +
SUITE B ENCRYPTION / SIPRNET DISTRIBUTION ONLY (SIPDIS)

** FILE COPY OF INCOMING TRANSMISSION ** FROM THE PENTAGON **

Phil, I don't know what's going on over at the DOD but it looks
like a nightmare.

A biological profile of your [CLASSIFIED SUBJECT] was just
presented to me—five minutes ago, in my own office—by
three of my aides as part of my four p.m. briefing.

As a security risk. Like [CLASSIFIED SUBJECT] was about to
invade the whole planet. Get on your best game. You cannot
take all of this [CODE:REDROCK] heat alone.

Stay low. Head down.

ARTIE

DEEP IN THE RAIN FORESTS OF THE AMAZÔNIA LEGAL, BRAZIL ONE HUNDRED KILOMETERS SOUTHWEST OF MANAUS

You will hear thunder and remember me, and think: she wanted storms.

It was a line from a Russian poem. Who had written it? Natasha couldn't remember now—not here, this far from Moscow. *Anna Akhmatova? As the bombs fell on Stalingrad?*

She thought so, but all Natasha knew for certain was that she found blue skies disturbing, even this one. The one she stared up at now from her current place in the mud, hidden inside a stand of teak trees sprouting from the middle of the jungle basin, with only the connective tissue of roots and moss and hardscrabble stones spreading beneath her. The unfamiliar patchwork of too-green rain forest crowded above her, and then that ridiculous blue sky.

Everyone who grew up in Moscow knew gray was the color of the sky. *The color of the sky and the color of truth,* Natasha said to herself. *The color of my heart, even.* Now, as she lay gripping her rifle in the muddy wash beneath the cloudless Amazonian sky, she recognized her old gray truth more than ever.

Blue is the color of hope, and hope is just the sound of people lying to themselves. You can't save the world. You can't even save one person, not the one person you want to save. Because Alexei's gone.

Proshli i Mertvykh. *Gone and dead.*

Natasha checked the safety on her high-powered rifle. She grimaced, yanking tight the Velcro waist strap of her body armor, beneath her flak jacket. *You're losing it. The closer you get to the Red Room, the harder it will get. So shake it off.* She rolled over onto her stomach. *Dostatochno!* Enough.

Natasha had been crawling her way through the mud beneath a canopy of teak and rubber and brazil-nut and mahogany and banana and acai palm trees (at least according to Tony Stark's environmental recognition software) all morning. The two Widows had broken the map into grids, and had been switching and shifting positions as they worked through it, but there was no sign of anyone or anything yet.

It was Ava's second mission, and it was the Amazon—tough terrain. The bullets weren't rubber and the enemies weren't a rival division of S.H.I.E.L.D. Academy.

You're going to hear about this from Coulson.

Natasha tried not to think about how little there was to go on for this op—one signature on one shipping document. One Veraport warehouse in the middle of the Amazon and one shot at linking it back to Somodorov's Luxport operations in Ukraine and Turkey.

To Yuri Somodorov. To the Red Room. To Alexei.

All Natasha knew was that if it was connected to Alexei's death, it was all going down. Weapons. Operations. Financing. Infrastructure. Personnel. Everything.

I'll kill everything you left behind, everything you ever cared about, the same way I killed you, you ghost of an old man. The way you killed my brother.

Natasha angled her face up at the sun until the blind burning sensation forced her eyelids shut again. She tried not to think anymore. Not about Ivan. Instead, she waited and listened. Ten more minutes and she would move on.

It's quiet—almost too quiet.

Even for a rain-forest jungle in the middle of nowhere.

She opened her eyes again, leaning on her elbows as she raised the double lens of her military-grade spotting scope and scanned the horizon.

These optics are meaningless. Nothing to see, nothing to track. The only chatter going on around here is a treeful of macaws. Natasha sighed. *Are you really surprised?*

That durak *Maks? That hacker would have said any-thing to get away from the Triad, not to mention two Widows. . . .*

Still, Yuri Somodorov's name had been in his files. And the Green Dress Girl had rigged her Cuff. And Maks had hacked her account to send her a message from someone he feared too much to name. That message had brought her this far, hadn't it? *THE LIVING AVENGE THE DEAD, NATASHK—*

Her thoughts were interrupted by a crashing sound in the distance, and she reacted instantly, every cell in her body contracting as she grabbed her rifle—

Then freezing—as she listened intently—

BOOM!

What the—?

Silence.

It could have been a rock slide. Maybe some kind of illegal mining operation? Or maybe— She tightened her grip on her rifle and glanced down at the drag bag by her side. If there really was something out there, she was going to need a little more firepower than even that. She began to mentally catalog her options as she waited. . . .

But there was still no sound, from any direction.

Now you're being paranoid. She checked the spotter again. She couldn't see anything, but when she breathed in, she thought she could smell the faint trace of spent gunpowder. *Or it could be one of the indigenous tribes building a fire. Who was it in this area, the Dessana? It could be them.* Natasha pocketed her spotter and rolled back onto her stomach, touching her S.H.I.E.L.D.-issue earpiece.

Or it's your imagination.

Natasha's voice was a whisper into her comm link. "Black to Red, you hear that? You got eyes on anything downstream? Friendlies or unfriendlies? Anyone showing up?" She waited. She had sent Ava ahead to clear a quick path down to the riverbank earlier, in hopes of getting a better look up and down the watery highway.

Maybe I shouldn't have let her go off on her own—why isn't she answering?

Water was the only way through the more deeply forested terrain, unless you went by chopper, and choppers made noise. *If Ivan Somodorov sent Yuri to establish a Red Room satellite as far away as the Amazon . . .* They wouldn't want to be found, and wouldn't take too kindly to visitors.

Natasha tried again. "Black to Red, you copy?" This time the response came with a burst of static almost louder than the voice speaking it, which was also a whisper now.

"Red to Black, that would be negative. I got a couple of monkeys going bananas and that's about it. After an hour of freaking bushwhacking in the heat. What's going on over there, *shishka?*" Big shot.

Ava was fine.

Natasha exhaled. *Thank God.*

"Stand by, Red," she said, ripping open a heavy-duty Velcro pocket, pulling out a square of transparent thermoplastic— a self-updating, heat-based, and environment-responsive combat plexi-map made by Stark Industries. ("I'm thinking of calling it ComPlex," Tony had said. "That, or Digital Polymerized Methyl Methacrylate, what do you think? Catchy?")

The ComPlex was just one of the thousands of patents Tony had Pepper Potts file for him. Last year had been a busy one; he'd gotten together a whole think tank of what he called "Like Minds," including promising students from all over the world. He'd begun a whole division dedicated to operational tools and toys—anything that could protect servicemen and -women, or minimize casualties in a combat situation. Some of his ideas were stupid—and many more had a habit of blowing themselves up in the prototype phase—but the ComPlex had come in handy on more than one occasion, and she'd started to rely on it.

Natasha stared at it before she touched her earpiece again. The jungle afternoon was so humid she almost couldn't see the holographic map projected on the plexi's surface, foggy air rolling over it like her own breath. The map flickered on and off; the heat seemed to have fried the screen.

She swore under her breath, shaking the plexi. "Black to Red, you sure? Thought for a second I heard a detonation, maybe SAM popping off down there? Some kind of portable MANPAD, like a bazooka or a Stinger?" It could have been anything. *Anything bigger than a shotgun and smaller than a tank . . .*

Ava's voice buzzed in her ear. "Negative on the fireworks, Black. I'm telling you, I got nothing on visual.

Though it's hard to hear over all the monkey screaming. Did you know monkeys could scream?"

Natasha frowned, tapping the clear square to zoom. The square shuddered and reset—and now a thin network of iridescent blue lines uncurled in front of her.

There—

"Affirmative, Red. I have, in fact, been to the Bronx Zoo. And ComPlex is back online. Now I'm seeing some sort of thermal signature. Looks like grid . . . D-9." Natasha waited—and another burst of static hit her earpiece, along with Ava's voice.

"Copy that. I can confirm, D-9 is lighting up for me too, *kapitan*. We've got company," Ava said.

Natasha didn't take her eyes off the pulsing red spot on the map, just over what looked to be the next ridge, on the far side of the Amazon river. "Affirmative. That's the one, Red. I'm seeing multiples, no clear read on how many." So there was at least something going on around here, whether or not it had anything to do with the Somodorovs. Either way, they hadn't come this far not to check it out.

"Copy that, Black. Rendezvous at perimeter D-9 for recon?" Ava sounded eager.

"Affirmative, Red. But do not approach. Wait on my command. I'm only a few clicks away. Black out," Natasha said, yanking her earpiece free of her head before Ava could respond.

As Natasha picked up her drag bag, she heard what she thought were the macaws, thrashing in the canopy as they finally flew away.

Something inside of her must have thought differently, however, because muscle memory kicked in, and she threw herself behind the nearest rubber tree without knowing why—

RATATAT TAT TAT—

RATATAT TAT TAT—

The mud she'd been lying in exploded into gunfire—

Pebbles and moss flew into the air—

Dragunovs. Which means Russians. Which means that was a SAM I heard—

Which means they've seen us, too—

Natasha spun and fled, diving for cover just as an RPG hit and her tree erupted, melting into a flaming black hole. And where there was one rocket-propelled grenade, there were always more.

"Ava," she shouted, but she couldn't hear anything.

Der'mo—

You wanted storms, Natashkaya?

Now you've got them.

S.H.I.E.L.D. EYES ONLY

CLEARANCE LEVEL X

SPECIAL CIRCUMSTANCES & INDIVIDUALS (SCI)
INVESTIGATION
AGENT IN COMMAND (AIC): PHILLIP COULSON
RE: AGENT NATASHA ROMANOFF A.K.A. BLACK WIDOW
A.K.A. NATASHA ROMANOVA
AAA HEARING TRANSCRIPT
CC: DEPARTMENT OF DEFENSE, SCI INQUIRY

COULSON: You realize how out of line that was? Taking a kid out into the field?

ROMANOFF: You're the one who told us to go away and bond.

COULSON: I meant minigolf, or bowling. You were supposed to take it easy on her.

ROMANOFF: Minigolf? Who do you think you're talking to?

COULSON: Bonding doesn't mean you take her with you to invade the Amazon. You weren't just her AIC, you were the only agent there. Period.

ROMANOFF: I wasn't thinking, okay? Neither one of us was.

COULSON: Someone had just tried to off you. You were out for blood. And for your brother.

ROMANOFF: You've been there. I know you have.

COULSON: We've all been there. It's just not a good place to be, not for a kid.

ROMANOFF: I know. But sometimes she doesn't feel like a kid. Not when she's in my head, remember?

COULSON: Maybe that's the problem. One of them.

ROMANOFF: How many do I have now?

COULSON: It doesn't matter. One or a hundred. They're all named Somodorov.

ROMANOFF: Not Romanoff?

COULSON: You tell me.

DEEP IN THE RAIN FORESTS OF THE AMAZÔNIA LEGAL, BRAZIL ONE HUNDRED KILOMETERS SOUTHWEST OF MANAUS

Ava watched as a plume of gray smoke billowed into the blue wash of sky above the forest canopy. The trees were so tall that she might not have noticed right away, except for the sudden, acrid smell of burning rubber—and the blast of static now shooting into her earpiece. *Der'mo—*

She'd yanked it away from her ear, but not before hearing Natasha shout her name. *A rocket-propelled grenade. RPG-7. Maybe three hundred meters away, no more than five.* She hadn't gotten the highest score in the class on the 1993 Mogadishu case study for nothing. Ava tapped again and again on her earpiece. "Black! Come in, Black!" She pressed harder on her receiver, but there was no response. She tried again—"Natasha!"

Nothing. She focused her mind and tried to reach out to the Widow using their Quantum connection, but her mind was racing as quickly as her heart was pounding, and she couldn't find a way out of herself.

Blue electricity sparked from her fingertips to the dirt surrounding her. If she didn't do something she was going to explode.

Come on. Think, Ava—

The comm link wasn't picking up even ambient noise now. There was no signal, which made no sense. The S.H.I.E.L.D. satellite wasn't down, unless . . .

It's a dead zone. Cell tower's been taken down. No repeater. No amplifier. No transponder.

So there's something here. Something big. And someone has gone to a whole lot of trouble to make sure we don't find it.

She could feel the surge of adrenaline in her veins. Her heart pounded, and sweat dripped down her face into her ears. She tried not to think about—

No! Don't say it! She's fine. Probably just on the move. She's freaking Natasha Romanoff, the Black Widow. It would take more than an RPG to slow her down—

Right?

Still—

Ava heard the *RATATAT TAT* of automatic rounds firing again. The jungle canopy above her rustled gently in the direction of the noise, still coughing up thick black curls of smoke.

Don't just stand there, you idiot.

Move—

Ava felt her boots begin to move up the riverbank as her mind raced even faster. *Now think—*

She took cover behind the nearest rocky outcropping and tried to assess the situation. *Meet her back at the chopper. That was the plan, for if we lost contact. Dust off at fourteen hundred. That's what she wants you to do.*

Ava jumped as she heard what sounded like the repeating echo of a Dragunov—

You know Natasha. She'll kill you if you don't follow protocol—

Then the low rumbling blast of another RPG-7—

But what if they kill her first?

As Ava crouched in the shadow of the rock, light spread from the double hourglass logo on her chest, and her hand moved unconsciously to the blades strapped to her thighs. Today a camo combat suit had replaced Alexei's old Kevlar fencing jacket, the one she'd used as the material to make her very first combat gear, but the double blades—one short, one long, both retractable, both electrified—never left her sides. She usually only felt safe when she was wearing them, when she knew the blue fire that came from deep inside her could find a way out through their steel.

Besides, they were Alexei's blades. When she wore them, she felt like she had part of him with her, which was exactly how she wanted to feel. Even now.

What would you have me do, Alexei? Am I just supposed to let her take that kind of fire alone? You tell me, she's your sister— The answer came instantly. Ava rose to her feet, sweeping her arms away from her body and pulling her blades into ready position. Clear blue light radiated out from her in every direction.

Suddenly he was there with her, crouching behind her in the shadow of the rock. "Go," he whispered. "But be careful. I'll kill you if you get shot."

She nodded. *I'm going.* Then she took a deep breath and threw herself into the tangle of rain-forest undergrowth that reached almost all the way to the riverbank—just as Natasha would absolutely not have wanted her to. *Sorry, sestra—you can ground me later.*

Ava stumbled over the uneven jungle floor, slicing at the undergrowth as she moved, advancing and attacking in almost one fluid motion—even if the only things she got to attack, for the moment, were plants. *That doesn't mean I'm not ready for combat.*

As she pushed forward toward the sound of the mortars, she tried not to let it rattle her. Suddenly this whole op seemed like a *terrible* idea, though Ava had no idea why the infamously fearless Black Widow had seemed to also feel that way. Sometimes she thought it was just the natural yin and yang of their relationship, that they were doomed to be in total and perpetual disagreement about everything.

Everything except Alexei. It was true; on that subject

the two Widows were in perfect accord. Anyone who had a hand in Alexei's death would be made to pay.

Anyone and everyone.

Ava ducked as she heard an erratic, staccato echo, this time louder than ever. *RATATAT TAT—*

RATATAT TAT—

She pushed on until she came to the clearing where she had last seen Natasha. The sudden *BOOM* of a long-range sniper sent her diving behind a clump of rubber trees. Ava found herself holding her breath, only exhaling when it began again—meaning it had yet to find its target.

BOOM.

There it was. Natasha was still alive, and Ava was jubilant. *Go ahead, shoot all you want. You're not going to hit that target. Not unless she wants you to.*

Another bullet whizzed past Ava's head, and she realized Natasha wasn't the only target; she had to get out of the line of fire. She took off running, jumping over the roots of an enormous teak tree, rolling herself expertly up and over the fallen trunk abutting it.

Ava forced herself to do the battle math, just like Natasha would. *What do you know? Heavily armed multiples. They've got the comm link down. So there's a they. At least four, by my count. One to pop the SAMs. One on the Dragunov. One sniper. One on the comm—*

Ava darted past a smoking crater in the mud. The wild green growth surrounding it was still on fire.

Breathe. Now. Natasha has to be here somewhere.

Look again. You know what you have to do. You at least have to try—

She dug deeper into her own psyche, calming herself down. She closed her eyes and slowed her breathing, one gulp of air at a time, until she felt her way past the boundaries of her own mind. Ava could still feel Natasha Romanoff at the edges of her conscious thought; that was their bond. For the moment, Ava didn't try to fight it. Instead, she pushed toward it, knowing that it was the fastest way to make certain Natasha was all right. *What do you see, Ava Anatalya?*

She glimpsed a scrap of blue sky—a canopy of green— and then a sleeve. The shooter's sleeve. He was hidden in the trees. She caught a glimpse of the elongated barrel of a Dragunov sniper rifle. Russian ground forces loved a Dragunov; Natasha had already taught her that much. *Make that two Dragunovs,* she thought as she spotted a second barrel attached to another camo-sleeved arm. And another . . .

Snipers at two and four and eleven, wedged in the trees like monkeys. Moscow boys. I can practically see the Red Army stars from here. That hammer-and-sickle stamp, just like on Maks's gear. They might as well be wearing THE RODINA *name tags.* She shivered, thinking of Recife. *So, Veraport? Yuri Somodorov? Did the Red Room hire your guns for you?*

Ava focused harder, trying to get a better look, but it wasn't easy; Natasha seemed more occupied by reloading the magazine of her own high-powered rifle. Then she looked out into her surroundings, and Ava caught a glimpse of the burned-out crater she had just passed.

There. She's right there. Now she could calculate Natasha's hidden position. *From here, I go three and eight—somewhere low—she's looking up at the trees from the ground—*

Ava restrapped her blades. They weren't going to help her cross the clearing, and no point in lighting herself up as target practice for the Russians. She fixed her eyes on a low clump of what looked like fern fronds across the way. *Hold on, Black. I'm coming. I've got your six, sestra.*

"Go," Alexei said in her ear. "Now—"

She took a breath and threw herself forward, charging across the clearing one more time.

RATATAT TAT—

The ground exploded behind her. Caught off guard, she screamed, exploding into a wreath of blue flame that shocked even herself, singeing the roots and trees surrounding her.

Get control—

Rolling forward, she dodged the next round, sprinting the rest of the way toward the cluster of ferns—and went flying into the air—

Der'mo—

A muddy hand had grabbed her combat-booted ankle as she ran past, tripping her up, sending her hurtling forward—

Then down into the mud.

Ava stumbled, rolling and sliding into what seemed like a small, dark cave. As she wiped mud from her face, she saw that she had landed inside a massive, rotting, and partly hollow teak trunk, wedged behind the ferns. Not her most ninja-worthy stealth moment. *So much for coming to Black's rescue.*

Ava used her elbows to drag herself deeper into the hollow. Natasha, too, had pushed her way up to the far end of the enormous trunk, leaving as much room for Ava as she could.

"What are you, stupid?" Natasha sounded angry. Furious, actually. If she hadn't been trying to keep her voice down, Ava knew she would be shouting. "You disobeyed a direct order."

"But—I heard the attack—so I—I came to save you." When Ava tried to whisper the words, she felt exactly how childish they sounded. She also found she could still taste the mud. *Could you make a bigger fool out of yourself?*

Ava's hands began to shake, and she felt for a moment like she could vomit right there in the tree, which she imagined would be the worst possible thing a person— any person—could do in front of Natasha Romanoff, Avenger, S.H.I.E.L.D. agent, hero of the people, woman of steel and stone. *Not Ava Anatalya Orlova, clown of the people, lover of ghosts, orphan of S.H.I.E.L.D.—*

Sometimes, to be honest, Ava found herself wishing that Ivan Somodorov had Entangled her brain with a more relatable or even less reliable counterpart—like Tony Stark, or Phil Coulson, or maybe a rock. Someone who had lost their nerve, told a stupid joke, or—yes—maybe tossed their lunch at an inopportune moment or two. Unlike the infamous Agent Romanoff, who had probably changed her own diapers from birth.

"Save me?" Natasha tried not to laugh as she reloaded her high-powered rifle. "That's pretty funny. Unless you're wearing an iron suit or swinging a god's hammer—or maybe you're big and green with a fist the size of a Prius—you're not going to be saving me anytime soon, kid."

"Don't call me that." Ava swallowed and forced herself to sound as normal as possible, aside from the whispering, as she inched her way down the length of the trunk, until she was within an arm's reach of Natasha.

Mosquitoes buzzed greedily around her mouth, and she ducked to hide her face in the mud of the trunk's narrow interior. *Leave it to Natasha to find an even wetter, hotter place—in the wettest, hottest place on earth—*

"I told you there would be mosquitoes," Natasha said.

"And I'm getting sick of how often people try to kill you," Ava snapped. She looked up to see Natasha slide the barrel of her sniper rifle through an empty knot in the trunk. As she did, she felt her cheek begin to sting beneath the flat black she'd caked on this morning.

"Ow—" Ava slapped herself on the face, crushing an insect the size of a peanut between her now-black fingers.

"Quiet," Natasha hissed.

Great. Ava took a deep breath.

Natasha didn't move her eyes from the sight on her rifle. "Sniper at two o'clock," she murmured. Her whole body was rigid as she targeted the distant canopy overhead. . . .

POP—

She paused to reload, sending the bullet casing flying past Ava's face.

POP POP POP—

The Russian snipers answered back.

Ava felt herself flinching and ducking instinctively, though the bullets only bit at the ancient bark of the fossilized teak that protected them. She was beginning to panic. *Be cool,* she thought. *You've got this. Pretend this is a drill. Pretend this isn't real. Pretend you're not here.*

POP POP POP—said the Russian guns.

You're not here and neither are those snipers . . . and those aren't mosquitoes . . . and it isn't a hundred degrees outside and a hundred and five in here . . .

Ava was so lost in her own thoughts that she didn't even notice Natasha had taken the next shot until another casing went flying.

"They're in the trees, between us and the chopper. Three unfriendlies, maybe more," Natasha said, keeping her voice down. She lowered her eye back down to the sight mounted on the barrel of her rifle. "Tangos in the trees. Sounds like a musical."

"Four," Ava said, under her breath. "I counted."

Natasha looked up, startled, but Ava knew she didn't have to explain. One basic fact about stepping on Natasha's brain from time to time was that Ava knew Natasha felt it, too.

"Now what?" Ava asked quietly, trying not to sound anything even close to how panicked she felt.

"Now?" Natasha rolled onto her back, dropping the rifle. She sighed. "Time for a new plan."

S.H.I.E.L.D. EYES ONLY

CLEARANCE LEVEL X

SPECIAL CIRCUMSTANCES & INDIVIDUALS (SCI) INVESTIGATION
AGENT IN COMMAND (AIC): PHILLIP COULSON
RE: AGENT NATASHA ROMANOFF A.K.A. BLACK WIDOW
A.K.A. NATASHA ROMANOVA
AAA HEARING TRANSCRIPT
CC: DEPARTMENT OF DEFENSE, SCI INQUIRY

COULSON: What about Ava? How was she doing, in all of this?
ROMANOFF: Better than expected, for a rookie.
COULSON: Better than you expected? You'd seen action together before.

ROMANOFF: Not like this. Only in Istanbul, and that was . . . Istanbul.
COULSON: Still. If Ava was in over her head, she would be the last to say it.
ROMANOFF: She was Russian. Taking a punch is in our DNA.

COULSON: But you two shared more than Russian DNA; did that help?
ROMANOFF: The Quantum link? There were some moments of connection.
COULSON: Some is a lot for a lone wolf like you, Romanoff.

ROMANOFF: I was handling it. Do we have to talk about this? Does this matter?
COULSON: This is an SCI investigation, Agent. It all matters. Especially if this is something we could be dealing with on a greater level in the future.

ROMANOFF: Ava Orlova is not the subject of this investigation, and neither is our QE link. You're barking up the wrong tree, Phil.

COULSON: With a forest this big, there's going to be a whole lot of barking.

ROMANOFF: That's what Ava and I were always afraid of.

DEEP IN THE RAIN FORESTS OF THE AMAZÔNIA LEGAL, BRAZIL ONE HUNDRED KILOMETERS SOUTHWEST OF MANAUS

"**W**hat we need is a distraction." Natasha breathed the words as she yanked her drag bag up next to her so she could rummage inside. She pulled out a S.H.I.E.L.D. PropX charge—Stark patent pending—short for proprietary explosive charge, the house favorite for covert ops, who traveled light and fast, with no room for traditional gear. It was small and smooth as an egg, heavy in her hand. Tony had promised her it would pack enough punch to buy her some time in close combat, if she ever really needed it.

"Is that what I think it is?" Ava said quietly, raising an eyebrow.

"One of Tony's little PropX bot poppers? Yeah, he really got on a patenting kick last year. This should do the trick." Natasha handed it to Ava with whispered instructions. "Toss that sucker as far to your right as you can. Aim for that low ridge over there."

Ava nodded and took the oval-shaped charge, which didn't look much like anything more harmful than an avocado pit. She pocketed it carefully, sliding it into the front of her jacket. "I've never seen a popper up close."

"No? Not in any of the Academy games? Not even a strat sim?" Natasha pulled out a second charge.

Ava shook her head. "I never really get to do any." She didn't elaborate.

Natasha shrugged, but it was all an act; she wasn't surprised.

I know, because I've seen the reports. Every instructor you've had, from Coulson on down, has made a point of pulling you out of anything even close to a combat sim. They probably don't even let you near a video game. They don't want to mess with the PTSD girl, don't want to screw with your already screwed-up head. I know, because I'm the one who gave them the order not to—

Natasha wondered if it had been the right choice. She hadn't wanted to take any chances—she was having a hard enough time on her own, after losing her brother—but she never knew what was right when it came to the kid.

Look where it left her—out in the field never having pulled the pin on a basic charge—and with powers she can't begin to understand. She's dangerous, and not just to an unfriendly. A rookie like that, she's her own easiest target—

It's almost like she keeps her own face in her crosshairs—

Natasha tried not to think about how familiar it all sounded. How those same words had probably been used to describe the Black Widow, in her early years in the field. *What did Yelena say, all those years ago? Your only true enemy is yourself?*

Yeah, right. Not counting Yelena, of course.

Yelena had also been through the Red Room and become a Black Widow, for a time impersonating Natasha herself.

A true enemy, and my old frenemy—across a sea and a lifetime ago.

She glanced at Ava.

Then again, when did you ever listen to Yelena Belova? And why are you even thinking of her now, at a time like this?

"You know what?" Natasha said, putting the idea out of her mind. "On second thought, I don't want you to blow your hand off. How about you just worry about getting to the chopper like you were supposed to? I can handle this."

"But I can help you handle it," Ava said stubbornly.

Natasha let out an exasperated sigh. "Did you ever think that maybe I don't want you to?"

"What are you talking about?" Ava stared. "You knew what that heat signature meant, didn't you? You wanted to draw the fire away from me. You purposely made yourself the target. You played dumb to get rid of me." Her voice rose with anger as she spoke.

"So what if I did? You think you're ready to take on the whole world with those funky blue lightsabers of yours?" Natasha said, rolling her eyes. "This isn't the Academy, Ava. It's the middle of the rain forest."

"So? Why does that spook you so much?"

"So if something happens out here, we're on our own. You know what that means? No Coulson hovering nearby to extract us. No high-security Triskelion to hide us. There's no backup. Nothing."

"Backup? How about, I *am* the backup?" Ava frowned.

"And how about if our friends are here, they're here for a reason, which means that we're getting close," Natasha said.

Ava nodded. "Which is only more proof that Maks's files were right. Veraport has to be Yuri Somodorov's front for the Red Room. This has to all lead back to Ivan."

"Maybe. But we can't presume anything. Not yet."

"All the more reason to bring some firepower to the fight," Ava said.

"Even if they are Red Room, we don't know how many friends these guys have in the neighborhood. Better not to draw attention before we have to. Right? Counter-surveillance 101. Which I'm guessing you haven't taken yet, either."

"Hey, *you* invited me on this trip. You were the one suggesting S.H.I.E.L.D. homeschool."

Natasha raised an eyebrow. "Well, now I'm inviting you to go home."

Ava looked at her.

Natasha hesitated. Finally, she nodded, pulling out her favorite Glock pistol. "Fine. You pop one, I'll pop the other. And I'll cover you."

"And we both run for it," Ava agreed. She looked out toward the edge of the clearing. "All right, then."

Natasha reached out to grab the sleeve of Ava's camo with her free hand. "I've got your six, kid," she said. "I mean, you know that, right?" She sounded gruff as she said it. She couldn't jam the feelings back down into any more words than that.

If something happened to you—happens to you— again—

If I lose Alexei and you—

Ava caught her eye for a second. "I know." Then she took a deep breath—

Reached her head out of the hollow, a rabbit venturing up out of its hole—

Scanned the clearing—

And froze.

Ava's expression changed, and she looked back at Natasha, wagging her head toward the open air beyond her. "Time to go."

"You said that." Natasha raised her Glock.

"Not us, them. Look." Ava backed entirely out of the hollow, and Natasha stuck her own head out into the warm jungle air, raising her spotter.

Then she lowered it.

Natasha didn't need the spotter to see the dark heads sliding into the fringe of palm along the facing ridge. The Russians were moving out.

"Maybe they think they've put us down already," Natasha said slowly.

"Problem solved." Ava grinned.

"No." Natasha frowned. "New problem. They'll want to confirm the kill. Find out who had eyes on them. I'd say we have three minutes."

"So what are we waiting for?" Ava asked, impatient. "Let's get out of here. Then we track them back to whatever hole it is they crawled out from."

"Take off your jacket." Natasha said suddenly. Hers was already halfway off.

"What?" Ava looked confused.

"Just do it."

Ava wriggled out of her jacket, dropping it into the mud next to her. Natasha tossed her own camo jacket into the hollow, then Ava's.

"Wait—I forgot the PropX. It's still in my pocket."

"Leave it," Natasha said. She pulled her Ka-Bar combat blade out of the sheath on her utility belt. The blade glinted as she turned it toward Ava. "Now give me your shoe."

"My what?" Ava scowled, but she began to unlace one combat boot. "Why?"

"We're supposed to be dead? Dead people usually bleed a little," Natasha said, dragging her blade across her palm.

As the red pooled in her hand, she reached down and grabbed Ava's boot, rubbing her hand along the inside.

Branches began to crack and snap in the nearby jungle undergrowth. Ava looked up, startled. "You hear that? They're cutting a path. Getting close."

"We've got about thirty seconds by my count," Natasha said as she measured what looked to be about ten paces from the tree trunk. "Plenty of time."

"Super," Ava said.

Natasha kicked up a clod of mud and knelt to bury the boot beneath it. Then she looked up at the canopy of leaves overhead, gesturing. "Don't just stand there. Cut me down those bottom three branches. We need them to find our remains."

"You mean my shoe?"

"Would you rather leave them your foot?"

Ava had her blades out almost before Natasha could finish the sentence. A pile of massive banana leaf fronds and dried husks and even a few bananas dropped atop the mud-buried boot. "Is that—?"

"Shh," Natasha said, looking up.

They could hear voices now—calling to each other from their respective pathways through the tangle of jungle—

"*Trista kilometrov*—" Three hundred kilometers.

"*Oni gde-to zdes'*—" They're here somewhere.

Russian voices. Rough-sounding. Tough guys.

Natasha sighed.

"Now would be a good time to start running," she said, pulling out the remaining PropX charge from her vest. She held it up, pressing her fingers along the base until a tiny row of lights appeared, one after the next.

She looked back over her shoulder at Ava. "Weapons forward. And tuck in your elbows on the way out. You don't want shrapnel in your arteries when this thing blows."

Ava faltered. "What about you?"

"I can take care of myself. Go—" Natasha hissed. She could already see the dark silhouettes moving toward the edge of the clearing.

"Slyshal chto?" Hear that?

"Do svidaniya—" Ava said, looking back at Natasha. Good-bye.

Then she took off running.

BOOM—

She didn't look back, and Natasha didn't want her to.

Not even when Natasha assumed blast position—diving into a tangle of green, expertly angling her boots to absorb the firepower as she landed—not when the heat and the smoke and shrapnel overtook them both—not when the shocked, shouting Russian grew louder—

Not when the first boom ignited the next—

BOO-OOM!

S.H.I.E.L.D. EYES ONLY

CLEARANCE LEVEL X

SPECIAL CIRCUMSTANCES & INDIVIDUALS (SCI)
INVESTIGATION
AGENT IN COMMAND (AIC): PHILLIP COULSON
RE: AGENT NATASHA ROMANOFF A.K.A. BLACK WIDOW
A.K.A. NATASHA ROMANOVA
AAA HEARING TRANSCRIPT
CC: DEPARTMENT OF DEFENSE, SCI INQUIRY

COULSON: Cutting it a little close, weren't you?
ROMANOFF: Seeing is believing, Phil. I wanted them to see
enough to cross us off.

COULSON: So you blew yourself up?
ROMANOFF: That was the general plan.
COULSON: Great plan.

ROMANOFF: Everyone's a critic. It was better than Plan B,
which was "get shot."
COULSON: You could have called for backup.
ROMANOFF: The area was a total dead zone. They were
jamming the signal. Even if the base at Manaus hadn't been
decommissioned, there was no way to get word to anyone.

COULSON: You call it in. That's how the protocol goes, Agent
Romanoff.
ROMANOFF: Sometimes the protocol is staying alive.
COULSON: But for how long?

ROMANOFF: This is the job. Things happen. You think I didn't
know that?
COULSON: You've lost one person in your life. You didn't want
to lose another.

ROMANOFF: I was doing the best that I could.
COULSON: Listening to this, I'm not so sure.

ROMANOFF: Is this an investigation or a lecture, Agent?
COULSON: Both, that's sort of my specialty.
ROMANOFF: You say that, but I'm not really feeling all that special.
COULSON: You'll get there. Keep talking.

DEEP IN THE RAIN FORESTS OF THE AMAZÔNIA LEGAL, BRAZIL ONE HUNDRED KILOMETERS SOUTHWEST OF MANAUS

Ava limped up the twisting jungle trail. She was a mess—wearing one boot, a dirty T-shirt, and no jacket. If the mosquitoes were eating her alive now, she didn't know and didn't care. *PropX 101: Field Experience. A+.* She'd like to see anyone else in her class take on these particular games.

Or not.

Once she was safely over the ridge from the blast site, Ava squeezed her eyes shut, feeling her way toward the Quantum link she shared with Natasha, the place where their minds connected.

Show me. Where are you, sestra?

Her mind was full of static—she was still reeling. She could only catch a momentary glimpse of Natasha, low crawling through the mud on her belly, but it was enough. *There. Thank God. You're alive.*

Ava focused again, this time catching the feel of damp earth oozing between Natasha's fingers, creeping down the front of her undershirt as she dragged herself forward. *So she's on the move.*

She caught one last glimpse of Natasha just as the uneven ground beneath the agent crested, sending her rolling down a sloping jungle hill.

Ava could feel Natasha giving up, letting herself fall, bumping over twisted roots and rocks, and when Ava opened her eyes again—

There Natasha was, well within sight of the trail Ava had cut into the jungle undergrowth on her way to the riverbank that morning.

Sestra—

Ava was at Natasha's side before Natasha could open her eyes, before she made a sound. Now that they were out of earshot from the bewildered Russians, and the ringing ordnance was just starting to fade from their eardrums, the adrenaline began to recede. Suddenly all that was left was the panic. Natasha was hurt, and Ava had to step up, whether or not she was trained for it, and whether or not she knew what she was doing. . . .

Basic first aid. I've got this. Field medics. I remember that unit.

"Come on." Ava bent over Natasha, dragging her to

the side of the trail where they both could rest under the shaded cover of a banana tree. "Oomph. You know, you're deceptively heavy for an Avenger. I thought you people were supposed to be in fighting shape or whatever."

"Bruce is heavier," Natasha said, her eyes still shut.

"Tony in his robo suit," Ava said. "Wouldn't want to be dragging the junk in his trunk around right now."

"Probably could have used Tony in his robo suit back there." Natasha coughed, opening her eyes. Her mouth was bruised and bloody.

"*Now* you're going to admit that?"

"It's fine," Natasha grunted, but it looked to Ava like it was still hard for her to speak. "I didn't know what Tony had put in that thing, and I underestimated the fireball. It happens. I'll be fine."

"You better be," Ava said fiercely.

"Really." Natasha sat back against a rock and brushed the mud from the front of her own filthy black tank. It made no difference. "I'm peachy." She felt her forehead, wincing. When she lowered her fingers, they were bloody.

"What? You are seriously screwed up," Ava said, sitting down next to her.

"Hey, I'm not going to say that was perfect, but it got the job done." Natasha wiped her bloody hand on her pants. "In fact, I'd classify that as your basic unscrew-it-up operations hack."

"You think?" Ava stared at her pointedly, then looked away. "If that was one of your better experiences in the field, remind me to start carrying around a body bag for you."

Natasha laughed, closing her eyes. "I feel like crap."

"You look like crap," Ava agreed. Then she sniffed. "And you smell like barbecue."

"That's my skin you're smelling. Maybe my hair. I did get pretty smoked," Natasha said.

"Excellent. I think I'm going to be sick."

"I've seen worse," Natasha said. "Felt worse, too."

"Why is that not a surprise?" Ava sighed.

Natasha shrugged. "I could maybe use a shower."

"You think? The smell right now is killing me."

"Bad? I can't smell it. I think I burned off whatever part of your nose does the smelling," Natasha said.

"I wish you didn't have to be such a freaking super hero all the time," Ava said, pulling her damp T-shirt over her head. She dropped it on the ground next to her, whipping out one blue-lit blade and slicing the fabric in half.

"It's a habit." Natasha leaned back against the rock behind her.

"I'm starting to get that." Ava wrapped the makeshift bandage around Natasha's head, blotting the gash at her temple. "Let's just get you back to the chopper," she said, standing up. She reached for Natasha's arm. "Can you make it that far?"

"Yeah. Really. I'm okay," Natasha said, taking Ava's hand and pulling herself up. She tried a few wobbly steps, by way of proof. "See? What about you?"

"Me? I'm fine," Ava said, tying the remnants of her shirt around her waist. Her tank undershirt was soaked all the way through with sweat and mud. "I just wish we could have followed them. They probably would have led us right back to the camp." She sat down on a rock next to Natasha.

Natasha looked at her slyly. "Yeah? Check this out." She pulled out the ComPlex, tapping it twice. The network of bright blue lights reappeared on the translucent square. She dragged one finger along the side, and a group of green blobs came into view. She pinched her fingers together and the image shrank until the river and the surrounding ridges of the basin came back into sight.

"You're tracking them? The Russians? How?" Ava squatted down in the mud next to Natasha to get a better look.

"A little PropX bonus—Tango Tracker. That's what Tony calls it, anyhow." Natasha shook her head. "That thing is genius. It's actually an old Russian intelligence trick from fifty years ago, spy dust. Now it's Stark's aerosolized way of marking anyone who shows up at a blast site after the fact. Seeing as it's not usually the good guys hanging out at the scene of the crime."

"Incredible." Ava stared at the plexi in disbelief.

"Yeah, just don't tell Tony that. I'm so tired of hearing about his Like Minds think tank, and his head is already big enough."

"No kidding," Ava said.

"But now for extra credit—" Natasha double-tapped

154

on one of the green figures and a window popped up. Inside it, a sequence of unintelligible numbers scrolled by. "There. Bingo."

"What are the numbers?"

"Me. Well, my DNA. So now we know the little green men have your boot." Natasha watched the parade of glowing shapes. "With luck, they'll think we blew ourselves up while trying to blow up them. Which, sadly, happens all the time."

"I know."

"From your munitions training?"

Ava shook her head. "From movie night. *Hurt Locker.*"

Natasha tried not to laugh. "Maybe I should have gone over your transcript a little more carefully before bringing you out into the field."

Ava's eyes stayed on the green blobs. "How long will it last? The—spy dust."

"Hopefully long enough for us to go back to Rio, pick back up the signal, and move to aerial. Drone and sat surveillance. All things we can do from New York."

"Great." Ava put her free hand on Natasha's shoulder. "Now let's get you back to the chopper. Do you think you'll be okay to fly, all banged up like that?"

"Yeah." Natasha held on to Ava's arm and pulled herself to her feet. "And don't worry. We'll get Five Eyes on it."

"Five Eyes?" Ava stooped to pick up Natasha's pack and slung it over her shoulder, in addition to her own.

"Didn't get to that one yet? Five Eyes. U.S., U.K., Canada, Australia, New Zealand. We move to electronic eyes, pull out, and then we can SWOT this black bag when we get home." Natasha leaned on Ava, and they started back in the direction of the chopper.

Ava frowned. "SWOT? Like a SWAT team?"

"What, are you kidding me?" Natasha pretended to look shocked. "*S-W-O-T.* Strengths, Weaknesses, Opportunities, Threats. Threat Assessment 101. You should have gotten that one on your first day of school. Right up there with the 'Who I Ganked on My Summer Vacation' essay."

"Ouch," Ava said. As they kept moving, she watched the ComPlex in her hand. "I don't know. It all looks pretty grim to me."

"Why?" Natasha asked. She sounded tired.

Ava shook her head. "It doesn't matter now."

"Why not?"

"Because. You're hurt and we should go."

Natasha rolled her eyes. "Oh, please. I've eaten chili dogs that have hurt worse than this."

"Must have been quite a chili dog."

"Chili German shepherd." Natasha smirked.

"Ah, I see. You just have to blow her up, *then* she makes jokes." Ava smiled, but she kept going. "Let's go. We'll leave it to five guys or five eyes or whatever. Just tell me one thing."

"Okay," Natasha said, stopping on the trail. "What?"

"I was just wondering." Ava hesitated. Then she handed over the ComPlex. "What's your take on the purple rain?"

"The Prince album?"

Ava pointed. "On the map. What does the purple rain stuff mean?"

"Radiation. Why?" Natasha looked down at the plexi and slowly answered her own question. "Because our glowing green friends are headed into a massive purple blast zone."

"It's getting brighter. What does that mean?"

"*Der'mo*—" Natasha studied the map. "It means we need to turn around." When she finally looked up, her eyes were serious. "Five minutes. We find their camp. Then we get in, we get eyes on, and we get out."

"You sure?" Ava asked.

"Sure enough." Natasha grabbed her pack back from Ava. "We can't walk away, not now. Not from that much radiation. I have to get close enough to see how bad it gets."

"Okay. Five minutes," Ava said as they headed off in the direction of the shifting green blobs and the pulsing purple stain.

How much is that much radiation?

It didn't matter.

They were going to find the camp, maybe even some answers.

Ava told herself she should feel relieved. She told herself she should feel excited. Ready for action, at least.

All she could feel was scared.

S.H.I.E.L.D. EYES ONLY

CLEARANCE LEVEL X

SPECIAL CIRCUMSTANCES & INDIVIDUALS (SCI)
INVESTIGATION
AGENT IN COMMAND (AIC): PHILLIP COULSON
RE: AGENT NATASHA ROMANOFF A.K.A. BLACK WIDOW,
A.K.A. NATASHA ROMANOVA
AAA HEARING TRANSCRIPT
CC: DEPARTMENT OF DEFENSE, SCI INQUIRY

COULSON: Who I Ganked on My Summer Vacation? That's your idea of a pep talk?

ROMANOFF: I was building bridges.

COULSON: A bridge to an Amazonian firefight, for all you knew.

ROMANOFF: What was I supposed to do? Walk away? The place was off-the-charts radioactive.

COULSON: Yes. Emphatically, yes. You were supposed to walk away.

ROMANOFF: That wasn't how it played out this time.

COULSON: Oh, believe me, I know. So do the joint chiefs, the D.O.D., and the Oval. Probably also the Kremlin and—should I keep going?

ROMANOFF: Should I keep talking?

COULSON: Are we going to cross the bridge?

ROMANOFF: Sometimes the only way out is through.

COULSON: I hate that saying. There's never only one way out.

ROMANOFF: Unless you're on a bridge, Coulson.

DEEP IN THE RAIN FORESTS OF THE AMAZÔNIA LEGAL, BRAZIL ONE HUNDRED KILOMETERS SOUTHWEST OF MANAUS

Fifty-five minutes later, the two Widows were still hidden in the thick tropical growth, a hundred meters out from where the green blobs now amassed, with eyes on what looked like some kind of World War II–era military depot—two stories of corroded steel, half overtaken by the jungle itself.

Veraport. That has to be it. At least, the local version.

Her head throbbed and her shoulder was probably dislocated, but somewhere beyond the pain it occurred to Natasha that she was impressed. Even with a spotter, she had to look twice before she noticed the sandbags built up by the building's doors and corners, where the mounted guns stood. The hired guns on overwatch, hidden in the ravine above. The perimeter of newly dug earth surrounding the structure, probably mined with antipersonnel explosives. Thick vines grew over every inch of the corrugated tin-looking rooftop; if Natasha and Ava hadn't watched with their own eyes as the Russian sniper patrol came sliding back through some sort of camo-draped loading dock, they might not have noticed it at all.

It wasn't an amateur operation, Natasha knew.

That was the problem.

You can't take that kid in there. You shouldn't even have her out here. She has no idea what she's getting herself into, and you do.

No matter what you think is in there—what you know is in there—this was the wrong move.

Also? Coulson is going to kill you.

Natasha pushed the thoughts off. There was no point. She couldn't walk away now—even if she could hardly walk without limping.

"Is that an airstrip? There's something catching the light, over in the next clearing." Ava pointed, and Natasha moved her spotter.

"Looks like an old NATO hangar, probably from military salvage. It would make sense. There has to be a way in and out of here, probably by air—and they have to be hiding those birds somewhere." Natasha handed Ava her spotter.

"I can't believe how well they've hidden it," Ava said,

looking through the double lens. "You'd never even know it was there."

But the digital footprint of the place was a different story. When Natasha took out the ComPlex, the pulsing purple circle that surrounded the blobby green figures on the screen of the sensitive instrument could not have been brighter.

The nearer they had come to the depot, the more brilliant the violet aura had become. *Now the whole thing's lit up like New York City at Christmas, like Rockefeller Center,* Natasha thought. *Only not in a good way—*

"That has to be it," Ava said, watching the plexi screen over her shoulder. "The source of our purple rain."

"I'm getting irregular gamma and neutron readings now. That's too much radiation for it to be nothing."

And nothing about this is good.

"What does that mean?" Ava looked somber. "Gamma what? What's in there, exactly?"

"We can't know for sure until we get closer," Natasha said. "You can measure plutonium and uranium at a great distance, but who knows how reinforced that structure is, with what kind of shielding. To get the full picture we need a much tighter range."

You shouldn't even be telling her this.

You know what all of this means, and it's crazy.

"How close?" Ava asked.

"Ten meters. Basically, just outside that bunker—or better yet, just inside."

"That's pretty close." Ava looked back at the building.

Natasha slid one map off the plexi, and another appeared in its place. "Forget the radiation for a second. Let me check the heat map—"

It would help to know the odds.

Before you get into direct action with a child.

"Right. How many hostiles are we looking at in there?" Ava asked, trying not to sound nervous.

Hostiles. It sounded strange to hear the word, coming out of a teenage mouth. "Ten, maybe fifteen. All clustered in one area, right here." Natasha tapped the screen. "What do you think, those are some kind of barracks?"

Ava thought about it. "Mess hall, maybe?"

"Ah yes, chow time. Probably. In that case, let's hope they eat real slow while I take a look around," Natasha said.

"We," Ava said.

Natasha looked at her. "You really think you're ready?"

Because I know you're not.

"It doesn't matter. This could be Yuri Somodorov, remember?" Ava was already moving toward the clearing.

Natasha grabbed her with her one good arm. "We're going in and out for recon, and that's it. Fact-finding only. A recce. Nothing more than an Amazon tourist op. Do you understand?"

Ava yanked her arm away. "I understand. Map and camera only. In and out, like you said."

"Just a recon?" Natasha looked at the kid, who already had a hand on the grip of each blade.

"Just a recon," Ava agreed.

"Fine." Natasha crouched low, moving to the farthest edge of their jungle cover. Ava followed.

If we're going to do this, let's do it quickly, Natasha thought. *Timing is everything.*

She scanned the building in the distance. "There isn't enough cover to try to stop for a radiation scan outside. We've got to get up and in. The largest purple mass seems to be on the second floor. Two adjoining rooms. I hate stairs, but I think we don't have a choice."

"You hate stairs? Why?"

Oh, kid, the things you don't know—

Natasha looked at her. "Because grenades roll down them," she said. "If you haven't learned that one yet, you will."

Truthfully, Natasha hadn't learned that one from S.H.I.E.L.D. at all. In fact, she could still see the yellowing paper of the old *britantsy* training manual—written by the MI5 to fight the Nazis—later stolen by Ivan Somodorov to fight the Brits.

Keep off streets when you can access yards and gardens and alleys. Never use stairs when someone can roll a grenade down them. Always shoot twice; once to kill, once to slow the nervous system more rapidly, for stealth. Only give a fake address when entering a taxi from the street. The best way to cross barbed wire is to have someone lie on it first and take the barbs for you—

"Got it." Ava eyed the stairs uneasily.

"Stay close," Natasha said, pushing off the ghosts. "I mean it."

"Go," Ava said, crossly. "I can do this, Grandma. You're worse than Coulson."

"Three. Two. One—" Natasha took off, keeping her head low and her body half-crouched. Tuck position. Light footfall.

She ignored the pain, focusing instead on what she could see and hear. Shadows and boots.

She kept listening, to make sure Ava was following, which she was.

They stayed in the perimeter shadows for as long as they could, only darting through the clearing surrounding the depot at the last possible moment.

Natasha could feel Ava watching her as they ran. To her credit, the kid never slowed and never faltered. As they moved closer to the building, they could hear the low hum of indistinguishable voices from the other side, but it was hard to make out anything more than the odd word.

"*Glupyy*—" Stupid. Always.

"*Glok*—" So they'd heard the sound of Natasha's Glock.

"*Amerikantsy*—" Americans. *Probably talking about the boot.*

Now for the rickety staircase. Natasha took them two at a time, pausing only at the second-floor landing to press her ear to the rusting aluminum door. *Clear.*

Ava followed right behind, staying in her shadow. One booted foot, one in socks. The corresponding steps even sounded off balance—*heavy soft, heavy soft, heavy soft.*

"Move it," Natasha whispered, backing up to the edge

of the landing. She'd need to pick up a little speed if she wanted to open that thing.

"What are you doing?" Ava hissed back.

"Kicking in the door."

Ava flipped open the shorter of her two energy blades—really, that one was closer to a dagger or a hunting knife—and sliced through the lock in three-quarters of a second of blue-lit energy. She powered off the blade and shoved the grip back into her utility belt before Natasha could say a word.

Now, that's not something they teach at the Academy.

Natasha looked at Ava. Ava shrugged. The door creaked open, and the Widows stepped inside.

Beyond the door was what looked like some kind of large, industrial storage room, stacked high with neatly organized rows of wooden shipping crates. It seemed prefabricated, though it was hard to tell with all the rusting joints and seams.

Definitely military, though. World War II, like I thought.

Bare lightbulbs hung from the interior ceiling scaffolding on single lengths of black rubberized wiring; but the high ceiling was only partially visible in the unlit space. The walls were striped with metal bracing, as if shelves had been removed to make more room for whatever merchandise was occupying the balance of the space.

Natasha cataloged all of the above within the first two seconds of entering the room; what she saw in the third second was slightly more problematic. An empty folding chair stood next to the door. On the plastic seat was an aluminum soda can that had been sawed in half, a make-shift ashtray. Smoke was still coiling up from the can into the air.

"Look." Ava grabbed Natasha by the arm, pointing.

"I know," Natasha said, keeping her voice low. "I see it. The Marlboro man can't be gone long, we have to move fast."

"Not sure I'd be smoking in a radioactive room," Ava whispered.

"Life choices."

Ava's eyes were wide as she looked over the room. "So whatever's in these crates, I guess it explains the shipping manifests," she whispered.

"Yep. Veraport. It's listed right here on the shipping labels. Christmas morning for all the bad little boys and girls." As Natasha spoke, her knife came out, and she quickly and quietly sliced through the sealed edge of the nearest crate. She began to pry open the lid. "Let's take a look at the coal."

"Coal?" Ava looked at her.

Natasha tugged harder on the wooden crate. "Well, seeing as we crossed the line to Naughty List hours ago—" She pulled harder and the lid ripped off.

Natasha peered inside. Whistled. "Holy crap."

"What is it?" Ava moved closer to take a better look. "Weapons?"

Natasha shook her head. "Forgive them, Father, for they have sinned."

Inside the crate, rows of Cristo replicas—miniature statuettes in the image of the world's most renowned religious icon, the white stone Messiah that rose from atop one of Rio's famed city hills—had been painstakingly stacked in neat rows. Natasha held one up. "Souvenirs."

"All this? That's it?" Ava asked in a whisper.

"Apparently our Russian friends are incredibly devout," Natasha said quietly, turning the statue over in her fingers. "Not a side of the Red Room I've ever seen before."

"Well, there you go. I guess you can't judge a book—"

"Hold that thought," Natasha said. She wrapped the statuette in her dirty shirt—to muffle the sound—and smashed it open on the side of the crate. The ceramic figure shattered, revealing a toothpaste-size, plastic-wrapped pouch of glistening black powder. "Oh, look. You can," Natasha said, grinning as she shook out her shirt. "Judge away."

Ava looked startled. "What is *that*?"

"It's product," Natasha said. "Which means money. Which means weapons and ordnance and boots on the ground to carry them." She tried to keep her voice low, but emotion was creeping into it.

"Product?"

"It's how dirtbags have come up with dirty money to pay for dirty habits going back thousands of years. Drugs. Oil. Smuggling. You have to have product if you want to start a war. It doesn't really matter which product, not for our purposes, anyways."

"So, you think this black stuff is some kind of drug?"

Ava took the bag from Natasha's hand, examining it closely. "Why would Veraport keep it in a radioactive bunker?" Ava asked.

Natasha searched through the rest of the crate. "Maybe because it's the last place anyone sane would go?"

"Or maybe this stuff is radioactive? Could it be setting off the radiation scans?"

"I don't know," Natasha said, weighing a bag of the black grit in her hand. "It's definitely not anything I've ever seen from our friends at the D.E.A. before. But yes— whatever this is, it's bad news being used to pay for bad guns that will make even worse headlines." She shoved the lid back on the crate and opened the next one.

It was full of money, zipped into plastic freezer bags and bound with silver duct tape. "Euros. Dollars. Look at all this cash—" She pulled out a bag of rubles. Russian money. "Not smart, to hide so much money in one place."

"Why?"

"Because someone like us calls in the coordinates and someone like Tony drops a bomb on it," Natasha said.

Her voice was emotionless, which required a huge expenditure of energy—because what she really wanted to do was scream. She had seen it a thousand times, the infrastructure of violence—the bomb maker's meticulous workshop, the terrorist cell's litter-strewn rental house, the sniper's abandoned rifle, still propped at the open window.

She knew she could never escape it; this was her job and her life.

But she could also never recall a time when she was so

utterly sick—so completely physically, emotionally sick—of fighting.

And now here I stand in Yuri Somodorov's drug cache, with signs of the struggle still to come, no matter how badly I want to escape it.

Natasha shoved the bag of cash back into the crate.

Ava stared at the black powder in her hand. "So our Moscow Station informant was right. The Red Room money does come through South America. Veraport, probably run by Yuri Somodorov, is somehow connected to the Red Room's European operation."

"You mean Ivan's operation," Natasha said. "This is how he funded Istanbul." The word hung over them like a ghost, and they both felt it.

This room killed my brother. These drugs. Somodorov money.

Ava nodded, slowly putting it all together. "This is the next connection. This room. We're going to do it. We're going to crack open the whole network."

"Don't get ahead of yourself." Natasha toggled her Cuff and began to scan and photograph the crates. "There's a whole lot more to the story somewhere. Where are they getting this stuff, and what is it? Where is it going? How can we use it to bring down the rest of the Red Room food chain? We won't know for certain until we run it through the S.H.I.E.L.D. labs. We may never know." She toggled off her Cuff and grabbed the plastic pouch from Ava's hand, dropping it into her pocket. "Let's keep moving. We'll get the readings and get out of here."

"*Yest' yemnogo vera,*" Ava said suddenly. Have a little faith.

"What?" Natasha gave her a strange look.

Ava pointed. "Look. There, on the side of the wood—"

A slogan was stamped on the crate in some kind of black industrial ink. One word, VERA, was larger than the others, and it wasn't just part of the name Veraport.

It was a Russian word, and they both knew it well.

FAITH.

S.H.I.E.L.D. EYES ONLY

CLEARANCE LEVEL X

**SPECIAL CIRCUMSTANCES & INDIVIDUALS (SCI)
INVESTIGATION**
AGENT IN COMMAND (AIC): PHILLIP COULSON
RE: AGENT NATASHA ROMANOFF A.K.A. BLACK WIDOW
A.K.A. NATASHA ROMANOVA
AAA HEARING TRANSCRIPT
CC: DEPARTMENT OF DEFENSE, SCI INQUIRY

COULSON: Really? You're going to stop there? When you're standing in the middle of a radioactive smuggling depot surrounded by armed Russian insurgents and unknown chemical substances?
ROMANOFF: Faith, Phil. You said you want to know the beginning. There was no way we could have known how many things were beginning right there, at that moment.

COULSON: Faith—that's ironic.
ROMANOFF: You know the Somodorov flair for drama.
COULSON: I guess a little drama makes sense when your cover is religion.
ROMANOFF: Nothing makes sense when you're talking about the Somodorovs.

COULSON: And you had never seen the drug before?
ROMANOFF: Never. It was like some kind of strange black sand, maybe dust.
COULSON: Not a compound you could identify? Not anywhere on earth?
ROMANOFF: I wasn't worried about the planets. I was worried about product.

COULSON: How this Veraport cover was using it to fund the missile op?

ROMANOFF: And what the op was—and how it tied back to the Red Room—and how I was going to take it all down.

COULSON: Life's greater questions, when you're a super hero.

ROMANOFF: Or just a Romanoff.

COULSON: Can we please get out of this missile depot now?

DEEP IN THE RAIN FORESTS OF
THE AMAZÔNIA LEGAL, BRAZIL
ONE HUNDRED KILOMETERS
SOUTHWEST OF MANAUS

"Faith," Ava repeated. "Veraport is suddenly a faith-based organization?"

"It's printed on the bags, too. Look—" Natasha held up the bag of black powder. There it was on the label: VERA. "So Faith could be the name they're using to sell the drug."

Alexei stood behind her. "You mean on the streets? To people? That is so messed up."

"So messed up," Ava said, slowly.

Natasha closed the last crate of statuettes. "It's all frightening, which is why we aren't sticking around to find out more. Let's take the reading and go before the Marlboro Man gets back on smoking duty."

"Right," Ava said. "The reading. I'm on it." She ripped open a Velcro pocket and removed her ComPlex from her utility belt. She tossed the plexi on top of the wooden crate, and the blue-lit map appeared.

"Faster," Natasha said, edging toward the window. "The Russians are on the move. We have to wrap this up."

"She's right," Alexei said. "It's too risky."

Ava tapped the screen, toggling to the radiation map. "I don't know what any of these numbers mean, but they're triple—no, quadruple—what we were seeing outside."

"So you've got the read? We're good to go?"

"Wait. It's not coming from the crates." Ava looked up. "The numbers double again on that side of the room."

"So what does that mean?" Alexei asked. "The numbers?"

"Something's over there," Ava said. She began to move as she scanned the room, finally stopping at the door opposite the stairs where they had entered. A brightly pulsing purple target now lit up the plexi screen. "It's almost definitely behind that door."

"What is?" Alexei took a step toward the door.

"Great. We've got the numbers now," Natasha said, shoving a crate back into place. "As soon as we get far enough away to get a signal, I'll call for air support. We have planes that can sniff out a radiation reading without going below ten thousand feet."

"Whatever it is, there are five of them." Ava looked up, stricken. She moved her fingers to the handle of the corroded steel door. "The handle's warm."

"Do you have to do this?" Alexei looked back at her.

Natasha shook her head. "Don't make me pick you up and carry you out, because I will."

Alexei disappeared through the door.

"Two minutes more," Ava said. Then she pulled the door wide open and stepped through it—saying nothing at all.

Ava didn't know what she was looking at, only that it was evil. They were evil.

"Bombs. They're bombs," Alexei said, *standing next to her.*

The bombs lying in the shadow room might as well have been five sharks moving through the water, with five sets of glinting teeth.

"Holy . . ." Her voice trailed off.

Natasha's voice came from behind her, in the other room. "Let me guess," she began. "Five stolen missiles, at least three meters long, judging from the numbers."

"Sounds about right," Alexei said.

"Steel casing. I'm going to say less than a meter in diameter. And based on the radiation, active warheads, so I'm thinking tactical ballistic missiles."

Alexei shook his head. "How active?"

"I'm also guessing there's nothing too short range about these suckers. So yeah, I'm thinking you're staring at a roomful of B-61s."

Alexei looked back through the open doorway to his sister.

Ava remained motionless, though she wanted to run.

"Yep." Natasha stepped up behind her. "Nailed it."

"I can't believe it," Ava said.

"What did you think it was going to be?" Natasha shook her head. "Plutonium's a pretty clear tell."

"I just never thought—I don't know."

Ava's face went even paler; she couldn't take her eyes off the five cylindrical bombs. "You think this is what Maks was so afraid of? Nuclear weapons?"

"He should be," Alexei said.

Natasha shrugged. "Something to do with this, anyways."

"Did you know?" Ava asked, quietly. "Before?"

"She knew," Alexei said. "She always knows."

Natasha's face was unreadable. "I just hoped I was wrong." With that, the Black Widow took over—moving closer, holding her Cuffs in front of her face, expertly pressing a three-millimeter sensor that appeared along one edge. A small burst of light projected out from her wrist as she scanned the room, digitally recording its contents.

Ava frowned. "So where did they come from?"

"We better find out," Natasha said.

Ava held up her ComPlex again. The ionizing radiation counter began to crackle with intensity, and she held it out to Natasha. "Check out those numbers. Does that remind you of something?"

"Yes," Alexei said.

Natasha looked up. "Istanbul? Yeah, I wasn't going to say it."

"She doesn't want to scare you," Alexei said.

Ava shook her head. "I'm not going through that again. Not what happened in Istanbul."

Natasha looked pained. "It's not the same. It won't be. Ivan's gone."

Alexei's gone.

"I'm not. I'm right here. Don't do this," Alexei said.

Ava shook her head. "No. We have to do something." She looked up at Natasha. "Let's torch them. Blow it all and get out of here."

"What?" Natasha sounded surprised.

"You heard me. Let's use Tony's PropX and blow this whole place to ash."

Alexei looked at her sadly. "That's not how it works, Ava."

"Listen to yourself, Ava." Natasha took the ComPlex out of Ava's hands, packing it away.

"I'm tired of listening." Ava's hand moved to her blades. "Maybe we don't even need the popper. You know what these things are? Not just steel. Pure energy. If I get one of these blades even close to those missiles, we could probably take this whole place down."

"Then what? What happens after that?" Even Alexei looked panicked.

"You're talking crazy and we don't have time for crazy," Natasha said. Already she was shoving Ava toward the door.

Ava pulled away, shaking her off. "Think about it. The

drugs, and the weapons. Why not blow one of the bad guys off the map?"

Natasha shook her head. "It's not that simple."

Alexei shook his head. "It's really not."

"You always say that."

"I do not," Natasha said.

"No, I don't," Alexei said.

Natasha grabbed Ava's arm again. "Look, you have to play a longer game. A long con, as Tony says."

"Nobody's playing anything. Not with these stakes," Ava said, looking back at the missile room.

"You want to blow the warehouse? Fine. But all you get out of that is a crater in the ground and a bunch of stuffed body bags—with a radiation cloud that will drift from here to India."

"Now you're being dramatic," Ava said.

"Should we talk about the fallout? Remember Fukushima? There is as much radiation in the U.S. now as there was in Japan when the reactors first blew. In five years, that toxic cloud crossed the entire Pacific Ocean."

Ava didn't say anything.

"She has a point," Alexei said.

Natasha shook her head. "You want to take down a whole black-market network? Actually stop one of the Big Bads? You use what you have, right in front of you."

Ava looked at her. Now she was surprised. "The bombs?"

Natasha pulled a smooth, slate-colored disc out of her pack.

"What is that thing?" Alexei stared.

It looked like some kind of DVD, except that when she held it against her hand, her personal handprint illuminated the surface for a moment—and the object sprang to life, now flickering with a series of five pulsing green dots.

"This is a tracker," Natasha said. "My tracker. Made out of the same tech that the major airline companies use for their black boxes."

"Is that another one of Tony's patents? I don't remember seeing it in class."

Natasha scoffed. "You think you guys get all the good stuff?" She slapped it on the side of the missile. "The second someone tries to launch this thing, we'll know where it's coming from, where it's headed, and we'll take it out before it ever lands. We don't just want the missiles. We want the guys who bought them, the guys who sold them, the guys who fired them."

"Yeah, but you don't care about the people they take out, on the other end? What about those guys?"

"The DOD has been intercepting crap like this since before you were born. In our atmosphere or even beyond it," Natasha said. "It's why we have a missile defense system. So do Russia, China, Israel, India, France . . . I mean, these are standard ops."

"Bombs? Standard?" Alexei whistled.

"The guy on the pointy end might not feel the same way about it. Or is that what S.H.I.E.L.D. would consider an acceptable loss?" The idea was incomprehensible to Ava.

Natasha attached another tracker. "I just want to know

who's calling the shots. Big fish to fry. If these stolen missiles track back to Ivan's network, I want proof."

"Big, deep-fried proof," Alexei said, examining the tracker.

Ava was unconvinced. "The only thing that's going to get fried will be the poor schmuck on the receiving end of these things when you let them back out into the wild."

But it was too late. There was no point in arguing. Natasha's mind seemed to be made up; in fact, she had attached a S.H.I.E.L.D. tracker to each missile now. "We can debate it back in Rio." Natasha glanced out the window. "Let's go."

"They're coming. Stairs. Now," Alexei said.

Ava sighed, but she let Natasha pull her through the first doorway, then the next—past the missiles, past the drugs, out the door into the fading light of the jungle sky. Finally, they had reached the rickety balcony, at the head of the even more rickety external stairs leading up to it. All they had to do now was get down the stairs and make their way across the clearing, back into the coverage of the jungle.

Cake, Ava thought, though she knew she was lying to herself.

As they began down the stairs, a voice floated up from the clearing, and they stopped moving.

A Russian voice.

A man.

"No," Alexei said.

"I'm not a sentimental man, but my brother was. Soldiers. They're all the same. They have to make even a pig's life and death into something meaningful. To pigs," the voice grunted.

It's familiar.

"*No, no, no,*" *Alexei repeated.*

The sound of clinking glasses followed the man's words.

A toast. They're drinking.

Celebrating.

"Ah, but you're the pig, Yuri," a second voice growled.

Ava froze.

Yuri.

The manifest from Maks's apartment was right. That must be why the voice seems so familiar.

Ivan's brother is here.

"*Ava, no.*" *Alexei shook his head.* "*Keep going.*"

The first voice scoffed. "My brother may have been a bastard, but he was a glorious bastard son of the Motherland. What we do now, we do to honor him."

More clinking, more grunting.

"True—"

"Aye—"

"To Ivan—"

"Old dog—"

Half a dozen of them, at least. So there's a crowd down there.

Yuri and his men.

The second voice chimed in. "We will have a thousand heads for every soul, every soldier we have lost. We will have vengeance—and the Somodorov name will be feared throughout the world."

"We have to go," Natasha hissed at Ava, shoving her down the stairs in front of her. Ava moved silently, wide-eyed. "Run. Now!"

"Listen to her. Get out of here! Go!" Alexei shouted.

Natasha shoved Ava as hard as she could, and the stairs shook beneath them.

"I'm not going anywhere," Ava said, the moment they were safely through the exposed clearing and back into the protective coverage of the surrounding jungle. "That's Yuri Somodorov."

"It doesn't matter," Alexei said, from the shadows. "You have to get out of here."

"We think it is," Natasha said. "We'll watch and listen. We'll make certain." She rotated one arm as she spoke, trying to put her shoulder back into place. She didn't look good.

Ava paced back and forth, picking her steps between the twisted roots of the immense trees surrounding them. "No, we know it's him. You know we both recognized that voice. He might as well be Ivan's twin."

Natasha sighed. "Am I going to have to knock you out and drag you back to the chopper on my back? Because I'll do that. You know I will."

"You know she means it. And you know she's right," Alexei said. "Even all busted up, she'll carry you out of here if she has to."

"What I know is that we both heard the name," Ava said. "*His* name. Yuri."

"Right." Natasha looked at Ava meaningfully. "So this is the part where we confirm what we've heard. We make a tactical plan. Support. Backup. Electronics. Firepower. That's how this goes down."

"Or, we go in there and thump him right now—" Ava's hands were already on the grips of her blades.

"Not an option," Alexei said.

Natasha stepped in front of her. "No. We're not going to take him and his arsenal of radioactive ballistics and his army of trained mercenaries alone. Not you and me, not like this. I can't take them all out, not injured—and you don't know what you're doing."

Ava was still pacing. "We can't leave him there. We have to stop him. All those weapons. The drugs. Look at him—"

"Or just don't," Alexei said.

Natasha looked.

In the distant shadows, at the bottom of the stairs, where soldiers still lounged around metal tables, a man walked a few paces apart from the others and lit a cigarette.

The smell was unmistakable, and it wasn't the Marlboro Man from the storage room. It was the distinctive scent of a particular brand, popular in the Ukraine. Ava found herself holding her breath. She would never forget that smell, and she knew Natasha wouldn't, either.

Belmorkanals. Ivan's favorite smokes.

The hound at Yuri's feet began to growl. His head snapped in their direction. Now he was barking, baring his teeth.

I don't care. I'm not afraid of you.

Light flashed through the clearing as Ava spun her blades—

Now Ava's blades were fully extended, both the long blade and the short. Their iridescent blue light spilled in every direction.

I hate you, just like I hated your brother.

Natasha shook her head, holding out her hands. "No. You don't want to do this, Ava."

"Listen to my sister," Alexei said.

"I'm pretty sure I do," Ava said, not even looking back at her.

Natasha took a step closer. "You're not. You aren't ready to shoulder that kind of guilt."

"You know she's right," Alexei said.

"Guilt? You don't know what I feel. You don't know what's on my shoulders," Ava said, backing away from Natasha.

You don't know I spend every day with ghosts.

The Somodorov name is death to me.

A death I'm still living.

"I understand you're frustrated, but you don't get it. You're still just a kid." Natasha reached out to grab her arm—but Ava swung her blades in front of her with a flash. The blue electricity flashed and surged, all around her.

Back off—

Natasha took a step back.

"A kid?" Ava scoffed. She had always had a good parry;

she'd come to rely on it even more since she'd come into her powers, though she'd always known how to keep people at a distance.

"*A kid?*" Ava took another step away from Natasha. "The thing is, *sestra*? I'm not. And the sooner you figure that out, the easier this is going to be for both of us."

"*AVA!*" *Alexei shouted.*

Before Natasha could answer, Ava began to sprint back out into the clearing.

"Ava—Ava wait—" Natasha cursed and followed.

But there was no waiting. No stopping. Nothing she could do to change what was about to happen. Ava knew that, and Natasha knew that.

Yuri Somodorov might have heard the commotion coming from the edge of the clearing, but he didn't look up in time to see her coming.

"*AVA— NO—*" *Alexei was still shouting.*

Ava flung herself into her advance, when she was still meters away. The scream was bloodcurdling, the attack was vicious. The blades went high over her head, and she hesitated, only for a second—

POP POP—

Two neat red stains blossomed across the man's chest, one after the next, in a steady, precise line.

The default double tap of Natasha Romanoff's training.

"*Der'mo—*" *Alexei said.*

Ava stumbled to a stop as the man she hated most in the world sank to the dirt, lifeless, and the closest thing she had to a sister dropped her rifle after him.

She froze, standing motionless until she heard the distant sound of Russian voices beginning to shout.

Alexei's voice was in her ear. "Move. Now."

She felt Natasha yank her back into the shadows of the underbrush, and the two Widows sprinted and tumbled through the root-ridden, uneven jungle floor, not stopping until they once again reached the chopper.

Even then, as the chopper lurched up and into the sky and the dark tangle of green shrank in the distance beneath them, Ava could only think one thing.

My God, what have we done?

S.H.I.E.L.D. EYES ONLY

CLEARANCE LEVEL X

SPECIAL CIRCUMSTANCES & INDIVIDUALS (SCI)
INVESTIGATION
AGENT IN COMMAND (AIC): PHILLIP COULSON
RE: AGENT NATASHA ROMANOFF A.K.A. BLACK WIDOW
A.K.A. NATASHA ROMANOVA
AAA HEARING TRANSCRIPT (TEXT EXCHANGE)
CC: DEPARTMENT OF DEFENSE, SCI INQUIRY

COULSON: Op status?
ROMANOFF: Op site was hot and heavily armed 4-plus
warheads/smuggling op.
ROMANOFF: Returning w/ product samples.

COULSON: Warheads? Pls confirm.
ROMANOFF: Nukes.
COULSON: . . .

ROMANOFF: + yuri somodorov.
COULSON: Ys is at the op site?
ROMANOFF: not anymore—game-time call.
COULSON: Uncle sam sends condolences.

ROMANOFF: Uploading recon images will use chopper secure
nav-link only.
COULSON: Need a house call to secure op site/cleanup.
ROMANOFF: Negative—site is still hot & not secure.
COULSON: Repeat?

ROMANOFF: Warheads still in play.
ROMANOFF: Needed a dangle—see who bites.
COULSON: Will ruffle a few feathers around here sparky with
you?

ROMANOFF: Affirmative—AO is not happy—wants to pick
more fights with bad guys.
COULSON: Sounds familiar.
ROMANOFF: I was happy to fight good guys, too.

ACT TWO: TARGETED

"THE EYES OF THE DEAD ARE WINDOWS
INTO A WORLD WE FEAR."
—CHRIS HEDGES

S.H.I.E.L.D. EAST RIVER TRISKELION
THE GREAT CITY OF NEW YORK

Five thousand kilometers north of Manaus and nearly a dozen gritty, sleep-deprived hours later, Natasha stared down at her bare, muddy feet. *They never tell you how dirty the life of a spy really is—*

She studied the generic gray tile floor of the institutional shower beneath her toes, letting the water splash off her bloody head and damaged shoulder.

Is that what I am? Am I a spy or a hero?

Natasha had known what she was before the Avengers Initiative had come along. *A Russian. An orphan. A Widow. A spy. A killer. A mess. A cynic. A defector. An American. A stone. A weapon.*

But since the Avengers, this whole business of saving the world had confused everything. As they had become household names across the planet, Natasha had become something more, at least to some of the population; more often than not, she'd been celebrated as a hero, even. And while other times she'd been called a villain or a vigilante (depending on the political climate of the moment), that never mattered to her, not personally. People could call her whatever they liked, and she could care less. Natasha Romanoff was a big girl. Growing up in the Red Room had seen to that.

But lately, Natasha had found herself wondering if she wanted something not better or worse—just less. Or at least, less public. *Hard to pull off covert ops when your face is on billboards—*

When Natasha had found Alexei, she had once again become something different, a sister, and she knew some small part of her had remembered and understood. She found her way all over again as she showed it to her little brother, just as she had when they walked to grammar school together along the Moskva River with their patched wool coats for warmth, their pails of *butterbrots* to eat, and their Heroes of the People textbooks to study.

But when the Red Room had swallowed her brother and left Natasha to walk the rivers with only Ava, the world and her place in it had changed yet again.

What is Ava to me?

And which Natasha Romanoff will take responsibility for that?

As Natasha stood in the shower back at base, she didn't feel like any of her previously lost or found selves.

She didn't feel like she'd been very heroic or particularly strategic or even sisterly. She felt tired and impatient and powerless, especially compared to that Veraport weapons depot.

Everything I did, every single thing, in South America was wrong.

The water blasted over her and the dirt and the soot and even the occasional leaf or twig swirled around her ankles, turning into mud—so much so that she thought she might have to move to another shower, as if S.H.I.E.L.D. plumbing was no match for the aftermath of an Amazon Basin op gone south.

And Ava's probably clogging up my apartment plumbing now. I should have made her shower here before I sent her back to Little Odessa.

But eventually, the layers of ash and exhaustion and perspiration and face paint dissolved away. At least the base's hot water was hot, unlike so many other S.H.I.E.L.D. facilities; by the time she got out, Natasha was beginning to feel better. Her toes were turning pink again and her ears had almost stopped ringing. When she finally pulled a pair of clean, black S.H.I.E.L.D.-issue sweatpants over her sore legs, and a clean, gray S.H.I.E.L.D.-issue T-shirt and fleece over her aching shoulder, she was a new person.

Almost.

Only the muddy boots gave her away, as well as the ragged gash on one side of her head—and profound darkness inside it. As Natasha left behind her little room and made her way down the halls and up the stairs that Alexei and Ava had escaped from, not so long ago, her mood only became darker. *Get your story straight. They are going to want to hear about more than the view from the Cristo—*

Natasha did not expect Coulson to let her off easy. Phil was a stand-up guy, and if there was one thing he had been clear on from the start, it was Ava. While he had wanted the kid to be with Natasha, his orders for Ava's conduct were clear; she had her blades for drilling, but no guns and no other weapons. The only actions she could take were in self-defense, and any target practice required dummy ammo.

So how are you going to tell him what happened at the weapons depot?

Maybe she wouldn't have to; Coulson had his hands full with whatever was going on with his Inhumans project. He wasn't exactly one for sharing, and Natasha wasn't one for asking. Between the two of them, they had managed to get on just fine with as much surviving and as little confiding as possible. But Coulson trusted Natasha, just like she did him. So what was she supposed to tell him now?

Ava would have killed Yuri Somodorov. She certainly would have tried to—and that alone might have killed her. At least it would have changed her life. Maybe even coming that close already has—

Natasha turned the corner to the elevator bay and waited, flattening her back against the wall. *You wanted me to help her? Now look—I've helped turn her into the same kind of monster I am.*

As if her life wasn't bad enough already.

A bell tone sounded, and the elevator doors slid open. Natasha took a breath and headed inside.

Who else will be in this debrief? She tried to think.

Maria Hill, probably, who was a good agent and a friend—even outside their poker game—but who wasn't going to advocate sending Ava back out into the field, either. Not after she got the report on Manaus.

Tony, probably. He'd want the full tactical download on how his gear had functioned, before anything. But the stolen warheads were going to throw him for a loop. He knew as well as Natasha how precariously the future of the world had been sitting atop its customary razor's edge, lately; the last thing he'd want to hear about would be nuclear weapons in the wild.

Wait until he sees them—

The images that the Widow's Cuff had recorded of the missiles were terrifying, even by S.H.I.E.L.D. standards. So were the drugs.

When it came to S.H.I.E.L.D., who could Natasha count on, and what could she really tell them?

Do my loyalties lie with Ava, who loved my family, or with Tony and Maria and Phil, who feel like family?

Natasha watched the lit numbers of the floors tick rhythmically by, one at a time. As one digit illuminated after the next, she found their sequential logic reassuring.

Seven leads to eight, which leads to nine and then ten—

That was what she needed now, to follow the logical path.

Rio leads to Recife, which leads to Manaus and then New York—

It would take her forward, all the way to the end, wouldn't it? She just needed to stay the course until she reached the very bottom of it all.

Rio to Recife to Manaus to New York.

One, two, three, four.

It made sense. She just had to keep going.

Five, the missiles will move.

Six, we will find who moves them.

Seven will connect all of it to the Red Room.

Eight will connect the Red Room to the surviving Somodorovs.

Nine, Ava will return to the Academy.

Which just leaves me with ten, the Green Dress Girl.

Ten is trying to kill me—

Each of those things was bad enough—but taken together, they all worried Natasha exponentially more.

What's the pattern I can't see?

All Natasha knew, when the reflective steel of the elevator doors slid open, was that she remembered the first life she had taken as clearly as if it had happened yesterday—and that she wouldn't wish that on anyone.

She was still lost in that thought when a familiar laugh interrupted her.

"Are you here for the big boy-girl dance, too? I came all the way down from Alpha Flight for this, it better be a good one."

"What?" Natasha turned to see Carol Danvers holding

open the door. The Widow felt a rush of relief. *Thank God.* Carol Danvers, a.k.a. Captain Marvel, was more than just one of strongest people Natasha had ever encountered, even among heroes.

Carol was also a steady force for right and truth and good, as unbelievably corny as it sounded. Soaring through the air in her red, blue, and gold suit, she was a symbol for something bigger than one person or one mission—though today she was in a flight jacket and cargo pants, with a cap covering up most of her trademark gold-blond hair.

It didn't matter what she was wearing, Carol was an old-fashioned hero, through and through; in that way she reminded Natasha of Cap on his good days—his best days, really. Natasha couldn't think of a greater ally in a time like this or in a room like this—and she found herself actually smiling, for the first time since she'd touched down at the base.

"This dance?" Natasha shrugged. "Whatever. I'm just here to spike the punch bowl and beat up the boys in the parking lot."

"My kind of girl." Carol grinned. "Let's get this party started." She clapped Natasha on her back, and Natasha tried not to wince from her raw shoulder.

Phil Coulson and Maria Hill were two of the most respected S.H.I.E.L.D. operatives in the history of the organization. There wasn't much either of them didn't know; between the two of them, Natasha had a hard time imagining there was anything.

Now they sat on the same side of the table; Tony and Carol and Natasha sat on the other. They had taken over the conference table in Natasha's favorite room of the Triskelion, a room everyone called the Brain Trust. It wasn't large; this morning it held only the five allies—some of the New York Triskelion's finest—but together they composed what was, even by S.H.I.E.L.D. standards, a remarkable team.

"You look like crap, N-Ro. Do you want something to eat, maybe a banana?" Tony looked her up and down. "Your face is green like you're thinking vomity thoughts. That's when Pepper makes me eat a banana."

"No thanks," Natasha said, quirking an eyebrow as she poured a cup of coffee from the electric pot in the center of the table. "No banana."

"Yeah, you don't really strike me as a fruit person," Coulson said.

What is with you people?

"Good to see you both, too." Natasha slammed the pot back onto its warming base. "For the record, I'm not *not* a fruit person. In fact, I might have an all-fruit dinner after this."

"You mean breakfast," Carol said, patting Natasha's arm. "I know it's hard to tell when you're a mile beneath the East River, but it's nine a.m."

"The only thing I'm tracking is those five missiles," Natasha said. "Which is why I hightailed it up here."

"Same reason I hightailed it down," Carol said.

"Good thing, too. We don't know when those five

missiles will go airborne. So we need to be smart and work quickly," Maria Hill said. She tapped a digital tablet in front of her, and the walls of the room began to animate with the flow of information. The message was clear: time for small talk was over.

Natasha let the hot black coffee seep into her system. Everyone in the room—heroes and operatives—stared silently up to the center of the Brain Trust's soaring ceiling, where holographic images began to take shape, composed of row after row of wire-thin beams of light. Now scans of the stolen missiles projected into the space, snapping themselves to a geometrical grid diagram and rotating in three dimensions. Radiological readings spun on either side of the images; the Brain Trust's data banks had automatically incorporated the readings from the ComPlex and Natasha's Cuff.

"Wow," Coulson said soberly. "You weren't kidding. Those really are B-61s."

"Whoa," Carol said, staring up from her seat at the table. "You know, when you said Somodorov had gotten out the big guns, I didn't think you were talking quite so literally. Where did you say you found them again?"

"Brazil," Natasha said. "An abandoned rubber factory in a forest preserve in the Amazon Basin, to be exact."

Tony chewed on the end of his pen as he studied the hologram. "Phil's wrong. Those aren't our B-61s. I had my Like Minds program redesigning ours all summer. They're not this."

Carol looked at Maria. "Are we really talking about this? It's a classified program."

Maria nodded, dropping five army-green folders on the table in front of them, all marked *top secret*. "Consider yourselves read in on it, as of now." *Read in* was army talk for *cleared to know*—something that didn't happen very often, around here.

Never a good sign, Natasha thought.

Maria sat back in her chair. "That's why I brought Carol in; she's been consulting on the NASA side, to try to keep toxin by-products out of the atmosphere."

"Not consulting, arguing. I don't build bombs, and I don't want them junking up our atmosphere. First we pollute our own planet, and then we move on to the whole solar system? I don't think so." Carol shook her head. "Now you're messing with *my* turf."

"I hear solar warming's a fiction." Tony shrugged.

"You try telling that to the sun," Carol groused.

"The missiles," Coulson prompted.

Carol continued. "The B-61 weapons program has been going on for years. The DOD's basically retrofitting old nukes for modern war; it's a classified weapons upgrade program they've undertaken with NASA."

"Yeah, yeah. Precision targeting, more controlled detonation," Tony said. "Building a better bomb, as if that's not an oxymoron."

"Exactly," Carol said. "The program was always pretty controversial."

"Because making better bombs only makes it more likely that you'll use them," Coulson said.

"Right. But looking at that hologram, I'm starting to think someone else has actually started upgrading our B-61 upgrade program."

"What?" Natasha looked surprised.

"Upgrading how?" Tony frowned.

"This looks to me like someone's taken up where the DOD left off," Carol said. She pointed to one end of the holographic missile. "See those back fins, the way they taper? NASA shot down that design a year ago because it was too unstable. The nose is different, the diameter is wrong, and from what I can tell, this missile segments differently, which means an entirely unpredictable detonation procedure."

Tony stared. "Are you telling me some unknown third party is experimenting on NASA's experimental nuclear weapons?"

"Basically. But, you know, it sounded cooler," Carol said. "The way I said it."

"We know, we know. You wrote a book," Tony said, rolling his eyes. "You're so great, *Captain Marvel.*" They teased each other like terrible twin siblings; sometimes Natasha thought it was because Danvers seemed like the only one of them actually strong enough to take it— without turning into a big green earthquake.

Carol shrugged. "And did mention I live in space?"

"Can we stick to the briefing?" Tony asked loudly.

"I can also fly," she whispered loudly.

"The missiles." Natasha glared at both heroes. "Who has that kind of infrastructure? It would have to be a foreign government, right? Or at least a pretty significant setup. The Manaus guys didn't exactly look like they were experts in nuclear physics. There wasn't a lab facility or anything like that," she said.

"Absolutely," Carol said. "You'd need a secure facility, component parts, and a whole lot of expertise."

"Like, Tony Stark–level expertise. And Tony Stark–level money," Tony said. "That's a whole lot of money."

"Which leads us back to our current set of problems. Who made them, who sold them, who bought them—?" Coulson dropped his top secret folder on the table.

"And how did the Manaus guys get their hands on them—?" Carol added.

Maria sighed. "And, of course, where are they planning to use them?"

"Nukes," Tony said, shaking his head. "Who stashes *nukes* in the Amazon?"

One, two, three, four.

Rio to Recife to Manaus to New York.

There had to be a pattern there somewhere—a sequence and an order, just like the numbers in the elevator. There always was, Natasha knew.

I just have to find a way to see it.

COULSON: How did we get here? What happened to the rest of your leads on the Red Room's South American network? I thought you found a guy in Panama.

ROMANOFF: Someone else found him first. Clean shot, right between the eyes. All we got from Panama was food poisoning.

COULSON: What about Buenos Aires? I seem to remember something about a sleazy internet café address?

ROMANOFF: A washout. Pipe bomb.

COULSON: That's actually a blowout.

ROMANOFF: Either way, it was closed before we got there. If by closed you can mean a smoking black crater in the ground.

COULSON: And São Paulo was a red herring, if I remember?

ROMANOFF: The reddest. Bloodred. We found him in a Dumpster.

COULSON: So no leads. There's your lead. Someone was working hard to cover their tracks.

ROMANOFF: That's how it looked. Dead ends. Dead operatives. Dead everything.

COULSON: The Red Room way.

RUDE BREWS COFFEE HOUSE
FORT GREENE, BROOKLYN

While Natasha was at the Triskelion, Ava was supposed to be waiting at her apartment. Instead, she had set out on a mission of her own—leaving behind the jungles of the Amazon Basin for the wilds of Flatbush Avenue, where her oldest friend, Oksana, worked. Ava had managed to make the same trip on the last Friday of every month for as long as she'd been at the Academy.

She took the subway, even in her filthy camo pants. She wasn't thinking; she was in robo-survival mode now. She'd stolen a sweatshirt and black rubber shower slippers out of the landing-bay locker room at the Triskelion.

Neither fit.

"You look terrible and you smell worse and you're still

the most beautiful girl on the train," Alexei said, *hanging from the rail in front of her.*

"I can always stop off and shower at the Y," she said, smiling.

"I bet." He laughed.

"That's the one good thing about having survived living on my own in a basement."

Alexei raised an eyebrow. "You know where to find all the free showers in Manhattan?"

"Mostly Brooklyn. But also all the free food." She smiled, resting her dirty hair back against the plastic seat beneath her.

The old man one seat down from her got up and shuffled to the back of the car with a glare.

Alexei burst into laughter. "Did you see? That was so good."

"I'm so glad I'm here to amuse you," Ava said, because it was how she felt.

Just let me feel it. I'm so tired of worrying all the time, about how I feel and how she feels and who will know what we feel—

If she let herself, she knew she would fall asleep right then, so she forced herself to sit back up, and spent the rest of the ride telling Alexei a story about trying to give Sasha a shower at the Y when she first found her, and when the poor kitten had looked as bedraggled as Ava herself did now.

It was so nice to be able to talk to him again, she almost missed her stop.

When Ava got to Flatbush Avenue, she immediately found her way to Rude Brews. It wasn't Starbucks. It was basic, a no-frills indie coffee shop—not too stylish and not too comfortable, so nobody felt inclined to stick around long enough to hog the tables and ask to use the wireless. And if they did, well, that's where the whole rude concept came in; the baristas would just insult you until you left. *"You got somewhere to be, pal? Or were you just planning on moving in?" "Oh, I see, you're 'writing.'" "You know we can hear your Adele through your earphones, right, buddy?"*

Sana had gotten a job as a Rude Brewista six months ago, which was why Ava found herself standing outside the window now. Making sure Sana was still okay was always Ava's first priority. Sana, and then Sasha Cat, who Ava had left in Sana's care. . . .

Ava looked at Alexei. "You have to go," she said, pausing pointedly at the door.

Alexei flattened himself against the glass in front of her. "What if I don't want to? Because I don't—"

"We can't make trouble for her. It's her job," Ava said, pushing him aside to pull open the door to the shop.

"Look," Alexei said, pointing to a slogan that had been scrawled on the glass in bleeding marker. "'To you it is just coffee. To us, it is . . . also just coffee.'" He laughed. "That has to be Sana, right?"

Ava looked at him affectionately. "I'll say hello for you."

"No you won't." He sighed.

"Nope," she said, disappearing inside.

Sana—pink cheeks, brown skin, her trademark headband holding up her curls—stood behind the counter of the coffee shop, which seemed to be thriving. The line for coffee was long, and Ava had time to stow away all the details she could gather: face fuller, hair cleaner, and a relatively new-looking T-shirt beneath her Rude Brews apron. *She's fine. More than fine.*

She's happy.

After Alexei died, the girls had tried to keep in touch, but Ava hadn't been capable of talking then, not to anyone. When she finally found enough strength to force herself to answer Sana's emails and texts and occasional calls, Ava felt like she'd become a different person. She hadn't been much of a friend to anyone since then; she imagined Sana had had to grieve her loss while Ava had been grieving hers.

And then there was the issue of Ava's new life. Though Sana had met Alexei, she didn't know the whole truth about him—or that he had been murdered. The only thing Sana knew about Ava and her S.H.I.E.L.D. Academy gig was that when Alex had died, his sister had used all her connections to get Ava some kind of rare scholarship to military school. It was true enough, in a way, and Ava couldn't correct her, anyhow.

But things were looking up for Sana. Since Ava had started at S.H.I.E.L.D. Academy, Sana seemed a little more settled. Ava knew she had moved back in with her taxi-driving father and his new family, and was working most days and fencing or studying most nights, for her

GED high-school-equivalency exam. Ava figured that the goal was college, whether Sana would admit it or not.

Good for you, Sana. You should get a regular life. At least one of us should.

Ava stepped up to the counter.

"Can I help you?" Oksana said, smiling in spite of their mutual pledge not to blow each other's cover—i.e., Sana wasn't supposed to have friends over during her shift, and Ava wasn't technically supposed to leave the Academy in her first year. But being the Black Widow's pet PTSD case had its perks. So did having few friends; there were fewer people to ask questions.

"One rude brew," Ava said, pretending to study the menu posted on the wall behind Sana. "Make it your rudest."

"That's four shots of espresso." Sana raised an eyebrow. "Sure you can handle that much lip?"

"I'm tougher than I look." Ava shrugged. "And I've had a long few days."

Sana looked her over, taking in every scratch on Ava's face, every inch of sunburn on her skin, and of course, the smell. "Yeah, okay. What size? Jittery, Wired, or High-Wired?"

"High-Wired. Like I said, tough week."

Sana raised an eyebrow. "That's what they all say." Her crabby-looking manager, India, who was foaming milk next to her, looked up, annoyed at all the chatter. India didn't believe they should be hiring girls who had formerly lived in the basements of community centers.

India barked, "Move, Sana. We've got a line—" Then she looked at Ava. "You smell."

Ava hurriedly stuffed a dollar in the tip jar and stepped away. Sana wouldn't pull the money out until later, when she'd have time to find the message Ava had scribbled on one side, just like always. That had been their code for the past year now.

This time it was a drawing of a fish, underlined with a single line—in their code, a stick—and the number seven. *Fish sticks.* In other words, a meeting. Tonight. At their old spot at the Stark Community Kitchen, where they'd spent too many nights eating fish sticks and plotting for a future they each doubted would ever really come.

Ava couldn't wait to catch up. It wasn't easy to sneak out when Natasha was home, but knowing Romanoff, she'd be at the Triskelion late into the night. Ava would have plenty of time to go home and shower before she came back.

At least, so she hoped.

Ava's hair was still wet when she walked up to the Stark Community Kitchen wearing borrowed clothes from Natasha's apartment. She hadn't had time to do laundry, and her South American clothes were all so filthy now they would probably have to be thrown into a furnace.

Good thing I know a few basements—

The borrowed black leather jacket was some Italian brand called Balenciaga—the dark Japanese denim jeans looked like they were vintage—and the simple fitted white T-shirt was from a French boutique whose name she couldn't pronounce. If you eliminated Natasha's work wardrobe—a combination of combat fatigues, body armor, wet suits, and what Ava had come to think of as S.H.I.E.L.D.-issue Widow-wear—there were only a dozen things in Natasha's closet. Ava was now wearing a good number of the ones that weren't meant for infiltrating a Monte Carlo casino.

As she stood in front of the Community Kitchen, she thought about how many times she'd walked through those doors in the past. In the snow, in the rain. When she'd had nothing to eat all day. When she'd felt like she was all alone in the world. And then on better days, brighter days, when Sana was at her side.

It had been a long road to now.

You had to hand it to Tony, Ava thought; the place was now nothing like the basic soup kitchen Ava and Oksana had known. It was sleek and modern and new—full of fresh produce and healthy food—even donated pet food, for the nonhuman strays. The place was so popular it now offered meals for purchase as well as for free to those who could not afford them. The Stark CK had become a community hangout in a place that badly needed one, and Ava was grateful that Tony had made good on his promise to mark Alexei's memory in a way that would be meaningful, if only to her.

Over the doorway, Tony had arranged for a few words to be painted, in Cyrillic. The phonetic translation of the Russian was roughly *Ne Teryayetsya, Ne Zabyli*—

Not Lost, Not Forgotten.

Never.

Ava avoided looking at the words even now, though she found it comforting that they were still there.

It was that feeling that made her look around for Alexei; she'd half expected him to be waiting for her when she'd walked up. There was no knowing why or how he came and went; it could be hours, it could be days. He wasn't here at the moment, but that didn't mean anything. He always came back to her.

And I will always be here when you do.

Ava moved inside and took a seat by the window. As she waited for Sana, she pulled out her iPod and scrolled through the last playlist her friend had uploaded for her. Song lyrics were how they most often communicated now, especially since Ava couldn't really talk to Sana about anything that was actually going on in her life—and they hadn't seen each other in months.

When Oksana sent her DJ Jazzy Jeff and the Fresh Prince's "Parents Just Don't Understand" for example, Ava knew Sana must be fighting with her dad again. When Ava countered with the Kinks' song "Two Sisters," she knew Sana would understand that life with Natasha wasn't all that easy, either. This was the first playlist Ava had gotten since she'd sent off Duran Duran's "Rio." *But I came back, Sana. To New York and to you, just like I promised.*

At least, for now.

Ava scrolled to a song, nodding as she clicked on it. "Run the World (Girls)" by Sana's idol, Queen Bey. So her friend really was feeling good. *Thank God.* Sana wouldn't pull out Beyoncé lightly. Maybe she'd gotten a promotion, or met someone. Ava made a mental note to ask her about it tonight.

"Is this seat taken?" A boy's voice came from behind her.

Of course. There you are—

"You goof. Just because I said you couldn't come to coffee"—Ava smiled, picking up her bag and moving it by her feet—"I didn't mean you had to disappear all afternoon."

"Wait, what?"

She froze. *That's not Alexei—*

Ava whirled around in her seat, surprised. She looked toward the Boy Who Was Not Alexei. "Yes, sorry—I thought you were—my friend is—"

Instead of Alexei, she saw a tan-skinned boy with a tight smile and hair that fell long into his warm brown eyes. He wore a Montclair Fencing Academy hoodie, and balanced a tray of french fries in one hand and his fencing bag over his shoulder.

You.

It's you.

Ava kept stammering. "I—I mean my French is—"

"Fried?" Dante Cruz asked with a smile. "Do you always talk to yourself?"

Her heart lurched. Dante had been Alexei's best friend. She knew him but she was surprised to see him.

Not just surprised. Flustered. Freaked out. Superstressed.

Say something—

"Dante Cruz? Is that you? What are you doing here?" Ava asked. She could feel her face turning red, which was even more embarrassing.

"What is he doing here?" Alexei whispered into her ear, suddenly sitting right beside her. "Did you have plans to see him?"

She glanced at Alexei and shook her head. *No.*

"Hey, am I interrupting something?" Dante shot her a strange look. "Maybe, like, a stroke or a nervous breakdown? Facial twitch?"

Alexei laughed out loud.

Ava blushed more. *Get ahold of yourself.* "No. I meant—no, you're not interrupting."

"This is awkward," Alexei said.

Ava tried not to look at him. Instead, she tried to smile at Dante—but Alexei was right; it was always this awkward between them. She didn't know what to say, didn't know how to talk to Alexei's former best friend in person, now that they were face-to-face. *And while Ghost Alexei is staring me in the face—*

"I'm sorry," Ava said, "I know I'm being really weird. I was just—I was expecting someone else."

"Someone dead." Alexei grinned.

Ava ignored him, focusing on Dante. "And you startled me. I didn't even know you knew about this place, to be honest."

"My memorial soup kitchen, and you wouldn't think

*my best friend would know about it? That's kind of cold,"
Alexei said.*

Dante shrugged, but at least he seemed to buy it. "I got the same letter you did, I guess. That form letter, from Stark Industries, about Alex's memorial soup kitchen or whatever? As if they even knew him."

"Cold," Alexei said again. "Dude, seriously."

Ava took a breath. *You mean the letter that went to you and me only? From Pepper and Tony? Who in fact knew and really liked Alexei?*

"Right," she said. Ava didn't want to set Dante off; he'd unloaded on her at Alexei's funeral, and ever since then she knew he'd always blame her for his friend's death. She blamed herself as well, so she didn't really see how she was going to be able to change his mind. As a result, she had never tried.

Dante shrugged. "I come down here and just hang out sometimes. I mean, the guy was my best friend."

"Dude," Alexei said. "I know. This sucks."

"Even though he could be a total tool." Dante smiled.

Alexei coughed.

Ava laughed.

Dante eyed her strangely. "And I kind of like the Russian on the front, even though I don't understand it. You know why it's there?" He sat down across from her, sliding his tray onto the table.

Alexei eyed his friend suspiciously.

Yes. Obviously.

"Why do you think?" Ava asked, choosing her words carefully.

"I guess there was this whole Russian family out there that he didn't even know he had. And, I mean, I never even saw it in him. Did you?" For a minute, Dante looked like he really wanted to know, like he was just relieved to have someone to talk to about it, so she answered him honestly.

"To be fair, I didn't even know about it," Alexei said. "Could you tell him that?"

"To be fair," she said, "he didn't even know about it, until right before—"

Dante looked away, trying to compose himself. Alexei ran his hand through his hair, looking down at the table. Ava didn't know what else to say.

Silence is better than a lie.

"Whatever," Dante said, looking back at her. Then he smiled and picked up a packet of mustard. "Plus, good fries."

Ava grinned back. "Looks like it."

Alexei looked at Ava. "Tell him that plain mustard is disgusting, and if I were here I'd have—"

Dante laughed to himself, holding up his mustard packet. "Al would have the barbecue sauce and the ketchup and the ranch dressing and the hot sauce, and all of it would be going on his fries at the same time." The timing was eerily perfect.

Alexei laughed so hard Ava was almost certain Dante could hear him.

"Disgusting boy," Ava said.

"Right?" Dante smiled.

"You two were really close, I know," she said. "I'm sorry."

"Yeah. Well. He was my best friend, that moron." He looked at her. "I guess I'm sorry for both of us."

Ava nodded.

Alexei banged the table. "Come on. If there's a sorry contest here, I think the dead guy sort of has that one in the bag."

Dante opened the packet of mustard and dumped it on his fries. "You never wrote me."

"You didn't?" Alexei looked surprised.

"I did. Didn't I? I mean, I thought I did," Ava said, lamely.

"No, I would remember. You didn't," Dante said again. "I thought it was weird. You wrote me back once, and then you just stopped."

"The guy has a point," Alexei said. "Why didn't you write him? I mean, he was my best friend. You at least had that to talk about."

"Stop," Ava said, irritated at both of them. "Just stop already. I don't want to talk about it, not with you." *Not either of you.*

They both shut up.

She knew exactly what she'd written—and what she hadn't. She just couldn't explain it, how sharing the pain with someone who knew such a different side of Alexei only seemed to make everything worse for both of them.

In Dante's letter, all he could talk about was whether or

not it was her fault that Alexei was gone. In Ava's response, all she could talk about was how she'd let Alexei down, and how guilty she felt.

How he would be here if he'd never met me. How I couldn't protect him. How he sacrificed everything for Natasha and me—

"Fine. If you're that upset, I don't know why you wanted to see me."

"Huh?" Alexei looked at her. "You did?"

"I didn't," Ava finally blurted out.

"That's not what Sana texted me." Dante sounded defensive.

"She did?" *Of course she did.*

"Uncool," Alexei muttered.

"Yeah, a few hours ago. She said you had some kind of break from school and that we should all meet up here and hang out." Dante shrugged. "Because you wanted to hang."

"With you?" Alexei raised an eyebrow—and disappeared.

Ava stared at the space where he had been, and then at Dante.

"Great," she said. *I'm going to kill her.*

"Wow." Dante picked up a fry and dropped it. "Don't sound so excited about it."

Ava tried again. "I mean, I'm not *not* excited."

"No, I get it." Dante shook his head. "I should go."

Ava could feel her face turning red.

"What does a girl have to do to get a fish stick around here, Mysh?" Oksana slid into the seat next to Ava.

"There you are!" Ava stood up and pulled her friend into a tight hug, leaving Dante sitting awkwardly at the table.

He cleared his throat. "Look, if I'm crashing, if you two would rather be alone—"

"Well—" Ava said, not letting go of Sana's arm.

"Of course not," Sana said, squeezing Ava like a kitten as she sat down. "So. Are you kids having fun? Because I gotta say, it looks like you're having a blast—"

S.H.I.E.L.D. EYES ONLY

CLEARANCE LEVEL X

SPECIAL CIRCUMSTANCES & INDIVIDUALS (SCI)
INVESTIGATION
AGENT IN COMMAND (AIC): PHILLIP COULSON
RE: AGENT NATASHA ROMANOFF A.K.A. BLACK WIDOW
A.K.A. NATASHA ROMANOVA
AAA HEARING TRANSCRIPT (EXCERPTED LETTER)
CC: DEPARTMENT OF DEFENSE, SCI INQUIRY

** FILE COPY **

Hi,

I thought I would see if you were okay. I know that's kind of a
stupid thing to say, because of the whole "last time I saw you
was at a funeral" thing. But anyways, I hope you are.

I wanted to say that I'm sorry for what I said. How I acted
like it was your fault when Al died. I knew it wasn't true even
when I was saying it. I mean, I thought it, of course I thought
it, because that's how it felt. I wanted it to be someone's
fault, and I wanted to punish that person.

I was angry.

But sometimes, when I think about it now, I can't remember if
I was angry at you for taking him away—or if I was just angry
at him for leaving. It's becoming a blur, like a memory, or a
ghost.

I know he wouldn't have left town if he hadn't met you, but
I don't think you meant for any of it to happen. That's what I
actually believe.

Anyways, it would be great if you could write back. It's supposed to help my grieving process. Which sounds really creepy, I know, like I work at a funeral parlor or something. But that's what this lady I go talk to tells me. I need a "community of loss" or something. My process sucks.

I know you got sent away to military school or something, but please try to write.

Dante

S.H.I.E.L.D. EAST RIVER TRISKELION, TENTH FLOOR
THE GREAT CITY OF NEW YORK

Maria Hill stood up. "We'll run this through the network, our guys, and then the International Atomic Energy Agency. Find out what is missing, what's been stolen, and from what NPT signers—" She paused, taking in Tony's blank look. "Non-Proliferation Treaty." She shook her head. "We need to see who just can't admit they've misplaced a few city-killers in some old, unnamed storage facility somewhere along the way."

"Ah yes. The dance of the lying liars that lie," Tony said. "I know it well."

Coulson looked unhappy. "We'll find out what

happened. It's not like five lost socks. But we'll have to confirm everything with the IAEA inspectors, the DOD, the joint chiefs."

"I'll check out the NASA side," Carol said, standing up. "See if I can find anything more about other abandoned proposals. Those weird-looking fins, for starters. It may not get us the names of the people who bought or sold them, but we could at least find out who worked on them."

Coulson looked up at the hologram. "Whoever these guys are working for, I'm pretty sure someone lifted a whole lot of this bang from a military base, and not too long ago."

"How can you tell?" Natasha asked.

"By the shiny," Coulson said, pointing to the gleaming casing on the hologram of the missile. "It's in too good of a shape to come from a scavenger who just digs the undetonated duds up out of the desert floor."

"He's right," Carol said. "These aren't exactly vintage."

"Yeah, well, that doesn't make me feel better. It means our insurgents are all up in there with some unknown government," Tony said.

Natasha shook her head. "Fine, but why? Who went to the trouble to steal these? Even if it's the Red Room, why risk it now? For what?"

"That," Tony said, "is the sixty-three-thousand-ruble question."

"Then I'll send it up the chain to the Oval, and to the U.N.," Maria said. She looked at Carol. "You're down here with me today, if you don't mind. I'm going to need at least one person who speaks NASA on my end of the phone."

Carol nodded and picked up her bag. "I speak NASA *and* Klingon."

"So you kids are about to have a great day," Tony said.

"Something tells me yours isn't going to be much better," Maria said. "You've got the wheel, Agent Coulson?"

Coulson nodded. "We'll make an operational plan and reconnect on the hour." He looked at Natasha. "Agent Romanoff will head it up, and we'll put together the support team as needed."

"Good luck," Maria said, her eyes meeting Natasha's. She disappeared out the door and into the hallway. Carol followed, pausing at the doorway.

"If you need me . . ." she said. She didn't finish the sentence.

"I know." Natasha nodded. She knew from a look what Earth's mightiest hero was thinking, and she agreed. Life would be a whole lot simpler without both missiles and senators.

How would that be? If we had no bigger problems than rent and poker night.

Then the door closed behind Maria and Carol, and the grim reality of the task ahead settled into the room.

"So. You want to know who stashes nukes in the Amazon?" Natasha asked.

"Now might be a good time to figure that out," Tony said.

"Veraport is the name of the front. The hired guns were Russian," she said. "I think the Red Room is involved, somehow. Even if I can't prove it yet. We were tipped off that they were running a financing racket through South America—and that looks like it could be true. Yuri Somodorov's name was listed on a shipping manifest for the weapons depot where we found the warheads, outside of Manaus."

"Yuri Somodorov was also found dead at the site," Coulson added.

Tony looked at Natasha.

"Game-time call." She shrugged. *I don't want to talk about it.* That was the message she telegraphed in the silence that followed.

Tony got the message. "All right," he said. "Fine."

Coulson looked back at Natasha. "Seriously?"

"I said I don't want to talk about it," Natasha said.

"But—Yuri Somodorov?" Tony asked. He couldn't resist, even though Natasha glared at him. "You didn't think we might want to get a few answers out of the guy?"

What do you think? Of course I did.

"Of course you did. You're the most strategic person I know. You would never do that." Tony put his pen down on the table. *Which means it wasn't you who dropped him.*

She knew he was thinking it, but he didn't say it. He just looked at her for a second—then turned to Coulson. "Forget Yuri. We don't have time for this. So—how are we going to handle those missiles?"

Natasha looked at him gratefully. "I tagged the missiles so we can track them. We have to be ready the moment someone tries to move them, but until then, I say we just let it play out."

"Tracked how?" Tony asked. "Please tell me it doesn't involve RFID tech, like last time. Seeing as we've only narrowed that search to 'not South America.'"

"Hey, we may not know Green Dress Girl's identity, but we were able to use her digital signature to get to Maks Mohawk. Don't knock baby steps," Natasha said.

"We have five stolen nuclear weapons. That's not a time for baby steps." Tony frowned.

"I've got a S.H.I.E.L.D.-issue hotbox sending out a timed cellular data signal. In other words, I put the equivalent of a cell phone on each one of them, just like you asked. It should run right through our satellite," Natasha said.

"That's more like it," Tony said begrudgingly.

"I've got another question," Coulson said. "What do we do now? Steal them back? Take out the Manaus depot?"

"No. We sit back and wait for someone to try to use them," Natasha said.

"Are we really doing this? We're going to use ten tons of nuclear missiles as the dangle in a smuggling op? Isn't that a little like the tail wagging the . . . whale?" Coulson asked. He didn't look at all convinced.

"Dog," Tony said. "The tail wags the dog."

Coulson shook his head. "No, I'm pretty sure this one's a whale."

"So we keep an eye on things, and make sure we move

in before anything happens." Natasha shrugged. "Not a problem."

"No, nuclear warheads in the wind. They're never a problem," Tony said.

"I'm not going to let anything happen," Natasha said. "We won't."

"How do you know?" Tony wasn't buying it. "It's not always up to you, or even us."

"How else are we going to prove who is behind it? How else can we expose the Red Room for what they are? How are we going to see what the endgame is, who they're targeting and why? How can we protect anyone if we don't know who to protect, and what we're protecting them from?" Natasha's voice was rising.

"Sometimes you can't know who to protect. Sometimes things just happen, N-Ro." Tony didn't say anything else, but everyone in the room heard what he was really saying.

"This isn't just about me," Natasha said. She could feel her face going red, which wasn't like her, and felt like a betrayal.

"I'm just saying, we all know your feelings about the Red Room and the Somodorovs. Don't make this personal," Coulson said.

"Don't tell me that. Of course it's personal," Natasha snapped.

"Maybe you should sit this one out," Tony said, gently.

Natasha bristled. "Who else is there? Cap? Bruce?"

Coulson looked at her for a long moment, playing with the edge of the folder in front of him. "And Ava? What about her? How's she doing with all this? Her first mission, first time in the field, after everything?" *After Istanbul.*

Nobody said it. *They only think it.*

Natasha looked out at the room in defiance.

How is Ava? She's halfway to crazy, she almost killed a man, she hallucinates my dead brother—and she's the only one of you who understands.

Natasha managed a smile. "Ava? Never better. I think you could say . . . she's a natural."

"What have we got on my trackers? Have any of the tagged warheads shown up?" Natasha asked the nerdy-looking desk jockey in the computer bank closest to the door.

He held up one hand and kept typing with the other, without glancing away from his computer. She briefly considered shooting out his plasma screen with her Glock, but thought better of it. Bullets were expensive.

Natasha was already in a foul mood; she hated coming into this part of any Triskelion—the tenth-floor war room. Every S.H.I.E.L.D. base had a war room like this one, which consisted of half an amphitheater of computer desks stacked with monitors and facing a curving wall of nine floor-to-ceiling screens, each covered with different map views of the world.

They were all the same, these rooms—not to mention these wonks—and you never found your way to any one of them unless you were in as much trouble as Natasha was in now.

Nuclear trouble.

"I'm sorry, am I disturbing you?" she asked again. In her mind, she was already hurling his office chair against the illuminated projection of the Eastern Seaboard occupying screen six on the wall across from them.

"Just give me a minute," the techie said, otherwise ignoring her. "This is supes important."

"*Supes* important?"

Maria Hill looked up from across the room, where she was engrossed in conversation with Coulson, and waved her over.

Natasha leaned in. "Supes? For reals?" On his screen, she saw a sniper on one side of a river bridge taking out a whole squadron on the other. "Let me get this straight. I'm asking you about the positioning of five actual, live, missing nuclear missiles, and you can't give me an update until you kill your pretend insurgents?"

"Sh-sh-sh-sh-sh," the guy said, still not looking up. "Can't talk. I'm the sniper. I'm on overwatch."

Is there not one part of you that isn't afraid of what I'm about to do to you? As, you know, an actual sniper?

"Yeah, okay," Natasha said. "Sniper." She shook her head.

Maria appeared by Natasha's side. "Let's leave Barry to do his thing."

Natasha raised an eyebrow. "His thing? Do you mean *his game*?"

"Either way we need him to keep playing," Maria said.

"Let me guess: because the twist is . . . that his game is real—and all my ops are fake?" Natasha asked.

Maria shrugged. "The game doesn't matter, just who he's playing it with."

Now Natasha was interested. "Yeah? And who is that?"

"We don't know. Barry was on missile watch, until fourteen minutes ago, when he got challenged from an UNSUB who somehow jacked into our secure mainframe through a *Warrior World* lobby, believe it or not."

"Oh, I believe it," Natasha said.

"Now he's playing against an account with an IP address registered to a high-ranking S.H.I.E.L.D. operative."

"And you're telling me this because?"

Maria looked at her. "Which high-ranking S.H.I.E.L.D. operative do you think that IP address belongs to?"

"Me?" Natasha looked back down at the screen. "No."

"Yep."

"And how would this soldier superfan have found— Barry?" Natasha asked. "Doesn't that seem a little suspicious?"

Maria shook her head. "That's what we're trying to find out." She nodded to someone standing in the far doorway and waved them over. In response, Coulson made his way through the room.

"Do we have a status update?" he asked.

"Are you talking about the IRL ops or the virtual ops?" Natasha said. "This is ops central."

"Either way, don't ask the kid by the door. He is *very busy*," Coulson said.

"But the more important status update: Was I winning?"

Natasha asked. Coulson looked confused. Maria looked past her to Barry.

Because suddenly Barry was standing up in front of his monitor. "Uh, guys? You might want to come see this."

"Pull it up on the big screen," Maria said to the wonk at the desk immediately in front of her.

Another text box, from another UNSUB. At least, she assumed it had to be another one. Then she read the message:

UNSUB: HAVE A LITTLE FAITH, PTNETS
UNSUB: VERUYUSCHIKH SREDI NAS—
UNSUB: THE FAITHFUL ARE AMONG US

It's from the same person.

But it can't be from Maks. He's locked up. This is the work of a second hacker. Maybe the person who hired Maks in the first place.

The one he was so afraid of.

Maybe even the one who ties him to Somodorov.

Despite everything S.H.I.E.L.D. had thrown at him, Maks still refused to give up the name of the person who had hired him.

Once again, the skull logo appeared on the screen— only this time the screen was nine screens tall and wide, and the image occupied the whole war-room wall.

No. Not again. Not here—

For probably the first time all day, every head in the

room snapped up from its monitor. You could almost hear the vertebrae collectively clack and shuffle as the rows of spines straightened.

That's how you know something is really wrong—

"How did that thing get into our network?" Maria roared, startling the tenth-floor wonks. "Get it out—Initiate X Protocol—now!"

As if on cue, the moment the words were out of her mouth, all the screens went black. "X Protocol initiating," the wonk next to Maria reported breathlessly. "The network is locked onto override."

Yeah, right— That was too easy—

"Thank you," Maria said, to the room.

"He's not done," Natasha said, keeping her voice low. But the rows of monitors flashed back with rotating columns of bright white numbers as they began to reboot themselves. Only the screens on the wall remained dead black.

What's he doing? The UNSUB? The one that isn't Maks? Whoever this guy is, he's not done. He can't be.

He's just showing me that he knows how to get to me.

Her mind went immediately to her vulnerabilities. Her phone. Her apartment. Her—

Ava.

Natasha pulled out her phone and began to text.

N_ROMANOFF: ava if up stay home stay offline don't open door
N_ROMANOFF: shield hacked so going dark
N_ROMANOFF: back soon

Natasha pulled the sim card out of her phone and broke it in half, dropping it into the mug of stale coffee on the nearest desk.

"You should probably trash your sim cards, too. Whatever he's written, it's nasty and it replicates. Ask Stark, he was ready to hire the guy. This hack is the viral equivalent of bedbugs."

"He?" Coulson quirked an eyebrow. "Who's he?"

Natasha wished she knew.

"Face-to-face, we've only gotten eyes on three people: Maks the hacker, the would-be Rio assassin, and Yuri Somodorov," Natasha said.

"One's a corpse and one's a convict," Maria observed. "Which leaves the Rio assassin."

"We know she's in contact with Maks Mohawk," Natasha said. "At least, we used her RFID tracker to find him. But that's as far as we've gotten."

"What is Maks's side of the story?" Maria asked.

Natasha shrugged. "So far? No comment. But I did have to shoot him, which might have gotten in the way of some of his talking points."

As she spoke, a tiny white dot appeared in the center of screen five, the middle screen of the middle row of the room.

It expanded into a light, and then words—

UNSUB: POVERNIS'
UNSUB: TURN AROUND

"He's back," Maria called out to the room. "How did he get in again? Shut down the network—where's my X Protocol?"

Natasha spun around. All she could see were the rows of heads looking up from their monitors once again—

Except one.

Barry had fallen forward, his purple face resting on his keyboard, blood running from his mouth and nose and pooling on his desk.

The room broke out in chaos, but not before Natasha bent to the floor beneath Barry's chair and picked up the empty glass vial.

Only a few of the sandy black granules still clung to the sides of the container, but it was enough. Natasha recognized them. She also knew they'd match the sample she'd brought back from the Veraport depot.

Barry from the war room—Barry the tenth-floor gamer—had kept the Faith, and then he'd died from it.

The Red Room was finally showing its hand.

VERUYUSCHIKH SREDI NAS—

The Faithful are among us.

She grabbed the sample and bolted.

"Where are you going?" Coulson called after her.

"Home," she yelled back. "No phones—"

Ava—

232

S.H.I.E.L.D. EYES ONLY

CLEARANCE LEVEL X

SPECIAL CIRCUMSTANCES & INDIVIDUALS (SCI)
INVESTIGATION
AGENT IN COMMAND (AIC): PHILLIP COULSON
RE: AGENT NATASHA ROMANOFF A.K.A. BLACK WIDOW
A.K.A. NATASHA ROMANOVA
AAA HEARING TRANSCRIPT (TEXT EXCHANGE)
CC: DEPARTMENT OF DEFENSE, SCI INQUIRY

N_ROMANOFF: ava where are you
N_ROMANOFF: ava pick up the phone
N_ROMANOFF: this is n

N_ROMANOFF: don't call my phone it doesn't work
N_ROMANOFF: I borrowed the super's phone now, from
downstairs
N_ROMANOFF: am home but you are not

N_ROMANOFF: ava pick up the phone
N_ROMANOFF: ava pick up the phone
N_ROMANOFF: not safe to call

N_ROMANOFF: not safe to be out
N_ROMANOFF: not sure how long it will be safe here
N_ROMANOFF: get your butt home

N_ROMANOFF: ava pick up the phone
N_ROMANOFF: ava pick up the phone
N_ROMANOFF: am waiting

N_ROMANOFF: also worried
N_ROMANOFF: also if one thing happens to that jacket
N_ROMANOFF: ava be safe

N_ROMANOFF: ava pick up the phone

CHAPTER **18**: AVA

STARK COMMUNITY SOUP KITCHEN
FORT GREENE, BROOKLYN

Dinner wasn't as bad as Ava had imagined it would be. There were no fish sticks, but there was a crusty oregano-laced lasagna, and a pungent vegetable soup with so much cabbage that Ava could close her eyes and almost pretend it was *shchi*, the cabbage soup her mother—and every other Russian mother—used to make in the winter.

Almost.

Across the table from Ava, Dante kept busy eating his weight in garlic bread while Sana told funny stories about her customers or fencing, or about her stepsisters and brothers. Even one about drawing a butt instead of a heart in the cappuccino foam and waiting for someone to notice.

It was only the part where Ava and Dante didn't manage

to speak to each other all night that was painful. That, and the fact that her phone was dead, so she couldn't dial star sixty-whatever and pretend to get a call and go. She hadn't charged it since Manaus, except for the few minutes she was in the shower at Natasha's apartment. *Things S.H.I.E.L.D. doesn't think about when building aircraft—*

By the time they were halfway through the chocolate pudding, Ava didn't think she could take it any longer. "You have to come with me to the restroom." She grabbed Sana by the hand and yanked her toward the bathrooms, leaving Dante behind at the Stark CK table. As soon as they were out of earshot, Ava hissed into her friend's ear. "Seriously? What are you trying to do, San?"

"Nothing." Sana pushed through the bathroom door.

"You set me up. Tonight was sabotage. You should go to friend prison," Ava said, following her in. "I'm not friends with him. He hates me. He blames me for—everything."

Sana crossed her arms, leaning against the edge of the sink counter. "Say it."

"Sana," Ava said. She was getting seriously annoyed.

"What does he blame you for? What is everything?" Sana said. "Say his name."

"Whatever. No. Stop being so weird. You know what I'm talking about."

"No." She shook her head. "Alexei. Say his name."

"Sana," Ava warned.

Sana grabbed her hands. "You never talk about him, Mysh. It's like it never happened, like he never happened."

Ava pulled her hands away. Sana might as well have slapped her. "That's a horrible thing to say—and it's not true."

"And I know that's not true, I saw the two of you together. I know how crushed you were when he—"

"Sana!"

Sana looked at her meaningfully. "When he *died*, Ava. Alexei died."

"I know that. Of course I know that. What are you, insane?" Ava could feel the tears starting to come; they were prickling and bubbling up to the front of her eyes.

"No, Ava. I'm worried. The two of you lived in your own little world when you were together, and now you live in your own little world with his memory, because you're apart."

Is it true?

Ava was reeling. "I'm not alone," she said. "I've been studying at the Academy. I've been with Natasha on the road. I'm almost never by myself, in fact."

"You might as well be," Sana said. Her mouth twisted, and for a moment she looked like she was about to start tearing up, too. "You're my best friend, Ava. I've let you try to work it out by yourself for too long, and I swore to myself that when you came back, I'd help you find your way."

"But what if I don't want to find it?" Ava's eyes were blurring now.

"You will. You have to." Sana leaned in, dropping a

hand gently to each of Ava's shoulders. "But you can't move on until you work through all this."

"Fine with me, I never asked to move on," Ava said, looking away. A tear rolled down her cheek and into her mouth; she tasted the salt on her lip.

"You have to, Mysh. You know you do. And I think that the boy waiting at our table might be the one person in the world who's as messed up about it as you."

All the more reason that we should stay away from each other.

"Okay? Are you okay?"

Ava wanted to tell her she was fine, that everything was okay, that she just didn't understand. But the moment she opened her mouth, all she could do was cry.

Sana wrapped her arms around Ava, squeezing her into a fierce hug. "Just try. You might as well talk to him about it. Because I can't fix this on my own, Mysh. I need that boy to help."

Ava buried her face in Sana's shoulder; her friend smelled like freshly ground coffee and cinnamon, and even that was only fleetingly comforting tonight.

"He knows what you lost—" Sana began.

Ava cut her off. "He doesn't. Nobody does."

Sana looked at Ava sadly. "Okay. But he knows *who* you lost, better than anyone else. And I'm sorry. I wish more than anything that I could be that person for you."

"Stop. Just stop." Ava pulled away. She tried to collect herself, nodding, rubbing her face. *All the signs people give that they are fine. I'll give you them all. Just let this conversation end.* "It's okay. I'll be okay."

"But you're not," Sana said.

"Let's just get through this. We can talk about it later." Ava pushed her way through the restroom doors and headed back toward their table. *My eyes are swollen. My face is red. My nose is running. And Dante can see it all. He's probably terrified—*

Dante stood up as she approached. "I'll go." He reached for his fencing bag. "You two can stay and talk." He couldn't get out of there fast enough.

Yeah. Terrified.

Ava looked at him, finally taking a deep breath. As she did she shuddered, like a toddler who was trying to stop crying after a tantrum. *Accurate.*

Then she looked at him. "Do you maybe just want to get out of here? Walk me back to the subway or something?"

He stared. "Are you sure?"

She shuddered again, and she realized this time it was from exhaustion. "Yeah. I'm kind of beat. I need to go home and crash."

"I know the feeling," Dante said. Seconds later, he was pushing the door open and following her into the cold night air.

They fell into the same pace within moments, walking in silence down Flatbush Avenue. "I'm sorry," Ava finally said. "Really. I know I've been acting really strange tonight. I'm just—I don't get out much."

"I hear you," Dante said. "Hey, my school's bad enough, now."

Without him. You can't say it, either, can you?

He shrugged. "I can't imagine what military school is like." *Military school.* "What?" That's what she had said. Now she remembered. Was it a lie? She was so tired of lies, of conspiracy and deception. On the other hand, was the Academy really all that different from military school?

I guess in a way it's true.

Dante shifted his fencing bag to his other arm, and Ava changed the subject. "Oh, right. How's fencing going for you?"

"Great. I mean, fine." He shrugged.

"Yeah?" Ava smiled. "Which is it?"

Dante stopped walking and handed her his bag. She realized, the moment she took it, that there were no blades in it. The nylon case was so light she could carry it between two fingertips; when she lifted it, the thing deflated, almost folding itself in half. "Where's your gear?"

He looked across the street to the traffic light. There were cars idling at the intersection. "Well, yeah. I quit."

Ava was surprised. "But I saw you in Philly. You were so—"

"He was better," Dante said, simply.

She stood perfectly still. "Everything was better," she said. Then she reached out and took his cold hand in hers.

When he finally looked up, she could see his face in the streetlight, streaked with tears. His fingers tightened around hers—then he wiped his face on his sleeve, nodding. "I know. Nothing's okay."

There it was. The truth. The unbelievable awfulness of everything. It simply was—whether or not they wanted it.

"That's why you couldn't write," Dante said.

Ava nodded. "Sometimes I could hardly breathe. I couldn't catch my breath."

"I couldn't listen to people talk," Dante said. "Like, I couldn't sit by strangers who were talking in restaurants. I kept having to move. They all seemed so stupid. The whole world seemed so stupid."

"I felt like I had my hand in the burner," Ava said. "Right there in the flames. I'd wake up in the morning and think, 'Is my hand still in the burner?' And then I would feel it, always still there."

They stood for a moment in silence. Alexei was gone and the world had fallen into a thousand awful pieces. Even the things that had survived were not the same.

Like us. We aren't the same.

"We better keep walking if you ever want to get that train." Dante cleared his throat, and Ava let go of his hand. He shoved it into his pocket, awkwardly, and they began to walk again.

He looked over at her. "What about you? You fence for your school? I know Army and Navy and Air Force all have really kicking teams."

She shook her head. "The Academy isn't—it's more, like—" *Like the only teams at S.H.I.E.L.D. are strike teams.*

She tried to think of how to describe this Triskelion as a school. "It's pretty military. So it's more ropes and target practice and drills and obstacle courses. And, you know, outdoors stuff." *Yeah, outside as in denied area ops with snipers and grenades.*

"So no fencing," he said.

She almost smiled. "I do some fencing, but it's more on my own." *And with an electric blade or two—*

"Is that how your face got all cut up?" He leaned his head, to try to see better in the streetlight.

Ava touched her forehead self-consciously. "Yeah, well. Kind of." *Actually, that happened when we were blowing ourselves up in Manaus.* "You should see the other guys."

"All right." Dante smiled. "That's pretty cool."

Ava smiled back. "It's sort of cool."

They were only a block from the subway entrance now. Dante hesitated. "Hey, can you have visitors? We could come, you know, see you or something. Do they have, like, visiting day?"

Ava hesitated. There was no way to talk around that one. *It's a covert intelligence organization, so yeah, no. No visiting day. Not ever—*

"Hello? Rude! What, were you just going to *ditch* me?" A figure appeared out of the shadows, just beyond the streetlight. "Group hug," Sana called, plowing into both of them, arms everywhere. Ava leaned her head against Sana's shoulder and Sana pulled Dante's head close with one arm.

"Now. Are we going to get on the subway or just stand here and freeze our butts off?" Sana began to push Ava and Dante toward the stairs. "And that wasn't really a question. . . ."

They ran after each other. The streets were dark and the steps down to the subway platform full of dim yellow light. At the bottom of the stairs, Sana pulled out a MetroCard—probably her first, Ava thought. "That's right," Sana said. "I'm a legit Rude Brewista now. My turnstile-hopping days are over. In fact, I got you both."

"Look who's living large," Ava said, quirking an eyebrow, moving through the turnstile and handing back the MetroCard.

"Well, you're starving students." Sana shrugged, handing Dante the card. "I don't want to stress you out."

"Awesome," Dante said, shoving through the turnstile. "I got to get all the way back to Jersey. Nine-oh-eight train, almost every night."

"What's that about?" Sana pushed through after him.

Dante pointed to his Montclair Alliance Fencing Club jacket. "My parents think I'm at a fencing club in the city now."

"You never told them you quit?" Ava asked. It had been so long since she'd had parents, she couldn't imagine what it would feel like to have to lie to the people you lived with. *Yes, you can imagine it. You're doing it right now. Natasha thinks you're at home, and you're off in Brooklyn wearing half her closet—*

"It works," Dante said. "I get a whole lot of lost time, and they don't have to worry about where I am."

"Ah, right. Cop dad," Ava remembered.

"Cop dad? Good thing I didn't jump the turnstiles." Sana whistled. "I'll bet you would have hauled me down to the precinct and turned me in to Daddy."

"That's Captain Daddy to you. And yeah, not tonight." Dante smiled. "We don't talk that much anymore. Like I said, lost time. It works out for everyone."

They moved through the turnstiles and out to the edge of the platform. It smelled and looked like home, and Ava breathed deeply. "You know when you're walking down the street and you step on one of those subway gratings and you get a big old blast of dirty New York City underground air?"

Sana wrinkled her nose. Dante laughed at her.

"Stop. Don't laugh. I'm not kidding. That's my favorite smell in the world," Ava said.

"No, it's not," Sana answered.

"Really?" Dante shook his head.

Sana crooked her arm around Ava's neck. "Baked apples with cinnamon. That's your favorite smell. You've told me a thousand times."

Ava smiled. "Maybe. I've been gone awhile, though. Maybe I miss different things now."

She leaned against the tiled wall of the subway. At the far end of the platform, where the pools of yellow light dissolved into shadow and depth, two figures stood back in the darkness. Something was going on.

Then she felt Sana poke her in the waist. "Don't look," she murmured. They had both spent enough time on the street to know how to stay out of everyone's business. This was either a drug deal or a mugging, and either way it was better not to see anything or anyone.

Ava nodded, almost imperceptibly.

Sana threaded her arm through Dante's and slowly drifted with him, farther down the platform.

Ava found her hand dropping to one of her concealed blades. Before she could stop herself, she began to walk in the other direction, toward the magazine kiosk that hid the two guys from view.

"Where are you going?" Sana asked, sharply.

"Beyoncé." Ava pointed, moving closer to the magazines.

"Ava," Sana said. A warning.

"Just a minute." Ava headed over to the kiosk. She picked up a magazine and pretended to leaf through it.

The guy behind the counter coughed. "You wanna read it, you gotta buy it, sweetheart." He spoke without bothering to look up.

She ignored him, angling herself so that she could see over the magazine and into the shadows behind the farthest support pillar of the platform. She turned a page and snuck a better look.

There they were. The same two guys. One in a Nike jacket, one in a Yankees cap. Nike handed Yankees a roll of cash. Yankees pulled something out of his pocket in a wadded-up brown paper bag, shoving it into Nike's hand. She could just see the edge of it, poking out of his pocket.

It was a head.

She turned the page and looked again. Her heart was

beating so quickly now she thought she was going to pass out.

She knew what she was seeing: Jesus. The head of Jesus, anyways.

She was looking at a Cristo statuette, just like the ones she and Natasha had found yesterday in the hidden missile depot outside of Manaus.

Faith.

The Russian drug was here on the streets of her own Fort Greene.

S.H.I.E.L.D. EYES ONLY

CLEARANCE LEVEL X

SPECIAL CIRCUMSTANCES & INDIVIDUALS (SCI) INVESTIGATION
AGENT IN COMMAND (AIC): PHILLIP COULSON
RE: AGENT NATASHA ROMANOFF A.K.A. BLACK WIDOW
A.K.A. NATASHA ROMANOVA
AAA HEARING TRANSCRIPT
CC: DEPARTMENT OF DEFENSE, SCI INQUIRY

COULSON: So Faith had arrived on the streets of New York City.
ROMANOFF: Before we had.

COULSON: Which means the shipment you found in the Amazon wasn't the first.
ROMANOFF: Not if they'd already sold enough to buy five nukes.

COULSON: Yeah, that's the thing about nuclear missiles. They're almost never free.
ROMANOFF: Apparently.

COULSON: Tough call for Ava, that dealer in the subway. On the one hand, Faith. On the other, no backup.
ROMANOFF: It happens.

COULSON: Except this is the part where I remind you that she wasn't like the rest of us.
ROMANOFF: I know.

COULSON: She was a rookie trainee with a few classes under her belt and almost zero experience.
ROMANOFF: I wouldn't say zero. She had a direct line to my brain. Don't forget that one.

COULSON: You're saying she used the Quantum connection to fight the guy?
ROMANOFF: I'm just saying the guy didn't know what hit him.

CHAPTER **19**: DANTE

FORT GREENE, BROOKLYN
THE GREAT CITY OF NEW YORK

It was hard to see what was happening, from where I was standing on the platform.

All I could see was that, one minute, Ava—that's my friend—she looked like she was reading a magazine alone by the newsstand, minding her own business—and the next, she was beating the crap out of two skeevy-looking low-life dudes.

I'm serious.

Wait—

With these crazy glowing, like, electric blades that looked more like lightsabers than épée blades.

I am not kidding, I swear.

The blades looked like they were made out of some kind of blue light, like the good Jedi, not the Sith.

And Ava—my friend, the girl—was attacking the low-life dudes with it, just like an advance on a fencing strip—only this time it was on a subway platform instead of a strip, and she had the two blades instead of one.

One short, one long. That's what I remember.

Then she was standing on top of the bench in the center of the platform, okay? And she was screaming for them to hand it over, hand it over. And the guys were acting like they didn't know what she was talking about.

But then the one guy, the one wearing a Nike shirt or something, began to shout at the other guy, the Yankees fan. You couldn't really hear why, and then he tossed this paper bag at Ava.

That really ticked off Yankees fan, right? So Yankees fan told Nike guy to go jump in front of a train. Whatever.

But the thing was, the Nike guy?

He did it.

He jumped.

I'm serious.

He jumped in front of a train, right as it was pulling up to the platform.

I have no idea why.

Ava was screaming at him to stop, but he wouldn't listen. And the whole platform was still rattling, because the train was coming.

So the dude fell, right in front of the train, and the Yankees fan bolted.

And my friend Sana—the other girl, there were two— Sana and I were just standing there, watching all this, thinking we were going to watch a man die.

Everything after that happened so fast I could hardly follow it, really. The train was pulling up, and Nike guy was screaming, and Ava was going nuts.

I saw those blue blades flashing like crazy again, and then I just heard them, because the lights went out across the whole platform—the electrical wiring failed or something.

And the trains all across the city had to stop. And the one pulling into our platform did, too, making this loud noise the whole time, screeching and sparking like crazy.

I couldn't really see what happened after that, because the lights had gone out. But it sounded like the Nike guy started to freak out, because I heard all this yelling, and then I saw Ava pulling him up from the tracks.

Then he took off running, just like Yankee fan did.

And then there she was again, walking up to Sana and me like nothing had happened. Except she was still holding those two crazy blades, right? Yeah, so I just freaked out and ran for it.

That's when I called you, Dad. Because I'm still pretty freaked out and I think I might need a ride—

Dante stopped talking and waited. "Hello? Dad? You still there?"

There was no answer. He looked down at his garbage cell phone, the one that had already been his father's, and then his mother's. He knew he was lucky he was the oldest of his brothers and sisters, or it would have been even worse.

How much worse could it get?

His cell was completely dead, and he hadn't even known. He'd just kept talking, spilling his guts out to his police-captain father, who like usual, probably didn't even have time to talk. Or had one eye on his paperwork the whole time. Or the game—

"Crap," Dante said.

When did the phone cut out? How much did my dad even hear?

He hung up the phone, slipping it back into his pocket, and sat back down on the curb. He was completely freaked out, freezing his butt off, and only three blocks from the subway station. The trains were off-line. A cab home was going to put him back more babysitting hours than he could even stand to think about.

Should he go back and wait at the subway stop? The one where he'd just seen something totally insane happen, if not completely impossible?

At least I wouldn't freeze to death in there.

Then he heard her voice—

"Dante. You okay? What are you doing?"

He knew it was Ava. He just didn't know what he had seen, aside from nothing that he'd ever seen before. He could feel his heart thumping in his chest.

He turned slowly around to face her. Sana was right behind her. "What *was* that back there?"

Ava walked toward him. "Don't overreact."

Sana caught up with them on the street corner. "I can see why he's losing it—what kind of sport was that?"

"Yeah," Dante said, looking at Ava suspiciously. "And how do we know you put the Jedi weapons away?"

Ava sighed, yanking open her jacket to show the handles of her blades shoved back inside her waistband. Then she held up her empty hands. "There. See? It's all good. No big thing."

"You've got Day-Glo power blades and you might be a ninja and I'm pretty sure you just mugged a mugger during a mugging. It's a big thing," Dante said.

"That wasn't a mugging, it was a drug deal," Ava said.

Dante looked at her. "Thanks for clearing that up."

Ava tried again. "Look, think of it as fencing. We've all seen each other at a tournament before. I've seen you, you've seen me. Try not to see me as anything different from that."

Sana laughed. "Yeah, right."

"Not different?" Dante was practically shouting. "Fencing happens in a gym. On a strip. With Kevlar protective gear. And both people have blades, by the way."

"I know, I know," Ava said. "In retrospect, there was probably a better example."

"You think?" He snorted.

Sana just shook her head. "How did I not know this about you, Mysh?"

"I wasn't always like this. Something happened in Istanbul," Ava said. "Something sort of complicated."

"You mean, *that* Istanbul?" *Where my best friend died?*

"There's kind of a lot more to that story," Ava said. She looked at Sana pleadingly. "I wanted to tell you, San, I swear. And not like this. I mean, I know this all seems a little weird—"

"A little weird?" Dante could feel himself starting to really lose it.

Sana tried to step between them. "Calm down, Kid Cop. Think about it. This probably isn't the wackest thing that's happened in a New York subway."

"I'm pretty sure it is, actually." He could feel his face going red. "And anyways—now you're going to take *her* side?"

Sana shrugged. "Probably not the wackest thing I've ever seen, either."

Ava took her friend by the hand with a smile. "Like I said, I would have told you if I could have. It's just, well . . ."

"What?" Dante wasn't buying it. "That every word coming out of your mouth is a lie?"

"No. That's not true," Ava said. She had gone pale, though, so Dante figured it probably was at least a little true. "Not every word."

He shook his head. "Are you really in school right now? Did you even know my best friend? Did you actually love him?"

There.

He'd finally said it. He'd only been thinking it for, what? A year now?

Ava looked crushed. Then mad. Like, crazy mad.

"You know what? You think my whole life is a lie? You

want to see what the *military school* I go to looks like? Come on, then. Let's go. Let's do this."

"Now?" Dante wasn't so sure about that.

Ava nodded, holding up a hand as a cab pulled magically over to the side of the curb. "Right now. I have to get back there. I have something important that the others need to see. We need to hurry."

Sana waved to the cabdriver, pulling open the front passenger door. Dante wondered why she was riding in the front when she didn't have to, but then, he also barely ever went in cabs enough to know or care.

"Your teachers?" Dante asked.

"Sure," Ava said, sounding tired. "Something like that." Then she looked at him. "Can I borrow your phone?"

S.H.I.E.L.D. EYES ONLY

CLEARANCE LEVEL X

SPECIAL CIRCUMSTANCES & INDIVIDUALS (SCI) INVESTIGATION
AGENT IN COMMAND (AIC): PHILLIP COULSON
RE: AGENT NATASHA ROMANOFF A.K.A. BLACK WIDOW
A.K.A. NATASHA ROMANOVA
AAA HEARING TRANSCRIPT
CC: DEPARTMENT OF DEFENSE, SCI INQUIRY

COULSON: So you were looking for Ava. She was looking for you. The Triskelion was under attack.
ROMANOFF: And all our secure phones are hacked.

COULSON: This was the first time you knew Faith could kill?
ROMANOFF: You mean, apart from how any street drug could? Yes. Poor Barry.
COULSON: Data scientist James J. Berrimore. Newly transferred from the CIA's new DDI, Directorate of Digital Innovation.

ROMANOFF: He was just a kid—he couldn't have been much older than Alexei.
COULSON: Seventeen months.
ROMANOFF: What?
COULSON: James Berrimore was a year and five months older than your brother.
ROMANOFF: Phil—
COULSON: I had the same thought. I looked up his file.

ROMANOFF: Of course. That was the point. To make me remember, as if I could forget.
COULSON: Another message. Like the way he died.

ROMANOFF: Bleeding from the nose and mouth, I'd seen it before. I knew there were toxins and poisons and even venoms that could cause those symptoms. Our military had experimented with all of them.

COULSON: You mean, you knew from your previous employment?

ROMANOFF: It's not a spoiler. You can say the words. I know what I was.

COULSON: When you were a Red Room operative?

ROMANOFF: When I was a Russian spy.

BLACK WIDOW'S APARTMENT, LITTLE ODESSA, BROOKLYN

Natasha tore through her apartment but it was no use. She couldn't find anything that would lead her to Ava. The dirty pile of clothes in the bathroom hamper revealed nothing. Aside from the laundry and the used towel, there was no sign that she'd been there at all.

Meow—

The cat—she didn't really think of it as her cat—wandered in through the open window by the fire escape. It leaped to the top of the counter, crossed the outer ledge of the sink, padded across the dish drain, and stuck its head into the trash can.

"Do you smell something?" Natasha picked up the cat

and dropped it to the floor. She reached into the can and pulled out a used paper coffee cup.

Rude Brews? That's where you were? But is that where you are?

She was frustrated. She'd been trying the super's phone, down on the first floor, but Ava wasn't picking up.

Or something's wrong—

She shook off the memory of Barry's bloody face resting against his computer screen. Whoever was after her had just demonstrated the ability to reach into S.H.I.E.L.D.'s Triskelion and take whatever life they wanted. Not even the wonks on the tenth floor were safe anymore. The threat wasn't just a hack on a secure line. It wasn't even a magnesium charge.

It was a life, her life, and Ava's, and the stakes had suddenly risen exponentially.

Natasha stared at the coffee cup in her hand.

Where are you, sestra?

For the first time in a long while, instead of cursing her Quantum connection to Ava, Natasha actually wanted to use it.

It was always Ava who could reach her. She wasn't so certain it even worked the other way. *How does she do it?* Natasha closed her eyes.

Where are you, Ava? Talk to me. How can I find you?

She focused harder. Her breathing slowed. She pushed past her own conscious thoughts, letting her mind go blank. . . .

Ava Anatalya Orlova—

A knock at the door startled her, and her eyes flew open. She pulled the Glock from the back of her waistband and pressed herself against the wall nearest to the door. "Yes?"

"You got a phone call, honey."

Natasha frowned and pulled open the door to see her building supervisor, the ten-thousand-year-old and four-foot-tall Mrs. Smalley, in a housecoat, holding out her phone.

"Make it snappy, I'm waiting for a call from the furnace repairman. And the next time you give out my number, it better be to that Iron Man guy."

The cat ran past Mrs. Smalley's legs with a hiss. The old lady hissed back, then looked at Natasha. "Take it."

Natasha eyed the phone like it could detonate at any second (possible, given the day, but also how she viewed all phones) and kept her distance. "Did they say who it is?"

"Your sister."

Natasha looked relieved and took the phone.

"Ava?"

There was no one on the line. All she could hear now was a dial tone, followed by a strange clicking sound—

"Get down!" She clutched Mrs. Smalley and dove down the stairwell as the apartment exploded into an angry ball of fire and smoke and flying debris behind them.

** FILE COPY OF INCOMING TRANSMISSION ** FROM THE PENTAGON **

Phil,

Just got word of the attack on S.H.I.E.L.D. Losing good people
was the hardest part of every tour of duty I ever pulled. Losing
a kid from a secure facility on American soil is even harder.

Assume you guys are doing a floor-to-ceiling wipe? Let me
know if there is anything we can do at JCOS to assist.

Also: just saw the cable re the attempted Romanoff hit. As
you can imagine, the Oval was not happy. He hears the word
S.H.I.E.L.D. and thinks Sokovia or Ultron or that hammer guy.

Me to you, Phil: if you've gotten yourselves into some
messed-up situation somehow, give me a heads-up. I'll run
interference as long as I can.

And buffalo wings soon.

ARTIE

OFFICE OF THE JOINT CHIEFS OF STAFF
9999 JOINT STAFF PENTAGON
WASHINGTON, D.C.

CHAPTER **21**: AVA

S.H.I.E.L.D. NEW YORK TRISKELION, EAST RIVER THE GREAT CITY OF NEW YORK

he first clue came from her fingertips, where the blue sparks flew in a shower to the industrial carpet covering the floor of Maria Hill's office.

Ava was already getting the lecture of a lifetime by the time she felt the explosion. It almost rocked her off her feet; her eyes went blank and bright, and for a moment she thought she was going to pass out.

Then came the searing pain.

Natasha.

"You were out of line, Cadet." Coulson sat on the edge of Maria's desk, glaring at Ava. "And as soon as Agent Romanoff gets back, she's going to have a few things of her own to add—"

"I know, sir," Ava stammered, though she could barely manage to get the words out. Her head hurt so badly she could barely stay on her feet.

Natasha—are you okay?

Maria shook her head, pacing behind him. "Now isn't the time for S.H.I.E.L.D. playdates—"

Ava stopped listening. Instead, she reached out in her mind, past the edges of her mind, of the base, of the East River. She pulled herself, one block at a time, closer and closer to Little Odessa, where Natasha's apartment stood.

Closer. I need to get closer—

She couldn't see her fingers turning blue with light, but she could feel the warmth moving up her arms, encircling her entire body.

She clenched her fists, and the electricity burned brighter—and she could feel her mind moving with increased speed and clarity.

There we go—

Maria was still talking. "We've just lost a good kid—and a valuable analyst—to some kind of unknown chemical agent, well inside our own base—"

What's happening? Talk to me—

Something's wrong, sestra.

Ava balled up her toes as the energy shot through them. Now she could feel the tiny pinpricks of blue light piercing each of her pupils.

"Not when people are getting killed for no apparent reason other than a glass vial full of black—"

Ava looked up. "Sand?" she asked.

Maria looked at her strangely.

Ava pulled something out of her pocket and held it out toward her. "Like this?" It was another small glass vial, this one half-full of the gleaming black sand.

"Where did you get that?" Coulson asked as Maria stared at the vial.

"From the hands of a man who had just jumped in front of a train," Ava said. Now the pain was so strong she had to bite the inside of her own cheek to try to focus on what the agents were saying to her.

Sestra—

"What? Why?" Coulson asked.

"Why did he jump? Because the guy holding this stuff told him to—" Ava pressed the vial into Maria's hand. "Which is even worse news than you realize, because this is the same stuff we found at the Amazonas encampment."

"How is that possible?" Coulson took the vial from Maria's hand to examine it more closely.

Ava shook her head. Sunspots were flashing behind her eyes, almost like lens flare, which made no sense because she was inside. *Der'mo.* "I don't know. I wouldn't have believed it, either, if I hadn't seen it. Ask the others. They're waiting in the hall."

"The others?" Maria asked. "Other . . . children?"

"This hall?" Coulson asked. "You mean, here?"

This secure hall? This classified military base? He didn't have to say it. Ava didn't care; she had bigger problems than Coulson. The entire room was spinning now, and she hurried to force the words out. "Sana and Dante. I brought them with me. Go ahead, I know. You're going to flip out." She shook her head. "But I can't talk about it now. I have to go."

She made it only as far as the door.

The moment her hand touched the sleek, steel handle, her eyes closed involuntarily as her mind was suddenly flooded with images of fire and smoke, of screaming and sirens. Then Ava heard a voice, very small, as if from very far away.

Ava—I can feel you but I can't hear you—

If you're safe, stay where you are—they're here.

Ava's eyes flew open. She opened her mouth and a flood of blue light poured out. She flung her arms wide and the blue streams pulsed out from her fingertips, spreading and crackling across the floor beneath her and the ceiling above her like the roots and branches of a tree, or maybe the dendrites of a neuron.

The sparks went scattering as she formed two words, with great difficulty.

"Natasha—

"Now."

Then her eyes rolled upward and the room went black.

When Ava awoke again she was lying on one of S.H.I.E.L.D.'s infamous aluminum-and-canvas "body bag" cots *(as in, you'd sleep better in one)* in the infirmary.

Her head ached at the base of her skull, like someone

had been drilling. She turned her head to one side—away from the ache—

Alexei was sitting in the chair next to her bed, his head in his hands.

She tried to say his name, but only a groan came out.

Alexei looked up, a nearly palpable expression of relief on his face. "Oh, thank God. You had me worried, Mysh. Don't ever do that again."

She smiled and moved her fingers toward him, dangling off the edge of her bed. "You left me," she murmured. "You just disappeared."

"I know, and I'm sorry." A shadow crossed his face. "I couldn't handle it. I got jealous, watching you talk to my own friend. How stupid is that?"

"You can't just leave a person behind like that," she said, quietly. "Not unless you promise to come back."

"I'm here now, aren't I?" Alexei climbed out of the chair and squatted next to the bed. Now her eyes were level with his. "I'll never leave you, Ava Anatalya Orlova. I swear it on my—death."

Another voice interrupted, this time from the other side of the room.

"I'm right here, Ava. I didn't disappear. I came back. You're just confused. Can you hear me?"

Natasha.

Ava heard a beeping sound, and a whisper. "I think she's hallucinating. Can someone send in the doctor?"

"No, I'm fine," Ava said, rolling back over. She was relieved to see that the Widow looked unhurt, sitting upright on the edge of the next cot, still holding a mustard-colored plastic cup with a bent straw. "And so are you, I see."

"Cranberry juice," Natasha said, handing it to her. "Why do S.H.I.E.L.D. nurses always want to give everyone cranberry juice?"

Ava sat up, taking the cup. "Thanks."

"How does that head of yours feel?"

"I think I fried something," Ava said, moving her head gingerly back and forth. "Maybe grilled it."

"Who were you talking to, over there?" Natasha studied her face.

"Don't tell her. She won't understand," Alexei said into her ear, sitting behind her on the cot.

"Where? I must have been dreaming," Ava lied, putting down the cup on a medical station crowded with gauze and scissors and a small plastic bowl shaped like a bean. "I'm glad you're okay. I was really worried."

"I'm okay," Natasha said, holding out one gauze-bound elbow. "Just black-and-blue as usual. Everyone made it out, thank God. Even Mrs. Smalley."

"Ouch," Ava said, imagining it.

Natasha winced. "Yeah, I kind of threw us down the stairs. She's very lightweight—and I think she still has at least one good hip left."

"Great." Ava swung her feet down off the side of the bed. "The last thing I can remember is Maria Hill going on about an attack on the tenth floor. And then I felt you go down—"

Natasha looked serious. "They took out a junior agent,

an innocent wonk. I don't know how they got to him. They had some kind of total control, and they timed the hit to go down right as they hacked the base."

"*Just like Rio,*" Alexei said. "*I'm worried.*"

Ava nodded. "It's the same pattern. The two-part attack—just like when they came after you with the hack and the exploding bike in Rio."

"Agreed," Natasha said. "Whether this Red Angel or Red Room or Red Dress—"

"Green," Ava corrected.

"Yeah, whatever. It's clearly one person calling the shots, and it's not Yuri Somodorov," Natasha said, shooting Ava a meaningful look. "At least, not anymore."

"*She's worried about you. She doesn't want you to get hurt. Can you blame her?*" Alexei whispered.

Ava sat up and swung her feet off the edge of the bed. "We don't have to talk about that." The last thing she wanted to do was hash out what had happened back at the Amazonas camp; she hardly knew herself, or where that particular tsunami of rage had come from, or how she was supposed to control it.

"*But you do know. You know exactly where it came from. And you also know it's getting harder and harder to control yourself,*" Alexei said. "*You're going to have to tell her sometime, Mysh.*"

Ava fixed her eyes on Natasha. She was not going to start into this with either Romanoff, real or ghost.

"Yes, we do have to talk about it." Natasha said. "And we will."

Ava tried to stand up. "Gotta go."

"Not so fast," Natasha said. "We should probably check you out and make sure everything's okay. Revisit the quantum entanglement situation. See what's going on in your head, and why you got so fried."

"*If you let Tony into your head, he'll see how strong it's getting,*" Alexei said. "*Your power. Are you ready for that?*"

"No," Ava said—to both of them—only more loudly than she had realized. Natasha shot her a strange look.

"I don't want any more of Tony and his electrodes," Ava said. "I'm not a Quantum lab rat, and neither are you."

"I can't stop him from coming," Natasha said. "He's on his way back from Switzerland now. And he's been working with quantum physicists all week. Prepare yourself."

"Oh, please," Ava said, grabbing one of her shoes. "We don't have time for this. Let's get out of here. Did Coulson tell you? I interrupted a Faith dealer—"

"By which you mean you *jumped* a drug dealer in the middle of a drug deal? While you were out with your civilian friends? Blowing your cover and bringing them to a highly classified S.H.I.E.L.D. Triskelion base? Yes, I heard." Natasha's voice was scathing.

"It wasn't just any drug deal. It was Faith," Ava said defensively.

"I know, and Maria Hill has the lab looking at the sample now. But getting yourself into a potentially dangerous situation when you were alone in the city was the wrong call. You could have been killed."

"She's right, you know." Alexei sighed. *"You really do need to be more careful. If something happens to you—"*

Ava rolled her eyes. "I don't know how he did it, but I swear to you I was watching as that dealer made his buyer throw himself in front of a train. Was I supposed to just sit there and watch him get squashed like a bug?"

"Yes," Natasha said. "That. Exactly." She folded her arms, looking like one of the Academy instructors proctoring an exam.

"You talk a big game, *sestra*, but you know you would have done exactly the same thing."

"She would, but she won't admit that to you," Alexei said.

"What I did do," Natasha said, taking a breath, "was speak to Coulson about you going back to school. You're starting on Monday."

Ava felt her face immediately flush with humiliation. "That's not fair. I can't go back to the Academy like nothing happened, not now. Just give me a chance. Let me show you what I can do," she said.

Natasha shook her head. "Not in the field. You belong at the Academy."

"Why?"

"Put it this way: You know that whole Spider-Man thing you see on all the T-shirts? *With great power comes great responsibility?* Those aren't just words. They're the truth."

"So you're saying that by using my power I'm being irresponsible?" Ava asked, her voice rising. She could almost feel the blue electricity snapping in her brain as she spoke, begging to come out—

"*Careful, Ava. Don't lose control. Not now,*" *Alexei warned.*

"No," Natasha said. "You're being stupid." She shrugged. "And *also* irresponsible."

"Thanks for the vote of confidence. And by the way, *you're welcome.*"

"For?"

"I just saved you, didn't I? Sent S.H.I.E.L.D. to your rescue? Isn't that what I'm doing in this stupid bed in the first place? Or are you mad I didn't show up for you myself?"

"What? I tried to tell you to stay here! I could have handled it."

"You need me. I know you need me. Why won't you admit it?"

"*Because she's a Romanoff,*" *Alexei said.* "*And because she's scared.*"

Natasha stood up "You know what your problem is? You don't even know how much you don't know—and that's the scary part. *That's* what I have a problem with."

Ava's eyes flashed. "Here's a thought. You do your thing, I'll do mine."

"That's not how this works. I'm responsible for you. Ask Coulson."

"Why, because you checked me out of the Academy like some kind of library book?" Ava said, now furious.

"Pretty much," Natasha answered.

"Well, news flash," Ava scoffed. "The only person who has ever been there for me is me. Everyone else leaves or gets taken away—"

"*I told you. I'm not going anywhere,*" Alexei said, *looking stricken.*

Ava stood up and pulled open the door. "So excuse me if I don't think I need you to worry about me."

"Ava," Natasha began.

But Ava almost walked into Maria Hill, who was now standing at the infirmary door. Her face was grim.

"We have a situation."

SPECIAL CIRCUMSTANCES & INDIVIDUALS (SCI)
INVESTIGATION

AGENT IN COMMAND (AIC): PHILLIP COULSON

RE: AGENT NATASHA ROMANOFF A.K.A. BLACK WIDOW

A.K.A. NATASHA ROMANOVA

AAA HEARING TRANSCRIPT

CC: DEPARTMENT OF DEFENSE, SCI INQUIRY

COULSON: So you had three samples of the Faith compound at that point?

ROMANOFF: Yes. The one from Amazonas, the one from Brooklyn, and . . . Barry's.

COULSON: Did you compare them?

ROMANOFF: We did. Maria Hill had already run the samples through S.H.I.E.L.D.'s lab by the time I got back to the Triskelion.

COULSON: After your apartment went to that big Triskelion in the sky.

ROMANOFF: They were identical matches. Same environmental markers, same rate of atmospheric decay. They seemed to come from one larger identical source.

COULSON: Strange for any drug. Even the kinds you can't buy in a subway station.

ROMANOFF: Right? One of the samples had to be on the street in New York long enough to exchange hands between smugglers and mules and dealers and distributors. The other sample we'd lifted only the previous day. Who knows how long Barry had his. Or how they got to him.

COULSON: But that wasn't the only thing that was off about the compound, right?

ROMANOFF: No. There was also the drug dealer somehow being able to control the behavior of the poor junkie trying to buy it off him.

COULSON: The guy who threw himself in front of the train? Any speculation?
ROMANOFF: Honestly? I was more focused on who was trying to kill me—and who had torched my last clean pair of jeans. And on Barry.

COULSON: So what happened to the samples?
ROMANOFF: Maria forwarded slides to Carol Danvers, Tony, and myself. The theory was we'd come across the compound in our . . . line of work . . . sooner or later.

COULSON: How'd that turn out for you?
ROMANOFF: I'd have to go with sooner.

S.H.I.E.L.D. NEW YORK TRISKELION, EAST RIVER THE GREAT CITY OF NEW YORK

When Ava followed Natasha and Maria Hill into the Brain Trust, the first thing she heard was Dante's voice.

"Let me see if I'm getting this: you're pretty much a mash-up of the CIA and the FBI and some Navy SEALs—and that's even before all the super hero stuff comes in?" Dante marveled as he looked around the endless data walls of the room surrounding them. Sana sat on the other side of him, wide-eyed and staring as she took it all in.

"Yeah, you know, I always like to add in James Bond, but that could just be because of the cars and gadgets," Agent Coulson said, from across the table.

"I know, right? I love M," Dante said.

But the moment they approached the table, Dante fell silent. His eyes were on Natasha as he pushed back his chair and stood.

She came around the table to face him. When she'd returned to the Triskelion and learned that her brother's best friend was on base, she'd understood there would be no avoiding this moment, and she wasn't trying to.

"You're—you're—" he stammered. Natasha knew all too well what he was going through; shock was the usual reaction people had when they recognized her, not that she'd ever get used to it.

The Avengers had saved humanity enough times to become celebrities. While each had responded differently, it was only Tony Stark (and to a certain extent, Thor) who naturally thrived in the spotlight. Cap saw it as a responsibility, and Bruce a liability. For Natasha, who had been trained for the secrecy of black ops and stealth fighters, it was mostly just confusing.

How many school essays and applications and reports had been written about the time someone got to meet Natasha Romanoff? How many thousands of kids had dressed as the Black Widow each Halloween? How many times had Santa Claus wrapped up a version of her face— or her body or her motorcycle or even her red hair—and stuck her under the tree? *Was the Black Widow a person? Was she a brand? Was she a secret weapon? The last hope of humanity? A lunch box?*

She suspected the boy in front of her was going through

all of those questions now. *Your guess is as good as mine, kid.*

"You," Dante said, at last. "You're Alexei's sister."

She nodded. "I am."

"And you're the Black Widow," he said, cocking his head slightly to one side, as if altering his physical point of view would actually alter his perspective.

"That's what they tell me," she said.

He hesitated—and then smiled. "Finally," Dante said. "Something that actually makes sense." He held out his arms and stepped toward her, and at that moment she liked the kid so much she almost hugged him back—

"I hate to break up a moment, but things are flying," Maria said, taking her seat at the table. Ava sat down next to her.

"Seriously, though?" Dante looked at Ava. "Military school?"

"Technically, it's true. I do go to school, sometimes," Ava said.

"When you're not in the Amazon?" Sana wagged her head toward Coulson. "Which is where that guy just said you were."

"What's going on?" Natasha asked, pulling out a chair.

Coulson tapped a tablet on the table. "Maria was being literal. Things are actually flying. The missiles. They're in the air, possibly all five of them."

All around them, the wall screens now showed the sophisticated detail of classified radar intelligence.

Ava looked stricken. "Five? They've acquired five targets at the same time?"

"Actually, it's worse than that," Maria said. "We've confirmed that five missiles have now departed the Amazonas depot, but only one is still being picked up by our radar."

Coulson tapped again—and now only the radar tracking the one identified warhead remained.

A vague continental outline was visible on the map in the background, as if the idea of the missile detonating was still only an abstraction.

"No." Natasha frowned. "Four nukes in the wind? Just vanished? That's not possible. I attached a tracker to every missile."

"It's not a problem with the trackers," Maria said. "They were working. Our system was still picking up the signal on those nukes hours ago."

"Wait, *nukes*? You're being serious? As in, nuclear missiles?" Dante looked at Ava in disbelief. "What kind of nuke?"

"What do you mean, what kind? The stolen kind," Ava said. "The kind bought by dealing that Faith drug we saw in the subway."

"You're not making this up? Nuke nukes? You mean, like in a movie with George Clooney?" Oksana looked as shocked as Dante now. "Or Stalin?"

"Nobody's making anything up, as much as we all wish we were," Natasha said. "But I still don't understand. You're telling me we had all four on radar, and then we didn't. What happened?"

"It seems that the past few hours, our friends in the Amazonas have somehow managed to shield them from us—whether or not they even realize they're doing it," Coulson said.

"How do you accidentally hide a nuke?" Ava asked.

"It could be as simple as whether or not the craft transporting them has a steel-reinforced cargo hold," Maria said.

Natasha was out of her chair and pacing the room now. "When did they start to move?"

Maria's eyes were still glued to the radar. "That's the thing. Sometime during the chaos."

Coulson nodded. "We think that's what the Faith hack and the blast at Natasha's apartment were really about."

"They were trying to distract us," Ava said. "And they did." She looked at Natasha sadly. "We were the dangle."

Natasha shrugged. "Yeah, well. We screwed up. You've got to keep your eye on the ball. That's part of the game."

And I know that. This is my fault. If I hadn't gone home, if I had made Ava come with me in the first place, we might still be tracking four nukes instead of one—

"It's definitely moving by air. We can tell that from the speed, as well as the trajectory," Maria said.

"It has to be," Ava said. "There are no roads that lead to that depot. The whole park was only accessible by air or waterway."

"How is this your life? You're talking about a bomb that is flying through the air and pointed at people," Dante said to her.

Ava shrugged. "Yeah. You don't really get used to it."

Dante looked incredulous. "I hope not."

Sana put a hand on his shoulder. "Hold it together, man."

He shook his head. "Look at that radar screen. That beeping white dot is a bomb. If there was a right time to lose it, this is probably it."

Not an option. Natasha looked to Maria. "Can we get a make on the bird?"

"NASA and the DOD are working on it," Maria answered.

Behind her, the workstations were now filling with military personnel, staff trained for precisely these scenarios. None of them looked much more comfortable with the moment than Dante had, though. *Yeah, if things get hot, these aren't the guys I want deciding when to push the big red button—*

"Should we be looping Carol in?" Coulson asked. "How far out is Tony?" Things were getting serious, and Natasha only hoped the teens were still too oblivious to pick up on *how* serious.

"Carol was the one who alerted us to the missile movement," Maria said. "She's locked into Natasha's tracking signal and is following along with our friends at NASA." She looked over her shoulder. "Can someone patch Carol in?"

"Who's doing the math on this?" Natasha asked, looking at the crowd of analysts now swarming the room. "You guys?"

"I've got it." It was Carol's voice now as her face popped up in a box on one of the Brain Trust's screens. "And it's done. We've got what looks like a pretty clear trajectory, with a margin of error we're just going to have to live with—"

"Don't tell me what we can live with. Just tell me where the thing is going to hit." Natasha stared at the radar screen as she spoke.

"Sicily. Palermo, Sicily. That's the target." The words cut through the room—and it immediately fell silent.

There you go, Sicily. You just won the unluckiest lottery on the planet.

"You sure about that?" Natasha asked, scanning the room for anyone who could give her a clue as to what was going on.

They've got people on the inside, right? They have to. They knew who to hit on the tenth. They could be working with any one of these guys.

"Palermo, Sicily. I'm sure enough, that's where it comes down." Then Carol caught something else. "Wait. Correcting. I'm three degrees off." She adjusted a calculation. "It's not going to the city center. It's going to the suburbs."

Better. Only by a margin.

Natasha looked back up at the screen. The virtual map on the walls of the Brain Trust began to adjust as soon as Carol spoke; as if she were the one moving them. That's how closely her words were being followed right now; Natasha knew they were echoing through the Situation Room, the Pentagon, as well as a number of secure facilities bearing no name that could ever be repeated. "Monreale, in the hills outside of Palermo," Carol finally said. "I'll put in the coordinates now, the map should tighten up."

The room roared into activity as soon as she stopped speaking.

Maria took control. "Send out the call. Do it." An aide nodded and disappeared.

She looked at another. "Evacuate the area, they have to evacuate. Local authorities, national, the U.N. Now!"

A third: "Use every possible channel. State, the DOD, the JCOS, even the Oval. Heck, call CNN and the BBC if that speeds things up. Just get the word out."

Finally, her eyes swept the room. "Stay ready. You've only got a few minutes, people, let's make them count. These moments don't come around twice in a lifetime."

"Nine," Natasha said, her eyes on the screen. "Now we have nine."

"You heard the agent. Nine minutes," Maria said. "I want eyes back on the screen every minute. You've only got nine. Stay aware of the time." The room broke back into the buzz of activity.

Coulson looked over at Natasha. "What's in Monreale?"

Natasha tried to remember. "Nothing. A town. A church. A *pasticceria* and a *gelateria*, I don't know, maybe a pizzeria. It's Sicily."

"You think they're after a military target, maybe our base at Sigonella? They don't call it the Hub of the Med for nothing," Coulson said.

"Maybe, but that's all the way over near Catania, on

the east side of the island." She looked back at the radar. "That's not the right trajectory to hit the Hub."

"The Hub?" Dante asked. "That's this Sigonella thing?"

Coulson looked at him. "Naval air base for U.S. ops in all of Western and Eastern Europe, and really a hub for all of special forces. There, or Naples."

Natasha looked at him. "I was at Sigonella with Hawkeye right after Budapest, and I had a second stay at the Hub Med back in the Yelena Belova days. Took down an old Soviet bomber she'd had her eye on, and even airlifted Stark up out of a mess near there on the way home."

"Yelena Belova days?" Ava interjected. "Another Russian? Because that's a Russian name, right? Was she— like us? Krasnaya Komnata?"

"That's a long Russian story," Natasha said, brushing her off. "We can talk about it in"—she checked her Cuff— "six minutes."

She turned back to Coulson. "Monreale is outside of Palermo, and even Palermo isn't exactly metropolitan New York City. Still." She shook her head. "Probably a million people in and around the urban center, and all they can do is sound the sirens and get everyone as far away as they can."

"But no strategic target?" Coulson asked. "No reason for the target selection?"

"Can't think of one," Natasha answered. "Can you?"

"Power plant? Weapons plant? Industrial target? Oil? Crops? Water storage? Anything?"

"No, not at that site," Natasha said. "There's no reason

to drop a nuclear bomb on Monreale. There's nothing but a church." She shrugged. "Well, a famous church."

Ava spoke up. "How famous?"

"I don't know, people wait in lines to go inside. Byzantine frescoes. Lots of gold. I met an informant there once. In a confessional."

"And?" Dante asked.

"Well, he confessed," Natasha said, her eyes still on the radar map. *He confessed all over the floor and the nuns chased me out with mops.*

"I still can't believe it," Sana said. "Who bombs a gold church?"

"A really big atheist." Ava frowned.

"Or a bigger sinner," Dante said.

"I'd guess a rival capo from the Casa Nostra." Coulson shrugged. "Sicilian Mafia aren't exactly choirboys, except for when they are."

"Four minutes. This isn't helping." Natasha spoke up. "Can we zoom in?" She pointed. "That's the cathedral. Those are the cloisters. The thing that looks like the outline of a box, surrounding the garden and the fountain, see?"

"What are cloisters again?" Ava looked at her.

"The rooms where the monks lived, a long time ago. I don't know if they do anymore," Natasha said. "I only remember it as the place where I hid my Harley."

"Of course." Ava nodded.

"Three minutes," Oksana said, staring in horror at the numbers.

Nobody said a word.

After that, it might have been better if the tracker hadn't been able to transmit the live feed. But it was able, and the view from the missile was literally dizzying; it was a roller-coaster ride that everyone in the room knew could only end very, very badly.

The moment the warhead stopped climbing and began to flatten out, the quieter the room became.

The missile could only sustain a level apex for so long.

As they watched, the flat arch of the missile began to break, and its nose tipped lower and lower until it began to drop through the atmosphere, heading directly down toward the landmass beneath it.

On the radar screen, the map zoomed in, one grid at a time, as the missile fell closer to first the boot-shaped Italian peninsula, then the toe of the boot, then the island it almost seemed to be kicking.

The city of Palermo grew from a tiny glowing dot on the screen to the size of a quarter, then a poker chip, an apple—the face of a baby, then a child, anyone—

Now most of the screen showed a satellite view of the city, broken into grids, crisscrossed with highways.

One highway snaked up and out of town, and they could see it connect to a smaller grid, separated only by a bit of hillside.

"Here we go," Natasha said, holding her breath.

"Here we go?" Dante asked. "Are you kidding me? You guys are going to stop this thing, right? You're not just going to sit there and let it blow some town off the map, are you?" Dante was shouting now.

Maria didn't look up from the screen. "Can someone shut the kid up?"

Ava looked at Dante. His face was white. She took his hand in hers, and then reached for Sana with her other one.

Natasha looked away.

All eyes were on the screen. The horror was too vivid to watch—and too vivid not to. They saw the city break into streets, and the streets break into buildings.

Make it fast. Make it clean. Don't come down in the middle of a school. Don't come down in the middle of the church during a service—

Natasha found she was unconsciously bracing herself against the side of her chair. She waited, her body half-curled with tension.

The missile kept falling.

Natasha found herself counting down as she watched; they all were. It was impossible not to.

Ten.

Nine.

Eight.

Seven.

Six.

Five.

Four.

Three.

At the last second, just before it seemed that it was going to strike the cathedral straight on, the missile swerved.

Two.

"Look—watch the fin move—"

One.

As if by some kind of saintly miracle, the missile didn't hit the church.

It hit the cloisters.

They heard the percussive *boom-boom-boom* as the detonation began, and then the camera shook and the feed went black as it hit.

The room sat in silence. Ava let go of the others' hands. Nobody said a word. Natasha felt the bile rising in her stomach.

She looked at Maria. "Can we switch over to satellite? Try the Stark Sat first?" Tony's feeds were always higher quality than the federal government's.

"Bring up the feed," Maria said.

The new feed was an aerial shot of the cathedral and the immediate buildings surrounding it.

It was hard to see over the billowing black smoke.

It was even harder to believe it had happened.

Because it's our job to keep this from happening, Natasha thought. *This one was supposed to be mine, and I failed. I lost. I couldn't keep that missile from hitting.*

That's on me. This one is personal.

As they watched, the smoke turned from black and gray to white. Flames were still coming up from the center of the cloisters, but the buildings themselves appeared to be largely intact.

How many of these have I seen, in my life? Not exactly a mushroom cloud, but not a cloud you'd want to see in person. But Natasha had—especially in person. More times than she could count.

"Does that blast look right to you?" she asked. She wasn't sure—and she wondered if there was anything particular about this warhead, something she needed to understand. A visual clue to why Yuri Somodorov and his men had stolen it, and how they were using it. How any of it had anything to do with the Red Angel hacker and Red Room and even the Green Dress Girl.

"I don't know," Carol said. "I've never seen the B-61 adjustable precision fin in action, live. That was a little more than just precision." The smoke continued to curl upward in a series of great and exploding plumes as she spoke. "Radiation count is high, but the lethal fallout is relatively contained."

"Now I see why someone bothered to steal it." Natasha nodded. "That's a pretty specific strike."

"Yeah, well, that's the latest trend in nuclear strikes. We've gone from city killers to neighborhood killers to street killers."

Natasha nodded. "I get it. If you can limit the fallout, it's easier to use. Fewer headlines reporting civilian casualties."

Ava spoke up. "That's what one of my teachers at the Academy said about the Cold War. The only thing that kept the Soviets and the Americans from blowing each other up was the fact that they knew they would take the world down with them."

"Take that fear away, and what's stopping you from pressing the button?" Natasha looked back up at the image of the burning church.

"Nothing." Carol's words echoed across the room. "And they just did. If only to demonstrate that they could."

"Will somebody tell me what is really happening here?" Dante asked. "Is this World War Three?"

It was a good question, which is why nobody answered.

S.H.I.E.L.D. EYES ONLY

CLEARANCE LEVEL X

SPECIAL CIRCUMSTANCES & INDIVIDUALS (SCI)
INVESTIGATION
AGENT IN COMMAND (AIC): PHILLIP COULSON
RE: AGENT NATASHA ROMANOFF A.K.A. BLACK WIDOW
A.K.A. NATASHA ROMANOVA
AAA HEARING TRANSCRIPT
CC: DEPARTMENT OF DEFENSE, SCI INQUIRY

COULSON: You left. We were sitting there reeling—and then you were gone.
ROMANOFF: I had to see for myself. So I went.

COULSON: Because you felt responsible?
ROMANOFF: I had touched that missile with my hands, Phil. I'd put my own tracker on it.

COULSON: I know. I also know it won't help to tell you how comparatively small the loss of life was. Or how great the humanitarian crisis would have been had the trajectory changed by three degrees.
ROMANOFF: That doesn't change anything.

COULSON: You just see the destruction.
ROMANOFF: It's so familiar now. I've seen it so many times.

COULSON: You aren't the reason bad things happen to the world, Natasha.
ROMANOFF: After a while it doesn't matter why they happen. All of those moments, the rubble and blood and fire and smoke—the children crying and the parents screaming and the loved ones losing each other, sometimes forever—they all belong to me.
COULSON: You can't let them.

ROMANOFF: That's where I live. It's all I see. We all have a job to do. That's mine.

COULSON: It's not all you have. It's also not all the world is.

ROMANOFF: Death and destruction. Loss and pain. That's what my dreams are made of.

COULSON: But that's not everything.

ROMANOFF: I know. I just can't remember why not.

CITTÀ DE MONREALE, PROVINCE OF PALERMO REGIONE SICILIANA, ITALIA

Looking down at the coastline, the black plume of smoke reaching into the sky was the sure sign. Monreale was going to be a mess.

Ava had expected nothing less, not since the Widows had met the Stark Jet at the Triskelion hangar. Tony, to his credit, did not say a word about his long flight from the CERN facility in Geneva. He had immediately turned his plane around and headed back over the Atlantic to Palermo.

"Remind me next time I get a hundred million dollars to pick up one of these things," Natasha had said as they passed Greenland in record time. She was copiloting; Tony had left the crew behind.

"Well, that wouldn't get you one of *these*," Tony had

answered, from the pilot's seat. "I mean, maybe your standard Gulfstream G650 comes with a top-of-the-line Rolls-Royce engine, which is good, but not Stark Jet good. Top speed is what, Mach .995? Ninety-two percent of the speed of sound?" He scoffed. "Come on, guys. I need a fast ride."

"And you can do better?" Ava looked at him.

"I did. I built and rebuilt this engine twenty-four times until I got it right."

"Of course you did," Ava said, from the jump seat. "When you weren't busy saving the world or whining about it."

"Ha!" Tony said, winking. "This baby can *fly.*" He lowered his aviator sunglasses. "*Rolls?* Please. This is how Stark rolls." Natasha shook her head.

The banter—any talking, really—had stopped as soon as the triangular coast of Sicily came into sight. The plume of black-and-gray smoke above Monreale and Palermo, on the northern shore, was visible from the air. It had been carried with the wind down the coast.

Now, Ava thought. *Now it really starts.*

It was impossible to think of anything else after that, although it was equally impossible to imagine what they would find when they arrived. Even after touching down at the tiny Boccadifalco Airport—an old World War II airstrip, nine kilometers from the site of the missile strike—all they could see was a sky full of thick black smoke and ash, as if nearby Mount Etna itself had erupted, instead of a disaster dropping from the sky.

What would they find at Monreale? After talking their way onto a Palermo police chopper, trudging up the hillside town's steep main street, and weaving between the sea of hurriedly parked emergency vehicles, Tony and Natasha and Ava found their answer.

Smoke and rubble and destruction. The crumbling remnants of a rectangular stone structure, just west of the cathedral itself. Crowds held back by police, soldiers crawling atop burning ruins as they searched for survivors. Scientists in radiological CBRN suits, moving like moonwalking spacemen across the very center of the strike.

And reporters—a fleet of local newspaper journalists and bloggers and television reporters, any crew that could find its way from anywhere in Europe to Sicily. Civilian journalists holding smartphones tweeted and posted and captioned and confirmed what little the professional media could not. The missile had already struck; the remaining chaos was purely civilian.

This is what it looks like, in our time, Ava thought. *The beginning of the end, or at least, the beginning of something that feels that way.*

An act of war.

The one miracle had been the near miss of the strike. So many variables had fallen on the side of the Sicilians; at the last moment, the missile had veered slightly to the west, missing the cathedral completely. Mass casualties had been avoided. The cities—both Palermo and Monreale—remained, for the most part, safe.

Given that, only hours ago, a nuclear missile had been

streaking down from the sky toward a million human lives, it was more than a miracle. "Makes you almost wish you believed in them," Tony said, stepping under the police tape and catching up with Natasha and Ava. All three of them now wore particulate masks over their faces, like everyone else at the site. Until the smoke surrounding them had been tested, nobody could say whether or not it had been weaponized. All anyone could agree on was that however improbable it sounded, there seemed to be virtually no loss of life, and little fallout.

"That can't have been a miracle. It had to be the plan," Natasha said. "Nobody gets that lucky. If there's one thing I've learned in my life, it's that."

"So what, then?" Ava asked.

"Maybe the target was never the cathedral," Natasha said, shading her eyes with one hand as she pushed through the forensics teams to the middle of the blast site.

"And not just the cloisters. Look." Tony pointed. "See that orange flag? Where those spaceman technicians have marked it?" Through the opening in the crumbling remains of the stone structure in front of them, they could see through to the center of what had been the courtyard of the cloisters.

"You mean in the middle?" Ava said.

"It's not just the middle. It looks like the exact midpoint. If you were to get out a massive protractor and measure a radius, I bet you five bucks it would connect precisely to the center, right where the missile struck." Tony stared at the flag.

Ava looked at him. "Why? What's the point?"

"I don't know, aside from someone trying to prove they could target a tin can," Tony said. "What used to be there where it hit? Does anyone know?"

"I remember a fountain," Natasha said. "A round one. There was never any water in it." Ava looked at her curiously. "Some more—confessing." Natasha shrugged.

Tony raised an eyebrow. "What, water torture?"

"Anyways." Natasha changed the subject. "Aside from that fountain, I'm not sure what could have been there."

"Excuse me, padre?" Tony flagged down an ancient Sicilian priest as he passed in front of them, awkwardly adjusting an equally ancient-looking black rubber gas mask over his clipped white hair. The padre looked startled.

"What are you doing?" Ava hissed, horrified.

Tony looked back at her as he pulled the particulate mask down to expose his mouth. "I can't talk with this thing on. And I was thinking my good friend the padre here may have some helpful information."

He turned back to the old man. *"Buona sera,* padre."

The padre did not seem to like having his arm held, and he unleashed on Tony in Sicilian, or Italian—it was hard to tell. *"Lascia andare! Sei pazzo!"*

"What did he say?" Natasha looked at him.

"That I should let go and I'm probably crazy." Tony sighed, and tried again. *"Al centro, la fontana? Quero che era li? Altre cose?"*

"And?" Ava asked.

"In the center, the fountain? What was there before? Other things?" Tony said, watching the man's face.

His mouth was red and spluttering under the mask. He tried again to pull his arm away. *"Sono occupato! Sprecare il mio tempo!"*

"He's busy and I'm wasting his time." Tony looked back at Natasha and Ava. "Any other bright ideas?"

"Si tratta di una emergenza, idiota!" the padre bellowed.

"Really?" Tony looked at him. "I know it's an emergency and I'm not an idiot."

"Ask him about the fountain. What did it look like?" Ava said.

Tony nodded. *"Descrivere la fontana, padre."*

"L'angelo alato in ferro?" the padre said.

Tony nodded. "Okay, so what he's saying is that there was an iron statue, of a cherub."

The padre berated him again. *"Non cherubino!"*

"Not a cherub, maybe just a baby."

"Non un bambino! Un angelo, idiota. Angelo."

"Okay, got it. Not a baby—an angel. I think." Tony held both hands up. "Sorry. *Scusa."* Natasha said nothing; her eyes were on the old man.

"Si, l'angelo di ferro." The padre slowly pulled down his mask. "The Iron Angel. Very beautiful. *Molto bello. E andato. Tutti finito.* Gone, all gone."

Natasha pulled down her particulates mask. "Iron angel? That's what was there?"

The padre smiled—revealing three missing teeth—and

reached forward to pat Natasha's face with his wrinkled fingers. *"Come te."*

"Like me?" Natasha asked.

The old man sighed and walked back into the smoke.

"What does that mean?" Ava watched him go. She looked at Tony. "And do you even speak Italian?"

Tony shrugged. "I speak *villa* and *trattoria* and *barista*. I'm fluent in *gelato* and *vino* and *espresso* and *limoncello*. I also learned *contessa* at a shockingly young age. You'd be surprised how much you can absorb from a life of debauchery."

"Really not that surprised," Ava said.

"That's okay, 'cause it's really not that much." Tony shrugged.

"Iron Angel," Natasha repeated. She hadn't been listening to them. "Why would someone go to all that trouble to blow up the fountain of a courtyard next to a cathedral outside of Sicily?" Her eyes were fixed on the target site. "With or without an iron angel?"

"Religious reasons?" Ava asked. "A message from some higher power, like a Burning Bush or whatever?"

Natasha frowned. "If this was a message to the Catholic Church, wouldn't you aim four or five hundred kilometers north and target St. Peter's?"

"Sure," Tony said. "But for all we know, this might be the St. Peter's of Sicily. Or at least Palermo. Definitely of Monreale."

"Definitely," Ava said. "That."

Now Natasha was climbing over the barricade and

heading back into the blast zone. "Maybe it's not about the results? Maybe it was about the process?"

"I don't think you can go in there," Tony called after her.

Natasha looked back at him. "What if this whole thing was just a test? A diagnostic tool?"

Ava ran to catch up with her. "A weapons test?"

"It's possible," Natasha said. "I mean, that's what we were struck by, right? The adjustable fin, and how well it worked?" She pulled out her ComPlex and knelt in the rubble.

Tony beamed. "Aw, really? You're using it? That just makes me feel so warm and fuzzy all over."

"Calm down." Natasha held the tablet up, tapping it on. "I just need to locate my tracker. I want to get it home and into the Triskelion lab, see what it can tell us about impact."

"There," Tony said, pointing at a brightly lit arrow on the screen. "That way." Natasha pulled herself back to her feet and they moved forward, Ava following. They edged forward, screen first, until they were in the direct center of the debris field—standing in a deeply recessed crater that broke into a rubble pile at the middle point. The whole area was covered by about ten centimeters of what looked like thick, gray-white snow.

"Careful," Natasha said. "That's not snow. It's ash, and somewhere beneath the surface, you'll find things a whole lot hotter than fire." She pointed again. "There."

Ava kicked at a lump with her boot until the tracker

came rolling out, battered and worn, but still flashing a single green light. "Got it."

Tony whistled. "Talk about taking a licking and keeping on ticking. *Man*."

Natasha picked it up and slid it into the side pack of her utility belt.

"You can't be here." A soldier grabbed Natasha by the arm, pointing at his own masked face. "Radiation."

"Okay, okay. We're going," Tony said, raising his hands again. "*Scuse*."

It wasn't until they were back in the air that they had a chance to look at the tracker. Natasha left Tony at the controls and laid her pack out on the glass coffee table, in the back of the plane.

Ava watched as Natasha dumped the tracker out onto the surface. Then she picked it up, turning it over in her fingers. "It's still warm," Natasha said.

"Wait, there—" Ava said. "It looks scratched."

Natasha brushed off the back of the device. "It's not just scratched. Those are letters."

"And you didn't put them there, right?"

"No. They weren't there before." Natasha sat back on her heels. "Which means someone found it, carved the letters, and put it back."

"Okay, I didn't see that coming," Ava said. "Why?"

"I'm guessing the missile isn't just a symbolic message," Natasha said, staring at the tracker. "It's an actual message."

Ava moved to look at it more closely. "What does it say?"

"They're words. Carved into the silica." Natasha brushed off the ash with her fingers. "It's Russian."

"Of course it is," Ava said.

YA PRIDU ZA TOBOY.

Ava read the words over Natasha's shoulder. They didn't bother to translate. They both spoke Russian, and even if they hadn't, by now they would have come to expect those particular words.

I will come for you.

"Who do you think would—" Just as Ava began to speak, the Stark Jet banked so steeply that the tracker went flying off the coffee table—and then the coffee table itself went flying. Natasha hung on to the side of the leather couch. Ava hurtled into Tony's desk chair, which rolled onto its side.

Tony's voice came over the speaker. "Sorry. We've got our second missile. Danvers caught it earlier this time; we may be able to land in Cyprus just before it does."

Ava looked at Natasha. "Just not in exactly the same spot, I hope."

Then the Widow's Cuff began to vibrate, as did Ava's cell phone, as did the phones in every newsroom, television station, military installation, government office, school, and hospital on the planet.

S.H.I.E.L.D. EYES ONLY

CLEARANCE LEVEL X

SPECIAL CIRCUMSTANCES & INDIVIDUALS (SCI)
INVESTIGATION
AGENT IN COMMAND (AIC): PHILLIP COULSON
RE: AGENT NATASHA ROMANOFF A.K.A. BLACK WIDOW
A.K.A. NATASHA ROMANOVA
TRANSCRIPT: NEWSWIRE, EXCERPTED
CC: DEPARTMENT OF DEFENSE, SCI INQUIRY HEARINGS

*[BREAKING] PALERMO AVOIDS; MONREALE ENDURES
NUCLEAR MISSILE SCORES MIRACULOUS MISS (AP)*

(ROME) BREAKING: Italian officials are confirming this morning that Sicily's largest city, Palermo, has been the target of a high-precision nuclear missile strike.

The attack apparently targeted Monreale, a small, suburban *commune* built atop the hillside of Monte Caputo, in the province of Palermo. When an evacuation order was issued by the provincial government early this morning, upon first hearing of the imminent attack, the majority of local residents were able to depart.

The town is renowned primarily for its twelfth-century cathedral, considered one of the finest remaining examples of Norman and Byzantine architecture, and containing some six thousand square meters of glass mosaic work.

In its final approach, the missile avoided hitting the Monreale Cathedral; its historic cloisters were destroyed. "It's a heartbreaking loss, but also a miraculous blessing that so many human lives were spared," said the press office of the Holy See, speaking on behalf of the Vatican.

Italian military personnel have not released any other information offering motivation for the Sicilian strike, or for the particular choice of Monreale as a target.

No group has stepped up to claim responsibility for the strike, which represents the first time that a nuclear missile has been launched on a civilian population since the United States bombed Nagasaki and Hiroshima in the final weeks of World War II in 1945. World leaders have offered Italy, Sicily, Palermo, and Monreale condolences in the wake of the sudden tragedy.

NEW YORK PORT AUTHORITY, PENN STATION
THE GREAT CITY OF NEW YORK

"**B**urner phones? What are we supposed to do with two burner phones?" Dante sounded disappointed as he stared at the disposable plastic phone in his hand. *Yeah, nuclear missiles are dropping on the world and all I can do is phone a friend. That's helpful.*

A grim-faced agent had driven them off base in an unmarked black SUV the moment Ava was gone. They had been dropped at Penn Station, presumably so Dante could get the train back to Montclair. Sana had gotten off with him, saying she had a cab coming for her, which he guessed was just an excuse to not ride around alone with the guy with the gun.

Not that I blame her.

But Dante had no intention of going home, and soon enough he figured Sana must have known that—mostly because they began to walk toward the subway together, without even discussing it.

"It's just a free phone." Sana shrugged. "What did you expect her to give us, ray guns?"

"Blasters. First of all, that would have been cool, and second of all, way more *Star Wars*," Dante said.

"Ava already got all Jedi on that dealer with her light-saber things. How much more do you want?"

"Whatever. That was awesome." Dante looked at Sana. "Also, how much cooler would fencing be if you could use those?"

"So much cooler," Sana agreed.

Cooler than fencing, cooler even than LARPing, Dante thought.

For a second he wished Alexei could have been there to see it—see her—until he remembered that Alexei already had seen all kinds of things like that, without even telling him.

Jerk. He could have told me the truth. I would have been able to understand.

It was too late for that. Dante had explained that to himself in the mirror, almost every morning of the past year. It was too late to wonder what would have happened if Alexei hadn't seen Ava at the tournament. If Dante hadn't let Alexei leave him. If Dante had even just kept him fighting Cap, their idiot of a former team captain, who had torn his ACL the very next week and been kicked off the team. Dante wished he could have at least told Alexei that.

And anyway, he wouldn't have needed me to explain how his girlfriend could kick butt like a Jedi in the Fort Greene subway stop.

That would have been the first thing Al noticed about her. Well, the second thing. I was there when he noticed the first thing.

He couldn't look away.

Then he felt Sana's eyes on him and his face turned red. Dante smiled. "Just thinking about LARPing."

"You must really like LARPing," Sana observed.

Dante changed the subject. "Look. Ava and Agent Romanoff and that whole secret intelligence agency—they can't honestly expect us to sit here doing nothing, now that we know all this stuff is happening."

Sana laughed. "Yeah, right."

"I mean, can they?" Dante asked.

"They can do whatever they want," she said. "They're not going to ask your opinion. That's the whole secret-agency vibe, remember?"

"Sucks," Dante said, feeling like a powerless loser. He'd felt that same helplessness about his life for the past year and he was sick of it.

"It's not personal," Sana said, looking at him.

Dante frowned. "It's also not like we have to get their permission to help out. They don't own saving the world."

"I still can't believe Ava is one of them," Sana said,

watching a train take off. "The Red Widow, do you believe that? You think there will be action figures of her, like Natasha Romanoff?"

"I don't know." Dante shrugged. "But here's what I'm thinking. Ava may be a spy or an agent or a hero in training or whatever, but I'm the son of a cop."

"So you keep telling me," Sana observed.

"I can't just sit around while people drop bombs on freaking churches. Can you?"

"No." She looked at him somberly. "What do you propose we should be doing?"

What can we do that would matter? What would Alexei and I do, if he was still here? What would I do, if I was the one at the secret agency?

Dante looked up. "What about the drugs? The Faith or whatever? That's here in the city—and Ava went after that dealer in the subway station like it was important, right?"

"She sure didn't hold back," Sana agreed.

Dante hoisted his fencing bag over his shoulder, shaking his head. "Man, she's a baller."

"Yeah?" Sana smiled, studying his face. "You say that about all the girls? Or just the ones training to be super heroes?"

"Just the ones who are ballers." Dante looked away, embarrassed. Alexei had been his best friend, and he wasn't about to go crushing on his girlfriend.

Why? Was that what you were doing?

"Whatever you say," Sana said.

"Just stating a fact," Dante finally said.

"Sure." Sana shrugged. "I believe you. You're the cop's son."

He looked at her, the beginnings of an idea slowly unfolding in his mind. "Well, maybe that's it. I *am* a cop's son."

Was there something he could do?

"We've established that," Sana said. "And moved on."

"No, I mean that's how we could do it," he said, thinking out loud. "Figure out the Faith situation. We go to the precinct, see what the cops can tell us."

"Tell us what?"

"Who knows? If we go back through all the records of recent drug busts, maybe we can find something about Faith," Dante said. "If it's been out on the street for more than a week, I guarantee you someone has been busted for it. Probably even with it."

Sana considered the idea. "It's true that we know what Faith looks like, and where it comes from. We might notice something the police would miss."

Dante nodded. "And we've seen that dude jump in front of a train just because his dealer made him. Maybe the NYPD will have more records about how people act when they're using."

"That was so creepy," she said.

"Like a zombie. Like mind control or something," he agreed.

Sana stared out at the tracks. "You're right," she said, finally. "Faith is bad news. We have to do what we can."

Dante thought about it. "Every precinct keeps a

photographic database of their evidence room. We might actually be able to track down more Faith samples, now that we know what to look for."

It could actually work. If only my dad would help, for once—

"You think we can just walk in a police station and say, 'His dad's a cop, now let us use your computers'?" She looked skeptical.

"No. But it's Friday now, right? Fridays my dad does swing shift at the Twenty-Sixth Precinct, in south Harlem. A Hundred Twenty-Sixth and Amsterdam, by Columbia. How about we take a subway uptown and ask him ourselves?"

At least it'll give him a chance to grill me. He'll like that.

"Let's go." Sana pulled her MetroCard back out of her pocket with a flourish. "Don't ever say I didn't do anything nice for you. Or, I guess, mankind."

Dante grinned. "Go nuts, big spender."

Dirt and cigarettes and coffee—with the occasional whiff of old booze and old weed and old pee, depending on who was waiting. *All these places smell the same.* Dante put on his game face and stepped up to the precinct's worn front counter.

"Hey, Lieutenant Mackey. You see my dad around lately?" Mackey was a burly cop drinking a too-small Styrofoam cup of coffee, a permanent fixture at the Twenty-Sixth.

"Sir Lancelot." Mackey nodded, winking. "The Cap's in the back." Then he looked at Sana. "You got a date, Lancey?"

"In his dreams," Sana said, dropping into a hard wooden chair along the wall next to the counter. "Also, I thought Lancelot was supposed to be the good-looking one?"

Mackey hooted. "Burn. You got a feisty one, kid."

"Just ignore him," Dante said, starting around the counter toward the back rooms of the station. "Mackey confuses fencing with jousting."

"No can do, Sir Talks-a-Lot," Mackey said, stepping in front of him. "Only officers allowed past this drawbridge, unless you happen to be wearing Cuffs."

"Can you send my dad out, then? It's important." Dante pulled out his phone, like he was about to start crushing candy. "I'll wait."

Mackey gave him a look.

Dante picked up Mackey's little coffee cup and handed it to him. "Go on. You know you need a refill anyways."

Mackey took it with a glare and disappeared around the corner.

"Nice move," Sana said. "Lancey. Is that your under-cover identity, Agent?" She laughed, which sounded out of place in the dimly lit front office of the institutional building.

Dante felt his face turning red again. "Laugh all you want. We're trying to save the world—I can take a few hits."

"Did you need me out here?" a booming voice asked.

Dante straightened himself tall—and Captain Cruz appeared at the desk, in full uniform. Sana sat up in her chair at the sight of him, just as Dante had known she would.

I wish for once he could just be chill.

But his dad always acted like that, and his friends always reacted like that. Only Alexei hadn't been intimidated by it. *Maybe it was the whole Russian thing,* Dante thought. His father was not and would never be chill. Captain Cruz sometimes looked more like a guy who played a police captain on television than the real thing. His pants were ironed into perfect creases. He texted in full sentences, with punctuation. He even shined his badge.

"Hey, Pop," Dante said, looking up from his phone.

Captain Cruz began to smile, but moved on into his regular stress-face before he could quite carry it out.

"Dante? Everything okay? What are you doing here? Shouldn't you be at the club?" He took in Sana, still sitting stiffly in the chair, without saying anything. Dante knew he was too good of a cop for that—but he'd hear plenty later.

"I didn't have fencing today," Dante improvised. *I don't have it any days anymore, but still technically true.* "That's not why I'm here."

"If you don't have fencing, you should be home doing your work or helping your mother," Captain Cruz said.

Ding-ding-ding!

And it's time to play today's round of Why Aren't You Helping Your Mother—

"I will," Dante said. "I just need to know something.

It's for a project about local crime. Drugs, specifically."

Also true, strictly speaking.

He was well-versed in the art of lying to his father, and the first rule of lying to his father was not to actually lie. Captain Cruz would know the second you even tried it.

Omit, never commit.

That was the critical concept.

"For school? Are the two of you in class together? Were you going to introduce your friend to me?" his father asked, pointedly not looking at Sana. "And can you put your phone away when you're talking to me?"

Just like clockwork.

Dante slipped his phone back into his pocket. "Sana is a . . . youth advocate . . . taking a stand against drugs . . . and street crime," he said. "She's here to save the world, basically."

True enough.

Sana stood up and approached the desk—which might as well have been the bench of a courtroom, because they were certainly being judged. "Nice to meet you, Captain Cruz."

She extended her hand, looking right into the captain's eyes. "I'm with the Fort Greene Y."

True? In a way?

"Dante and I are both fencers."

True-ish? We both know how to fence.

"We met at a tournament."

True-like? From across the room, but okay.

Captain Cruz smiled dismissively, and Dante knew they were past the first challenge. *One down—*

"Have you been watching the news?" His father shook his head. "This isn't a good time for a project. None of us are safe until these stolen missiles are locked down. And there's a whole lot more to that than you guys can ever know."

We know. That's why we're here. That's why we're trying to help. We sat in a room with a black ops team and watched the missile drop—

"I get it," Dante said. "Completely."

Sana looked away.

"We're about to go to a red alert," Captain Cruz said. "Red. That's the category representing 'severe'—the highest terror alert status we've had since 9/11. I can't talk right now, and you both should get back to your homes and stay there."

Yeah, didn't think so.

Dante gave it another try, just for the sake of appearances; it seemed like the kind of thing a son would do. "But Dad—"

"Dante. That's it. I'm done here. I'll see you at home. Go help your mother." He looked at Sana. "Nice to meet you, Sandra. Good luck with the Y. I see what goes on out there, and we need all the help we can get."

And then Captain Cruz was gone.

Dante and Sana left the building almost as quickly. "Well, that sucked," Sana said as soon as they got back to the frozen sidewalk. "I can't believe that's your father."

Dante had his phone back out. He hit save and grinned. "Are you kidding? That went great."

"My dad has a whole new family. I don't even live with him half the time and he's nicer to me than that. I mean, at least he drives me around in his cab." Sana shook her head. "Is your dad always so rough?"

Dante could feel himself turning into a stone, the way he always did when people talked about his father.

What do you want me to say? Because I got nothing.

There's no explanation, and the only person who never asked for one and never cared is dead. Okay? Does that answer the question? Can we move on?

The only person who understands me is dead.

He fast-forwarded through that part of the conversation in his head, which was the other thing he did when the subject came up.

"It's okay," Dante said, walking faster now. "Don't worry. We got what we needed."

"We did?"

"Of course."

"Which was?"

"This. We were trying to get this." Dante held up his phone.

Sana looked. "What are those numbers?"

"My dad's badge number. I already know his password, he uses the same one for everything."

"Old people." Sana shook her head.

"With that and his NYPD email, we can get into the police database. I even got a picture of the badge when he wasn't looking, as insurance."

"Not bad, Lance." Sana smiled.

He bowed. "Any ideas where we can find a computer around here?"

"Please." Sana snorted. "I know how to get on a computer *and* get a free chocolate chip cookie. Come on."

A few minutes later, they were heading through the gates of Columbia and into the business school, where Sana waved at a cute blond boy behind the desk. He buzzed her in without a word, and she pulled Dante through the barrier behind her. "Fencers," she whispered. "Hook you all the way up."

Dante followed her as they cut through the volunteers' lounge, grabbed a handful of cookies out of a jar, and headed straight to the computers.

After that, it took three minutes to get into the NYPD police database—seven minutes to find a searchable directory of precinct evidence records—four more to find the image database. (Three to watch a video about fainting goats, but they were waiting for the database to load.)

And so, eleven minutes later, they'd found eight recorded instances of a mysterious black drug, previously unseen on the street, in altercations occurring in three different boroughs.

The nearest was right up the street, at 134th and Broadway.

In other words, Faith was all around them, even now. All they had to do was score some.

"Maybe this is a bad idea," Sana said, shivering. They had begun at 134th and worked their way down Broadway. Now they were almost to 120th, and they'd still found nothing. Nobody suspicious, nobody loitering. Nobody trying to score or to sell.

"Whatever," Dante said. "We give it a few more blocks and then we move on to the next place. Either way, we're at least ruling something out, right?"

"Fine. Okay, sure." She nodded. "But my butt is freezing off and I feel like it's going to snow, so let's make it fast." He was already moving down the block.

The closer they got to the black wrought-iron gates of Columbia's interior campus, the more students crowded the streets. By 116th, the sidewalks were crammed full of a whole range of twentysomethings with nose rings and purple hair—or with preppy wool coats and expensive-looking leather satchels. That seemed to be the basic division.

"Rich kids," Sana said, sounding disgusted.

"Probably not all of them," Dante said, surveying the scene, "but enough so that it makes sense that there was a Faith bust here." As he spoke, he shivered. Sana was right; now that the sun had gone down, the cold was almost unbearable.

"Seems like college kids are stupid, and college kids party. So yeah, there probably does have to be a dealer somewhere around here," she said, scanning the street.

Dante wasn't so certain anymore. They'd been out awhile, and he couldn't feel his ears. Maybe it was time to pack it in.

We tried. And we can try again tomorrow.

At least we can tell ourselves that—

"There," Sana said, in a low voice. Dante looked up—and she panicked, yanking his arm. "Don't look at him!"

"How do you know that's our guy?"

"Bus stop," she hissed.

"Taking a bus doesn't make you a drug dealer."

She sighed. "Are you going to make me spell it out for you?"

He nodded.

"He can't risk going on campus, because he's not a student and he'll get kicked off. So he waits there across from the entrance, sitting on that bus stop like he's going to get on a bus. But the bus just left, and he didn't move." She shrugged. "Ava and me, we've pulled that trick a thousand times. Bus bench, that's the best place to nap in the city. They can't make you leave and they can't prove you shouldn't be there."

Dante studied her face. He couldn't even begin to imagine the things she and Ava had been through, and at his same age.

And here I am, complaining about my family life—

He took a breath and nodded. "Okay. I'm going to talk to him."

She almost laughed. "You? You wouldn't know what to say to a drug dealer."

"Like you would?"

"No, but at least I lived in a shelter. I know how to talk to people on the street, Jersey."

"Hey, we have streets in New Jersey, friend." It was a dare, and he couldn't not take it. Dante jammed his hands in his pockets and casually moved over to the bus stop. He sat down and looked straight ahead.

"Hey, man," Dante said, keeping his eyes focused on the street in front of him, just like he had when he had to ride the eighth-grade bus as a sixth grader. "What's happenin'?"

The guy on the bench, who wore a ragged army salvage jacket and a Yankees sweatshirt with the hood up, didn't answer. He stank like the street, and for once Dante was glad that it was so cold. The freezing air seemed to kill the smell faster.

"I'm lookin' to score," Dante said. It sounded like a bad line from a movie, and it was hard to keep a straight face. Plus, he wasn't exactly sure what to say, so he just stuck to the point. "Something new. Looks like black sand. Called Faith, you heard of it?" He improvised. "Saw it at a party last weekend."

Yeah, right. Last weekend you were sitting in your house playing League of Legends. *Same with the weekend before that. And before that. And before that—*

Army Jacket scowled. "What are you talking about, clown face?"

"I'm talking about Faith. I'm looking for some. You know, Death Meth?" That was what one of the police reports had called it.

"Death Meth? That's a pretty messed-up name." Army Jacket laughed.

"I don't care what you call it." Dante shrugged. "I heard it's mind-blowing." *As in, it blows out your mind and turns you into a zombie. Stay in school, kids—*

Army Jacket shook his head. "I don't got any."

"Okay. Thanks," Dante said. Army Jacket scowled. *Oh, right. You probably don't thank drug dealers.* "I mean, whatever." He stood up, turning his back to the guy.

"I know a guy who knows a guy who could maybe hook you up," Army Jacket said, but only as Dante was about to walk away.

So that's how it works.

He turned around again. "Now?" Dante said. "Because I need it, like, today."

"No promises." Army Jacket shook his head. "Meet me back here tonight."

"When?" Dante asked.

"Midnight," Army Jacket answered.

"Too long," Dante said.

Army Jacket stood up. "Then forget it."

"Fine. Midnight. Make sure it's the real thing," Dante said, feeling a little more confident. "I don't want to get ripped off."

"What, you don't trust me?" Army Jacket looked at him, tilting his head and sweeping aside the greasy lock of straw-colored hair in his face. The look was—

Murderous? Is that the word for it? It was all Dante could do not to run.

"Five hundred large, right here. Midnight." Army Jacket reached toward Dante, who froze as the dude pulled the burner phone out of his pocket. "I'll keep this. Insurance."

"Great," Dante said, already walking away. He grabbed Sana by the arm, and they fled.

Midnight.

S.H.I.E.L.D. EYES ONLY

CLEARANCE LEVEL X

CONFIDENTIAL: PHILLIP COULSON

CLASSIFIED / FOR OFFICIAL USE ONLY (FOUO) / CRITICAL PROGRAM INFORMATION (CPI) / LAW ENFORCEMENT SENSITIVE (LES) / TOP SECRET / SUITE AB ENCRYPTION / SIPRNET DISTRIBUTION ONLY (SIPDIS) / JCOS / S.H.I.E.L.D.

** FILE COPY OF INCOMING TRANSMISSION ** FROM THE PENTAGON **

Phil,

I know you haven't forgotten the Geneva Protocol. The Hague Conventions. The BWC or the CWC. The U.S. does not engage in chemical or biological warfare.

Tell me there is zero chance you have any chemical, bacterial, or viral samples—on any Triskelion bases—that could be construed by the CDC as weaponized.

In the last 24 hours, a S.H.I.E.L.D. lab facility has processed a sample that the CDC has flagged as "questionable." The DOD and the JCOS have been alerted. Oval is next.

I'm trying to help, but you gotta help me help you, Phil.

ARTIE

OFFICE OF THE JOINT CHIEFS OF STAFF
9999 JOINT STAFF PENTAGON
WASHINGTON, D.C.

AMPHIBIOUS ASSAULT SHIP, U.S. NAVY SIXTH FLEET COASTAL REPUBLIC OF CYPRUS, THE MEDITERRANEAN SEA

Ava and Natasha watched the skies as Tony read the news off his tablet. They leaned, all three, against the upper-deck railing of an amphibious assault ship named the USS *Kirby*; it was the one U.S. ship in the region with an LHD (landing helicopter deck) large enough to allow the Stark Jet to land.

Coulson had friends in every department of the U.S. military, and he had scrambled to get clearance. The six F-35 fighter jets already stacked in a row along one side of the deck didn't exactly appreciate how close Tony came to toppling them into the ocean, but it had all worked out in the end. Even fighter pilots were susceptible to the Stark charm, especially when he wanted to talk laser modifications.

That was the only luck they'd experienced so far. The breaking news was grim, according to S.H.I.E.L.D.—and even according to CNN.

The second missile would hit part of a Russian carrier group in the waters just off the coast of the Greek island of Cyprus. Russian MiGs were scrambling on a course to intercept now, and the Russian carrier *Admiral Kuznetsov* had its infamous antiaircraft weapons and an entire air defense system at the ready.

The attack was heralded as no accident; the *Kuznetsov* was rarely in the region, and was considered a high-value target. It was, after all, Russia's only aircraft carrier—which only made the attack more grievous. The entire country was incensed.

Sicily had already spooked the entire world; with Cyprus, global order rested on a knife's edge.

"If you seek to threaten any part of the *Rodina*," the Russian president told the international press, "know this: we will respond tenfold. We join with our Sicilian compatriots to stand against these cowardly acts, and we vow to protect our maritime deployments, surface and undersea. We are now a country at war, and will fight as one."

"And that's coming from the guy who puts attack subs in the Black Sea." Tony sighed as he finished reading the latest from his tablet. "He's not messing around."

"We can't just sit here and watch," Natasha said, frustrated. "I don't care how many MiGs are up there. That missile could take out more than just the *Kuznetsov*. You saw how the Monreale missile drifted. This thing could chew through a good chunk of Cyprus."

"Or it could be fine-tuned to hit one highly decorative Iron Angel fountain," Ava pointed out. "We don't know."

"Cyprus as a target actually makes more sense than Monreale," Tony said as he raised a military-grade spotter to his eyes. "Cyprus is like one big Laundromat for most of Eastern Europe. You steal it, we'll deal it."

"Yeah? Is that on the flag now?" Natasha asked wryly.

Tony surveyed the coast in front of them. "I guess it's more of an unofficial motto."

Ava looked at him. "Money laundering?"

Tony handed her his spotter. "Well, last time I was there, it sure wasn't the shirts that were all that clean."

"I still don't understand why Iron Man isn't out there Hulk-smashing those missiles out of the sky." Ava frowned, peering through the lens.

"Iron Man doesn't Hulk-smash. And I offered, but I guess Russia must want to notch her own win, because that offer was firmly declined," Tony said.

"Of course it was. The *Rodina* does not need your help," Natasha said, staring at the sky. "Or anyone else's."

"Except when it does," Tony said.

"There," Ava said, looking through the scope. "It's coming. I see it."

The missile was visible from the water now. The steel casing flashed in the sun as it cut across the sky, a trail of white smoke spewing after it. They watched it from below this time as it headed straight into the water, picking up speed as it neared the earth.

A trio of Russian MiGs fell into place behind it.

They fired on the falling missile, one after the other. As the fighter jets attacked, the missile swerved.

The powerful guns on the *Kuznetsov* swerved with it, delivering the final rounds.

BOOM—

The missile exploded in the air, a few hundred meters above the surface of the water. A cloud of fire turned black and then white, spraying debris across the water beneath it for hundreds, maybe thousands of meters.

"Thank God," Ava said, gripping the rail of the deck.

"Two down." Tony nodded, his eyes on the smoke in front of them.

"Moscow isn't going to like that." Natasha sounded ominous.

"I'm guessing that was the point?" Tony looked at her.

"What point? Someone is threatening Sicily and Moscow? By way of Greece? What kind of bizarre board-game strategy is that?" Ava shook her head.

Natasha touched her earpiece. "I have Danvers on the line. She thinks this had to be another missile test."

"More targeting?" Tony asked.

Natasha shook her head. "She's thinking that what we just saw was a demonstration of the ten-second route reset."

"The swerving?" Tony asked.

She nodded. "Danvers thinks the guys firing the missiles are checking to see if their modifications worked."

"And sending a Russian message in a missile instead of a bottle," Tony said.

"Yeah, well, too bad Natasha's tracker is in a million little pieces floating on the water now." Ava was still watching the spreading waves of debris through the lens of the spotter. "I don't think anyone's going to be reading a message off of that one."

Then she lowered her spotter and pointed out to a dark shape at the far edge of the debris, still on the water. "Check it out. Look at that boat. The one with the people watching the target site with binoculars. See it?"

"So they're watching the debris field. A missile explodes in front of you and you're going to watch," Tony said. "Even us."

Natasha frowned. "Except the Cypriot authorities restricted the whole area. Only military craft are supposed to be here now."

"And look at the name of the boat," Ava said. She handed Natasha her spotter, and Natasha raised it to her eyes.

"*Zheleza Prizrak?*" Natasha frowned. "That's strange."

"Remind me what that means?" Tony asked.

Ava looked at him. "*Iron Ghost.*"

He raised an eyebrow. "Wait—Iron Angel, that was the statue where the first missile hit, right? And this one almost came down on *Iron Ghost*?"

Natasha lowered the spotter. "And then there's our hacker going on about the Red Angel." She shook her head. "It's all so—"

"*Russian,*" Ava said.

"Ah yes. The return of the great *Rodina,*" Tony said, raising his tablet. "Well, we might as well ask the *Rodina* what she knows about that yacht, then."

He hit a few keystrokes and waited. "*Nyet.* There is no Russian company registered to the Federal Tax Service—which is the Russian IRS—called Zheleza Prizrak, or Iron Ghost." He looked up. "And believe me, if there was, it would be paying more than ghost taxes. The Kremlin takes revenue pretty seriously. They're practically the Howard Stark of foreign governments."

"Did you try searching for Iron Angel?" Natasha asked. "*Zheleza Serafimy?*" She spelled it out letter by letter until he had it right.

Tony tapped out the words again. "*Nyet.*"

"What about Red Angel?" Ava suggested. "*Krasnyy Serafim?*"

More tapping. "Also *nyet.*"

Natasha gripped her fingers on the railing. "Maybe that's not the name that yacht uses for the Federal Tax Service. Every ship has to register with its flag state, though; that's international maritime law. In Russia, that's the RS, I think. The Russian Maritime Register of Shipping."

Ava looked at her. Natasha shrugged. "So I forged a few naval papers. Easier than passports."

Tony pulled up the site and entered the name. "There are zero Russian ships registered through Cyprus, but there is one ship registered to Russia operating in Cyprus."

Ava looked over his shoulder. "And?"

"The *Iron Ghost*. Registered to—"

Natasha held her breath.

"Wow." He looked up. "Veraport is a subsidiary of Luxport International."

"Otherwise known as the Red Room," Natasha said.

"It says that?" Ava asked.

He nodded. "I'm serious. Look, that's what the recognition certificate says. It's apparently also the name the document of compliance was issued in."

"Oh my God," Ava said, staring at the screen in his hands. "I don't believe it. We found it. The link to the Red Room and to the Faith operation. It's Luxport, just like Ivan's Ukranian warehouse."

"So after Luxport, the Red Room rebranded itself as Veraport?" Tony looked at Natasha. She didn't answer. Instead, she stared out at the smoking, debris-filled ocean. Oil still burned on the surface of the distant waves.

"Does this Veraport-slash-Luxport have an owner? Aside from the registering body?" Ava asked.

"You looking for the paperwork to actually say Krasnaya Komnata? You want to see a big red stamp with the words *Red Room*?" Tony studied the screen.

"I wouldn't mind," Natasha said, with a shrug. "Especially not when bombs are involved."

"Fine." He shook his head and went back to the RS archive. "Hold on." But as he began to tap out the search terms, the screen went dark—

Tony frowned. "I've powered down. We lost the connection."

Ava sighed. "I hate it when that happens."

"No. It never happens. Not to me. Not when you own your own Stark Satellite." He looked up to the sky, then back to the Widows. "It's them."

"We got too curious," Natasha said.

"Which means we got too close," Ava said, looking spooked.

Natasha took a breath. "All right. So tell me this: Why would a Russian company threaten its own government?"

"A message," Tony said. "A revolution. A conspiracy."

"A hoax," Ava said. "A Russian company would never threaten its own government, you know that."

Natasha nodded. "The only Russians who would threaten the Russian government are the Russian government." *Welcome to the theater of war—emphasis on the theatrics. I don't like this game, and I don't know this dance.*

Something about all of this feels off.

"Well then," Tony said, turning back to the water. "This isn't an attack. It's a puppet show." He rubbed his face with one hand, looking exhausted. "What's the moral of your story, little bomb?"

Natasha hated losing, she hated lying, but more than anything, she hated being a puppet. As far as she was concerned, it was time to cut the strings and get her questions answered.

Starting with this one, in particular—

God help us, where are those last three missiles headed?

A young officer, looking shorn and shaven in his

uniform, raced down the deck until he reached them. He snapped to attention in front of Tony and Natasha.

"Sir, yes, sir." Then his eyes flickered to Natasha. "Sir, yes—ma'am."

Natasha looked amused.

"Admiral Sanchez requests that you report immediately to the bridge, sir." The junior officer looked over to Ava. "All three of you, sir. And ma'am, ma'am."

"At ease, sailor. All right, then." Tony looked back at Ava and Natasha. "Let's go pull some strings."

SPECIAL CIRCUMSTANCES & INDIVIDUALS (SCI)
INVESTIGATION

AGENT IN COMMAND (AIC): PHILLIP COULSON

RE: AGENT NATASHA ROMANOFF A.K.A. BLACK WIDOW
A.K.A. NATASHA ROMANOVA

TRANSCRIPT: NEWSWIRE, EXCERPTED

CC: DEPARTMENT OF DEFENSE, SCI INQUIRY HEARINGS

*[BREAKING] RUSSIA SCRAMBLES FIGHTERS AS NUKES FALL ON CYPRUS
DESTROYER SILENCES SKIES WITH ANTIAIRCRAFT ARMS (AP)*

(ATHENS) BREAKING: A rogue nuclear missile seemingly targeting a Russian carrier group in the eastern Mediterranean has been peacefully detonated over the coastal waters of Cyprus, without loss of life.

The *Admiral Kuznetsov*, the sole aircraft carrier of the Russian navy, employed so-called missile-killer weapons, as well as robust air defense measures, supported by a full squadron of MiG fighter jets. While three MiGs fired upon the descending missile, it was the *Kuznetsov* that finally struck the nuclear projectile only a few hundred meters above the surface of the water.

Speaking from a podium erected to address the growing crowd waiting in front of the Ministry of Defense in Arbatskaya Square, Pavel Petrov, current minister of defense of the Russian Federation, blamed Western interests for stoking the fires of international discord, before urging the crowds to seek justice.

"Those who would punish Russia will be punished. Those who would harm us will be harmed. Those would believe they can defeat us will be shown to be mistaken. The *Rodina*'s memory is longer and more punishing than her winters."

Now that both the European Union and Russia have been targeted with what appear to be one arsenal of nuclear missiles, world leaders have been put on notice.

"None among us can be certain they are safe," said Cypriot president Constantinos Louka. "Until the terrorists who threaten our international community are stopped, who knows which city of the world will be targeted next." [Developing.]

AMPHIBIOUS ASSAULT SHIP, U.S. NAVY SIXTH FLEET COASTAL REPUBLIC OF CYPRUS, THE MEDITERRANEAN SEA

Admiral Sanchez's unlit cigar tapped out strategic places on the map while he spoke. He used words like *roll back* and *fall out* and *boots on the ground* and *imminent threat* and Ava felt like she could have been on the set of a war movie—and not the kind that ended with Wookiees getting medals.

How did I get here? To the bridge of an amphibious assault ship in the Mediterranean? Watching missiles drop and fighter jets scramble? Whose life is that?

Ava had thought she had known what she was getting into—back when she was first getting into it. Vengeance, against a man who had destroyed her childhood, her family, the love of her life, and her only chance at happiness.

It was simple, and it was fair.

It was justice.

But was that still true? Was that why she was here now? In the middle of a nuclear missile crisis?

What is happening to the world? What is happening to me?

The cigar tapped again, and she tried to focus on it.

"The Russian MiGs have vectored off. Their destroyer is maintaining a ready position, but then ours is, too. That's all just noise. Not our primary concern," said the admiral, in his steady Texan drawl. He had introduced himself as a self-proclaimed "big fan of the Avengers."

It never ceased to amaze Ava, how much further celebrity got the Avengers than the fact of their own military clearances and credentials.

Natasha looked at the admiral skeptically. "If you don't mind my asking, what's more *primary* than an entire squad of deployed and angry Russians, Admiral?"

"Guangdong," the admiral said, brusquely. "Radar's just picked it up. That's the next target, and it's a real problem." He tapped his cigar again.

Ava looked up. "Excuse me?"

He tapped the radar map on the table in front of them. "China. You want something to keep you up nights it's not going to be Russia. It's that one, right there."

Tony nodded. "What's the exact target in Guangdong?"

"Still working it out, but far as we can tell, a mostly defunct power plant. This one. Guangdong is full a' them."

"Mostly?" Ava asked.

"How defunct?" Natasha frowned.

"I guess we'll find out. But that's not our main concern now."

Tony looked at Admiral Sanchez. "If you don't mind me saying, Admiral, you look pretty concerned for someone with so much *not* to be concerned about."

"See, that's what I like about you, Iron Man. You're the funny one." The admiral nodded. "Well, son, this time it's more about the missiles."

"Yeah, that's not *so* funny," Tony said.

"Wait." Natasha straightened. "Missiles—plural?"

Ava stared. "How many of them?"

"Three, looks like. In the skies now." Admiral Sanchez dragged his cigar across the radar map, from the center of the enormous blank space that was northern Russia to the crowded coast of China. "Crossing out of Siberian airspace as we speak, which is probably for the best, given the whole carnival of crap we just watched in these waters."

Ava looked at Natasha. "Is this a test again?"

"I don't know," Natasha said, her eyes narrowing as she studied the map. "Maybe? If they're evaluating anything, I'm guessing it would be range. Looks like these last missiles will be traversing some long-range distances."

"But that makes no sense," Tony said. "What's the point of a missile test that uses up your last three remaining missiles? It's like practicing for a game you're never going to play, or a show you're never going to get to put on."

"For one thing, you scare a lot of folks," Admiral Sanchez said. "For another, you scare up a whole lot of attention."

"Sir, you have a call." The shaved and shorn officer who had brought them up to the bridge now stepped forward to hand the admiral a satellite phone.

"Yeah?" The admiral dropped the cigar and held the receiver to his ear. "This is Admiral Sanchez of the USS *Kirby*." He listened, raising an eyebrow. Then he held out the phone to Natasha.

"That's NASA calling, and it's not for me."

Danvers had been clear about the targeting. She'd run the numbers and come up with a scenario, delivered in three separate pairs of latitudes and longitudes.

By the end of the call, Natasha had asked for a satellite map of the Guangdong reactor to be pulled up on the radar table.

The individual buildings of the plant were now visible, and she had three different makeshift place markers—a saltshaker, a plastic inhaler bottle of nose spray, and the admiral's engraved watch—balanced over the images of three different structures.

As Natasha maneuvered the map and measured off

the markers, everyone else in the room stood around the table, staring at something that now resembled an enormous board game. "Look at the individual buildings of the plant," she said, pointing. "The way the missiles are targeted, Danvers is calculating that they'll hit here, here, and here." She moved the watch and the salt; the nose spray was already in the right spot.

"And?" Ava asked. She was leaning her elbows on the table, resting her chin in her hands. The last time she'd slept, she realized, was when she was unconscious in the Triskelion. *At this rate, I will achieve one hundred percent zombie status before the last missile is even close to hitting.*

"I'm not seeing it," Admiral Sanchez said. "That's a dead reactor. There's nothing there, it's like a ghost town. At least that's what I'm hearing from the DOD."

"Then why bother to target it? Where's the message there?" Tony folded his arms, still not moving his eyes from the table.

"Maybe it signifies something. I mean, it doesn't look like a coincidence, right?" Ava asked. "Maybe it's one of those mathematical things—"

Tony shot her an annoyed look. "Those mathematical things? Could you be more specific?"

"Come on," Ava said, dropping her head. She was exhausted. "You know what I'm talking about, where the numbers add up to the golden mean or the eternal ratio or pi-r-squared or something—and we just can't see it."

"Once again, we know this is the Red Room messing with our heads. We know who to blame, and we know what they're doing. Why don't we just go rolling into Moscow, find those suckers, and end this." Tony was ripping mad.

"Calm down," Natasha said wearily. "We don't know enough to say that."

Tony frowned. "Yeah? Well, I, for one, am tired of feeling that way. For once, I would just like something clearly spelled out for me."

"How clearly?" Ava said suddenly. Her chin was still resting on her hands, but her eyes were moving rapidly from one place to another on the map.

She sat up.

"Because if I'm not mistaken, that's not just a pattern. It's a letter, see?" Ava moved the saltshaker to one side of the targeted building, and the nose spray to a parallel point on the targeted building next to it.

"Not really," Tony said.

Finally, Ava shoved the watch to the bottom of a long passage that connected to them, from two rows below—another one of the three targets.

"I think it's literally spelling something out for you. It could just be that I'm delirious, but I think that's the letter Y. Does that mean anything to anyone?"

She looked at Natasha.

"Red Angel. Iron Angel. Iron Ghost. The letter Y. Each having something to do with the *Rodina*," Ava said. "And the Red Room."

Natasha said nothing.

Ava kept going. "The Russian hackers. The Green Dress Girl. The Russian fountain. The Russian yacht. What does that say to you?"

"Or who," Tony said.

Natasha stared at the table for a long moment. When she looked up, it wasn't clarity that Ava could see in her face. It wasn't understanding, or any particular answer. Her eyes had narrowed and her jaw had set. This was something else.

This was anger and steel and determination.

"I have to go," Natasha said, pushing out the swinging door that led from the bridge to the narrow hall of the upper decks.

"But—" Ava began.

Tony shook his head. "No point."

She frowned. "You think we're going to Guangdong?"

He smiled somberly and clapped his hand on Ava's shoulder. "I don't think *we're* going anywhere, buddy."

She didn't understand what he meant until it became clear that Natasha was never returning to the bridge—a fact that was underscored when the lone Sikorsky chopper lifted off from the deck without being cleared, and with a pilot whose identity was classified.

Tony shrugged. "They're just lucky she didn't take an F-35." He looked at Ava. "Sometimes I forget what a badass pilot she is."

"I don't," Ava said. She tapped her forefinger against her temple. "It's all right here, if I push hard enough."

"Let's get out of here." Tony reached out and put his arm around Ava, letting her lean against him as they walked back to the plane.

"We'll work it out, kid. Don't worry."

But I am *worried.*

What are you doing, Natashskaya?

Ava closed her eyes and let her mind roll outward—feeling her way out into the sky, toward the horizon and the person she had last seen disappear into it—but Natasha didn't answer.

It almost felt like she was actively keeping Ava out.

Is that even possible?

The deck was quiet.

Nobody on the USS *Kirby* had given their missing chopper too much thought; they were all too busy watching the live feed from Guangdong, where a drone camera recorded the first images of the three enormous hits simultaneously taken by the reactor—which now burned in, as one pundit noted, "the shape of a single threatening *kanji of violence,* not unlike the Roman alphabet's letter Y."

"I've never been threatened by kanji before," Tony said as he ducked into the cockpit of the Stark Jet. "Or even the alphabet. But maybe that's why N-Ro bailed on us."

"I guess. Wow." Ava buckled herself into the copilot seat, to his right. "She's really gone. I did not see that coming."

Tony glanced over at her. "Is this your first time in the big-kid seat?"

Ava nodded. "I'm pretty sure you're breaking about a thousand federal regulations by letting me sit up here."

"You should take a picture. You might not get into that chair again for a long, long time." Tony flipped a row of unmarked switches, and Ava knew he was readying the plane for takeoff.

"Good idea," she said, sliding open the camera app.

"Best selfie ever." Tony grinned. "How would you top that, a moonwalk?" He thought about it. "Though I just took a good shot in front of the CERN Hadron Collider. Where, by the way, there is a whole lot of good research going on right now. Something you and N-Ro might want to think about, if she ever lands."

"I have a great one of myself getting photobombed by a monkey in Rio," Ava said, not paying attention. "Wait, I'll show you."

She scrolled through her phone. "You think a monkey will be all sweet and cute, but then you actually meet one and—"

Her voice cut off.

"That bad, eh?" Tony checked his radio, then saw her face and stopped. "What?"

"These are my Rio pictures." Ava was staring at her phone, frozen. "Why have I never looked at these?"

He shrugged. "I don't know, maybe because you were busy taking out a hacker and a jungleful of smugglers-slash-drug-runners-slash-arms-dealers-slash-terrorists, while fighting off drug dealers in Brooklyn subways and chasing down a handful of stolen nukes?" He shrugged. "But that's just a hunch."

Ava stared at one particular image—then dragged her fingers across it, to zoom in on the frame and make it as large as she could.

"Tony—" But beyond that, she didn't seem to be able to get the words out.

It was the picture.

She'd scrolled past it before, but she'd only looked at the two big faces that were the focus of it—her face and the monkey's.

But there were three faces in this photograph, and she could see that now.

Down in the right-hand corner of the frame, there was a third blurry profile, hidden by shadows that she now slowly began to filter out.

"I think the monkey wasn't the only photobomber in this picture," Ava said, still in shock. She held out the cell phone to Tony.

There she was.

The Girl in the Green Dress—accidentally captured on screen as she fled the monument—minutes before the Harley attack. The face was blurry, but it was nothing the facial recognition protocols at S.H.I.E.L.D. couldn't deal with, she suspected.

"Is that her?" He was incredulous.

Ava nodded. "Just after the brush pass. I didn't know I had it."

"Do you know what this means?" He studied the photo with a growing smile.

Ava nodded. "Now we can run it through the database. We can get a name, maybe even a GPS for her."

"Hallelujah," Tony said. "Finally a way around that crappy RFID tracker. We have to get this back to S.H.I.E.L.D."

He handed her the phone, and Ava immediately hit the number for Natasha. It went straight to voice mail.

Tony slid on his aviators. "Times like this, my young friend, are why going ninety-two percent of the speed of sound just isn't fast enough."

But as the Stark Jet ripped into the sky, Ava couldn't help but wonder what exactly it was that they were speeding toward.

Ava had fallen asleep sitting up in her seat; she didn't wake up until the Statue of Liberty was in front of them. The Stark Jet flew straight to the East River base, and Tony seemed antsy the moment they left his plane for the Triskelion hangar. "You get that image to the lab. I have somewhere to be."

Ava looked at him curiously. "What's the rush?"

"I blew off an investors meeting for CERN." He sighed. "Now Pepper is punishing me by making me show up for everything on my calendar."

"So?"

"So I never show up for *anything* on my calendar. Do

you know how full my calendar is? It's sadistic. Who are all these people?"

"Don't ask me, I don't have a calendar." Ava smiled. "I'll let you know if the database comes up with anything. Have fun at your—whatever."

"Parade," Tony said, looking glum.

"Of course." She shook her head. "Other people have lunch plans. Only Tony Stark would have parade plans."

He looked miserable. "Honorary grandmaster. The first annual Stark Parade of Holiday Heroes."

"Ah, right." She nodded. "There are posters for it in the subway."

"I'm the guy who throws candy at the screaming children."

"*To* the children, I think. Not *at* them," Ava said.

"I tried to get out of it, but you know these big monster-balloon parades," Tony said.

"Not really."

"They don't wait for anyone. Once you inflate those suckers, they're full of hot air and it's go time. And the crowds are vicious. Did you ever try to get near that tree at Rockefeller Center during the month of December?"

"No," Ava said. "Is it December?"

Tony grinned. "Spoken like an almost-Romanoff."

She looked at him strangely. "I'm the wrong person to ask. I always hated balloons. They had them at the Moscow Zoo, and I walked around with a finger in each ear, in case one popped."

"Well, these balloons are the size of houses, so I suggest you skip the parade. They don't make a finger or an ear big enough for that."

"No problem." Ava held up her phone. "I have a criminal mastermind to ID, remember?"

"You have your fun, I'll have—well, at least you'll have your fun," Tony said with a sigh. "Let's leave it at that."

ACT THREE: REVEALED

"NEVER FORGET THAT JUSTICE IS WHAT LOVE LOOKS LIKE IN PUBLIC."
—CORNEL WEST

S.H.I.E.L.D. EYES ONLY

CLEARANCE LEVEL X

SPECIAL CIRCUMSTANCES & INDIVIDUALS (SCI) INVESTIGATION
AGENT IN COMMAND (AIC): PHILLIP COULSON
RE: AGENT NATASHA ROMANOFF A.K.A. BLACK WIDOW
A.K.A. NATASHA ROMANOVA
TRANSCRIPT: NEWSWIRE, EXCERPTED
CC: DEPARTMENT OF DEFENSE, SCI INQUIRY HEARINGS

[BREAKING] NUCLEAR MISSILES STRIKE CHINESE REACTORS IN GUANGDONG; ROGUE WARHEADS AS YET UNCLAIMED (AP)

(BEIJING) BREAKING: The latest report issued by the Central Military Commission of the People's Liberation Army and the People's Republic of China has confirmed that three armed nuclear missiles have struck the coastal Chinese region known as Guangdong.

Regional authorities prepared for the worst, evacuating all nonessential personnel and shutting down the area's power grid in the minutes before the attack.

Bordering the two key economic growth sectors of Macao and Hong Kong, Guangdong houses a defunct nuclear reactor that was considered the likely target for the strike, according to several unconfirmed sources in the U.S. Department of Defense.

The president of China has made it clear that the author of these attacks would be apprehended and punished. "Let the missiles fall. China is a world superpower that will not be subdued—not by terrorist action, nor by Western governments hiding behind the pretense of rogue insurrection. We intend to demonstrate this resolve, and our military might, in the days to come."

NATO, the United Nations, the European Union, and the member states of the G7 have joined together in condemnation of the attacks. [Developing.]

CHAPTER **27**: DANTE

QUEENS WAREHOUSE, NEW YORK
THE GREAT CITY OF NEW YORK

While saving the world and fighting crime by intercepting drug dealers at midnight in Morningside Heights had sounded dramatic at first, Dante's plan had a few obvious flaws. For one thing, he had an ironclad curfew. For another, he had a suspicious mother and a cop father, and it hadn't been lost on either of them that Dante hadn't left the house at night for a year now, since Alexei was gone.

By the time Dante faked going to sleep, crawled out his window and over the garage overlook, rode his bike to the bus stop, got the NJ Transit in downtown Montclair, took the PATH from Newark Penn Station to New York Penn Station, not to mention the subway up to 116th—he was late.

When he got to the bus stop where he'd met Army Jacket that afternoon, nobody was there.

Great.

He checked the time on his phone.

Twelve fifteen. I'm late. But where's Sana?

She wasn't answering her regular cell, and hadn't since he'd gotten on the bus. And he couldn't call her burner phone; that number was in *his* burner, which Army Jacket had taken.

Crap.

The only other people on the street were a group of girls laughing and clinging to each other in the cold as they crossed the street to Barnard College.

What if they already came? What if Sana was here and something happened? How stupid, to think I could come on the scene and play hero—

Maybe his father was right. Maybe he needed to get a new plan for his life, because it didn't look like law enforcement was exactly his speed.

Then Dante noticed a beat-up-looking white van on the side of Broadway, in front of a closed-up fruit stand. The motor was running, and white smoke blasted out into the cold. *Is that the dealer? Why else would they be sitting there? None of the shops are open. What are they waiting for, if not me?*

He stared for a moment, then pulled up his hood and crossed the street toward the van. *They might have seen something. They might know if she left with someone.*

The driver's window was dark when Dante knocked on

it. "Hey. Can I talk to you for a second? I just have a question—"

When the window rolled down, the first thing he saw was Sana's face, wide-eyed, bound and gagged, in the passenger seat. When he turned to see the driver, he got something that felt like a can of Mace in his eyes. It stung as badly as he imagined Mace did, but when he rubbed his eyes, it felt like granules of sand were inside.

Dante didn't have to be a genius or a scientist to know what it was.

Faith. I've been exposed—

Then he heard the crack of metal against bone—felt the flash of pain trigger across his body—saw Sana's eyes widen as he pitched forward and landed in a pool of inky-black nothingness.

It was the pain in Dante's head that woke him up.

Holy crap, does that hurt—

It stabbed down from the crown of his skull, shooting all the way to the deep interior of his brain, Humpty-Dumpty-style—only the king's horsemen seemed to be spooning out his soft-boiled brain for breakfast.

Every pain receptor in my head is on fire.

Every single one.

Even the follicles of his hair hurt where they touched the top of his head. His skin burned and the nerves behind his eyes were bulging against his eyeballs. He wanted to stick a fork inside and pop them, to let the pressure out.

I'm dying. This is what it feels like to be dying.

It has to be.

I can't imagine feeling worse—

Then it hurt too much to think, and he faded away.

The world was still blurred, dark around the edges, lighter in the center, when Dante realized he was conscious again.

He tried to see. He waited for a moment, but his eyes couldn't focus the way eyes were supposed to. He was stuck in some kind of perpetual haze, half-awake, half-dreaming.

Fight it off.

His body was heavy and sluggish, and his mind just wanted to go back into the warm darkness he'd just emerged from.

No.

Don't let it take you.

You don't even know how long you've already been out.

Dante thought of the man on the subway tracks.

Faith—

Remember. That's what this is. You won't be able to resist forever, but you have to try—

He closed his eyes.

He tried to touch his throbbing eye, but found he could not move his hand. He was a motionless puppet, a stiff form. Probably some part of his brain was already messed up enough to be stalled out, waiting for more instructions. He still had his conscious mind, though, and that was something.

Okay. So you can't see? Don't look, genius.

You have other senses. Listen.

What's out there?

Voices, echoing.

A sharp, brief clanging sound.

Something heavy, scraping against something hard.

Is that concrete?

Somewhere industrial.

Not a place meant for people.

Now he could make out the indistinct murmur of many voices, some at a distance, others much closer. All coming from above, high over his head.

So I'm on the ground. They're standing above me.

The echo means the space is big. Maybe even huge.

A warehouse.

How many other voices did he hear? Hundreds? Thousands? He tried to tell one from the next, but they all began to blur together, and he found he lost count when he tried to define them.

YOU ARE THE FAITHFUL—

The voice came into the background of his mind, fuzzy with some kind of neural static, as if from an immense loudspeaker lodged in his skull.

The Faithful—

Dante tried to focus on other sounds, the ones not coming from his own mind. The ones coming from the space around him.

Working.

That's the clanging noise, tools.

Machinery.

IN YOU WE WILL ACHIEVE GLORY—
How did that voice get in my head?
WITH YOU WE SHARE ALL—
How can I get it to stop?
OUR GLORIOUS RETURN TO POWER—
I think I'm going to be sick.
Dante opened one eye.

He saw the blurry outline of trucks, tankers almost. A rectangle of sky behind them. A garage door, but bigger.

A cargo door.

Coming in from the street.

The voice returned a third time.

YOU WILL NOT STRAY—

I will not stray, Dante thought.

YOU WILL NOT BETRAY US—

I will not betray you, Dante thought.

WE SHARE ONE GREAT CAUSE—

One cause, Dante thought.

Wait—

He tried to force himself to think about the words.

Don't listen—

It was harder than it seemed.

Stop-stop-stop-stop-stop—

He tried to tune out anything coming into his mind.

Dante strained to see with his peripheral vision. Out in the warehouse space, he saw massive teams of people, crawling all over the floor, working on something, though he couldn't see well enough to know what it was.

A giant puzzle?

TODAY IS THE DAY WE ACT—

Today is the— Today is the day— Today-bee-cee-dee-ee-ef-geeeeeeeeee—

Come on. Just keep thinking anything but the words, Dante thought.

THE DAY WE MAKE OURSELVES HEARD—

The day—bee-cee-dee-ee-ef-geeeeeeeeee—

He couldn't take it anymore.

Grunting, he rolled slowly to his side, sweating from the effort.

He saw a blurry face, the only one he could make out in the watery distortion around him. He knew that it belonged to the girl lying next to him, out of focus as she was. Because he knew her—

Sana, he tried to shout.

His lips barely moved, and no sound came out.

He summoned all his strength and flung one hand out, pitching and rolling himself toward her—and as he began to move, he saw something.

There, a dark stain in an otherwise indistinct blur of grays, was an object lying next to her pocket.

A phone.

Her burner phone.

She must have had it with her.

He strained to reach, his fingers crawling across the rough concrete, a few centimeters at a time. Slowly, finally, his fingers reached the phone, tightening around it as he rolled onto his back.

He pressed one random button, then another.

"Hello?"

In the distance, far over his head, a face came into view.

"Is anyone there?"

It was blurry, almost low resolution, but from where he lay, it had to be massive.

"Sana? Dante? Is that you?"

The face was eerie. It stared down at him as if from great heights, but Dante had lost all sense of time and space, so he didn't know what he was actually seeing.

He knew he must be falling under the influence of the drug, though, because everything around him was becoming more and more unreal.

Even the face he was looking up at now.

Especially the face.

Impossible.

Could it be—? No—

I'm hallucinating.

It's the Faith.

But he opened his eyes wide and looked a second time, just to be certain.

Is that—

Iron Man?

S.H.I.E.L.D. EYES ONLY

CLEARANCE LEVEL X

SPECIAL CIRCUMSTANCES & INDIVIDUALS (SCI)
INVESTIGATION
AGENT IN COMMAND (AIC): PHILLIP COULSON
RE: AGENT NATASHA ROMANOFF A.K.A. BLACK WIDOW
A.K.A. NATASHA ROMANOVA
TRANSCRIPT: NEWSWIRE, EXCERPTED
CC: DEPARTMENT OF DEFENSE, SCI INQUIRY HEARINGS

[BREAKING] WORLD LEADERS ASSEMBLE AT U.N.;
MONREALE, CYPRUS, GUANGDONG REMAIN A MYSTERY (AP)

(NEW YORK) BREAKING: An emergency session of the United
Nations convened in Manhattan today as global leaders
attempted to reach a consensus response to the nuclear
missile crisis of the past forty-eight hours.

While no one organization or government has claimed
responsibility for the attacks, which saw five unaccounted-
for nuclear missiles deployed directly over the populated
land and water regions, or military assets, of the European
Union, Russia, and China, some aspects of the crisis are
indisputable, according to U.N. secretary-general Jean-
Bertrand Allois:

"Nuclear missiles are not free, nor are they easy to acquire.
No coalition on the planet would threaten a sovereign
nation—let alone three in one day—without the assurance of
some powerful allies. The world community will not rest until
these alliances are brought to light, and the perpetrators are
punished."

Some military analysts have pointed to the lack of mass casualties as proof that the strikes were not the work of traditional terror groups, though a credible alternative scenario has yet to be offered, other than what Arthur Bailey, press liaison for the U.S. Office of the Joint Chiefs has called "the work of madmen." [Developing]

CHAPTER **28**: NATASHA

NATO RAPID REACTION FORCE TRAINING CAMP, ADAZI BASE FIFTY KILOMETERS FROM RIGA, LATVIA

By the time Natasha touched down at NATO's Adazi encampment, she had been in the air for nearly four hours. Most of that time had been occupied by reliving old missions, revisiting old failures. Seeing ghost after ghost of her past, sometimes even ghosts of herself.

She recognized them all.

The image of the fiery, burning Y was what had done it.

That was when she had known.

You—

Of course it's you—

But it would have been impossible to forget, with or without the direct connection.

I'm no angel, she had said.

Neither am I, Natasha had answered.

That was the curse of the Black Widow: adrenaline memories, indelible, forever imprinted, no matter how layered the palimpsest grew. The more she wanted to forget, the harder it became not to remember. Not to see the face in the crowd. Not to feel the shadow falling over her shoulder.

Because some ghosts were always there, and always would be.

Ivan. Alexei. Clint, the way we used to be. Bruce, the way we might have been. Cap and Tony, back when the Avengers Initiative still brought out the best in all of us. Coulson and Maria and Fury, before Hydra.

One day Ava will be a ghost as well—just like I am.

Just like Green Dress Girl.

Just like—

She picked up the radio, restless.

I should have known.

She didn't want to think about this now, not any more than she'd wanted to think about it ever. She wondered why it had taken her this long to put it together, if there was some small part of her that hadn't wanted to know, wouldn't allow herself to see it.

As if anything could keep the inevitable away.

Not this time.

"Mission Control, this is Natasha Romanoff. I am entering Latvian airspace under the aegis of the U.S. Department of Defense, from the USS *Kirby*. Someone from joint chiefs should have given you a heads-up. Do you copy?"

Static.

Honestly? Sometimes Natasha thought it was easier to fight aliens.

Too bad, guys.

I can't get where I'm going in a U.S. military vehicle, and you're the closest taxi stand in the neighborhood.

But when her radio crackled again, she knew she had nothing to worry about. "Good morning, Natasha! Welcome to Adazi base and NATO's Operation Atlantic Resolve. We heard you might be stopping by. You are cleared to approach."

She took a deep breath. Half an hour to get rid of the chopper, half an hour to grab the chartered flight from Riga airport. Ninety minutes after takeoff, Aeroflot flight 2103 would land at Sheremetyevo Airport, north of the city that was home to the one ghost she desperately needed to speak to, right now.

Moskva.

Moscow, city of red angels and iron ghosts.

Your city, Yelena. You made your point.

I'm coming. Are you happy?

Finally? Is this what you wanted?

Be careful what you wish for, dear Widow.

Four million tons of cargo. Four million opportunities to push Faith beyond the borders of the *Rodina*.

That's why Natasha was here.

The Moscow offices of Veraport Global Shipping, a division of Luxport Holdings International, occupied a squat beige building in a nondescript business park on the east side of the city center. Veraport had been jammed beneath a freeway overpass and between two rings of the Moskva River.

Natasha sat inside the Kofemaniya across the street—eating bread and cheese and drinking strong, bitter coffee—while she ignored the women in fur collars around her and instead watched the building through the glass window.

She checked her Cuff. Veraport booked through Moscow but connected by rail through to Vladivostok, where the big commercial port on Golden Horn Bay stayed open all year round, despite the ice. Four million tons of cargo moved through Vladivostok each year, and who knew how many of those containers went unregulated by border patrol, for what? A few thousand in bribes, probably paid in euros, an easier currency to work with when taking your mistresses to Paris for the weekend?

How many of those shipping containers also carried Faith?

How long had it taken, to spread it from Eastern Europe to South and North America?

And where else is it now?

She looked back out the window and sighed. She knew she couldn't wait any longer. It was time to face reality.

He's not coming.

You're going to have to do this alone.

Which is fine. You should be used to that by now.
You are.

She closed her eyes and drew a long breath. She didn't have the mental capacity that Ava did. They didn't connect to the Quantum link in the same way and never had. Just because Ava could experience some unexplained part of the quantum universe didn't mean that Natasha could.

No matter what you wanted to call a spirit, or even a ghost—

No matter how much you miss—

"We aren't doing this. Tell me we aren't doing this."

That voice. His voice.

When she opened her eyes, her brother, Alexei—whatever this was, that Ava saw of him—was sitting in the seat across from her. "Are you casing the joint? Is that what this is? Joint casing?"

His hair was rumpled. His skin was tanned. His eyes were sharp and bright. It was the Alexei she remembered—the Alexei she and Ava loved—the Alexei they walked the streets of Istanbul with, the one who walked into battle by their side.

Now he was dressed in S.H.I.E.L.D. workout clothes, as if he were a classmate of Ava's. A person with a future, instead of only a past.

He looked down at himself. "Really?"

She found herself smiling back at him, even in the oddness of the moment. "It's good to see you. I wasn't sure you'd come," she said, pushing her coffee cup around in a circle. She stared down at the cup now, as if she couldn't keep looking at him. She was too afraid, sitting here in Kofemaniya surrounded by fur hats, that she was going to come undone.

"Yeah, well, next time someone says 'You pick the place for lunch,' don't say Moscow."

She looked at him. "I don't know exactly how Ava does it, when she sees you. But I thought there was a chance—since I've seen glimpses of you, when she talks to you—maybe I could see you myself." She shrugged. "With or without Ava."

"And?" Alexei said, raising an eyebrow. "What's going on, Tasha?"

She frowned. "I can't explain, but I think it's all in that building over there. Everything. Answers. The Red Room, Ivan, all of it. What the whole thing has always been about. The one person yet to figure into the equation."

She'll be there. That's what I'm afraid of. That's why I need you, only I can't say those words.

Not even to a dead person.

"Yelena Belova." He looked out the window. "At Veraport? You really think she has something to do with all of this? More than just a connection to the Red Room?"

Her eyes were still fixed on the building across the way. All she could do was nod. She tried to speak, but her throat caught, and she cleared it. When she looked back at him, she composed herself; she composed herself by looking at him, which is why she needed him here, now.

"That's what I'm going to find out. And I guess I just—I needed someone to watch my back," she said.

"*Except you know you don't,*" he said, looking at her. "*Yelena or not. You never have. You watch your own back. But I'm here, if that makes you feel better.*"

He looked almost disappointed, which was funny, Natasha thought, since he wasn't even really there. *Why would I imagine my own brother to come back from the grave disappointed? Not missing me? His only sister? What kind of broken head do I have?*

"*You're not broken. You're fine. It's me. I really don't get out much,*" Alexei said. He leaned forward. "*And of course I've missed you, Tash. Don't be an idiot.*"

Natasha smiled as she looked out the window to the building in front of them. "Good. We may have to blow a few things up."

Alexei smiled. "Now you're talking."

Natasha snapped the handle off the wire-grid doors holding the Dumpsters in place. Other than smelling a little more like sour milk and old cabbage than midtown Manhattan, it was a pretty standard basement.

Parking, garbage, and a server room. Professional-looking elevators going up to the office levels. Service stairs leading down to the furnace and up to the roof.

Natasha scanned the brass-framed list by the elevators. *There it is.*

VERAPORT. *Seventh floor.*

Alexei stood next to her. "You got a plan, or is this your standard storm-the-room, take-out-the-bad-guys deal?"

She glanced at him sideways. "You know for once I

actually don't know the answer to that. I don't know what she wants from me."

Yelena. I know this is all coming from you. It has to be. There's no other explanation.

What do you want?

"*That can't be good.*" Alexei sighed.

"No." She shook her head. "So how about we storm and secure, rather than storm and shoot? Just because, you know, talking."

"*Since when did Natasha Romanoff care about talking?*"

"Well, interrogating."

"*Ah. Fine. You handle the talking, I'll stick to the rocking.*" He winked.

"You sound like Tony. That's scary. At least you've been spared more whole years of Tony, now that you've—" She didn't finish the sentence.

"*Moved on?*" He smiled. "*That's okay. It's not like I don't know what's happened.*" He raised an eyebrow. "*Now that would be awkward.*"

Then the elevator door opened suddenly, and they found themselves staring at the inside of an empty mirrored box.

"*Did you push the button?*" Alexei asked.

"I thought you did," Natasha said, her eyes narrowing.

He held up his noncorporeal hands. "Sorry. No can do."

She looked at him questioningly, and he shrugged. They stepped inside. A digital panel above the buttons still showed the elevator's origin.

The seventh floor.

"I get the feeling this is the express," Natasha said,

taking her Glock from her waistband and checking the safety.

"*Wish I could help more.*" *Alexei nodded.* "*But hey, at least you don't have to worry about me getting hurt.*" He looked at her, and she smiled sadly.

"For once," she said.

Six floors later, the elevator chimed as it slowed to a stop.

The doors slid open, and the two heroes stepped out into the lobby of Veraport Global Shipping—

Or at least, what was left of it.

Weapon still drawn, Natasha cleared the space—though there didn't seem to be anyone there. The place had been torched, floor to ceiling. Crumbling black ash was all that was left of the walls and floors. Most of the interior doorways were blown out. Only the windows remained intact. The space was empty, with the exception of debris and a few blackened chairs turned sideways.

She picked up a burned tin trash can and dropped it again. Then she smelled her fingers—even licked one.

Magnesium. You must really like the stuff. Pretty basic, but okay.

You had to use a whole lot of it to blow this place up, I'd say ten or twenty times more than you used on the Harley.

"*Hey, Nat?*" *Alexei called to her from the next room.* "*I'm not sure who you thought you would find here, but looks to me like someone else found them first.*"

"Maybe," Natasha said, walking through the rubble to join him.

The next room was equally grim. She pulled a warped ceiling tile off of the remains of a file cabinet, tossing it to the floor. When she tugged on the handle of the top file drawer, though, it was still locked.

She frowned. "Does that seem weird to you? That this whole place is wrecked but there's one piece of furniture still here—and it's locked?"

Alexei shrugged. "Someone left in a hurry."

"Or just left something behind," Natasha said.

Alexei nodded. "And then sent us straight up here on the elevator to find it?" He frowned. "You think we're being watched?"

She shrugged. "How many security cameras did you count in the lobby?"

"One by the elevators, two in the front lobby, one by the door we came through, four more, in the corners of the basement," he fired off.

"Nice," she said. "Eight security cameras and not a single car in the parking basement. What does that tell you?"

"Tells me we better get a move on opening up that file cabinet."

She pointed her Glock with two hands at close range and fired two successive rounds.

"The old double tap." Alexei sighed.

The file drawer slid open—and now she could see something was inside. A black notebook computer, also covered with ash.

"That thing has to be fried. It must have baked in there like in an oven," Alexei said.

She shook her head. "It wasn't in there. Not during the fire. There wouldn't be ash—there isn't any in the cabinet. It's steel."

She knelt and swept an arm's worth of concrete floor clear of rubble. Then she placed the computer carefully in front of her, and opened it.

A prompt flashed in the middle of the screen.

CLICK ME.

She frowned, but slipped her finger across the touchpad until the cursor moved, and double-clicked on the words.

A window opened on screen.

"It's some kind of uplink. Video chat or something," she said.

"But not a video?" Alexei asked, squatting in the rubble next to her.

"I think it's live," she said. "It must be her."

"Yelena?" Alexei asked.

Then Natasha heard laughter—and a blond girl appeared in the window on the screen in front of her.

Natasha stared.

It wasn't Yelena Belova.

"Are you talking to yourself? Is that the great Black Widow's secret operational strategy? Insanity?"

Slavic bone structure, Natasha thought. *Wide-set eyes, dark as coal. Broad features. A trace of the Urals—*

It's her—the Green Dress Girl.

The girl's hair was cropped in a blond bob now, and Natasha realized the long, brunette hair had been a wig.

She sat in front of a computer, and the room behind her looked like some kind of a lab, industrial, with corrugated metal walls, and heavy equipment surrounding her.

But—you? It's not supposed to be you, Natasha thought. *You're not my ghost.*

Not the right ghost, anyways.

And you're so young. Too young.

Something's wrong.

This is all wrong.

"Stop staring. It's rude," the girl said. "Manners, Natasha Romanoff? Were you raised by animals?"

"No," Natasha said. "But you aren't who I was expecting."

"It's no mistake. I'm *much* more than you were expecting," the girl said, laughing again. "I'm also more than you'll ever be. You or your sad little pseudo *sestra*. I don't know what Uncle Ivan ever found at all interesting about either one of you, to be honest. But then, when has honesty ever helped anything, I ask you?"

"Ah. So you're Red Room," Natasha said. "Like Yelena. Like me."

It was a statement of fact, not a question. It was a truth manifest in every word the girl spoke, in her every move. *The confidence. The cruelty. The strategy.*

Natasha could almost hear Ivan pontificating now. *It's a mental game,* ptnets. *Don't play if you can't win, and never, ever show less than a winning hand—*

"Red Room? I'm much more than that, *ptnets*." The girl

smiled, raising an eyebrow and a challenge—as if the nickname amused her, as if Natasha's whole childhood amused her—and she dared Natasha to say otherwise.

Ptnets. Baby bird. Ivan's pet name for his pet Romanoff. The word set Natasha's blood boiling; it always had.

Natasha raised an eyebrow. *Oh, I've been playing that game a lot longer than you, little girl. So why don't you go shove yourself right back up into that nest?* She smiled. *Come back again when you're ready for me.*

Now Natasha held her voice steady. "You belonged to Ivan, then? You were the *devushki Ivana* of your day?" Ivan's girls. That was what they were called at the Red Room. His special pets. Natasha had been one of them, and the memory made her physically sick.

"Belonged to Ivan? Of course not." The blond girl looked bitter for a moment, then scoffed. "Ivan and Yuri didn't just raise me. *They* belonged to me." Her lip smiled—or snarled—almost triumphantly. She was gloating. Then, as quickly as it had come, the smile faded. "Until you took them away, both of my uncles, and I had to take over for them."

"Uncles? Ivan Somodorov had a sister?" Natasha tried to think of it. *Was it possible? Did I miss something? Could Ivan have hidden something as big as his own sister from me?*

"Ivan had my mother. I had Ivan. Yuri was—oh, I don't know, more of a brother, maybe a cousin? I guess that's how you could see it."

Why does she look so familiar?

"My name is Helen Samuels."

And why is that name so familiar? The two women stared at each other across the video link. Natasha tried to feel her way through the situation. "Can I help you with something, Helen? Things are a little busy these days— what with the missile attacks—even when you aren't trying to kill me."

"Sorry about that. I've been trying to get your attention, but it turns out you're an *awfully* hard girl to get attention from."

"Like I said, kind of busy." Natasha shrugged.

"I tried the magnesium, but you didn't remember it was how we first learned basic detonations in the Red Room."

"I remembered," Natasha said, carefully. *Keep talking, psycho—*

Helen pouted. "I tried the hack, but you didn't seem to understand I was your Red Angel."

Natasha looked at her. "I guess I was distracted by the whole 'coming to kill you' thing."

"So then I had to employ a slightly bigger canvas. What a shame."

Natasha was having a harder time keeping her composure, now. "Iron Angel? Iron Ghost? You randomly obliterated eight centuries of Sicilian culture; you threatened—what, three cities? Took on the Russian navy—and let's not forget about the Chinese nuclear reactors—on top of terrifying, say, most of the planet, for a *word game?*"

Helen shrugged. "Yet here you are."

"Next time try texting," Natasha said.

"There's no next time. Why do you think I had to bring you all the way to Moscow? Yuri had so many plans for his precious bombs, his Faith, the spread of our network across the world—but in the end, what did he really want? Power. Fear. Why waste time? I did the math and jumped straight to the end." Helen sighed. "You're still not getting it. And here I thought we were kindred spirits. You know, like minds . . ."

Like minds . . . where was that from? Stark had said something similar, hadn't he? Suddenly the pieces clicked into place.

"It's Tony," Natasha said suddenly. "Of course. You're one of his 'Like Minds.' You interned for Tony Stark. The think tank."

"I did," Helen said. "Now I've moved on to explore other opportunities. Isn't that how they say it in job interviews?"

"You're the Rhodes scholar he went on and on about. The teen Tony Stark of Russia, that's what he calls you. You won the Stark Award in quantum physics."

"And molecular chemistry, though I admit, there's something about the word *quantum* that always seems to grab the spotlight."

"Why are you doing any of this, Helen? Tony said you had so much promise."

"I did. And I do. Wait, I'll show you what I'm *promising* to do." The camera angle swung around suddenly, erratically. "Which is, to ruin your life the way you've ruined mine. Kill your baby chicks, *ptnets*, the way you killed Ivan and Yuri."

She's picked up her computer. What am I looking at?

"You're there because I'm here," Helen's voice said.

The screen now showed a warehouse full of workers in bright yellow shirts, moving industriously around the cavernous space.

Helen spoke again. "And while I'm here, I'm busy, and I need you to leave me alone."

That place has to be the size of a football stadium.

In the center, Natasha could see three giant shapes, brightly colored, though it was difficult to determine what they were.

Sails? For a boat? Fabric, for a tent?

A shipping container marked VERAPORT was parked at one end of the warehouse.

"You'll be in Moscow, so you won't get to see the show in person, but I promise you it will be *spectacular.* Even for New York."

Of course she's in New York. That's why she made certain I'm not.

Natasha could feel herself starting to lose control. "I don't know. New Yorkers are pretty jaded. Now that you've used up all your fireworks, I think you're probably old news."

"Oh, believe me. The fireworks are just getting started. Have a little faith, Natasha."

That line is really starting to get to me—

"Even your friends do," Helen said, offscreen—and she let the camera drop, so that for a split second, Natasha could see the two people lying on her floor.

Dante and Oksana? How did they get there? And where are they—? Where's Ava?

Helen had flipped the camera back to her own face, and she smiled into it.

"Helen," Natasha said, carefully. "Why are you doing this? What does this have to do with me? Or your precious Faith?"

"It was Yuri who wanted to terrorize the world. I just want to terrorize you. Let me put it this way: mathematically speaking, the most effective dispersal method for the Faith particulate is aerosol, and the per-square-foot population density of New York City increases by four hundred percent during a few particular weekends of the year. Two, actually. New Year's Eve in Times Square, and—"

"The Stark Holiday Parade," Natasha said, stunned.

Helen smiled at the camera, her face angling off-kilter, close to the screen. "You know, I absolutely love balloons—don't you? I hope your friends do. And your city."

Static overwhelmed the video feed.

"Don't do it." Natasha raised her voice. "Helen!"

The images on the screen grew blurry—and Natasha felt a wave of anger.

"Where's Yelena, Helen? I know she's behind this. Tell her to come out and fight me in the open. Don't pretend she isn't involved in this somehow—"

"Don't worry about anyone but the Alpha, who can control every exposed inhabitant of New York City. That's my advice, *ptnets*."

But then the video link cut out—and the screen went to black. "Helen!"

Only the ghost of a voice lingered. "I was going to kill you, but I decided that would be too merciful. Now I'm going to strip the baby birds from your nest while you watch. It's a steep drop to the ground, Natasha. You'll be surprised to see how fast they fall."

On the last syllable, the laptop sparked and burst into flame.

"*Der'mo—*" Natasha cursed, throwing the computer against the wall as hard as she could. It broke into halves and went skittering into the rubble, sparking and shorting to black.

Natasha was reeling. It wasn't a side of herself that she showed very often, but she couldn't stop it now.

She felt like the burned-out walls were closing in on her, and she couldn't think, couldn't strategize, couldn't do any of the things that had kept her alive—and made her who she was, really—for most of her life.

"Are you okay, Tash?" Alexei's voice came from behind her.

She tapped her earpiece. "Coulson? Coulson, can you hear me?" She tapped it again. "Tony? Are you there?" Now she tapped it three times. "Ava? Ava, it's me."

"Tasha!" Alexei stepped through her, turning around to look at her. He looked like he wanted to grab her and shake her, but his hands hovered in their immaterial state.

She looked at him with wild eyes.

"Look at me, Tash." Alexei moved his face directly in

front of hers. *"Get it together. You're in Moscow. She's in New York. You have a few hours to get back to the city, and you have to move quickly now. One step at a time. Just think about that."*

She tried to look at him but her eyes were blurry with tears.

You're not really here, Alexei.

You're gone. My brother's gone.

I can't think what to do, because you died.

They're all going to die because you died and I can't think.

Because I couldn't save you.

She closed her eyes.

Because of Ivan and Yuri Somodorov. Helen Samuels. Yelena, tangled up somehow in all of this.

And me.

Because of me.

Because I'm lost and I'm tired and my brain is full of cotton, only it's the kind of cotton that hurts—

"Natashkaya!" *Alexei was shouting now.* "Stop it! I'm here. I'm right here. Stay with me."

"It's too late. That psychopath, Helen. She's got Faith. Who knows how much?" Natasha looked at her brother with despair. "Who knows what damage she can do?"

"It doesn't matter." Alexei shook his head. "Forget the Faith. One step at a time. You can't do anything until you get out of here, right?"

Natasha stared at her brother for a long moment.

"I have to find Yelena," she said, finally. "I know she has something to do with all of this. And I have to tell Ava. She has to help her friends."

"We will." Alexei looked at her. *"We'll work it out. You can do this. You can stop Helen Samuels. You're not alone. I'm here. Let's go."*

She nodded.

Then she followed her dead brother out the door, once again determined to do the impossible.

S.H.I.E.L.D. EYES ONLY

CLEARANCE LEVEL X

SPECIAL CIRCUMSTANCES & INDIVIDUALS (SCI) INVESTIGATION
AGENT IN COMMAND (AIC): PHILLIP COULSON
RE: AGENT NATASHA ROMANOFF A.K.A. BLACK WIDOW
A.K.A. NATASHA ROMANOVA
AAA HEARING TRANSCRIPT
CC: DEPARTMENT OF DEFENSE, SCI INQUIRY

COULSON: Are you saying that you and Ava shared a delusion? Alexei "appeared" to you, too?

ROMANOFF: I'm not saying anything. Or maybe I don't know what I'm saying.

COULSON: And Yelena Belova? Allegedly also a Black Widow, also from the Red Room. Do you want to elaborate? Seeing as she's supposed to be dead?

ROMANOFF: You're one to talk, Phil.

COULSON: Too bad your files were wiped. I'm sure we could have read all about her there.

ROMANOFF: That's why she had Maks wipe them, I'm guessing.

COULSON: So Ivan was an opportunist. Yuri a terrorist. Helen's a psychopath—who really hates you.

ROMANOFF: She can get in line.

COULSON: How does Yelena fit in to this circus?

ROMANOFF: My guess? Not the clowns.

S.H.I.E.L.D.
NEW YORK TRISKELION, EAST RIVER,
THE GREAT CITY OF NEW YORK

Helen Samuels. A.k.a. Elena Somodorova. According to the S.H.I.E.L.D. database, that was her name, Green Dress Girl. Now that Ava finally had the file, she found it difficult to put down.

It was a wild story.

Elena Somodorova was born in Moscow and taken to one of the many government-run orphanages, with other wards of the state; she was legally adopted by Ivan Somodorov at the age of six, then privately schooled in a succession of Ivan's laboratories before transferring to an accelerated high school program at Beijing University.

Adopted by Ivan Somodorov. Ava had stumbled on that one the first time she'd read it. *So she's Red Room, like we thought. Clearly, she has to be. Ivan wouldn't have bothered with her otherwise.*

She studied at Ivan's labs? Did she study at my mother's lab? She's older than I am, but not by much. Did we eat at the same table? Were we subjected to the same tortures? No, because who would survive all of that and still call Ivan family?

Ava kept reading.

Elena Somodorova eventually graduated from Oxford and returned to Moscow, earning certificates in physics, chemistry, mechanical engineering, and something about data structures that Ava didn't fully understand.

Elena was athletic, pretty, blond, outgoing, and smart; one teacher described her as "terrifyingly gifted." Another found that she "lacked empathy." A third more specifically defined her as "pathological."

Of course she's pathological. That's why Ivan wanted her, and what Ivan wanted her to be. She tried to blow up the Harley while we were still on it. What wouldn't she do?

But something more was going on here; the longer Ava spent reading over Helen Samuels's file, the more certain she was of it. There were too many redacted pages, too many holes.

Ava tried reaching out to Natasha again, though she'd had no luck in the past few hours. She closed her eyes and stretched her consciousness as far as she could, reaching back across the water—

Natasha. Where are you? I need to talk to you.

I can't do this on my own.

Tony was still with Pepper, getting ready for his parade. Dante and Oksana weren't answering any phones, not even the burner phones she'd swiped for them out of the S.H.I.E.L.D. Academy supply room.

I can't wait any longer—

She took the file with her and left the Triskelion.

Tony was standing on the grandstand, being interviewed by three different networks, when Ava pushed through to the edge of the platform.

She held up the file. "Helen Samuels," she said.

"Sorry, guys. I'm going to need five minutes." He hopped off the platform, walking over to Ava with a panicked look on his face. "There are animals and I have been told to hold them."

"Helen Samuels," Ava said, holding up the file.

Tony looked startled. "Did something happen to Ellie? Is she all right?" He sounded concerned, which threw Ava off.

"What do you mean?"

"Ellie. Helen. What about her? Aside from the obvious?" Tony asked.

Ava paused, confused. "Wait, which thing do you think is obvious?"

"Winner of the Stark Prize in Physics and Chemistry, of course," he said, as if the size of her brain should be as universally obvious as the color of her hair or her height.

"Okay, so she's supposed to be some kind of genius, right?" Ava asked. "That's what I was getting from the file."

"Ellie's not just supposed to be. She is one. She's a Stark Industries 'Like Mind.' "

"You mean your think-tank thing?" Ava asked. "With all the crazy patents?"

"Exactly. Who do you think designed the neural interface for the ComPlex? Who do you think created the trigger for the PopX?"

"You had her designing weapons?" Ava's eyes were huge now.

"Not weapons. Triggers. Safeties. Redundancies. Little pieces of larger puzzles, that's what she was good at. Solving individual steps. Ellie wasn't a big-picture person, in fact I always found it to be fairly strange, how disconnected those two parts of her brain could be. But why are you asking me about Ellie?"

"Helen Samuels is the Green Dress Girl," Ava said, helplessly. "Elena Somodorova."

"Impossible." Tony grabbed the file out of her hand and opened it. "Are you telling me that the person who tried to kill both of you is the same person I had designing weapons in my lab?" He looked stricken.

"Tony! You just told me Helen Samuels didn't—"

"Ellie—Helen—this 'Elena' person—shouldn't have even touched *pieces* of them. They're still weapons. I did that. I had her doing that."

"You didn't know," Ava said. "Hard to check a hacked record."

Tony was irate. "It's bad enough that they don't examine everyone who *buys* a weapon. The very least we could do is examine everyone who *makes* a weapon."

"I need to find Natasha, and I can't find anyone," Ava said.

"I have to shut down the manufacturing. I don't even know what we're fabricating right now. She could have rigged all of it." Tony was pulling out his phone.

"Natasha," Ava said.

"You're the one who shares a conscious seam . . . reach out."

She shook her head. "Is that really what you're calling it now? A conscious seam?"

"How am I supposed to know what to call it? Neither one of you ever lets me examine you." Tony sighed. "Why do you think I went to CERN? At least they're willing to research Quantums—"

"What about Dante and Sana?" Ava wasn't listening to him. "Is there any way to track a burner phone?"

As she said it, her own phone rang, and she picked it up.

All she could hear was the seemingly random mashing of buttons. She looked at the number and then put the receiver back to her ear. "Dante? Sana? Is that you guys? I think you're butt-dialing me—"

At that moment, Ava thought she heard a whisper, someone trying to speak to her from the other end.

Then it cut off.

Tony looked at Ava. She pointed at the phone while still trying to hear.

"Burner phone? Can you locate it?"

He held out his hand.

"This doesn't make sense. It's here. The signal." Tony frowned. He and Ava were sitting in his trailer, just across from Rockefeller Center, the centerpiece of the parade this afternoon—and really, the center of the holidays for New York City.

The crowds had been swarming onto the sidewalks on either side of the road since early this morning. Tony's trailer was the only place they could get out of the crowd long enough to hear each other.

"Where?"

"Not here. It's at the head of the parade. Where all the floats are assembled. Some are in the streets at the top of the route, some are in a warehouse a bit farther back."

"Why would Dante and Sana be in there?"

"Fun? An interest in helium? Aerodynamics? Aerosol?"

Ava looked up, grabbing Tony's arm. "Did your Like Minds think tank work on anything to do with this parade?"

"Not really. Nothing important. Maybe the aerosol delivery system. Ellie volunteered to head up a team that took my PropX design and use the same trigger system to inflate the balloons in like, a tenth of the time—"

"Helen Samuels worked on incorporating an explosive device into your parade balloons?"

"Well, it sounds bad when you say it like that, but—essentially, yes."

Ava sat up on the edge of the suede couch. "Tony. Balloons?"

He got it the same second she did. "Balloons."

"Tony. The Faith."

He looked grim. "That wasn't a parade Helen Samuels was working on. It was the dispersal system for a chemical weapon that could take down all of Manhattan."

Ava shot out the door and into the crowd before he could say anything else.

Tony was right behind her.

S.H.I.E.L.D. EYES ONLY

CLEARANCE LEVEL X

SPECIAL CIRCUMSTANCES & INDIVIDUALS (SCI)
INVESTIGATION

AGENT IN COMMAND (AIC): PHILLIP COULSON

RE: AGENT NATASHA ROMANOFF A.K.A. BLACK WIDOW

A.K.A. NATASHA ROMANOVA

AAA HEARING TRANSCRIPT / CALL EXCERPT

CC: DEPARTMENT OF DEFENSE, SCI INQUIRY

COULSON: Tony. I can't hear you.
TONY: I'm running in the middle of a parade. We have a
situation. Stark Holiday Parade of Heroes.

COULSON: Bad?
TONY: You need the whole house, Phil. And a hazmat team,
and a radiation drone. We need to start taking readings now.

COULSON: Missile strike?
TONY: Right now, Coulson—

COULSON: What are we fighting, Tony? More warheads?
TONY: Worse.
COULSON: What's worse than a missile hitting New York?

TONY: When New York is the missile, Phil.

CHAPTER **30**: DANTE

STARK HOLIDAY PARADE OF HEROES,
PARADE WAREHOUSE
THE GREAT CITY OF NEW YORK

Dante awoke to the tramp of boots. Something was happening—and now.

He staggered to his feet, using the edge of a shipping crate to pull himself up by the elbow. His eyes had finally begun to adjust to the altered chemical state of his blood, and he found that now he could move, albeit slowly, and make out distinct shapes and faces.

The Faithful had dispersed, pulling laminated lanyards and neon-yellow T-shirts on over their clothes.

STARK HOLIDAY PARADE OF HEROES.

Holy crap. Was that today? Suddenly all the pieces began to fall into place. *The helium trucks, and the tanks.*

387

The massive shapes, the colorful sails, only that's not what they were.

The teams of Faithful.

The sound of the commotion around him.

Now they were indistinguishable from the other parade volunteers filling the room in front of him, wheeling giant tanks of helium to the row of enormous balloon figures that lined the floor in front of him.

It was only if you looked carefully that you saw the Faithful were using tanks stamped VERAPORT. *That's not helium.*

One by one, the three balloon floats slowly began to inflate.

No—

Each balloon—full of Faith particulates?

What could that do?

And to how many people?

Aerial dispersal?

The entire city could be exposed.

He looked down at Oksana, still motionless. "Come on, Sana. Wake up. You've got to wake up." He pulled her to a sitting position, leaning her against the crate, but her body was still limp and her eyes still closed. She struggled to open them.

It's affecting her worse than it's affecting me.

Why is that?

He grabbed her phone and dialed the same series of numbers, again and again.

Ava has to pick up—I have to warn someone—

"Dropped call? Don't you just hate the service on those S.H.I.E.L.D. satellite phones? At least, I know I do mine."

He turned to see a blond woman, small and spry, standing in front of him. Waving an identical phone to the one he was holding.

"You know, you'd think if S.H.I.E.L.D. could send a satellite into space, targeting it at just X, and at precisely Y miles above the earth's crust, that they could get the freaking signal to work, am I right?" She grinned. "That's okay, you don't have to answer. I know I am."

Dante didn't react. His hand moved to shove the phone into his back pocket, as if he could keep it—or anything he knew—from her.

"I'm so excited that you woke up, my friend. I've been waiting for you. This is going to be so fun."

"Yeah? I don't think I know you." Dante was wary.

"Of course you do. I'm Ellie. You're Dante. And we're *thisclose*." She held up her fingers, crossed. "I work with Tony. Or at least, I did. Until I got a better offer. From myself."

Dante froze.

At first, something about her voice was just familiar—but then he realized who she was. The woman with the megaphone, commanding the fleet of refueling trucks, the one he had seen at the cargo loading doors, before.

The Queen Bee. Their commander.

Their Alpha.

The one giving the orders, the one the Faithful lived to serve.

He could feel it in his own mind, even now, though it didn't seem to control him the way it did the others. It was a hunger, like desire, but somehow stronger. He could tell even without the megaphone that it was her. You could hear it in her voice. The entitlement. The confidence. The darkness.

It was almost like she wasn't human, but like—

What?

A goddess—

Stop.

You're doing it again.

Don't listen.

You can't drop your guard.

Not for a second.

"What do you think, boys? Should we give our friend Dante a little something, to make him feel better?" She gestured with one hand, and the enormous security guard next to her stepped forward with a silver aluminum case, flipping it open and holding it out in front of her.

He was one of them. Dante could tell by the way he moved, by the way his eyes fixed on the Ellie person, no matter who else was in the room.

"I don't know, I think I'll pass," Dante said.

He eyed the case, which looked like it was full of some kind of glass vials, holding black water. Black as Faith.

That can't be good.

"Oh, come now. Life is so painful as it is. Haven't you been through enough? Hasn't she taken everything from you? Your best friend? Your life? You can't be enjoying any of this."

Dante's eyes narrowed. "I don't know who you're talking about."

"Of course you do. Her. Them. It doesn't really matter, if you're talking about one or twenty, they're all the same."

"Who?"

Ellie sighed. "The Widows. The Black Widow. The Red Widow. What's next, the Blue Widow?"

She moved toward him. "Should that be me? What do you think? I could stand for the red, white, and blue, the way she does for Mother Russia."

She dangled her arms around Dante's neck, and he bristled.

"The Widow America? I could run around with Captain America in his little tight man-pajamas?" She leaned her face close to him.

He shook his head. "I think maybe you got a little of that stuff in your own head, lady."

"Of course I have." She kissed his cheek, then pulled a vial out from the precision-cut black foam lining of the case.

She reached again into the lining, pulling out a long, slender hypodermic needle. "And now you will, too."

Dante's eyes found the door, and he threw himself toward it.

The security guard grabbed him and flung him backward, now holding his arms pinned behind his body.

"Running for it? A little late for that, don't you think?

Besides, what would Daddy think about that? Running away, when you could be standing up for the more unfortunate, doing your civic duty?"

"You don't know anything about me or my duty," Dante said, through his teeth, as the guard twisted his arms.

"Really? And if you ran now, what would your beloved Widows say? Would you be worthy of them, then? Are you a hero or not, Dante Cruz?" Her voice wrapped around him, tightening until it felt like he was going to choke.

I'm going insane. She's crazy and she's making me crazy.

"How do you know my name?" Dante shook his head. "How do you know anything about me?"

"I know everything about all the Widows." She leaned over Dante's face. "All three of them."

"Three?"

"Natasha, Ava, and Yelena." She was whispering now. "They're like the Three Musketeers, except deep down they all hate each other."

"I don't know who you're talking about." *Don't take the bait. Don't listen to anything she says.* "And I don't care. None of this has anything to do with me. Just let me walk out of here and you can go ahead and do whatever you want."

"Of course I can. I always do." She walked closer to Dante, who pulled backward, away from her. "Hold him tight, boys. He's a slippery sucker. Practically a snake."

Dante glared. "Pretty sure I'm not the snake around here."

"You? Of course not." She patted Dante's face. "You're

Alexei Romanoff's best and most loyal friend. You have to live with the knowledge that he died for no reason, after being taken from you with no warning."

No. He died because of people like you. You were the reason. You took him from me with no warning.

Dante said nothing.

Ellie brushed the hair out of his eyes coyly.

"It's hard, isn't it? Carrying around all that hate? You have every reason to hate Natasha Romanoff as much as I do. But without the Faith, all that hatred, it can really drag a person down, don't you think?"

I don't hate anyone except you.

Dante closed his eyes. "You tell me."

"The Black Widow . . . now, she's the real snake. She destroyed someone I loved very much. Two someones, actually. She destroyed someone you cared about, just the same." She pulled the plastic cap off the hypodermic needle. "We have to hold her responsible, Dante. Someone has to."

The words came out before he could stop them.

"It was an accident," Dante said, stubbornly. "She didn't kill her own brother. Don't be stupid."

She held up the needle, examining it in the dim warehouse light. "In Istanbul, in a militarized underground base, surrounded by a private army, under the command of a literal mad scientist. *Whoopsie.*"

Dante said nothing.

In her own insane way, Ellie was right about that. At least, he couldn't argue with her logic.

She shook the vial of black liquid in her other hand. "Now that she's spawned another Widow—equally stupid, and as insufferable as the original—well, there just isn't enough ego in the world to tolerate the two of them."

Dante shrugged. "Yeah, well. Like I said. Not my jam."

"Of course. Our jam is going to be the future. We're going to be the best of friends, Dante. You and I." She examined the vial, giving it one last shake.

"Yeah, I'm not your friend."

Ellie smiled, raising the now-naked needle in front of his face. "Oh, but you will be. I'm about to take care of that. We're about to have even more in common than the three Widows."

Dante stared at the needle as she stuck it into the vial with one swift move of her hand. Then she withdrew it, letting the empty vial drop to the floor. It shattered, and she laughed. "You know, I think Natasha is really going to like seeing us together. It'll be a little reminder for her, of the brother she never had."

"Great. Just what I always wanted."

She smoothed the skin on the inside of his elbow with the other hand. "You know what this is, Dante?"

"Yeah."

"But you don't. It's Faith, you know that much. But it's not anything like what the others were exposed to. It's pure Faith, more than any human has ever endured. There are only a dozen vials of it in the entire world, and all of them are right there in that case."

"So?"

"Ah yes. Elegantly put. So, it's highly experimental, and very dangerous. And beyond that, who knows? It could kill you. It could render you a drooling idiot. It could eat away at your brain from the inside."

"Super."

"But the one thing it will do, beyond anything else, is affect you. And as you can see, for some reason, you seem to be less affected by the aerosolized form of the compound, which I find most peculiar, and somewhat irritating."

It was true.

Dante had come to realize it hours ago.

He had been temporarily paralyzed, and his vision had blurred—and his head pounded like he'd just gotten a major beating—but he had never for a moment completely lost his will. He had stayed himself, never become one of the Faithful.

Why me? Why not them?

"It's possible that some human minds are simply, naturally immune. Certainly something we should study in the future. Consider yourself a chemical trial. With the added bonus that, after I baste you like a turkey, I'll drop you off on Natasha Romanoff's doorstep. A little present, a souvenir, really. Something for the holidays, to remind her of her beloved brother."

"Sounds great," Dante said. "But you forgot one thing, Ellie."

"What's that?"

"Her."

Ellie's face clouded—and as she looked in the direction of Sana, lying on the floor . . . but no one was there—and, with all the energy she could summon, Sana came flying out of the shadows behind the soldiers, behind Dante.

She lunged at Ellie, cracking a wooden balloon stake over her head.

Dante shoved the two soldiers nearest him against each other, cracking their skulls together like two halves of a clamshell. As one soldier dropped his small-caliber weapon, Dante scooped it up, firing rapidly.

BOOM.

BOOM.

BOOM.

BOOM.

Faith darts went flying, and each of the four soldiers sank to the ground.

He turned the pistol on Ellie, who was struggling with Oksana—

Pulled the trigger—

CLICK.

It was empty.

"No!" Dante shouted. "Watch out! Sana—"

Oksana looked up, surprised—

As Ellie—Helen Samuels—sank the hypodermic needle into the softest part of Sana's stomach.

[REUTERS] [BREAKING] *STARK HOLIDAY PARADE OF HEROES KICKS OFF;
BIGGER BALLOONS, BELOVED HEROES TAKE BROADWAY*

*[New York City] Santa has come to Manhattan—in the form of
Tony Stark, CEO of Stark Industries, who will be kicking off a
heroic holiday season in style—and live!—any minute now,
as soon as the football game ends. (Please set DVRs to allow
thirty extra minutes on either end of programming.)*

*Join us as thousands of heroic balloon handlers, super-
marching-band musicians, and cape-able clowns—as well as
a host of other performers—parade through the streets of New
York City. Help us bring SuperSanta himself from all the way
uptown to his favorite tree at Rockefeller Center, along with
more than forty-three of your favorite new and returning super
hero characters, now starring in balloon form!*

*Will Captain Marvel do the Big Apple proud in her first parade
appearance? Will Grand Marshal Tony Stark be forced to put
on his Iron Man super suit to save the day—or will the balloon
Iron Man save it for him?*

*Join with us in welcoming the holidays to the Big Apple—
stream the festivities live* **here** *and* **here**.

FIFTY-ONE THOUSAND FEET OVER THE ATLANTIC SOMEWHERE OFF THE COAST OF NEW YORK CITY

Putting a plan in place always calmed Natasha down. The first step of this particular plan had involved grabbing a taxi to Vnukovo, Moscow's private airport. The second had required grabbing a plane. In between those two steps, there had been only three or four small, irrelevant details—haphazard private security, flight plans, passenger manifests—and then suddenly there she was, in the air on the way across the Atlantic.

Natasha had been almost disappointed in her old motherland.

By the time her Widow's Cuff began to buzz, she had started to descend out of the clouds. She could just make out the Statue of Liberty and the far edge of the city where her plans would become more . . . complex.

Her Cuff buzzed again. "Sorry, I have to take this call," she said to the man in the expensive-looking suit duct-taped to the copilot's seat.

He nodded, eyes wide over his duct-taped mouth. He had been the fourth small, irrelevant detail standing between Natasha and liftoff. She'd locked his pilot in the private bathroom in back, but there hadn't been room enough for both of them, so she'd given up and duct-taped him into his chair. That had been five hours ago—and he still looked terrified.

Natasha tapped on her Cuff, pressing her earpiece into her ear. "Phil? Is that you? You gotta start calling people back." A burst of static answered her. The connection was bad, but what did you expect when you were higher than any cell tower?

"Where are you now?" Coulson's words finally erupted in a single burst over the garbled line.

She raised her voice. "Just a little longer. I told you I'd take the fastest ride I could find. We're almost there."

"We? Are you on a military transport?"

"Not exactly. I got a ride with . . ." She pulled a wallet from the inside jacket pocket of the man next to her. "Vladimir Milosovich." She glanced up at her copilot with a laugh. "Hey, you're *Vlad the Dad*? Small world! I'm a friend of Maks—why didn't you say something?"

The man looked at her. Very funny.

"Natasha?" Coulson was buzzing in her ear again.

"Don't ask." Natasha tossed the wallet back to Vladimir. "You don't want to know, Phil. I sort of hijacked a plane. It's fine. It was just a little one—"

"*Natasha!*"

"Let me rephrase." She adjusted her earpiece. "I took a short-term volunteer position as the personal pilot of a billionaire entrepreneur headed from Moscow to New York City." She raised an eyebrow at Vlad. He shrugged. It was almost true. "And he's going to fire me as soon as we touch down at the Triskelion."

The man nodded. That was definitely true.

Natasha tapped her Cuff and pulled out her earpiece.

She didn't have the capacity to talk about it anymore. Not when she was the one who was going to have to make the call on when to take out Rockefeller Center to contain the Faithful before they spread to other cities, taking other lives. As if that made her some kind of hero.

She felt like a fool. How had her instincts betrayed her so badly? How had she not seen it coming? How had she not known?

Known what, exactly?

But she knew the answer, whether or not she wanted to admit it. She'd known it since that day in Rio.

That they were coming for me.

That she was.

For a moment, Natasha felt herself slipping out of the machine focus of combat mode. She cross-examined herself as she studied first the East River in front of her, then the Triskelion landing strip.

She scanned up and down her mind for any detail she could recall about one person in particular—the one who was about to turn the city into a hellhole.

But how could anyone have known that?

That Ivan had raised Helen Samuels, someone so powerful—and so ruthless—

And that some of my best old dead enemies may not be as good or as old or as dead as I thought. . . .

For the first time, she wondered if the day wasn't about faith, but about pride. Natasha had stupidly believed she was in control of her destiny, when really her fate—and her future—was just a tragic web spun by the deadliest of friends and the deadliest of assassins, all along.

From the Red Room to Ivan to Alexei to Clint to Fury to Yelena to Tony to Cap to Bruce to S.H.I.E.L.D. to Coulson to Ava and back again to Alexei.

And then to me. To this day. To now.

She had thought she had lost everything already—and yet here she was, preparing to lose again.

As the wheels touched down, she made up her mind.

Helen Samuels was going down, no matter who or what it cost.

No matter what her connection was to Yelena Belova.

More likely, because of it.

S.H.I.E.L.D. EYES ONLY

CLEARANCE LEVEL X

SPECIAL CIRCUMSTANCES & INDIVIDUALS (SCI)
INVESTIGATION
AGENT IN COMMAND (AIC): PHILLIP COULSON
RE: AGENT NATASHA ROMANOFF A.K.A. BLACK WIDOW
A.K.A. NATASHA ROMANOVA
AAA HEARING TRANSCRIPT
CC: DEPARTMENT OF DEFENSE, SCI INQUIRY

** FILE COPY **

*[EYEWITNESS ACCOUNT OBTAINED BY S.H.I.E.L.D. /
RECOUNTED BY CRUZ, DANTE—SEE ROMANOFF, ALEXEI /
TRANSCRIPTED PER AAA PROTOCOLS / COULSON, P.]*

So Helen, Ellie, whoever the crazy person is, she stabs Sana
in the stomach with this needle from one of those glass vials
with the black Faith inside. And I'm freaking out, because that
was about to be me, but also because it ended up being Sana.
And I'm only still standing there because Sana's just jumped
Helen and these burly zombie guards to help me get free. Only
now I realize Helen's gone.

I'm yelling, and Sana just curls up on the floor in a ball. I see
her eyes roll back into her head, and then all I can see is the
whites. And this greenish-whitish foam starts to bubble from
her lips and, like, ooze out of her ears. I'm screaming and
shaking her and asking if she can still hear me—and then she
starts to kind of moan—and her whole body starts to shake,
like she's having a seizure. Then I say all this stupid stuff to
her, like how she can fight it, and that I know she's strong
enough.

Then I just shut up, because I can see she's changing, like,
transforming.

And that's when everything gets off-the-hook crazy.

CHAPTER **32**: AVA

STARK HOLIDAY PARADE
OF HEROES ROUTE
THE GREAT CITY OF NEW YORK

Ava and Tony ran through Rockefeller Center. The snow was thick and the crowd was thicker, on and off the street. They edged past the giant holiday tree, slipping and darting through the crush of humanity.

That's so strange, Ava thought. *Natasha and I even talked about going to see the tree this year. I never imagined I'd be seeing it like this.*

I wonder if it will still be here tomorrow.

If any of this will be.

Now Tony was shouting into his earpiece, reading numbers off the sophisticated computer Ava knew only looked like a wristwatch. "Coulson, we're not even there and we're hitting an INES rating of four or five. We need to widen the exclusion zone, do you copy?" He looked at his wrist. "I'd say—twenty clicks."

Ava slid in her own earpiece, just in time to hear Coulson's voice crackle. "You realize twenty kilometers means all of Manhattan?"

"And we may be talking about more than that if we don't take the source down," Tony said. "We know the balloons are bad news, but we can't start a stampede."

"What's the play?" Coulson asked.

Ava looked at Tony. "We're making it up as we go."

"Yeah, well, *pop the giant weaponized balloon heroes* isn't exactly one from the playbook," Tony said.

"Just find your friend Helen and take her out before she can trigger dispersal," Coulson said. "Helen or this Alpha or whoever is calling the shots."

"On it. At least the high radiation means we're getting close," Tony said. "And Romanoff says there's only one Alpha."

"Coulson—" Ava tapped her own ear, cutting in. "Is she back yet?"

Ava could feel something stirring in her mind. If Natasha wasn't here, she had to be near.

"She just landed—gearing up and heading your way now," Coulson said. "Should be online in five."

Tony looked grim. "Tell her to put on a MOP suit. If things don't go our way, we're going to have to light the place up. Unless S.H.I.E.L.D. can find a way to cure a whole city full of Barrys. And by S.H.I.E.L.D. I mean me—but even I'm not that fast."

"Copy that." Coulson's voice was bleak.

Tony pulled out his earpiece and looked at Ava, shaking his head. "The parade route begins up ahead." He pointed. "We'll never make it. The crowd isn't even moving. This is crazy. I've got to get in a suit."

"I'll keep going." Ava nodded.

"You sure?" He looked uncertain, but she knew they had no choice. "Coulson's got the perimeter, and Danvers is probably already on overwatch."

"Probably?"

"Hopefully?" He looked at her. "Be careful. And stay away from any giant balloon heroes. Or, you know, any of my interns."

"Got it," she said, pocketing her earpiece.

When she looked up again, he was gone.

S.H.I.E.L.D. EYES ONLY

CLEARANCE LEVEL X

SPECIAL CIRCUMSTANCES & INDIVIDUALS (SCI)
INVESTIGATION
AGENT IN COMMAND (AIC): PHILLIP COULSON
RE: AGENT NATASHA ROMANOFF A.K.A. BLACK WIDOW
A.K.A. NATASHA ROMANOVA
AAA HEARING TRANSCRIPT
CC: DEPARTMENT OF DEFENSE, SCI INQUIRY

** FILE COPY **

*[EYEWITNESS ACCOUNT OBTAINED BY S.H.I.E.L.D. /
RECOUNTED BY CRUZ, DANTE—SEE ROMANOFF, ALEXEI /
TRANSCRIBED PER AAA PROTOCOLS / COULSON, P.]*

As I watch, I see the black stuff, the Faith, it starts coming
to the surface of Sana's skin, all over. It's shining like salt
crystals or something. I realize I smell something burning, and
then I see it's my own hand.

It's hot from touching her skin, like she's on fire.

Then I hear noise coming from down below, and I realize the
three balloon floats are all gone, and the parade must be
starting. And the Faith, it's inside them, three of them, and I
don't know how to stop any of it, or even when it's going off.

That's when Ava finds us—only when I look at her, I see
it's Helen that she's found—and I see those crazy blue
lightsabers flashing. I want to go help her, but I can't leave
Sana, and I know Ava wouldn't want me to.

So all I can do is watch.

STARK HOLIDAY PARADE OF HEROES, PARADE WAREHOUSE, THE GREAT CITY OF NEW YORK

"**W**hat have you done to Sana?" Ava had her back to Dante, but he didn't need to see her face. He could hear it in her voice.

Rage.

And now he saw the answer in Helen Samuels's eyes.

Fear.

It only flashed there for a second, but he recognized it instantly. And it was enough to draw one conclusion: this wasn't going to end well.

"You're too late," Helen jeered. "The Red Widow and the Black Widow. Late again."

"I don't know about that," Ava said, keeping her luminous blades between them. Dante watched as the energy seemed to ripple from the center of her chest to the farthest tip of her blades.

Incredible.

"You and I are still here, *Elena*. It can't be much of a party without us, can it?"

Helen smiled. "I hate to *pop your balloon*, friend, but this sort of party can. In fact, it might be even better. Especially without you—"

She grabbed a syringe from the top of a nearby crate and swung it at Ava.

Ava dodged the needle, striking back.

The blue light flashed and the blade cut through the air between them with a loud *whoosh*. Dante felt himself holding his breath.

Come on, Ava—

He watched with awe. This wasn't the Ava he knew. It was the Ava from the subway—the Red Widow. She was . . . *baller*, he thought, as Ava moved in on Helen.

Helen shrugged—then dove at her again, stumbling closer.

Ava's second blade flew through the still air.

Swoosh, swoosh—

Helen dodged the blows, then straightened.

"This is getting dull. Do you want me to tell you a story, Ava Anatalya Orlova? An old Russian story? About Yelena Belova and Natasha Romanova?" She pronounced Natasha's name the Russian way. "The *real* Widows?"

"Why not? I love a good story," Ava said.

"Then let me tell you this one: Once upon a time, whatever you thought you knew about your precious Black Widow was a lie. Whatever bond you imagined you had with her, it was weak."

"Is this where *Baba Yaga* comes in?" Ava mocked, swinging her blade at the mention of the infamous Russian witch.

"In a way. Let me tell you how this story always ends. You, Ava Anatalya Orlova—not she—you sacrifice everything— the people you love—your soul mate, your best friend, your family? And she, Natasha Romanova, crawls away to spread her poison somewhere else in her web."

Ava moved both blades in front of her now. "You know what? I lied."

Helen raised an eyebrow.

"I'm not really a story person."

And with that, Ava hurled her short blade at Helen's face. As Helen ducked, Ava attacked with her long blade.

The warehouse exploded in blinding blue light—and when it faded, Helen Samuels lay sprawled on her face on the floor, cowering beneath raised hands.

Ava lifted her electric blades higher. "Where's your army of Faithful now, Elena Somodorova? Not much of an Alpha, are you?"

Helen dropped her hands. "Do it. I dare you. That's what a Widow would do, isn't it? A real one? What Natasha did to my family?"

Ava hesitated as Dante watched.

The deathblow, he thought. Didn't she deserve it? Ridding the earth of Helen Samuels would be a public service, wouldn't it?

Ava's eyes narrowed.

Helen sneered. "Well?"

Dante shook his head. "It's your call. She's the Alpha, right?"

"Am I?" Helen smiled.

And with that, Ava dropped the blades and punched Helen in the jaw as hard as she could.

Dante watched, relieved as Helen slumped motionless to the floor. He looked at Ava questioningly.

"I have enough ghosts in my life already," Ava said.

Dante said nothing. He got the feeling Ava wasn't talking to him anyway.

Ava ran to her friend's side. A moment later she was cradling her head. With blue electricity still crackling along Ava's torso, the heat from Sana's body didn't seem to bother Ava.

Sana didn't respond, except to keep rocking back and forth as she had been for minutes now.

Ava turned to Dante next to her, her eyes dark. "What is this?"

"Pure Faith," he said. "Or something like that. That's what Helen called it, anyways. Before she stabbed Sana with it." He looked over to where Helen now lay on the floor. "Is she—?"

Ava shook her head. "No. She's just out cold. I had to get her to stop talking. We have a city to save."

But it was hard to even think about anything but Sana as she wailed, rolling to one side. Ava held her as she thrashed back and forth, coughing up what looked like black blood.

Dante looked out at the street. "The balloons are rigged. I don't know how or when they will blow, I just know we have to get rid of them, cut them loose somehow, keep them from detonating. Especially if Helen's not the Alpha . . ."

"How many?" Ava asked, smoothing a loose curl from Sana's forehead. "Faith balloons?"

"They aren't all weaponized. It's only three of them," Dante said.

"Let me guess. The Black Widow?"

"And Iron Man and Captain Marvel," Dante said. "Helen Samuels has kind of a twisted sense of humor."

"We can't leave Sana," Ava said. "If you think you can handle her, I'll go after the balloons while you call an ambulance."

"Really?" Dante looked at Sana uncertainly. "Even if S.H.I.E.L.D. let us, what kind of hospital do you think we can take someone who looks like—"

"Like *my friend*?" Ava asked, forcefully.

That's some powerful denial, Dante thought.

Before Dante could answer, a red, gold, and blue blur streaked down from the sky with a wave, pulling up to hover and then land just inside the warehouse doors.

Carol Danvers stood firmly planted back on the earth, her hands on her hips. "I've got your six, guys. I can take it from here. You've done enough."

Ava looked relieved. "Is that you, Captain Marvel?" She'd never seen her in person, in her full regalia.

Carol smiled. "Well, it's not Iron Man. I mean, do I look like I need a freaking suit?"

"Copy that, kid. Air support is within five." Iron Man saluted, landing next to Captain Marvel. "And bite me, Danvers. Suits *rule*."

They turned back to Ava and Dante—and Sana.

"That thing's Sana?" Iron Man's face slid up to reveal Tony. "Sheesh. We better hurry up with those balloons."

"Stop," Ava said. "*That thing* is still my best friend. And she'll be fine. She's not the problem."

But Dante knew Tony had a point. There was nothing in the creature that reminded him of their former friend— or at least very little. No matter how badly Ava refused to admit it.

The Faith had overtaken Sana's entire human form, from the look of it—and the result looked like nothing Dante had ever seen before—though it was still eerily familiar.

Faith. That thing is pure Faith.

The drug we've been chasing—it's right here, and it's alive. I can feel it, somehow.

And it's hurting Sana.

Swirling clouds of black emanated from her nostrils, spiraling down around her torn clothing. Her fingers had stretched and curled into something that looked more like enormous claws.

Her skin glittered with gray crystals, rippling across her

body, shining like the mysterious compound. As Dante watched, the crystals shifted into drifts of Faith that formed and re-formed, hardening in some places only to suddenly give way in others.

Sana—the thing that Sana had become—was huge and solid. From the look of it, maybe almost three meters, taller than the average person. Her face, if you could still call it that, now reflected only the basic features of a human face—two eyes, a mouth, some kind of nose.

Then the Not-Sana opened her mouth—its mouth—and screamed.

"We've got to get her out of here," Ava said.

"And take her where?" Dante asked.

Captain Marvel shook her head. "We can't let civilians near her, not now. Whatever's going on, your friend isn't in control of herself."

Now the Not-Sana threw herself against the corrugated steel wall, screaming. Strangely, Dante found he had to fight the urge to scream back. *Why is that?*

Carol and Tony and Ava stared, almost in disbelief.

"We'll get her back to the Triskelion. I'll radio ahead to Coulson and tell him to get a unit ready," Tony finally said.

"He has a room that can hold her?" Ava frowned.

"Oh yeah." Tony nodded. "Believe me, this isn't Phil's first does-he-have-a-room-that-can-hold-her rodeo."

Captain Marvel looked at Ava. "Can you guys just keep Sana here while we get rid of the Faith threat? Then we'll bring her home?"

The Not-Sana hurled herself against the steel girders holding up the structure again and again, until the whole warehouse felt like it was going to collapse. Dante felt his own head start to pound.

Ava nodded. "I don't think she'd hurt us. I don't think she'd hurt anyone. Not if she can help it."

"That's not what I'm worried about," Dante said. "It's just the chaos. I mean, bullets are going to start flying and innocent people are going to get hurt."

"Spoken like the son of a cop," Ava said, but she hesitated. "He's right. We'll be careful."

Captain Marvel clenched a fist.

Iron Man clenched a robo-fist.

And like that, the heroes were gone.

S.H.I.E.L.D. EYES ONLY

CLEARANCE LEVEL X

SPECIAL CIRCUMSTANCES & INDIVIDUALS (SCI) INVESTIGATION
AGENT IN COMMAND (AIC): PHILLIP COULSON
RE: AGENT NATASHA ROMANOFF A.K.A. BLACK WIDOW
A.K.A. NATASHA ROMANOVA
AAA HEARING TRANSCRIPT
CC: DEPARTMENT OF DEFENSE, SCI INQUIRY

** FILE COPY ** NYPD INCIDENT REPORT **

DISPATCH:

At about ████ hours, Dispatch advised that there had been a report of a disturbance in the vicinity of ████ and ███████, the approximate location of the Stark Parade of Heroes warehouse.

ARRIVAL & OBSERVATIONS:

On arrival at the scene, responding officer noted the destroyed perimeter wall of the structure.

Further investigation was interrupted by the emergence of an unknown individual dressed in a horror-type costume, extremely tall, physically intimidating.

After the individual fled the scene, Captain Cruz determined they were most likely a cast member of the Stark Parade of Heroes.

We proceeded with caution.

CASE NUMBER: 0572910

THE SIXTH AVENUE PARADE ROUTE
THE GREAT CITY OF NEW YORK

The enormous balloon was still bobbing down the avenue when Captain Marvel spied it.

Within moments, Carol Danvers grabbed the inflated Carol Danvers by the foot. *This is kinda surreal,* she thought.

With one twist, she snapped half the cords binding the balloon free from its twenty-six handlers below.

Then she streaked upward, dragging Captain Balloon after her, until she could lob her latex self as hard and as far as she could, sending it spinning into the atmosphere.

Where Alpha Flight and I will just have to clean it up later, because that's what we do for you, Earth. Clean up your stupid space trash.

Captain Marvel sighed.

And people think I have an inflated ego.

Only the faintest *BOOM* let anyone know the deed was done.

By the time she headed back down for the Balloon Widow, Captain Marvel was almost enjoying herself.

Always knew you were full of hot air, Romanoff.

BOOM.

S.H.I.E.L.D. EYES ONLY

CLEARANCE LEVEL X

SPECIAL CIRCUMSTANCES & INDIVIDUALS (SCI)
INVESTIGATION
AGENT IN COMMAND (AIC): PHILLIP COULSON
RE: AGENT NATASHA ROMANOFF A.K.A. BLACK WIDOW
A.K.A. NATASHA ROMANOVA
AAA HEARING TRANSCRIPT
CC: DEPARTMENT OF DEFENSE, SCI INQUIRY

** FILE COPY ** NYPD INCIDENT REPORT **

DISPATCH:

Dispatch requested additional units report to the Stark Parade
of Heroes warehouse.

ARRIVAL & OBSERVATIONS:

As Capt. Cruz began questioning the two minor teens present
on-site, it became clear that he had a personal relationship
with the minor male. It was later made clear to me that the
minor male was indeed the eldest son of Capt. Cruz. The
minor female was apparently no relation to either Cruz.

Both teens were described as "agitated" or "hysterical" by
multiple officers at the scene.
When Capt. Cruz asked both minors to return with him to the
precinct, the minor female reacted in an aggressive manner.

At that point, she retreated into the warehouse, saying she
needed to retrieve personal belongings. Five or ten minutes
later, it was determined that the minor female had broken out
a first-floor window and exited the scene entirely.

CASE NUMBER: 0572910

CHAPTER **35**: TONY

THE SIXTH AVENUE PARADE ROUTE
THE GREAT CITY OF NEW YORK

The second Iron Man heard the first *boom*, he knew Captain Marvel had destroyed her inflated twin.

Fine.

That was her call.

It was the next *boom* that made up his mind.

He himself knew better than to throw away a research opportunity like this. Especially for a compound with no known antidote.

He flew the inflated Tony into the airplane hangar where he normally kept his older-model Stark Jets.

As the doors sealed shut, he wondered what the lab would come up with, when he launched the ten thousand samples this one balloon would generate.

Then he went back for Sana, the biggest sample of them all.

"Where's Ava? Sana?" Tony's mask was off now. Captain Marvel landed behind him in the street in front of the warehouse. Which was surrounded by both the paramedics and the NYPD—

"I can explain," Dante said as he walked out.

"I'd like to see you try," Tony said.

An unconscious Helen Samuels emerged on a gurney, flanked by a paramedic holding up an IV bag, as well as one paramedic steering either end of the cart.

"The minute you guys left," Dante said, "Sana freaked and busted out of here. Ava went after her, and Ellie— Helen—started to wake up. I panicked."

"You did the right thing, kid." Carol Danvers nodded.

"Calling the cops? When is that ever the right thing?" Tony asked.

"I didn't! Not exactly," Dante said, uncomfortably. "Sort of the opposite, actually."

"Huh?" Carol looked confused.

"The cops called me," he said, looking less than happy about it. "I didn't come home last night, and my parents are pretty mad. So I guess my dad traced my phone and— well, he's been following me—"

Dante shrugged as Captain Cruz came out of the warehouse and slammed shut the ambulance doors.

"Yeah, I'm grounded for life."

"Been there myself, kid." Tony clapped a hand on Dante's shoulder.

"Not me. I was a saint," Carol said.

"There's something else," Dante said, looking uncomfortable. "About Sana."

"Spill," Tony said.

"I think—I can hear her, in my head. Telling me what to do. Where to go. Weird things, things she'd never say. It's like, her voice, but it's not *her*."

Tony looked at Carol, who nodded. "I think we found our Alpha."

S.H.I.E.L.D. EYES ONLY

CLEARANCE LEVEL X

SPECIAL CIRCUMSTANCES & INDIVIDUALS (SCI)
INVESTIGATION

AGENT IN COMMAND (AIC): PHILLIP COULSON

RE: AGENT NATASHA ROMANOFF A.K.A. BLACK WIDOW

A.K.A. NATASHA ROMANOVA

AAA HEARING TRANSCRIPT

CC: DEPARTMENT OF DEFENSE, SCI INQUIRY

** FILE COPY ** NYPD INCIDENT REPORT **

DISPATCH:

Dispatch requested backup as officers on the scene followed
the costumed individual and the minor female into the Stark
Parade of Heroes.

ARRIVAL & OBSERVATIONS:

As helicopter units tracked the two fleeing individuals down
the parade route, coordinates were relayed to all responding
squad cars.

Near the intersection of Rockefeller Center and Fifth Avenue,
one air unit radioed that the female minor had engaged in
an altercation between the costumed individual and a third
unknown female.

Three to five minutes later, both the female minor and the
unknown female had drawn weapons. At that point, the
costumed individual began to lose control and attack the
surrounding environment until more units were called to the
scene.

CASE NUMBER: 0572910

THE SIXTH AVENUE PARADE ROUTE
THE GREAT CITY OF NEW YORK

"**N**atashkaya!" She heard Ava's voice while her back was still turned. "I found the Alpha. There's just one thing—"

Natasha heard it in Ava's voice before she saw it. The flinty hardness, the push of adrenaline that inflected every syllable. Her hand went immediately to the back of her waistband.

It's not there—

She must have come from behind me.

"Touch one hair on that Alpha's head and I'll shoot," Ava said. "I mean it."

"I know," Natasha said, raising her hands in surrender.

And as she slowly turned to face all that remained of her family, she also found herself staring down the barrel of her own Glock revolver.

She looked up the street to Ava. Behind Ava, she could see what remained of the enormous parade of balloons lining the street. She saw a creature, surrounded by policemen, and squad cars, and flashing lights. It was the end of *King Kong*, without the Empire State Building—and just as tragic.

She felt for Ava, but it was surreal to see her holding a gun.

Natasha stepped toward her, reaching out.

"Ava. I don't know what's going on with you, but it's going to be all right."

"That's not just the Alpha, Natasha. That's not Helen Samuels. It's Sana."

"What?"

"That's *my* Sana. Helen gave her a shot of pure Faith, and it's not only a drug. It's some kind of slow-acting chemical weapon."

"I know," Natasha said. "I mean, I suspected."

"Within a month, everyone who has been exposed to it could already be dead. There's no cure. Nobody knows anything about it. That's what Dante said. He was in there with Helen, all night." Ava looked distraught.

"We can help Sana. Just put the gun down."

"No. You forget, I'm in your head. I know what you're going to do."

"I'll do what I have to do," Natasha said. "Nothing more."

"And this is what I have to do," Ava said. "She's my oldest friend. My only friend. I've got to help her and get her out of the city."

Natasha could see Ava starting to panic. "Helen's twisted. She wants to spread the pain she feels. Her father's wrath. Ivan's wrath. He was her adopted father," Natasha said. "Yuri was her uncle."

"Why is she so angry?" Ava held her chin up and stood tall. "Is it because of what you did to Yelena?"

What does she know about that? Steady—

Natasha took another step toward Ava. "What do you know about Yelena?"

"I only know what I could get Tony to tell me." Ava backed away. "I know you tried to protect her from being like you. I know you did everything you could to keep her from being a Widow. I also know that you failed."

Natasha's voice was impassive. "Since you know everything, where is she?"

"You couldn't protect her, and you couldn't stop her. She did what she wanted to do, and that was her choice," Ava said, her hands shaking as they held the Glock. "And she died."

"Why are you telling me this?" Natasha asked.

"Because you can't protect me, either, and you have to stop trying. I'm not Alexei, and I'm not you. I'm not your responsibility, not any more than he was."

What if I want you to be? Isn't that what a family is?

Ava's hand wavered again.

First my brother. Now this—

Natasha's mind retreated to the thought of her own colossal losses, and she shivered. *Get over it. Alexei's gone and Ava's—*

Gone another way.

Natasha telegraphed her message before she could stop herself, just as a stray bolt of lightning might suddenly catch in the electrical wire strung between different city blocks.

Please. I'm begging you. Put down your weapons and step aside—

We can still help Sana. It's not too late.

Talk to me—

Still nothing.

Natasha sighed and pulled her spare pistol from her boot. Maybe she could scare Ava into dropping the Glock.

Moy sestra.

"You're on the wrong side of this one." Natasha's voice hung in the air amid the confetti. "Put down the weapon and step away."

"I'm not leaving Sana. I have to get her out of here. I don't trust S.H.I.E.L.D., and I don't trust the police. I don't trust anyone. They'll see her as collateral damage, and she's not. Not to me." Ava took a breath. "So I won't give her up."

Not even to you.

Natasha raised her voice again. "This is your last chance,

Ava. Put the gun down. Take another step and I'll send you to meet my brother in the grave."

She knows I'm bluffing. I know I'm bluffing. What else can I do?

Ava's voice cut through the cold air of the avenue. "Do what you have to do. As for Alexei's grave, I think you know we both already live there, *sestra*—"

Fine. Natasha tightened her grip on her revolver and began to count.

One—

Ava's voice echoed across the street. "Like you, I'm not afraid."

Two—

"But unlike you, I don't desert the people I love—"

Thr—

Two shots rang out, just like always.

The first shot to hit the target, the second shot to slow the flow of blood to the nervous system. A proper double tap, exactly as S.H.I.E.L.D. had trained their operatives for more than a century now to do—

Ava screamed.

Natasha spun around.

In the street behind them, the creature that was Sana dropped, her legs collapsing under her.

A police captain stood tall, surveying his shot.

Sana sank to the ground. Her face was visible now. As the blood ran from her body, the Faith slowly began to lose its hold.

Ava ran to her friend's side in horror.

Natasha stooped to pick up the forgotten Glock from the asphalt.

As Sana's blood ran across the pavement, one heart quieted, but strangely enough, it was the other that had never felt so alone.

S.H.I.E.L.D. EYES ONLY
CLEARANCE LEVEL X

SPECIAL CIRCUMSTANCES & INDIVIDUALS (SCI)
INVESTIGATION
AGENT IN COMMAND (AIC): PHILLIP COULSON
RE: AGENT NATASHA ROMANOFF A.K.A. BLACK WIDOW,
A.K.A. NATASHA ROMANOVA
AAA HEARING TRANSCRIPT
CC: DEPARTMENT OF DEFENSE, SCI INQUIRY

COULSON: I can't believe you didn't destroy a chemical
weapon. I mean, I can.
STARK: It's a little complex. This isn't any of your standard
chemical weapons.

COULSON: Can you work with it or not?
STARK: You don't get it. This compound—the thing Romanoff
keeps calling Faith—it doesn't exist. Not on Earth, anyways.

COULSON: Don't tell me.
STARK: I'm telling you. I think it's Terrigen based.

COULSON: You think Helen Samuels is an Inhuman?
STARK: All I know is, she tried to gas Manhattan with a giant
bubble of my chiseled face full of an alien-derived compound
that is looking increasingly like Terrigen mist.

COULSON: Keep me posted.
STARK: I will. Also, the CERN project? It's ready for them.

COULSON: Do they know?
STARK: About the other Quantums? I wonder.

COULSON: But a Quantum Inhuman? That's just not something
I want to think about.

** FILE COPY OF INCOMING TRANSMISSION ** FROM THE PENTAGON **

Phil,

I don't know how you did it, but I just saw that [CLASSIFIED
SUBJECT] was placed back on my Restricted Handling Assets
circulation list.

Also see that [CODE:REDROCK] AAA hearing transcripts are
officially closed. So let's hope we've seen the last Red Room
threat to Rockefeller Center, at least during the holidays.

Congratulations to you, but especially to her. I think it's
safe to say that she can stay at S.H.I.E.L.D. with you for
the time being, especially as you continue to research the
interplanetary nature of the [CLASSIFIED SUBJECT] cloud
threat.

Next round of nachos is on me.

ARTIE

OFFICE OF THE JOINT CHIEFS OF STAFF
9999 JOINT STAFF PENTAGON
WASHINGTON, D.C.

CHAPTER **37**: AVA

S.H.I.E.L.D. NEW YORK TRISKELION, EAST RIVER
THE GREAT CITY OF NEW YORK

Sana lay on a metal table, a white sheet draped over her bruised and battered body. Only the shining gray-black crystals remaining on her human form gave any hint of the creature she had become.

"Thank God she's alive," Ava's voice said.

Adhesive electrodes connected her skin to a maze of thin blue and red wires that apparently allowed the roomful of S.H.I.E.L.D. agents on the other side of the mirror full information on her vitals.

"What's going to happen to her?" Ava stared through the window.

"I don't know." Coulson shook his head. "It's ironic,

though. That gunshot slowed her heart just enough to halt the permanent transformation. Captain Cruz probably saved her life."

"I hope that makes Dante feel better," Ava said.

They both knew it wouldn't.

"As for Sana, we'll just have to wait and see, then follow protocol." Coulson looked over to Ava.

"I hate that word. *Protocol*," Ava said, still watching the room. "It's just a thing people say when they can't admit they're doing something horrible."

"Life can be horrible sometimes, as I think you know." Agent Coulson turned back to the window. "And this particular horrible thing is for Oksana's own safety, as much as everyone else's. We'd do the same to you or me or anyone."

Ava glared. "She's not anyone. She's my oldest friend."

"I know it's tough. Be patient. Bodies take time to heal. She'll wake up soon. For all we know, she'll still be herself. . . ."

"Don't say that." Ava pushed on the glass with one finger, wistfully. "Don't lie." She closed her eyes, wishing it away. Wishing everything was different. Wishing her friend was still her friend.

Come back to me, Sana.

Agent Coulson put a hand on her shoulder. "I know whoever Sana is, she'll be needing you. And when she does wake up, we can talk about next steps all together."

* * *

Ava pulled herself toward the gym ceiling, arm over burning arm. She'd done it every day this week, faster and faster. The next time she had to break into a seedy hotel room off an alley in Recife, she'd be ready. For now, her arms felt like rubber—

Rubber couldn't ache like this.

"Looking good, spaghetti arms," a voice called.

Ava looked down to see Dante Cruz, the newest recruit at S.H.I.E.L.D. Academy, looking up at her from the bottom of her rope. Tony was still testing every cell in his body to find the source of his Faith resistance.

He saluted.

She turned back to the rope and smiled to herself.

By the time she reached the top, he was gone.

On her way out of the gym, she found him standing in the lobby, staring at the place where Alexei's name had been carved into the Wall of Heroes among the names of the lost. She left him alone. She let him feel it. Feeling it was better than feeling nothing at all.

Right, Alexei?

Her flickering hallucination of a boyfriend appeared at her side.

"So strange. To see Dante here at the base, and Sana . . . like that," he said quietly.

"Everything is different now," Ava said.

Alexei looked at her. "Everything?"

Ava didn't answer.

"You two still need each other, Ava."

"Why? Because of some random brain connection?"

"*Because you don't get to pick your family, and she's yours. Whether or not you like it. Whether or not she's your legal guardian. You're all each other has.*"

"I have you," Ava said softly.

Alexei raised an eyebrow.

"I have Sana," Ava said.

Alexei looked away. "I will love you forever, perraya lyubov."

"My first and only love," Ava smiled wistfully.

"*But I'm not the only one who loves you, Ava Anatalya. So go talk to her. For me.*"

Ava stood silently for minutes after he was gone. She knew he was right. She'd do it. For him.

No, she thought. *For me.*

Natasha stood outside the Triskelion, next to a shiny red Harley. "What is this?"

"It yours. It's a present, sort of. If you ignore the fact that you bought it for yourself," Ava said.

"No, I bought it for you. For your birthday."

"Turns out I'm not really a Harley girl. And I think you need a new friend." Ava patted the seat fondly. "Harley misses you."

Natasha looked at the bike. "Wow. I don't know what to say."

"I know. But I do." Ava looked out at the East River. "Here's what I've figured out. There's more than one way of being Entangled. We need to accept that we are—but more than that—*how* we are."

"Yeah? And how's that?"

"We're family, whether or not you want to admit it. It might have started because of quantum physics, or the Red Room, or Alexei, but that's not all it is anymore."

Natasha looked at her, a small smile on her lips. "You think?"

"And I think what that also means is, while maybe we can share a cat or a closet or plumbing or takeout, we can't fight together."

"We made a pretty good team, though," Natasha said, gently. "Didn't we?"

"We did. But whether it's you and Yelena, or you and me, or even maybe you and the Avengers—we need to go our own way."

Ava took a breath. "I have to find my own way, and become my own person. Even my own Widow."

"Like Helen and Yelena?" Natasha raised an eyebrow.

Ava laughed. "Maybe. Although I get the feeling those two sort of deserve each other. Even if no one will tell me why."

"And us?" Natasha slid one leg over the side of the Harley. "What do we deserve?"

Ava handed her a shiny red helmet. "Whatever we want."

"Even ghosts?" Natasha asked.

"Especially ghosts." Ava smiled.

Alexei waved to his sister as she sped away, one red curl blowing free of her helmet.

Ellie lay on her cot in her cell, staring at the iron manacles on her wrists, thinking about circles.

There was something perfect about the pale circle of *dosai* batter sizzling with coconut curry on a Tamil street vendor's hot iron in Kuala Lumpur, in Malaysia.

The white-bright moon over Kowloon, hanging over the bay in Hong Kong.

A single egg boiled in strong tea, eaten in a paper napkin while overlooking the drifting boats of honeymooners on Taiwan's Moon Lake.

A heavy cast-iron pan of saffron rice shared with random Real Madrid fans after a victory at Estadio Santiago Bernabéu.

The view of Rio from the Cristo at the top of Mount Corcovado.

She didn't know what it was, exactly—but it was something. She felt it in her bones. In her blood.

Five minutes after walking into Tony's apartment—her own was uninhabitable now, thanks to Helen—Natasha stared at the blinking message in front of her.

UNSUB: Natalyska.
UNSUB: Please, Natalyska.
N_ROMANOFF: Nyet.

N_ROMANOFF: You're an enemy of the state, Yelena.

N_ROMANOFF: You're also an enemy of mine.

UNSUB: You think you're so different from me? You just betrayed a different state.

N_ROMANOFF: Was that what you told yourself when mini-you almost took out New York?

UNSUB: She was young.

N_ROMANOFF: Around here, the young don't generally dabble in chemical weapons.

UNSUB: Everyone makes mistakes. Ellie will pay for hers.

N_ROMANOFF: Oh, I'll make sure of that.

UNSUB: Is it true, what they say? That nothing of the old Natasha remains?

N_ROMANOFF: Maybe just the hair.

UNSUB: What a shame. She was something. The real Black Widow, unreduced, undiluted. Before she encountered Western moral equivocation.

N_ROMANOFF: The real Black Widow? Do you mean the one who killed you?

UNSUB: And yet apparently not.

N_ROMANOFF: What happened to you, Yelena?

UNSUB: You left me for dead. The Red Room brought me back again.

N_ROMANOFF: So Ivan Somodorov was your Frankenstein's Bride?

UNSUB: I wasn't the Frankenstein, Natalyska.

N_ROMANOFF: What are you saying?

UNSUB: Helen Samuels. Her real name is Yelena Somodorova.

N_ROMANOFF: We got that. But you and Ivan? That's low, even for you.

UNSUB: Ellie's not my child. That's what I'm trying to tell you. She's an exact genetic duplicate.

N_ROMANOFF: Let me get this straight. You were my impostor, and she's your—clone?

UNSUB: No . . .

UNSUB: Not mine.

ACKNOWLEDGMENTS

Writing with the Widows is always a joy; I have been fortunate to spend the better part of another amazing year with Natasha Romanoff and Ava Orlova—not to mention Tony Stark, Phil Coulson, Carol Danvers . . . the list goes on and on.

This is the part where the thanking generally goes, but seeing as we're on our second round with Black Widow now—I think this is my tenth YA book, actually—all the people I can't live without already know exactly how much they mean to me: it's a small club. That said, I can't write a book and not mention Sarah Burnes, who is not just an agent but an everything. Equally larger than life are Disney's Editor-In-Chief Emily Meehan and Marvel's Director of Content & Character Development, Sana Amanat. Each of these three women is someone I consider myself lucky to know. (I think the technical term is *baller.*) Working on their behalf are at least a hundred other people who have contributed meaningfully and often to this book and to my life. To each one of them I am deeply and truly grateful.

Beyond that, my friends (both YALL & civilian) and my family (both furless & furry) are my life—you know who you are. I acknowledge that freely, not just here but everywhere, and not just when I'm publishing a book. You guys are what matters.

Finally: Women of Marvel (plus squirrels), you rock. Whether you're in the audience or at the mic, you are my people. Let us continue our path to world domination. *Shh.*

M. Stohl
July 2016